A Murder for Miss Hortense

A Murder for Miss Hortense

Mel Pennant

Pantheon Books, New York

Published by Pantheon Books, a division of Penguin Random House LLC, 1745 Broadway, New York, NY 10019.

Pantheon Books and the colophon are registered trademarks of Penguin Random House LLC.

The Library of Congress Cataloging-in-Publication Data is available.
LCCN 2025934848
ISBN: 978-0-593-70162-1 (hardcover)
ISBN: 978-0-593-70163-8 (ebook)

penguinrandomhouse.com | pantheonbooks.com

Printed in the United States of America
10 9 8 7 6 5 4 3 2 1

The authorized representative in the EU for product safety and compliance is Penguin Random House Ireland, Morrison Chambers, 32 Nassau Street, Dublin D02 YH68, Ireland, https://eu-contact.penguin.ie.

To my grandparents, Miss Dolly, Baby, Bobsie and John,
and to your whole generation

"Don't underestimate her," I say. "Old women can be very fierce."
Rosalind Stopps, *A Beginner's Guide to Murder*

Not everything that is faced can be changed, but nothing can be changed until it is faced.

James Baldwin

The Original Members of the Pardner Network of Bigglesweigh

Miss Hortense

Blossom

Constance

Dimples

Errol

Fitz

Pastor Williams

Mr. McKenzie

A Murder for Miss Hortense

1

The Pardner Lady Is Dead

On the morning Blossom brought the news that the Pardner Lady, also known as Constance Margorie Brown, was dead, Miss Hortense had not long finished watching *Kilroy* and was in the back garden pruning the Deep Secrets. Her bloodred roses, which she had planted a lifetime ago, were put there to stop her forgetting something that was, by its own nature, quite unforgettable. The sun hadn't yet risen to its highest point, and as she knelt down, it filtered in through the leaves, playing a kind of peekaboo against her back.

Blossom, who said she had rushed off the number 64 bus and all the way to Miss Hortense's home, could barely get the words out: "Dead! And I never saw it!"

She carried the news all the way from Bridge Street Market, where she had been in conversation with Mr. Wright. That was the Mr. Wright who Blossom had once said favored Engelbert Humperdinck, but, apart from the light skin and sideburns, Miss Hortense couldn't see the resemblance. It was Mr. Wright who saw the ambulance as it pulled up at a quarter to seven outside Constance's home, number 52 Percival Road, which was the house on the corner. The ambulance didn't leave until something like 8:15 a.m., which meant, according to Mr. Wright, that they must have been working on her hard. Mr. Wright, as they knew, lived in the council flats opposite, so although he didn't quite have direct access into Constance's front room, if he went out on his balcony (which he did upon hearing the sirens and seeing the flash of blue lights) and stood with his neck tilted heavily to the side, he could just about see into the front right corner of Constance's bedroom.

Blossom took a deep breath and stopped fiddling with the chiffon scarf that hung unevenly about her neck. There was a slight tremor at the corner of her mouth. Blossom was a woman who didn't step out of her yard without two layers of foundation and several pins in her hair. Her nails were always immaculately polished in a magenta pink. But on that morning, something had gone wrong, and one eyebrow sat higher than the other and her skin tone was uneven. She licked her lips and continued.

Constance, like Miss Hortense and Blossom, lived by herself, although unlike them, Constance had children—a son and daughter—but Mr. Wright was quite sure that it was *she* in the body bag that was zipped up all the way to the top. "Body bag" was whispered by Blossom, and she crossed herself before repeating the words and then crossing again, despite the fact that Blossom wasn't a Catholic or in any way a follower of any religion—except, if there were such a religion as Love Thy Money, then it's fair to say that Blossom would have been a very devoted member.

Blossom was quite sure that the information she had was correct. There was no mistaking it. And then, just like that, when she'd got it all out, Blossom deflated like a balloon and nearly lost her footing on Miss Hortense's doorstep because it was *a shock*. The shock of having Constance be quite alive and full of life, taking up even more space than was strictly necessary, for so many years, to the unbelievable realization that she had now become a Hope No More.

For once, this was not a death that Blossom was claiming she had foretold. That was what the "I never saw it!" bit was about. Blossom generally knew everything that was going to happen after it had happened, but she was particularly accurate when it came to death.

"I can't believe it," she said again, the sweat dripping from her brow. It was normally at least an eighteen-minute walk from the bus stop to Miss Hortense's, but this day, according to Blossom, she made it in four and a half minutes.

There was nothing for it but to let Blossom in and get the little glasses from the cabinet and pour the neat white rum, Wray & Nephew, all the way to the top of each.

"I . . ." said Blossom, gripping the glass hard. But nothing further came out. It was rare for Blossom to be without words. It had happened only once before, in the summer of 1968, after her second husband, Lester (the one with the funny eye), hit her and she had boxed him so hard that he flew across the room and hit his head on the sideboard. She had rushed all the way to Miss Hortense's then too.

Now both of them fell silent as they contemplated what it meant for the Pardner, indeed for them all, now that the Pardner Lady was dead.

2

No Place for Our Money

The Pardner had begun on the night Hortense first met Blossom, a miserable Friday evening in the summer of 1963. Despite the season, clouds hung in the sky like they had dropsy and there was a chill that ran right through Miss Hortense's bones. Errol had come to find her after he'd heard she'd moved to Bigglesweigh and had insisted she leave her box room to join him at a blues dance. "Come na, man." Although she didn't mind a good party, it was her sister who had loved them.

Hortense and Errol hadn't seen each other since the spring of 1958. On the night he came to find her, she was soon to turn twenty-nine and was thicker-set with a more ample bosom and wider hips. But, despite nearly three years in England, her skin tone, a deep, dark mahogany, hadn't lost any of its depth. He was twenty-seven, but still the same scrawny pipsqueak. She noted, however, that his copper hair no longer sparkled. He had just acquired a wife called Precious, and very shortly before that, a daughter, both of whom Hortense had yet to meet. As they walked side by side, they talked briefly about Hortense's sister Evie. Evie, whom she followed to England in September 1960. Evie, who was lost to her.

"Is just how it is here," he tried to rationalize. "Na worry 'bout it."

"Well, I going find a place for the two of we and the pickney," said Hortense, giving away more than was characteristic. "I going tek her and me nephew away from that man."

As they arrived at Blossom's little house, a brass horn rose to greet them, and Hortense shook out her headscarf to the pulsating "Madness" of Prince Buster.

A sudden commotion came from further inside the house. In the front room, a small table was squashed in the middle, with a man sat at each of the four sides, staring each other down. Behind the men was a gathering of people watching the unfolding drama, including a woman the color of yellow yam with a mouth full of little shark teeth, whom Miss Hortense would later come to know as Constance Margorie Brown. She was peering over shoulders.

"Rahted! How him do it?" said a man stood next to Constance. He had noble, chiseled features as if carved from the granite of a gravestone. This was Mr. McKenzie. He shook his head. "That na make no sense. Brown can't play."

"I win. Fair and square," said a man sat at the table with a prominent forehead and slicked-back hair who turned out to be Mr. Brown, Constance's husband. He rose, not very far, to his feet—he was a short man—and gestured to the dominoes tiles on the table, all akilter now.

"Is I win! You fe give me my winnings."

Another man at the table rose slowly. He had broad shoulders and a fighter's ready stance. This was Fitz.

"Is dere anyone here who this man don't owe no money to?" asked Fitz to the room.

Someone in the corner shouted, "Brown owe the whole world to rahted," and Mr. Brown, with his big forehead, seemed to shrink into the carpet, before sliding towards the door.

Miss Hortense watched as whatever smile Constance Margorie Brown had previously disappeared. She leaned away from her husband as he passed her on his way out, her shark teeth revealing more of themselves.

"See the real player deh so," shouted a large man with a funny eye, sat at the table.

His name was Lester, but that wasn't the name Miss Hortense had for him. He motioned, with a bulbous finger, for Errol.

"Come now," Errol said, turning back to Hortense and easing both of them further into the room. "Hortense a go tek me place," he shouted across the crowd. Errol was practically pushing Hortense towards the space Mr. Brown had left.

The Bullfrog (the name Hortense had for the large man with the funny eye) said, "No."

So Errol fished in his pocket and took out four single-pound notes and a handful of change, which he counted and put on the table. *Slam.*

"All right, then," said the Bullfrog. "Come na, darling. I going tek you money," he taunted Errol and the third man at the table, whose name was Bigsy. "I going whip you backsides tonight."

Hortense shook her head at Errol, removed her coat and sat at the table. To her right, Fitz—she could smell the spice in his aftershave. To her left, Bigsy. In front of her, the Bullfrog, breathing heavily.

They were playing the dominoes game Six. In order to win, you needed to win six games in a row. One break in the pattern and you started back at square one. The game could go on for hours. Hortense rolled up her sleeves. The Bullfrog said in Errol's direction, "She know how fe play?" Hortense looked across at him. He was an ugly-looking man if ever she'd seen one. She put down her handbag and picked out her seven bones, the tiles she was going to play with.

The first five games were taken by the Bullfrog. He belched into the room. A smile played at the corner of his wet mouth as he eyed the money on the table.

When the Bullfrog was about to play his first domino of the sixth game, Bigsy deployed the common tactic of distraction and shouted towards the kitchen. "Dee? Tell them what happened to you at the bank."

His wife, Dimples, a sickly-looking slip of a woman with no dimples in sight, emerged from the kitchen a few moments later. "Well, on Monday, I went to the Royal National Bank," Dimples began into the room. Her voice was watery. She frowned, and Miss Hortense spotted the dimple for the first time.

"I said I wanted to open a little bank account." Sniffle. Frown. Dimple. "The cashier said they didn't do that. So I said," continued Dimples, *"But I thought this was a bank."*

"Pass," said Bigsy, slapping the table. He didn't put a domino into play.

"And then she said that they didn't have any place for my kind of money."

6

"But don't all banks have place fe money?" said a high-pitched voice. Miss Hortense looked up to see a tall, fair-skinned woman who had entered the room with a tray of over-stewed stewed chicken. It was Blossom. The Bullfrog tutted.

"Well, that's what I said, and I even showed them I had it. Five pounds," said Dimples. "But, *Oh no*, said the cashier. *We can't take that*," mimicked Dimples, frowning. Dimple.

"And what did you say back?" Hortense asked, cool and composed. It was the first time her voice had entered the room. She continued to study her dominoes.

"Say back?" asked Dimples, looking puzzled. "Well, I didn't say anything back. I left. As quickly as I could."

"I heard it's the same at the First Union Bank up on George Street," said another woman, now standing in front of Mr. McKenzie, with a resemblance at the mouth to Constance. This was Mr. McKenzie's wife, Myrtle, a prim-looking, buttoned-up woman. She was staring across the room at a man wearing a baggy beige suit who was continually wiping at his brow. His name was Pastor Williams.

"Better if you seeking to accumulate riches to go to Luke. Verse twelve, thirty-three through to thirty-four: *Provide yourselves a treasure in the heavens that faileth not, where no thief approacheth, neither moth corrupt . . .*" Myrtle continued, seeking to get the pastor's attention, but the room had moved on.

"It's because you wasn't with you husband," shouted the Bullfrog, licking down a domino. "Bigsy, you fe go back with her to the bank, you hear? Is we fe do de talking and manage de money," he continued. He belched again.

Bigsy sat up. "Well, yes," he said. "Dee, I could go back with you next week."

"Pass," said Fitz, tapping his hand on the table. He didn't have a domino to put into play.

Hortense, who had heard quite enough from the Bullfrog, shifted in her seat and eased off her shoes.

"All I wanted to do was put a likkle savings aside," said Dimples.

"Dem scared we a go rob up the place," said Fitz, not looking up from his dominoes.

7

"Union can boycott bank, Errol?" asked Mr. McKenzie from behind Myrtle, who was still quoting the Bible.

"But that na what dem want?" said Bigsy.

"Why don't you just start a Pardner?" asked Hortense, gently putting down a double blank. No one except for Errol had seen it coming. There was an intake of breath from the room. Miss Hortense had blocked the game.

The Bullfrog pushed his chair back so violently that it fell over, and he cursed a bad word beginning with *b*. He stood on his stumpy legs and slammed his heavy fist onto the table so hard that several of the tiles jumped off in fright and landed on the floor. Fitz looked across at Hortense; something danced behind his eyes. A broad smile appeared on Errol's face.

But Miss Hortense noticed how Blossom had flinched, just as the tiles had done, when the Bullfrog brought his hand down onto the table.

The next three games Hortense won straight. Errol was practically laughing. The Bullfrog's neck pulsated. It grew increasingly quiet as the guests in the room gathered around the table to witness the Bullfrog being licked by the nurse woman Errol had brought.

Dimples said, "This Pardner, who would be the banker?"

"I could do it," said Blossom. This time she had with her a bowl of clumpy rice and peas that had clearly caught the bottom of the pot.

"You?" roared the Bullfrog, who it turned out was Blossom's husband—no wonder the flinching. He whipped his head around and lashed out his tongue. "You stupid or what? You can't even breed pickney."

The room fell silent. Miss Hortense looked up to see that Blossom had almost completely disappeared in her own house.

"Anyway," said the Bullfrog, "Pardner a no good business. Old-time foolishness from back home. What can Pardner do for we here inna England?" He slapped down another domino.

"Well, yes, maybe you right," said Bigsy, blinking at his dominoes.

"What about Hortense?" asked Errol as Hortense won another game. "She's good with money and a nurse to rahted. Can't get nothing more trustworthy than a nurse."

"No thank you," said Miss Hortense as she picked out the bones for the next game. She had no desire to take on this raggedy group of people.

"And what about that house you was talking about for you and your sister?" asked Errol. Hortense looked up from her dominoes and glared at him. He knew full well not to put her business into a room of strangers. He turned quickly to Dimples. "And you, Miss Dimples, you is wanting to build a place back home. And, Fitz, you is always talking about getting a boxing gym for you and the boys dem. And you, Pastor, how about a proper church for you and your disciples; Miss Myrtle could help you build it. Why wait for them to accept us and our money?" asked Errol, as if he were at a rally.

The next game Hortense deliberately lost to the Bullfrog, and then quickly the next four games in succession. When the Bullfrog won the sixth game in a row, he rubbed his hands together and pocketed the four pound notes and one pound in change; there were no casualties on the floor and Blossom wasn't flinching. Errol slapped his thigh; the party was over. Even Millie Small with her "My Boy Lollipop" couldn't raise the mood.

"I know," said Dimples. "Why we don't start a Pardner right now? It's Friday, everyone must still have a likkle something left inna them pocket? What about five pounds? Pass me you hat, Fitzroy." Fitz passed his hat to Dimples and fished out five pounds to drop in. Pastor Williams dithered, then said he would put in five pounds the following day. Dimples put in the five pounds she was going to deposit in the bank. Mr. McKenzie put in five pounds, and, after Myrtle insisted, another five pounds for her second cousin Constance. The Bullfrog refused to put a single penny in, of course, and wouldn't let Blossom do so either; but when Hortense returned with a slice of her rich moist black cake the following day, Blossom had five pounds (which she told Hortense she had been hiding under a floorboard) waiting for her.

Errol leaned down to whisper in Hortense's ear. "What happen, man? You could have taken him. That was my last money. You can sub me?"

Miss Hortense cussed her teeth and put her wages in the hat for her and Errol.

9

The hat contained, or would contain, forty pounds.

It was more money gathered in ten minutes than many would see in months.

"Now, Miss Banker," said Errol, directing himself to Miss Hortense, his spirit buoyed again by seeing what was achieved in the hat. "Who going bag first draw? Who going get the whole of this money first?" For that person, it would come like a loan. It would take another seven weeks before they would pay it back with their weekly contributions, and eight before they would get another lump sum themselves. But it was so much more than a loan, as the faces of each of those who had contributed attested as they looked from Miss Hortense to the hat. It was the face of a loved one they could send for and hold close; it was a means to start a little business and to become the person they wrote back home and boasted that they were; it was a little piece of land, a refuge, a house, a church hall, a boxing gym, a community center. It was a future they could plan for, and finally see a path to, and it was a finger up to the Royal National Bank.

No longer were they just a group of individuals striving to make a home for themselves in a foreign land. They were part of something bigger; integral to each other like organs of a body. And Miss Hortense was right at the heart of it.

On that miserable Friday evening in the summer of 1963, Miss Hortense became the banker, also known as the Pardner Lady of Bigglesweigh. She didn't put herself forward willingly, but she took her responsibilities deadly seriously, and she would not stop being the Pardner Lady, nor taking those responsibilities seriously, until seven years later. That was when she was kicked out of the Pardner in the most humiliating way you could imagine after the thing that no one spoke about happened. Another thirty years would pass, and Constance Brown would have to die, before the remaining members of the original Pardner—well, at least those who were able to walk, that is—were all in the same room again.

3

Bricks and Mortar

For Hortense, the Pardner had meant many things, but by far the most precious of things was her own front door.

Hortense had lived at 37 Vernon Road, Bigglesweigh, Birmingham, England, for over half her life. At the ripe age of sixty-five, Miss Hortense, even up close, could be mistaken for being two decades younger than she was. Her skin was still soft and plump despite the years in England. But for the occasional visit to Mane Attraction on the High Street, she still hot-combed her own hair using the traditional method of the hot iron on the gas cooker with newspaper and Dax. She dyed her hair herself too, but she wasn't afraid to let the gray show, and the silver of it streaked through her hair like sugar glistening through a stick of rock. It was that silver that shone through now, catching the sunlight, as Miss Hortense stood in contemplation at the window in her front room.

She was thinking about their Pardner and how it had never been ordinary. How it had had more than three lives. Its first life had enabled the eight of them to chase their dreams—37 Vernon Road an example. It evolved, in its second life, into a community investment scheme that had benefited not just the eight of them, but the whole of Bigglesweigh. In its third life, it had pivoted again into something entirely different and far more dangerous. It had moved into the "Looking Into Bones" business: "Bones" the shorthand word for the quick-fire dominoes game they played, but also the word they used to describe the murders, disappearances and kidnappings they had investigated, back when it was too dangerous to use the names of those involved.

Miss Hortense turned briefly to look at Blossom, sat behind her on the settee, still speechless at Constance's death. She thought about how she had sought to protect her by losing that dominoes game all those years ago, and how she had been protecting her ever since. If it wasn't for that game, she pondered, the Pardner Network of Bigglesweigh, in its many guises, would never have existed.

Number 37 Vernon Road was Miss Hortense's little "always" house, with the hanging basket beside the door, bloodred roses and hydrangeas spilling out of the back and front gardens; with the doorstep that was always polished to a high cherry sheen, the net curtains starched bright white; where, up until thirty years ago, the door was always kept on the latch for anyone to come and go as they pleased. The number, the road, the city, the country all mattered. Bricks and mortar obtained at a time when a Black woman acquiring bricks and mortar in Bigglesweigh was almost as unheard of as England winning a World Cup.

It was a two-up two-down on a small plot of land in a nondescript road. The only standout neighborhood features were a post office at the bottom on the corner of Lancet Road, where an infamous robbery had taken place in 1965, and, on the other side, opposite Miss Hortense, the Richardsons, a white family with seven girls (not, despite what the mother would have you believe, connected to *those* Richardsons), who had been so cantankerous that the eldest daughter knew how most of the local policemen liked their tea. There wasn't anything remarkable about Bigglesweigh. It was a place you went through, not to. It was a place where ideas might originate but were never quite realized. It was one of the first places in the West Midlands to get a cinema, but that became a bingo hall and then, years later, was boarded up.

It had taken nineteen Pardner draws, from the summer of 1963 to the semifinals of the World Cup in 1966, for Hortense to save towards the seven hundred pounds and sixty-two shillings to put down as the deposit. Back then, number 37 was not much more than a broken-down shell that hadn't been lived in for donkey's years. Miss Hortense saw the possibility, though. It was going to be an "always" home for her, her sister Evie and her nephew Gregory (which Hortense pronounced *Gregry*). A place of safety and permanence.

Miss Hortense often thought about what the house would have looked like if Evie had made it in with her son. If she'd taken the big room facing the road, sewn the curtains to go at the front, helped pick out the carpets and the wallpaper. As it was, it had always been just she one. In a house she had fallen in love with, not because it was anything to look at, or in the best area, but because it was hers: *her* number on *her* road, *her* postcode in *her* town, in *her* country. Her home.

There had been instances throughout the years and, in particular, just after Hortense had moved in, when she got letters through the letter box, and sometimes stuck to a brick thrown through the front-room window, and once on a piece of feces squashed to the door, telling her she must go back home. But how could she possibly have taken such correspondence seriously when the author couldn't even spell "banana" and was stupid enough to reuse her Family Allowance envelope? Damn fools. As if living in a country for twice as many years as the one she had come from didn't make this her home.

In 1966, after Miss Hortense had moved into 37 Vernon Road, she'd invite anyone who came to her door—Black, white or purple—in for a drink and one of her famous gizzada pastries, and every invitation accepted was a small victory against that road that had so obviously been repelled by her.

That house on Vernon Road represented the long journey away from her parents when she had come to England to find Evie. It was every shift she had ever worked at the hospital, every insult she had swallowed down to her stomach, the relationship she had sacrificed and more. But it was the Pardner and all those draws that had given her the start, and for that she would be eternally grateful.

When Miss Hortense saved up enough for the deposit, the Pardner had the same original eight members: Miss Hortense decided it was Dimples who bagged first draw, second Blossom, third Constance, fifth Fitz, sixth Pastor Williams, seventh Mr. McKenzie and eighth Miss Hortense. The fourth person's name she found too difficult to consider.

When Precious's daughter, Likkle, was old enough, she would run all the way from the top of Ebley Street to bring the family's hard-earned income; the little girl had strict instructions not to stop until she'd reached Miss Hortense. Except the one time she tripped, her dress wet and muddy, her knees all cut up and bruised.

"I can't find it," she said, her lip trembling, her hands empty and those big eyes full of water. Miss Hortense didn't know how long she'd been standing inside the gate in the freezing cold, building up the courage to tell her so. They both went out to look for the envelope along the main road and in the hedgerow that ran alongside it. But nothing could be found.

"Our little secret, then," Miss Hortense assured the girl, squeezing her hand tight. "Now run home and don't mention this to you mother." She often wondered what had become of the girl.

Fitz would travel all the way from Wolverhampton after a long shift at the rubber factory to bring his hand as soon as he had been paid. They never talked about why the urgency, but Miss Hortense knew: it was because of what happened that one time with the horses, when his first wife kicked him out. He was a man who didn't trust himself, and it was true that for some, money could really burn a hole inna dem pocket.

For Blossom, the Pardner was first and foremost an escape route. A way out from under a brooding husband, otherwise known as the Bullfrog, who had used her body like a punching bag. When Miss Hortense had handed over Blossom's first draw, she grabbed it with iron in her grip, declaring: *I will never be inclining on a man again and I will kill any man who tries to put a finger 'pon me.*

The Pardner Network of Bigglesweigh had provided entrances and exits, ways and means, for the eight members of the Pardner for a good number of years. Back then, the Pardner represented possibility, and that was enough to make the sacrifice. And back then, all they had was possibility—after all, it's what they had first come to the country with. That and a trust that each one would come through for the other seven. The Pardner bound them together irrevocably in their dreams, hopes and desperation.

But it wasn't until Bigsy's funeral in 1964 that the Pardner really found its feet and moved into its second life.

The funny thing is, that only happened because of the mix-up with the bodies.

4

The Geriatric Mafia

Back in Miss Hortense's front room, Miss Hortense switched on the TV. Mr. Blair, the prime minister, was outraged about guerrillas and gardeners or some such thing. Miss Hortense switched it off again.

As the rum reached the pit of her stomach, Blossom began to retrieve her words. She reached a shaky, heavily ringed hand to her mouth and said: "Hortense, you think is our meeting yesterday had someting to do with Constance's death?"

Miss Hortense walked back towards Blossom and sank into her favorite leather armchair. The chair protested against her weight as she adjusted herself. She looked down at her right leg, which was starting to swell, as it did in the heat, or sometimes when she was about to tell a lie.

Blossom was referring to the meeting she and Hortense had had with Constance and Pastor Williams the previous day. They had sat right across from Constance, at the small *plinkety-plinkety* glass table that rocked whenever anyone so much as breathed on it. Hortense had been summoned by the two of them—that was the right word: "summoned"—to Constance's house in Musgrove Park, and then, it was fair to say, Hortense was ambushed.

"What the two of them can possibly want with me now, Lawd?" Hortense had asked at the time she received the invitation, in the vicinity of Blossom, not really believing that Blossom would have the answer. Thirty years later, Blossom was still on the inside of the Pardner, but she wasn't on the *inside* inside, and that was because Blossom and Miss Hortense had remained close, despite what the others had said about her.

15

"All I know," Blossom had said, fiddling with her brightly colored scarf, "is there mussy something gone very wrong with de money because I don't see my draw fe five weeks now."

In retrospect, Miss Hortense should have paid more attention to the fiddling.

Of course, Miss Hortense could have chosen not to go. She wasn't a somebody to be summoned by anybody, not least by Constance Brown or Pastor Williams, but she was intrigued about the money problems Blossom had been complaining about for several weeks and why Constance and the pastor wished to put aside thirty-odd years of ostracism to have Hortense's company. She had also recently come into the possession of some information that she felt it was only right that Constance, as the current Pardner Lady, should be made aware of.

"Well, I might as well go," Miss Hortense told Blossom casually. "There is something I wish to show Constance Brown in any case." And she looked across to her handbag on the coffee table.

Like Constance herself, the suburb of Musgrove Park had always been two-faced. The last time Miss Hortense paid a visit to Constance was in 1964, when Constance and her husband, Mr. Brown, had lived on the ghetto side of it, renting a room from the now infamous white slum landlord, in a shared boardinghouse riddled with rot. That was before said landlord set fire to the boardinghouse, and Constance's husband, Mr. Brown, had died.

Before the fire, Miss Hortense knew that Constance was barely making ends meet. This wasn't unusual among her people, particularly in those days, but even then Constance had been a proud woman. Nothing wrong with that, but it was her Small Island ways that Miss Hortense couldn't stand. In any case, Constance's fortunes had changed significantly in the decades that followed and with them, her accommodation.

"To the manor born," Miss Hortense said sarcastically as she looked up at the oversize windows on the corner plot. Blossom turned to Miss Hortense.

"Now don't say anything you are going to regret, Hortense. Just listen." Which was advice indeed, coming from Blossom. And then

16

she added in a whisper, "Don't forget—don't mention our Black Cake investigations."

There was an expensive shiny black car taking up the driveway. The front garden was not as well kept as it could have been, the evidence in the half-hearted attempt at manicured shrubs around the border. The entrance was vast and reminded Hortense of the old plantation houses in Jamaica. It was obvious they were being watched. A curtain at the front of the house moved as a distorted figure came towards them through the frosted glass panels of the heavy timber front door, which swung slowly open to reveal Constance with her frozen half-and-half smile. Her yellow-yam hue was even duller in the shadowy light. She was wearing pearls (though probably fake ones), a salmon-pink cardigan and low-heeled navy court shoes, all inside her own house. The inside of the house was neat enough, though Miss Hortense noted the cobwebs and dust fluttering along the high ceilings; a side effect of having too large a house and too small a ladder. Inside smelled like Constance: the scent of Pears soap and bandages. Not important enough to go into the sitting room or whatever room that was on their right, which Constance was quick to firmly close the door to, they were led towards the back of the house. Constance's Jheri curl glistened as she shimmied in front of them, leading them into a kitchen that had a strong smell of burnt toast and overdone porridge. Not like Constance to burn things.

"Sister Hortense," said Pastor Williams, who was already sat at the glass table. A whiff of mothballs emanated from him. The table wobbled as he said, "Good to see you, Sister." Yet his eyes said something different. Constance directed her and Blossom to take a seat. No one offered either of them so much as a glass of water, and for a moment no one said a thing; such, she supposed, was the gravity of the occasion.

Miss Hortense watched the two of them on the other side of the table looking like the Black geriatric mafia: Constance, with her mouth pushed up in that stiff smile, her shark teeth barely showing, her stare aloof; then there was Pastor Williams, looking like an excuse in his suit and overly tight waistcoat. The shine from the table matched his bald head. He swiped a rag across it to mop it up. To Miss Hortense's left, Blossom fiddled with her scarf.

The pastor ended the silence by tapping the table. He cleared his throat, the master of volume starting off almost at a whisper.

"We might as well cut straight to it, Sister Hortense." He paused for breath. "We all, sitting around this table, understand, and I would say, agree on, the importance of the Pardner."

You had to lean in to get it all. Blossom was nodding; Constance was nodding.

"It is fair to say, we, around this table, have a better understanding of what the Pardner is than most. It is an institution, an institution that rests on its discretion and confidential nature."

So it was to be a sermon, thought Miss Hortense, as she adjusted her seat and inhaled deeply.

"It is a valuable institution, and despite some knocks and hardships along the way, the Pardner, yes, I say it again, the Pardner has flourished."

His words rose and fell, and in the dip, Miss Hortense sniffed and said: "Lined your pockets and rinsed off de Pardner money more like." Miss Hortense was not a person to say things under her breath. She didn't care who heard or who might be offended. Blossom gave her a kick all the same; Constance adjusted her position in her seat.

He paused. "Yes indeed, the Pardner has, in its time, been profitable, and that has assisted the community greatly." He looked to Constance. Hortense detected an uncertainty in his eyes. "But given your previous, and it would seem still current criticism," he said, now addressing Miss Hortense, "of the way we run this Pardner, we were somewhat"—he was choosing his words carefully—"surprised by your rekindled interest in rejoining it."

Miss Hortense opened her mouth and managed to say, "What the . . . ," and was on the verge of saying a word beginning with *b* (even though Miss Hortense didn't like swear words) when she felt another sharp dig in her shin and saw Blossom glaring at her.

"Just listen na, man," Blossom whispered.

"Yes. Sister Blossom here"—the pastor looked over to Blossom, who nodded her head and smiled as she adjusted the scarf again—"has been a strong supporter of you of late," he continued.

Hortense glared back at Blossom, who beamed.

"She brought your recent interest in rejoining the Pardner to our attention, and I felt"—Pastor Williams looked at Constance, who looked away—"it was only fair to think on it. Given the current circumstances." He damped his hands as if trying to quell a fire.

"With McKenzie, poor thing, on him deathbed," interjected Blossom.

"Yes, well, that," continued the pastor. "It might, as Sister Blossom here suggested to us, mek some sense for us to think on our membership some. Particularly with certain recessionary circumstances that have, um, temporarily diverted certain mortgage payments." He was clearly on the verge of trying to say something more, but Blossom's face turned to confusion and Constance kicked him under the table and he changed tack. "Well, we used to be eight, and then, what with you and Brother Fitz deciding to leave—"

"I was turfed out," said Hortense, not under her breath.

Pastor Williams cleared his throat and continued. "Yes, well, that, and then with various deaths and ting over de years it went down to four, but now, since Brother McKenzie have him stroke, we is only really three—Sister Constance, Sister Blossom and me. Having another somebody, like you, come back, who understand the Pardner and de money, and who was there right from the beginning, well, that could be good. That could work."

Hortense huffed. Constance chewed on the inside of her cheek; Blossom continued nodding.

"But something very concerning has come to our attention," said the pastor carefully, looking at Constance. "Or let me put it another way"—the volume rising—"we were recently approached by a young man who raised with us some grave concerns."

"What young man?" said Blossom in an even higher pitch than normal.

"I'm coming to that, Sister Blossom," he said. "The young man in question is a Germaine Banton. You know him?" the pastor asked Hortense.

"Who?" asked Blossom, leaning forwards.

"Germaine Banton. He is the owner of the business called G&T," said Constance.

"This young man said you threatened him, Sister Hortense. Is that right?" the pastor asked.

19

"What is that?" asked Blossom. "Who? Hortense? You?" She turned to Miss Hortense with an open mouth.

Pastor Williams didn't wait for an answer.

"We do not run our Pardner in that way, Sister Hortense."

"Not anymore, at least," Constance said, not quite under her breath.

"We are not," said the pastor, "in the business of threatening people."

"We are," said Constance, "in the investment business."

"We understand that it must have been Sister Blossom who told you about our interest in this young man's business," said Pastor Williams.

Blossom started coughing. Miss Hortense shot her another look.

"Our investments are strictly confidential, as Blossom knows. But we shall deal with that later," said Constance with a lick of velvet in her tone.

"As you may already now know, Miss Hortense, G&T, nothing to do with the drink as far as I understand it"—he was looking again at Constance for confirmation—"is a very promising business. A very promising business," Pastor said again, as if to convince himself of the fact.

"A very promising business," repeated Constance, but Miss Hortense observed that she was wringing her hands.

"It is starting to make some good returns," the pastor continued. "And we are very hopeful that the Pardner will benefit from them. So we have no idea"—he motioned to Constance, whose half-and-half smile was returning—"what your concerns with this young man's business could possibly be, and why you felt the need to threaten him on our behalf." He tapped the table.

There was a silence as Miss Hortense shifted. Blossom fiddled so hard with the scarf it wouldn't have surprised Miss Hortense if the stitching started to come apart. Miss Hortense looked at Constance.

"Turmeric," Miss Hortense said finally.

"What?" asked the pastor, nonplussed.

"They na use it," said Miss Hortense. "Inna dem patty."

Blossom's mouth opened wide.

"Food coloring can give the patty the yellow but it's not the same as turmeric. Not at all. And how can you trust a patty that don't have any turmeric?"

Constance gave off a sort of victorious sigh.

"A patty . . ." said Miss Hortense, hearing her pronunciation change, aping that of her host, with a touch of the St. Andrew, "supposed to have turmeric. That is the traditional, well-tested, *Jamaican* way. I don't trust something that call itself one thing but don't have all the ingredients to justify the name."

Miss Hortense gave her own half-and-half smile, mimicking the woman on the other side of the table, and looked directly at the pastor. She could see out of the corner of her eye that Constance's gritted teeth were beginning to reveal more of themselves.

"That is what you call a fraud, don't it?" said Miss Hortense, underlining her point to the pastor, who seemed not to know what to do with his hands. Uncomfortable under the glare of all three women, he mopped his head again.

Constance snatched the baton. "You see, Pastor? How could you even have considered this? The current membership of the Pardner is just fine, thank you very much, and just because Mr. McKenzie is not well don't mean we need any more members, and definitely not that woman sitting over thereso." She generally directed her hand towards Miss Hortense.

"Well, why would you share you pension?" asked Miss Hortense. Blossom kicked her again.

Constance continued addressing Pastor Williams. "Like I said, even before this poor, shaken-up young man told us what she had done, Miss Hortense is not a suitable candidate for this Pardner. And we don't need nor want her interfering in our investments neither. She is not to put her nose in our business again." Then, drawing out her sharpened knife, whetted over the course of thirty years, she said under her breath, "And we don't need to remind ourselves what happened the last time she interfered, do we? People get hurt." She fake coughed. "People get killed."

There it was. The knife pushed deep into the open wound that Miss Hortense had hoped might have, in some part, healed. There it was still: oozing in her chest, on display for everyone to see. Miss Hortense suddenly felt hot in Constance's kitchen as she pushed her chair back and it scraped on the cold hard tiles. But her leg had swelled right up and she couldn't stand up as quickly as she would have liked. The table rocked with the motion of her.

Miss Hortense leaned across the table and said very directly: "You better watch yourself, ya hear? Don't think I don't know who you are, Constance Brown. Don't think I don't know what you is capable of."

Constance started to turn red, and the smile completely disappeared.

"But not to worry," Miss Hortense said, leaning back again. "I shan't get myself involved inna any of your business, my dear."

Miss Hortense wasn't one to break her promises. So, with that, she walked out of that big old house with the information she had recently discovered tucked into her handbag, with no intention of having any further conversation with Constance Brown, Pastor Williams or perhaps even with Blossom, who had led her into the trap, ever again.

Oh, it was true that right at that moment, if looks and wishes could kill, Miss Hortense would have killed that ignorant, flat-bottomed, Small Island, false-smiling, butter-wouldn't-melt, fake-pearls, goat-mouthed woman a thousand times over. And enjoyed every moment. However, it seemed that, despite ample provocation, something else was destined to beat her to it instead.

5

The Second Life of the Pardner

It was after all the drama at Bigsy's funeral, in August 1964, just over a year after the Pardner started, that they really got into the swing of things. That was when the Pardner grew from being a personal loan scheme for its eight members to representing something the whole community would benefit from.

Bigsy was Dimples's husband and it was Dimples who bagged the first draw back in 1963. When, three days after they'd decided to start the Pardner, Miss Hortense had brought an envelope with forty pounds in cash to her door, no words were necessary. A person could reveal a great deal about themselves to Miss Hortense without uttering a single word. She believed that everything you wanted to know about a person was written in the body. All the secrets were there to behold, if you only took time to decipher the signals and opened your eyes wide enough to look. It was in their clothes and how they were worn, in the smell that lingered, in the way a person held themselves; if they leaned slightly to the left, it could be because there was pain coming from the right; it was in the pallor and condition of the skin, the way that they breathed, shallow or deep. Miss Hortense was an expert in all these things because of her nursing. She could tell you whether a person was hiding something even before they themselves were aware of the thing they were hiding; and nine times out of ten, she was right.

Dimples was a woman who was homesick. You could tell that by the yellow-ocher green that rested just below the surface of her light brown skin and the runny nose that she had even in summer; the way that her cardigan constantly slipped from her left shoulder, as if there were no point in pulling it back up properly; the water in her voice and her eyes, which were dull, except for when she was talking about that little patch of land she and her husband were saving up for.

"You don't know what this means, Miss Hortense." Dimples's eyes in that moment were pools of light. "We going buy a plot of land in Stony Hill," she had said, holding on to Miss Hortense's hands long after the envelope of cash had been passed between them. Her hands, despite the sickness for back home, were warm. Miss Hortense knew well and good what the Pardner meant. Patience, sacrifice and reward. But Dimples never did get her reward.

That was because, in August 1964, Dimples's husband, Bigsy, whose name on his passport said Livingston Turner, was killed. Dimples described it as a cold-blooded killing, and everyone else came to agree.

Bigsy was an ordinary Jamaican man, a welder who lived on Fore Street and worked at the Metal Works Factory in Drews Lane. Before that he had lived in Lawrence Tavern in the St. Andrew Parish, Jamaica. He was a good man, with a good family, who lived a good life. Until his untimely death, there was nothing remarkable about him, which for a Black man in those days was a blessing.

On Wednesday, August 26, one of the hottest days of the year, he went to work at 7:30 a.m. and never returned home. He died aged thirty-five, in the back room of the loading bay of the depot of Metal Works, the factory where he had worked for the past six years, never a day late, never a sore word, even when the company had dropped its standards in an attempt to save costs. The details of his passing were gruesome—the sleeve of his very well-pressed overall got stuck in the machine they used to press the hinges. The ring finger, middle finger, whole wrist and shoulder all followed, and as the emergency stop button hadn't worked for many months, his whole arm and most of the left side of his body joined them before the machine was eventually shut down at the mains. Metal Works said that it was Bigsy's inexperience that had caused the accident. He didn't, according to them, have the right qualifications. They didn't add that no one in the factory had the so-called right qualifications either. But they did send some lovely flowers to Dimples expressing their *greatest sympathy for her loss.* With a very big full stop after the last *s*. They refused to engage in any further correspondence with her.

Overnight, the sickly yellow-ocher green of Dimples's skin tone was replaced by a deep blue and she decided that, given the Metal Works Factory was trying to blame her husband for his own death, his funeral was going to be an eye-opener: Bigsy was going to have an open casket. If Metal Works wasn't going to take responsibility for its own failures, then she was going to show it, and anybody else who cared to look, what its barbaric failures had caused.

Until the death of Bigsy, if a Black person died in Bigglesweigh, it was the local undertaker, Thompson & Sons, that they were carted off to. The Thompson family had been in the undertaking business for at least half a century before Bigsy died. They were, according to them, top professionals in the field of dead people. They had never stepped out of the West Midlands, "didn't fraternize with any person they didn't trust including nignogs, didn't want any of their daughters fraternizing with nignogs and they certainly didn't want any living nignogs living on their road." Though they didn't have any problem taking their money when they were dead.

When the coffin was opened at the funeral, Dimples, who was standing next to it, fainted. Mr. McKenzie, a toolmaker at the Metal Works Factory, had come to see Bigsy off and was in the viewing line to the side of the Thompson brothers. He overheard the youngest Thompson as he leaned over to the oldest Thompson and whispered, "Well, we can't help it if they all look the bloody same."

McKenzie was a good man, with a son of his own called Michael, who McKenzie had dreamed would one day be able to achieve much more than him. When he looked into the open coffin, he was so appalled by the disrespect shown to Bigsy and his family that he decided then and there that he would hand in his notice.

Dimples fainted not because of how bad Bigsy looked in the coffin (she was the one who identified his body), but because it wasn't Bigsy in the coffin at all. In fact, it wasn't even a man. None of the funeral attendees had any idea who the old woman was.

McKenzie decided that no longer would any member of his community need to rely on the services of bigots who couldn't even give a decent Black man a decent send-off. But how did a Black toolmaker with no experience of undertaking start an undertaking business? You think the National Bank would lend to him? That's how the Pardner Network of Bigglesweigh started all those years ago in the community investment business.

6

Black Cake Investigations

"Hortense," said Blossom, easing off her shoes and elevating her left leg on the pouf in Hortense's living room.

"Yes, Blossom."

"When we was at Constance's house yesterday, you said that you was going show her something? What was the something you was going show her?"

Hortense reached across for her day handbag on the top of the coffee table.

Miss Hortense had two handbags that she was very fond of. Both were soft black leather with a short handle to hold in the crook of her arm, with a large zipped pocket at the front and plenty of zipped pockets on the inside. The two bags were almost identical, except that one of them had a small piece of red ribbon tied onto the handle. The bag with the ribbon was her night bag. The one she reached for now didn't have the ribbon.

Hortense rooted around in it, cussed her teeth, and emptied the contents of the bag one by one onto the coffee table: a bottle of Mackenzie's Smelling Salts, a small bottle of rum, a hairpin, two credit cards (one marginally thicker than the other), an almost-empty packet of cigarettes, the King James Version Bible, a hymn book, a cleaner's dark blue tabard, a pair of knickers, a large yellow dusting cloth, a bottle of bleach, a name tag, a lanyard and a passport (the names on all three were different). She left the syringe, which contained 5 milliliters of succinylcholine, in the zipped pocket inside the bag, noting that the wallet definitely wouldn't be in that pocket and the sight of the needle would make Blossom queasy. Finally, she reached into the bag and pulled out her wallet. She fished around in the wallet, took out a five-pound note and showed Blossom.

"Money?" asked Blossom.

"You don't see how dirty it is?" said Hortense, holding it up to the light. The queen's face was all marked up and a chunk was missing from the side.

"Don't all money dirty like that?" asked Blossom.

"Oh no," said Hortense, putting the note away. "Some money is much dirtier than others." She began repacking the items back into her handbag.

"And what that got to do with Constance?" asked Blossom.

"The big black expensive car," said Hortense enigmatically, not looking up.

"Oh," said Blossom. Sometimes she found it very hard to follow Hortense, so she didn't bother to ask any more questions about that. Instead, she said, "You thinking what I'm thinking?"

"How would I know what you is thinking?"

"Well, now Constance is dead, there isn't anybody stopping you from getting back inna de Pardner. Pastor man—him couldn't stop a clock."

"Oh no you don't," replied Hortense.

"But—" said Blossom, but Miss Hortense stopped her right there.

"Mek me tell you something. Never again. Not in my lifetime," she said. "I know the Pardner may be short of members, but you just going haffy find somebody from somewhere else."

Miss Hortense had in truth thought about it, but not in the way that Blossom was suggesting. The meeting with Constance Brown and Pastor Williams had reminded her of a time she couldn't let herself forget. She hadn't slept the whole night, and neither the cerasee tea nor the smelling salts were helping. She took up the bottle of smelling salts now, waved it briefly under her nose and sniffed sharply.

"Nope," she said. "Me finish with that long time."

"Hortense?"

"Yes, Blossom."

"Me sorry," said Blossom very quietly.

Blossom had told Constance and Pastor Williams, of all people, that Miss Hortense had wanted to return to the Pardner, like a dog with a begging bowl, when, in fact, she did not. As Hortense remembered that smug expression on Constance's face, her chest got hot again and her leg started to tingle.

Miss Hortense couldn't think of any time before, in the whole thirty-seven years of knowing Blossom, that she had come straight out with an apology. But of course, it wasn't ever as straightforward as that with Blossom.

Blossom took a sip of her rum. "But don't you think it's strange, Hortense? That first McKenzie, poor thing, have a stroke and now Constance is dead, all in a matter of weeks? Two people in the Pardner more or less gone, just like that? Well, that to me seems very strange indeed."

Miss Hortense didn't think that illness and death were, in and of themselves, strange. It was the circumstances that could make them so. Constance died of a heart attack. Though as far as Hortense was concerned, Constance had never shown any weakness of the heart. Mr. McKenzie had his first stroke months before Constance died, though it wasn't until the third stroke that he was taken to St. Anne's Hospital. St. Anne's was known as the Knackers' Yard because the people who went in there either came out dead or mostly dead. A third of Mr. McKenzie was discharged the weekend before Constance passed away. He had lost all feeling and function on his left side and his speech had completely disappeared. Of course, before the strokes, you couldn't say the McKenzie name without thinking about the tragic loss of their only son, Michael, in 1967; hence the "poor thing" from Blossom.

For the past thirty-odd years, Blossom had been coming to Miss Hortense in secret every Wednesday for a slice of Miss Hortense's black cake generously soaked in Rich Ruby wine and white rum. The recipe had been handed down from Miss Hortense's mother, and her mother before her, and Miss Hortense had no intention of adapting it for anybody.

After Blossom had finished digging out the raisins, she would hand Hortense a small, folded-up piece of paper. On the piece of paper was a name or names written in Blossom's barely legible handwriting. Such was the need for confidentiality that Blossom would say, "After you finish you background checks, Hortense, don't forget to burn it when you done. If Pastor or she ever find out, you see . . ." Blossom would whisper. "Hell to pay."

The names were in relation to various community investments that the Pardner was contemplating making. "Top secret," Blossom would say under her breath, because walls have ears. After Blossom had finished with her crumbs and left, Miss Hortense would start the background checks, and that's what had happened when, one week before Constance died, Blossom had passed her the note that read *C&T*. Miss Hortense had put on her glasses and said out loud, "C&T?"

Blossom had looked at her indecipherable handwriting on the paper. "No, that is not a *C*, it's a *G*," she had said, and continued eating her crumbs.

"You know what the *G* and *T* stand for?" Miss Hortense had asked. Blossom had shaken her head no.

Miss Hortense's "background checks" weren't the usual type of background checks one might associate with someone trying to investigate an investment opportunity. Miss Hortense didn't give a fig about how financially "promising" the business was or was not. Her checks were purely about one thing: the person. The person behind the business, because it was that person who could make or break the community, and as her own mother used to say: *One bad apple can spoil the whole cart.*

Miss Hortense would simply, after her look into the person, provide a "recommendation": a green flag meaning: *Nothing to worry about, go right ahead.* Or it might be a red flag, which meant: *Stay well clear and don't touch that person or their business with a bargepole.* That secret recommendation to Blossom would translate into two Pardner votes on the investment opportunity: one vote from Blossom, one vote from their friend, Mr. McKenzie.

In that way, Miss Hortense was very much at the heart of the Pardner, despite no longer being a paid-up member. She didn't consider it interfering. She considered it a duty to her community because it only took one bad apple—and, it seemed, she was the only one looking for them. Up until the meeting the day before, as far as Miss Hortense was aware, her involvement had been very much hidden from Pastor Williams and Constance Brown, and the majority of the people over the years had received green flags from Miss Hortense's Black Cake investigations, even when the Pardner broadened its investment portfolio. Blossom would come with more names, and Miss Hortense would step up her checks, and in that way ensure that the Pardner continued, in some small part, to be the organization that had been created all those years ago when Dimples fainted at the funeral: to provide doors to good people who wanted to do good for the community.

In fact, there were many wonderful initiatives that the Pardner had invested in over the years: the Bigglesweigh Afro-Caribbean Social Organization, and the land and buildings the Pardner helped to acquire for it in 1968, which had acted as a hub for the community ever since, or the kick start it gave Fitz to set up a local boxing gym in the railway arches to help youths turn their lives around, as well as McKenzie's undertaker's on Chappel Road. But then there were the red flags, and when C—no, G—&T had produced a red flag, Miss Hortense knew that she would have to do something out of the ordinary, because with McKenzie's strokes, Blossom's one vote against Constance and Pastor's two meant that for the first time in over three decades, the cart was about to receive its first bad apple in the form of the G&T investment.

"But . . ." said Blossom, wiggling her bunion foot on the pouf. Not only had she finally found her words, but there seemed to be no end to them now. "You don't think it's strange, Hortense? All this death? You don't think there is something funny going on? Maybe you should start Looking Into it?" Blossom whispered the last three words.

The investment business was not the only out-of-the-ordinary activity that the Pardner Network of Bigglesweigh had participated in. It was another set of tragic events that happened just over three years after Bigsy's funeral that catapulted the Pardner into its third life.

It was when Mr. McKenzie's nineteen-year-old son, Michael, was found dead on Cuckoo Lane, and the police had claimed it was from a heart attack, that the "Looking Into Bones" business—otherwise known as the detective arm of the Pardner—started. When it became clear that the police weren't going to investigate, the Pardner members inadvertently became unofficial sleuths in their own community, locating the two Chapman cousins who had beaten Michael to death, and discovering their uncle was Charlie Reynolds. It was they who had exposed that nasty piece of work, and the two rotten seeds he had planted, to the world.

During that case and subsequent ones, the Pardner utilized intelligence Pastor Williams received from his congregation; the influence Errol had in the trade union; the contacts Fitz had in the underground world that he had once been a part of. Constance exploited her official position in the local council; Blossom's obsession with death brought surprising insights; Dimples, when she partially recovered from Bigsy's death, shared information she acquired from other people's houses where she worked as a domestic cleaner; and Hortense brought her medical skills as a nurse.

Miss Hortense cussed her teeth at Blossom's suggestion.

"How can a woman like Constance just drop down dead," continued Blossom, "without any warning? That na make sense to me. Constance dead? That don't seem strange? What if something *bad* happened to Constance? What if it's only *we* can help? You not going do someting 'bout it, Hortense?"

Blossom went on and on until it got dark and a weary Miss Hortense told her it was time to leave.

Truth be told, Hortense was starting to think that the circumstances surrounding Constance's death were odd; but to keep her out of harm's way, she was never going to admit that to Blossom.

7

A Bright Red Flag

The strange circumstances surrounding Constance's death involved her son. A week before Constance died, and the morning after Blossom passed her the note that read *G&T*, Miss Hortense visited the library.

"They're not Apples," said Joel, looking at the dark screen. "But most of the time they work all right." Miss Hortense had not a clue why the boy was talking about fruit. The only thing she knew about computers was that on the first of January, they were all meant to catch some kind of killer bug and mash up the world. Well, here they were in April 2000, and the world still seemed to be functioning fine. He hit the top of the monitor a few times.

"There," said Joel as he pointed to the computer screen, which had lit up again. "It's come up now."

Whenever Miss Hortense came to the library, even though Joel was often the only security guard on duty, he made sure he was on his break to assist her. So when she asked him, "How you turn this thing on, why de screen gone black again, what am I to do with this mice-rat?" he would not only do the magic to turn on the computer for her, but he would put down his radio, pull up a chair, and put in and pull out any details that she required.

"G&T is . . ." said Joel, scrolling the screen, "a model agency, a talent agency and a catering dynasty."

"All of that?" said Miss Hortense, looking at the computer. There were glitzy pictures of girls in half frocks, a glass of something fizzy with a palm tree in the distance and a plate of steaming ackee and salt fish. Germaine Banton, according to the flashy website they were now looking at, was the business owner. He was doing very well for himself, going by his sparkly watch and shiny jacket, a young man who was going places—or so it seemed to those who perhaps didn't look too closely.

The radio was making a crackling sound and Joel said, "I better be getting back."

"Hold on," Miss Hortense instructed Joel as she raised her hand. "Go back a minute." Joel went to the previous page. Miss Hortense leaned in to the screen and looked hard. In the picture on display, in the background, almost hidden at the very edge of it, was a short man with a big forehead whom she recognized. Miss Hortense looked at the sign in the photograph—*Rushden Industrial Estate*—and she leaned back.

"Well, well," she said to herself.

"What?" asked Joel, but Miss Hortense lifted herself up and was already on her way to the door.

Miss Hortense caught the number 122 bus to the Rushden Industrial Estate, handbag clasped firmly on her lap. It was a fifty-two-minute journey to the outskirts of town and the bus ride was bumpy. Miss Hortense didn't like cars. Her preferred method of transportation was the bus. She knew most of the bus routes in Bigglesweigh, a number of the drivers, and many of the bus timetables by heart.

When she arrived, she went to the unit that looked most similar to the one on the computer, Unit 44. The shutters were down and there were no lights on. "What time dem open?" Miss Hortense asked a man in front of an adjoining unit, with grease on his hands and face.

"Couldn't tell you, love. But they don't open during the day."

What kind of business can afford not to open during the day? Miss Hortense asked herself. The man went back to working on a car, a big shiny black one.

"But when it is open," Miss Hortense shouted to get the man's attention again, "does a short man with a big forehead and big belly go inside?" She was describing Nigel Brown. The man shrugged at her, but she could tell from the way he had started to vigorously poke underneath the car that something she had said had impacted his pace.

Next, she went to the address for G&T Catering Dynasty, Talent and Model Agency. This turned out to be a small takeaway shop around the corner from the High Street. There were no palm trees in sight but plenty of paint peeling off the walls. There was a young-looking girl, whom Miss Hortense recognized from the computer: one of those with hardly any frock on, who appeared rushed off her feet, despite the fact that there wasn't anybody, save for Miss Hortense, in the shop for her to serve.

"What would you like, aunty?" the girl asked, wiping her hands nervously on her small blue apron. She was mixed-race, with an elaborate hairstyle piled on top of her head, a curly strand falling into her face.

"Hmm," said Miss Hortense, wanting to flick the nuisance curl away. She looked up at the menu above the counter, which was in bright primary colors. "What you recommend?"

"I don't know," said the girl, fidgeting. "People say the beef patties are nice?"

"One of them then, please."

The girl smiled briefly. "I'll warm it up, yeah?"

Miss Hortense nodded.

It was midday, but the only other person to come into the shop was a white man, tall and lean like a pole, most of his face covered by an Aston Villa baseball cap, asking for change for a ten-pound note. The girl, in a strop, refused to give him any, and the man left in an equal strop. There were two red plastic chairs and a beaten-up table. Miss Hortense took an uncomfortable seat. Thirty seconds later, a microwave pinged and the girl brought what Miss Hortense wouldn't call a patty on a paper plate. The girl smiled again, wiped her hands down her thighs and went back behind the counter.

"Is you mek dis, dear?" Miss Hortense asked, eyeing up the soggy pastry.

"No, aunty. We buy them in," said the girl.

Miss Hortense squeezed it open.

"It have turmeric inna it?" Miss Hortense poked at the vivid sogginess.

Before the girl could answer, a dry-skinned boy Miss Hortense

35

recognized from the computer as Germaine Banton rushed in off the street, looking a lot less shiny than he had on the computer. He bounced around the back of the shop and the young girl followed him like she was being swept up in his tailwind. Voices rose from behind the closed door and Miss Hortense rose from her seat to listen in better:

". . . but, G . . ." The girl's voice. "I just don't want him in the shop."

Germaine swore.

The girl's voice: "Okay, sorry, G, yeah. Sorry . . ."

There was a silence and Miss Hortense moved nearer. The door suddenly opened and Miss Hortense made like she was studying the over-bright menu as the boy stormed out. The young girl came back to the counter a few seconds later, eyes red.

After Hortense left the shop, she called her nephew, the policeman.

"Gregry?"

"Yes, Aunty?"

"You know any tall mawga white men?" she asked him.

"That's quite a broad description, Aunty," he said. "Can you narrow it down a bit?"

"The one I'm interested in wears one of them Aston Villa caps."

"A football supporter? Aunty, that could be anyone. But if he's very tall . . ."

"Yes."

"And slim . . ."

"Yes. Yes."

"And supports Aston Villa, then I suppose it could be Richard Dudney—goes by the name of Dice. He works as a bouncer at the club on the High Street. He's a nasty piece of work." And then he said, "Why d'you want to know, Aunty?"

But Miss Hortense had already put the phone down on him.

Later that evening, when she headed to the Oasis nightclub on the High Street, Miss Hortense carried her night bag.

The items in her night bag were identical to those in her day bag, except that in Miss Hortense's night bag, you would also find two bottles of perfume. One was a purple crystal round bottle that she had received one Christmas from her nephew and his ex-wife. It had a fancy and unnecessary atomizer with stupid black tassels at the end. The bottle was empty (she had thrown out the dreadful-smelling liquid when she was given it) and the atomizer emitted air only. The other was a thin gold bottle, and when Miss Hortense was forced to use it, it gave out a particular form of cocktail that could be used to great effect to provide temporary, but agonizing, blindness.

When she got to the Oasis nightclub, she already had the tabard on underneath her raincoat. She walked straight past the long queue that wound around the corner and entered at the front, where she nodded at the burly security guard who was stood next to the tall mawga man with the Aston Villa baseball cap. They parted to let her in and then she nodded again at a blond girl on the front desk who was stamping ink on the backs of hands.

Hortense went directly to the ladies' toilets at the back of the club, took out the bottle of bleach and the purple perfume bottle and sat on the uncomfortable stool with both, pretending to be a toilet attendant. She stayed there listening to pointless drunken conversations until one of the girls mentioned something about a "G." Miss Hortense eased herself off the stool, went to the dance floor, found her target, and then followed him to the exit of the club, where she stood in full view near the doorway with a single dirty unlit cigarette in her hand, watching as the white man in the Aston Villa baseball cap and Germaine Banton exchanged plastic bags.

The third time Miss Hortense came across Germaine Banton was after she encountered his handiwork hidden behind a pair of sunglasses. It was the day after she had been to the nightclub. She went back to the shop intending to show the girl with all the hair on her head how pastry for patties *should* be made. Whoever had made the one presented to her made the mistake of overworking the dough and adding too much water, and had completely left out the turmeric. But when she got there, the young girl was wearing sunglasses indoors, even though it was an overcast day with no sign that the sun was going to make an appearance.

"What can I get for you?" asked the girl, lowering her head and rocking on her left foot.

"What happen to you face?" Miss Hortense demanded.

* * *

37

Normally, Miss Hortense would have left her investigation at three checks. She certainly had enough information for a bright red flag. But because of McKenzie's strokes, Blossom's one vote against any G&T dirty investment was likely to be worth naught; and, most importantly, because of the girl, she knew there would have to be a fourth encounter.

So the fourth time Miss Hortense encountered Germaine Banton was four days before Constance died, in his own flat, the one that he shared with the young girl from the shop, whose name was Tamisha. The flat was also shared with a two-year-old baby boy; a Thomas the Tank Engine card that sat on the fake fireplace told her his age. Miss Hortense made sure the flat was empty before gaining entry using the thicker credit card. She was inside their front room when he came home. It was a neat little place: Tamisha's efforts, Miss Hortense suspected. In the main bedroom, it was predominantly Germaine's things on show—a whole heap of white trainers lined up as if to attention and three gold watches, in their boxes, marking time. The bathroom was clean enough, the laundry basket empty. The contents of the fridge were sparse, but of what was in there, all the labels were facing out. In the front room there were a few fluffy toys and a play box, but they were all packed up into a corner as if sorry for their presence. It was too orderly; and in the order and exactness was a silent violence all too familiar to Miss Hortense. It probably didn't take much to tip the balance.

Miss Hortense perched on the settee with a cup of tea.

"What the . . ." Germaine swore, as he entered the room. "What you doing in my fuckin' yard?"

"Don't worry," Miss Hortense said, taking a sip of the tea, with her other hand resting inside her bag. "Is just me one." Nevertheless, he bounced around the flat, calling for his girlfriend and threatening to ring the police, all while pulling at his trousers and flinging doors open and closed. Miss Hortense was not concerned. If necessary, she had something in her handbag that would calm him right down.

When he'd done the rounds, Miss Hortense had almost finished the tea. As he entered the front room again Miss Hortense patted her bag and said, "I understand you looking for investment."

"Who the fuck *are* you?" he asked her again.

"You ever hear of the Pardner?" she continued calmly.

He stopped, his eyes narrowed, but didn't answer.

"Should they decide to forward any money to you, I would politely decline. Don't tek a penny, you hear?" she continued jovially.

"Why would I do that?" He was still on high alert, as if waiting for someone to jump through the window.

"For a start, you have a rat infestation inna your catering dynasty."

Miss Hortense put a bag of what looked like rodent droppings on his coffee table.

He leapt back. "What the fuck is that?"

"And if you lay so much as a fingernail on that young lady again, I will tell the food hygiene people where I found it."

They weren't rodent droppings, but she knew he wouldn't know the difference. And it wasn't an untruth. When she had leaned against the counter to hear the argument, she saw evidence of the animal friends.

He smirked then and said, "All right, grandma."

"Oh, me nearly forget," she said. She kicked at a plastic bag that was under the coffee table until it was in full view.

"This was in you likkle boy's toy box," she said. The smirk quickly disappeared from Germaine's face. Inside the bag was a five-inch knife, one thousand pounds in cash, which she had counted (less the dirty five-pound note, which she put in her wallet), and several small bags of white powder.

"You should really be more careful," Miss Hortense said, "about where you hide you things. I know you, boy, and I am always watching. And don't worry—you na have to see me again if you listen. But if you don't, I know people too. People who aren't as nice as I am the first time, you hear me?"

Germaine looked across at the box and then up at Miss Hortense and down again. In the moment of his indecision, she stood up.

"Thank you for the tea," she said politely, and quietly left him standing, mouth open wide.

Oh yes, there was plenty of evidence to provide a red flag for Germaine Banton. And Miss Hortense had also discovered in the course of her investigations who Germaine Banton worked for, a fact that had direct implications for Constance. Unfortunately, because Constance had drawn her knife and pushed it deep into Miss Hortense's oozing wound, Miss Hortense never got the chance to warn her.

8

Upsetting the Apple Cart

After that awful encounter with Constance Brown and Pastor Williams in Constance's big old house, Miss Hortense hadn't gone directly home.

Now she had discovered that Germaine Banton hadn't taken her advice, she had taken the bus to Alcock Street and then walked five minutes to the underpass where the ring road meets Southbury Road. This was an area known commonly as the End, where half people, many with nothing left it seemed but a drug habit, ended up, living like ghosts, half in this world, half in another. It was there that she asked for Stanley Thomas and was directed to a huddle of cardboard boxes at the end of one of the rows.

Miss Hortense believed that just like a medicine in the body found its way to the area that needed it most, so a word or a gesture carried some part of its truth to the heart. In Stanley's presence she often said "love," because that is exactly what for most of his life he had not had and had needed most.

The truth comes in many forms and looks like many different things, depending on where you are standing. Stanley's truth was four white men in blue uniforms with set faces who busted open his front door on a wet Wednesday morning in 1970, punched him to the ground so that his jaw was broken in two places and dragged him in only his Y-fronts and one sock, kicking and screaming, into a police van, his bare foot that had been dragged along the concrete floor bloodied and blistered. He disappeared into a black hole that Wednesday morning that he never emerged from. It was the same black hole she found him in that day, the day before Constance's death. The same black hole that Miss Hortense felt responsible for creating.

"Stanley, love?" she shouted down at the pile of stained cardboard boxes. There were groans.

"Stanley? Is me, Hortense."

"Miss Hortense?" came an ashy voice. "A you that? You can lend me a five-pound note?" The cardboard boxes rustled. He slowly emerged, his hair uncombed and balding in places. One of his shoes was almost worn down through the sole, and a sour stench followed him.

She looked directly into his creased face. "You eat?"

He blinked at her with bloodshot eyes.

"Come," she said, and she walked on. He followed slowly behind her, dragging the foot that was still troublesome.

Stanley never entered Miss Hortense's house, despite her telling him that he could. He sat outside on the wall in the front garden. Miss Hortense warmed Mannish water and brought it out to him because he needed the iron. The last time she had invited him into her home, he had taken the china bowl with him. The last time he was there, she had told him he could take anything he wanted, including a bath, but he never took her up on the offer if it meant entering her house. She knew he was afraid of the front door.

"You can always stay here," said Miss Hortense. "Get youself cleaned up." It was a conversation they had been having for years.

He let out a bitter laugh. "Miss Hortense, me too old."

"But you not cold," she replied.

"But me is going there soon," he said with a resignation that still sent a chill through Miss Hortense.

"Well, me best be getting on," he said, slurping the last of the soup from the bowl.

"There is a white man, wears one of them Aston Villa hats, tall and mawga like a pole, goes by the name of Dice, you know him?" If the man was conducting his business in the way Miss Hortense feared, there was a big chance Stanley did.

Stanley raised his head like it carried the weight of lead and looked at Miss Hortense with those uneasy red-yellow eyes. "And what if me do?" His left hand shook with the itch of the drug. Miss Hortense took a deep breath. A decision to be made. Her leg started to tingle. She went back into the house, took out the dirty five-pound note from her wallet and handed it to him. They both knew where it was going, back to the nasty place it had come from.

"Dice's boss," Stanley said, scrunching the money into a ball, "send him come a the yard come deal."

"And you know him boss?" asked Miss Hortense.

"No," replied Stanley, scratching. Not true, thought Miss Hortense. But in any case, she felt sure it was the "G" of G&T, otherwise known as Germaine Banton.

"And Cuttah know 'bout any a this?" Miss Hortense asked. Stanley shrugged.

"Cuttah's blade gone rusty long time," he said. "But that white boy, Dice?" Stanley smiled, exposing decaying and missing teeth. "Him na 'fraid fe slice." He nodded once at Miss Hortense, got up and left. The bowl remained on the wall.

Later that evening, Miss Hortense headed to Bridge Street Market. When she got there she took a left, crossed the road and entered the infamous Belvedere Estate. She walked up to the second floor of the second block and, after a pause to catch her breath, walked to the flat right at the end. Even before she knocked, the door was opening. A heavy, big-eared man in a leather jacket, who favored a large male donkey, was standing behind it. He nodded in her direction. Miss Hortense cussed her teeth and cursed him out.

"Stupid ass," she said, and went straight past him into the back before he directed her to do so. Sitting on a leather settee was a little old man. Gray tufts of hair sprouted from his dark brown creased-up head; dry feet emerged from worn brown leather slippers. This was Cuttah.

Cuttah aka Nine Lives had been a badman, a rude boy; what some people, not Miss Hortense, mind, might call a Yardie, before the word "Yardie" had been invented. That was a word Miss Hortense despised.

Back in the day, Cuttah had been one of the original and top-ranking badmen. Famous for fingernail and toenail detachment, chains (the stupid gold ones around his neck and the ones that you could swing whole men from) and, perhaps surprisingly, his love of Maine Coon cats. Back in the day, you only needed to say Cuttah or Nine Lives and that meant terror. Yes, there was Vincent "Ivanhoe" Martin, and Melvin "Red" Bright, and then there were men like Cuttah Nine Lives who came to England determined to make their fortunes any which way. Back in the day, if there was badness in Bigglesweigh and a Black man was involved, Cuttah was somewhere in it. Back in the day, if the Pardner was the good, then this man was the bad, and when Miss Hortense and the Pardner were looking for investment opportunities, he was looking for the same but for opposite reasons.

That was of course back in the day, before he took "sick" when his daughter went missing and he wouldn't let anybody, except for one particular person, treat his malady.

He looked up from the TV to see that one particular person standing in front of him, handbag at her side. "Miss Hortense," he said warmly. "You watch this?" He pointed to the balding man on the TV talking in an American accent like he had a mouth full of marbles. "Take a seat na man. Is what pleasure I owe this ya visit now?"

Miss Hortense pushed up her nose and remained very firmly on her feet. Two of his cats came and rubbed themselves against her leg and she kicked them away.

"You run out already?" he asked her. Miss Hortense held firmly on to her handbag. After her retirement from the hospital, it was mostly from Cuttah that she got the contents of her syringes.

"We have an agreement," Miss Hortense said, overarticulating.

"What you talking 'bout now?" Cuttah asked her, looking back at the TV. They were about to enter the house through the keyhole.

"I'm talking about the fact that someone is running drugs in Bigglesweigh."

"I tell you before, small-time dealers," he said, waving her away. "You dry the well, water a go get in from somewhere."

"Not small-time. Not on my information," said Miss Hortense. She reached into her bag, took out the slip of paper that Blossom had given her last Black Cake day and handed it to the old man. Cuttah narrowed his eyes at the scrawled handwriting.

"C&T you say?"

"No, that is a *G*," said Miss Hortense.

He sat up in his chair. "Here? In Bigglesweigh?"

Hortense nodded.

"Leave it with me," he said. And they both knew what that meant.

The dry-skinned boy, Germaine Banton, might have been stupid enough to report her back to the Pardner, and might have been stupid enough to accept the Pardner money, whatever was left of it, but Miss Hortense's visit to Cuttah made well and sure that that bad apple would be permanently removed from the cart.

9

In Not-So-Loving Memory

It wasn't a good day for a funeral. The weather couldn't make up its mind, one minute glaring sunshine, the next gray with the wind picking up and threatening to blow in the wrong direction. They all knew what that meant for the cemetery. And just like the weather, Miss Hortense was feeling increasingly unsettled about the death of Constance Brown.

When, two weeks after her passing, Gregory, Blossom and Miss Hortense entered the redbrick reception lobby of the Pentecostal church, it suddenly became so quiet you'd be mistaken for thinking it was them who had brought death.

Blossom leaned into Miss Hortense and whispered, "Plenty people have heart attacks nowadays and is fine. Personally, I have a feeling she was inflicted by something much more *deliberate*." Miss Hortense agreed but she wasn't going to tell Blossom that.

Miss Hortense's nephew had called her on the Thursday after Constance died.

"Aunty?"

"Yes, Gregry?"

"You all right, Aunty?"

"Yes, Gregry."

"You sure, Aunty?"

"Yes, Gregry. Why wouldn't I be all right, boy?" After all, it wasn't Hortense who was dead.

"I heard Miss Constance passed away," he said. "Are you going to the funeral?"

When she replied of course she was, he said that he was going to

46

try to make it too. Damn fool, using up all his good annual leave on a funeral he thought might take Miss Hortense to some kind of edge. What did he think she was going to do? What did any of them think she was going to do? Jump up in the service and start hollering about how Constance had taken her place as the Pardner Lady?

"Gregry, nutting na wrong wid me," she sighed.

Still, he knocked on the door an hour before the service, looking more and more like her sister Evie every day.

"Now, you sure you all right, Aunty?" he asked Miss Hortense again.

"Lawd Jesus, boy," she said. "If you ask me that one more time . . ."

They picked Blossom up twenty minutes later, her unnecessarily wide-brimmed hat rubbing up against the roof of the car and the nylon of her jacket crackling as she pushed her big body into the back seat.

"I'm not doing too good, you know," Blossom whined, in response to a question that Gregory didn't ask. "Don't know if it something me eat, but me belly not feeling good at all, at all, at all. And me chest it feel like a weight de 'pon it and me foot been playing me up since morning."

And so it went on, all the way to the hall.

After the stony welcome, in which nobody looked directly at them, one of the Mavises handed Blossom (not Hortense) a glossy order of service. There were two Mavises—a little one and a large one. The little one, Mavis Buchanan, was like a clucking lizard, with small black beady eyes always on the move and twitching. The large one, Mavis Campbell, was like a chugging train, slow and full of steam. It took a while to get her going, but boy, once she did it was best to get out of her way.

Inside the order of service were twelve whole pages of glossy pictures of Constance taken over many years: sitting, standing, lying on a beach in the sun (looking much younger than Miss Hortense had ever remembered her looking), with her two children, with big foreheads like their father; sat at a desk with a pen in her hand and certificate on the wall; and one in particular that caught Miss Hortense's eye in which the trademark smile was missing and there was an expression on Constance's face that looked like fear. The picture was cut in half so you couldn't see who was on the other side of it, but the way her body was leaned away, Miss Hortense suspected it was the husband, Mr. Brown, who died in the fire.

They took their places towards the back of the church, which was almost filled up. Constance's family—her son, Nigel; daughter, Camille; and granddaughter, Jasmine—were in the front row. On the stage, Pastor Williams, surrounded by his entourage, wiped his brow. He looked unexpectedly nervous. Next to him, Mavis B adjusted her wig.

They were instructed to rise as the pallbearers carried Constance's coffin to the front of the hall. Miss Hortense wondered if, inside the coffin, the shark teeth were still on display.

When the coffin arrived at the front, the pastor stood up and mopped his brow again. Miss Hortense reflected how, despite the good finances the Pardner had brought him, he never seemed to have a suit that fitted him properly. The brown suit he was wearing today was too big and very creased and it looked like it was swallowing him up in the sweltering heat of the hall. He unfolded his arms. He began with a whisper, which, like a spell, made the congregation fall silent.

"We are here today, ladies and gentlemen, to pay tribute to the life of a very special lady, Constance Brown, known to many of us as Sister Constance." He mopped again.

Blossom leaned over to Miss Hortense and whispered, "Him still don't give me me Pardner money."

"Sister Constance had been a righteous and upstanding member of this congregation for as long as we have been here," continued the pastor. There were some coughs.

"Many of you in the congregational hall today knew Sister Constance. Any of you who knew her, raise your hand."

Most hands went up. Gregory looked at Blossom; Blossom looked at Miss Hortense, who kept her hands tight to her sides.

"Those of you who knew her knew she was always smiling."

There was an echo of assent in the hall.

"You prayed with her and approached her for advice. Yes indeed. She always had advice."

There were some amens.

"But there were many things about Sister Constance that you may not have known."

"Amen," said Miss Hortense. Blossom nudged Hortense; Hortense cussed her teeth.

"For example," continued the pastor, "she was a woman who invested greatly in our community. She was a local councillor for many years. She was a mother and grandmother. A woman who knew how to get things done." The volume increased a notch. "When someone leaves so suddenly, we question. There was no long illness, no opportunity to get used to the fact that this wonderful woman would no longer be a part of our lives. I saw her the day before she sadly passed away but never had a chance to say goodbye."

Miss Hortense thought about that day. The meeting at the big old house; Constance wringing her hands at the table and the smell of the burnt toast and porridge. Something wasn't right.

"We question," continued the pastor, "why does God take life so? But no matter how she went, most importantly she knew her *maker*." Amens. The volume became thunderous. The familiar crescendo rising to its climax.

"She knew the value of salvation."

He stopped then as if at the edge of a cliff and moved to barely above a whisper again. "Which one of us can say that we are better than the next? We have all done things we regret. Who here is without sin, raise your hand? We all deserve an opportunity for salvation. Don't it?"

The two Mavises said, "Um-hum."

Pastor dipped at his knees. "'How Great Thou Art.' Let us stand."

The congregation stood, including Miss Hortense, though not immediately. Constance's daughter, Camille, walked at pace out of the hall. Miss Hortense turned to watch her as she disappeared out of sight. She wondered where she was going.

The chorus reached a crescendo. "*Then sings my soul, my savior God, to Thee . . .*" Miss Hortense could hear one of the Mavises at the top of the note. "*How great Thou art. How great Thou art.*" Gregory turned to Miss Hortense and smiled. She frowned. The singing continued. "*How . . . great . . . Thou . . . art.*" The song was over, the sound of many clothes creasing to sit down and of bottoms reaching seats. There was a silence.

Constance's granddaughter, a boxy young woman with the telltale forehead and round rosy cheeks, climbed onto the stage, her head bowed.

"My grandma," Jasmine said. She unfolded a piece of paper, sniffling. "You taught me how to be strong. To never let anybody take advantage and make you wrong. I will never forget what you taught me about achieving your goals and in life to make sure you always play the right roles. Never to let anyone get in your way and to always make sure that you have your say. I'm so sorry, Grandma. I wished I hadn't . . ." Her voice caught and Miss Hortense didn't get to hear what word she had found to rhyme with "Grandma." Jasmine started blubbering. The mother appeared again at the other end of the hall and rushed down the aisle to rescue her.

"Sorry. As you can tell," said Camille, leaning in too close to the microphone, "Jasmine was very close to Mum." She led her daughter away.

Then the son, Nigel, who according to Blossom was a big-time property developer, stood up. Miss Hortense watched him closely. He moved quietly to the microphone. A good-looking man ten years ago maybe, but now very much on the turn. Too much good living, Miss Hortense suspected, watching his belly wobble as he cleared his throat. Miss Hortense thought about the expensive black car and the dirty five-pound note.

"*Yea, though I walk through the valley of the shadow of death . . .*" He was not a good speaker. "*I will fear no evil.*" He looked into the crowd, his broad forehead furrowing, as he focused on someone behind them. Miss Hortense turned slyly; it was a man three rows behind them, five seats in from the aisle. He was heavyset, with big ears, like a donkey, and sweating in a leather jacket. Miss Hortense recognized him immediately. Nigel quickly looked back to his sheet of paper.

Blossom leaned into Miss Hortense and whispered, "It was the son who found Constance dying. Poor thing." Although Blossom didn't always impart useful information, this piece was, and Miss Hortense considered it carefully. Nigel clearly wasn't what he made himself out to be and she needed to keep her eye on him.

Camille stood up next, gently hushing the granddaughter, Jasmine, before moving to face the crowd.

"Many of you," she began, "knew Mum. Many of you knew her as Sister Constance, but to me she was just Mum. I say just Mum, but for those of you who knew her, you would know that she was never 'just' anything. I admit she wasn't always the easiest person to get along with."

Blossom leaned into Hortense and whispered once again, "I knew it! Is the daughter had something to do with her death," and she nodded at Hortense knowingly.

"But she loved her community," continued Camille. "She decided she wanted to serve and so she did just that. She was a single mum to me and Nigel for a long time. Things were tough but she never gave up. Her going, well, it was a big shock, but she was as tough as old boots and she didn't do anything she didn't want to."

There were some laughs from the congregation. Miss Hortense looked to see who wasn't laughing. The pastor was looking very serious.

"She had high standards and she made sure we had them same standards instilled in us. Me and my brother, we want to say thanks, Mum, for all you did for us. I promise you I'm gonna continue your work in the community. Rest in peace." There were a number of amens and she left the stage. Gregory cleared his throat.

Pastor Williams stood back up to talk about a roof that needed fixing and carpets that needed replacing. Blossom whispered to Miss Hortense again, "I going toilet," and she eased herself out of the row. The tributes continued as several tithe plates were distributed. Too many, it seemed to Miss Hortense. Another song, some further words from the pastor, and the coffin was being lifted and taken out of the hall.

Gregory loosened a button on his suit jacket. The time for any hollering from Miss Hortense had passed.

10

A Ghost at the Graveside

When they left the hall, they found Blossom sitting outside in the lobby area twirling her scarf impatiently. "You all right, Miss Blossom?" Gregory asked.

"It was basic," Blossom replied. "You can tell McKenzie, poor thing, never do it. Look like costs were cut. Very. Basic."

The interment was to be at the Brayfields cemetery, which was a fifteen-minute drive in good traffic. In the car, Gregory turned on the radio. "Rise," by Gabrielle, momentarily blasted out. Miss Hortense didn't say a word until they arrived. Brayfields cemetery was an over-flow off the main Westmill Hill cemetery. It was tucked away and difficult to find unless you knew where you were going.

Westmill Hill had been opened in the 1800s, though the first Black person wasn't officially laid to rest there until 1925. At the front were an earl and Sir George Lovely, engineer, industrialist, philanthropist, and slave owner—though the Black-people-owning part didn't feature anywhere on his headstone. Constance's husband, Mr. Brown, poor Bigsy and Dimples, and nineteen-year-old Michael McKenzie, the under-taker's son, were all in the Westmill Hill part of the cemetery; but to be clear, none of their people were at the front.

Also buried there were two people who had meant the world to Miss Hortense, her sister Evie and her old friend Errol.

The Brayfields part of the cemetery wasn't opened until 1991 and was where most of the Black residents from the surrounding areas were now laid to rest. Gradually over the years the rows were filled with more and more.

Miss Hortense or Blossom could tell you with their eyes closed how to get to the overflow Brayfields cemetery. It was built on a landfill site that when the wind was blowing in the wrong direction smelled like rotting eggs due to being waterlogged. But if you didn't know the cemetery, or you hadn't been to a funeral in Bigglesweigh since 1965, it was safe to say you wouldn't have a clue how to find it.

They stopped off in Westmill Hill so that Miss Hortense and Gregory could spend a few moments with Evie, Gregory's mother. Miss Hortense brushed down her grave, pulled out a few weeds and said some quiet words. Gregory then drove them to the Brayfields part and they hopped their way through the marshy grass to the graveside where Constance was being buried.

Miss Hortense, Gregory and Blossom stood together. They were given a wide berth; no doubt on account of Miss Hortense, and Gregory's profession. Mr. Wright, Blossom's friend, came to join them too. He kept reminding them how he was the first person to find out the news that Constance was dead.

"I see them not burying her with the husband then," noted Blossom.

Constance was getting a fresh new space. Neither Blossom nor Mr. Wright could work out why.

The usual groups were scattered around the grave. Some long-standing members of the community stood back by the oak trees, walking sticks pushed into the ground, a hand in a pocket, mumbling low. Miss Hortense spied Fitz among them. He had left the Pardner when she had, in solidarity with her, but they hadn't been in each other's company much since; the thirty-year silence hadn't just been with Constance Brown and Pastor Williams. Save for Blossom, she hadn't kept up with any of them, even Fitz. It was too painful, and she had backed away, even from those friends who stood by her.

The immediate family stood at the front but well apart from each other. Nigel stood a few steps in front of his wife. Camille stood with Jasmine, who was still sobbing and leaning on her shoulder, away to the left, the only connection between her and her brother that telltale forehead.

Nigel's wife, an ebony-colored woman with a mole on her left cheek, was at least a foot taller than him in her heels. She was dripping in jewelry, and shades covered two-thirds of her face.

Camille was a divorcée, Miss Hortense remembered. She had the bruised look of her mother but was more a cornmeal to Constance's yellow yam. She kept looking over her shoulder and Miss Hortense wondered who for. As Miss Hortense watched them, she observed how, save for the granddaughter, all of their eyes were dry.

Pastor Williams stepped forwards. "And now we must lay Sister Constance to rest. Earth to earth, ashes to ashes, dust to dust. This was a good woman." He dipped at his knees. "She was well respected amongst us." He dipped again. "So, dear Lawd Jesus, soften the hearts of those who try to malign the character of this good woman with their wicked ways."

Out of the corner of their eyes, Blossom and Miss Hortense exchanged a look.

"Those," said the pastor, dipping again and glancing across at Blossom and then at Nigel, "whose hearts covet material goods and money. Let them see it in their *hearts* to relinquish that which does not belong to them."

"Yes, Lawd," came one of the Mavises; the other Mavis said, "Amen."

"God be with you," the pastor signaled. A tambourine was whipped out of a bag and a hymn was struck up as clumps of earth were scattered onto the coffin.

When the song finished, the rattle of the tambourine started up again. A woman who sounded like a foghorn started crying and Nigel turned and started walking towards the cars. His wife strutted her way behind him. It seemed the foghorn had set the granddaughter, Jasmine, off again, and she started bawling loudly as Camille led her away too.

The pastor hopped after them. As he did so, Miss Hortense noted a strange movement across the road beyond the row of parked cars. A shadowy figure who at first appeared to be moving with the breeze. It wasn't unusual to see ghosts in a cemetery, but she distinctly saw what she thought was a ghost leaning up and doing what appeared to be a pee-pee against a tree. But no, it couldn't be. Mr. Wright was looking in the same direction but when she nudged Blossom to have a look too, Blossom was pulling at the scarf around her neck with one hand and clutching her chest with the other.

"Help," she gasped, her breathing shallow. "I can't catch me breath." She clawed at the scarf, which had tightened around her neck, and her hat dropped to the ground.

"I'm dying!" she gasped. "I'm dying."

11

A Death in Harrow

One week had passed since Constance's funeral, and across the country, another woman was dying, though there would be far fewer mourners this time.

"Mum?" Sonia didn't know what to do with her mother's hand. But then it dawned on her that she wouldn't get to feel it again, so she should keep holding on to it, for at least a few moments more. Every second counted now, she supposed, though the hand wasn't holding back, it was just there, limp; well, dead now. She'd gone. Finally, what they'd both been hoping for had happened.

Sonia placed her mother's hand next to her side, then looked up at the nurse. She hesitated, grabbed the hand once more and there were the motions for tears, but none came. She rose up from her knees, not in an elegant manner, her thighs chafing against each other and her tights slipping on the laminate floor. How long had she been kneeling?

She suddenly felt quite dizzy. Well, she'd never been in the presence of a dead body before. She felt quite sick at the sight of it.

"Would you like us to call someone for you?" asked the nurse.

"Oh, no. Thank you," said Sonia. There wasn't anyone to call anyway.

Sonia took a deep breath and exited the hospital room where her mother had spent the last few drawn-out weeks of her life. She had a question that she was on the verge of asking the nurse: *Had my mother ever mentioned the Pardner Lady before?* But there was no real point now.

* * *

Sonia sat in her mother's house on the end of her mother's bed with all the boxes around her. Her mother had been closed, strict, quiet and, not to forget, violent. But who was her mother, really? Shut away for more years than Sonia cared to remember, a fear she never shared always etched across her face. Deeply religious but with no congregation, reading her Bible and encouraging Sonia to do the same.

Sonia pulled up the last remaining box and roughly emptied it onto the bed. This one had been pushed away from the rest, deep in the loft. In it were scraps of paper, old banking books and more photographs, like in the other boxes. But these photographs were ones she didn't remember seeing before, a black-and-white tunnel into the past. She picked one out at random. Was this a picture of her father? Sonia didn't even know her mother still had pictures of him. All those times Sonia had sought to ask her about him when she was a child. After a while she gave up.

Her father had been a gaping absence. All she knew was that he had been in a road accident when she was little and that when he died they had to move. He was handsome, Sonia thought; even in the colorless photo, his hair looked somehow copperish.

She riffled through some more of the papers, found an old passport her mother had used to come to England. She was looking dutifully optimistic. Sonia hadn't known that woman.

Sonia flicked through the deeds for their old house in Birmingham: the house that her mother didn't want to sell but also never wanted to visit. The house that she rented out. She flicked through the banking books. Adding and subtracting had been Sonia's profession before she lost her job, but everything was not explicable with an equal sign. Life had always felt unbalanced to Sonia; something had always been missing.

In the banking book, Sonia noticed a recurring payment on the first of each month. It was the same in every one of the books. For years. She riffled through to find the earliest book. Jesus, the year she was born, 1963? The payee was an A. Williams. Who was that? A scrap of paper with her mother's handwriting on it slipped out of one of the books onto the bed: *The Pardner Lady, 52 Percival Road, Bigglesweigh.* The same suburb of Birmingham where her mother's house was?

The days merged as Sonia put her mother's affairs in final order. She binned most of her mother's prized possessions—that old purple dressing gown, the turned-gray nightdresses, those worn-out slippers—but Sonia decided to keep the earliest bank book and the picture of her father. Now with her mother gone, she could do anything, have a fresh slate. With her mother's money she could go on the holiday of a lifetime, a trip to the Caribbean. If only it hadn't been for her mother's last words. They weren't *I'm sorry for everything I've ever done to you.* Instead her mother had said:

It's Bone Twelve. The Pardner Lady is watching. It's her fault.

Sonia knew as she heard the words over and over again in her head that she would have to find out who this Pardner Lady was. That she wouldn't be finally rid of her mother until she did.

12

Blossom's Prediction

Of course, Blossom wasn't dead. She was what might be called a hypochondriac: a woman obsessed with other people's ailments as well as her own, and also quite obsessed with death.

Anyone else might have been embarrassed to take all the attention from the deceased at a funeral, but not Blossom. Two weeks had passed since she lay on the ground with her feet spread-eagled and her thighs and stockings on show. An ambulance had to be called and the road blocked off to let it come into the cemetery. And of course, Blossom insisted on the siren all the way to the Queen Elizabeth, the hospital where Miss Hortense used to work and had retired from six years ago. After all that, it turned out she had nothing more than mild indigestion and slightly elevated blood pressure.

Since the funeral, Blossom had taken to visiting Miss Hortense almost every day, hobbling in and plonking herself on the settee with a heavy sigh. She was there again now.

"Don't worry 'bout me," she would say, fanning her face with her hand. "Forget I am even here. Me soon dead anyway."

Despite the rift with the Pardner all those years ago, and the rumors that followed, Blossom had always stood by Miss Hortense. Yes, Hortense wasn't always the easiest somebody to get on with and could be stubborn like a mule. But Miss Hortense was the bravest person Blossom knew and she could always be relied upon in a time of crosses. Also, as a retired nurse, Miss Hortense was a very good person to be in the vicinity of if you were in any way concerned about your health.

It wasn't the first time someone had craved Miss Hortense's company just in case medical assistance might be required.

When, in July 1966, the white neighbor opposite, Maggie Richardson, had discovered Miss Hortense was a nurse, there was no rest. Every five minutes there was a knock at the door and her familiar singsong:

"Hiya, Horty, Zoe's stabbed Carly in her leg with a fork. Could you stitch it for me?"

"Hiya, Horty, my husband drank too much and I can't wake him up, do you have anything that could help?"

"Hiya, Donna's been having contractions every six minutes, would you mind seeing if there's a crown?"

"But you can deliver a baby," Maggie Richardson had said one time when she and the husband had crossed the road to check on her after another of Hortense's windows had been broken. The unintended inference being that if Miss Hortense hadn't been a nurse, the brick might have been justified.

"Did I ever tell you the story?" said the husband, settling into Hortense's settee after she had offered them both a cup of tea and a gizzada.

"Oh God, not *the story*," said Maggie Richardson, waving a hand.

"Well, last year," began the husband.

"Oh, Jesus," said the wife. "Horty doesn't want to hear about this again."

He continued. "The post office, the one at the bottom of the road, was robbed. They never found the bloody Yam Yam that did it. And the police only went and thought it was me because of what that bitch, Millicent Granwaithe, had said." He looked at Hortense, his shaggy hair falling into his eyes.

"Well, I've said it before and I'll say it again. I don't shit where I eat," the husband said.

"Your mouth!" said the wife.

"She doesn't mind. Do you, love?" he said to Hortense. "It's just, well, it wasn't us. The brick. We don't shit where we eat. And anyway, you can deliver babies."

* * *

Miss Hortense sat down next to Blossom in her favorite chair.

The shy ambulance man, who wouldn't make eye contact with Miss Hortense, had assumed that Blossom was a rational person. He had said that Blossom's heart was probably healthier than his. Blossom cussed her teeth.

"He na know what him a talk 'bout."

And the doctor at the hospital where she had been taken, at Blossom's insistence, just as a precaution, mind, had said that she was "as right as rain."

"What make rain right?" asked Blossom now. "These doctors no have no clue. I'm telling you me sick."

Her lips quivered.

"Something not right at all. I feel it inna me bones. You have to look inna dis thing, Hortense. You have to do the Looking Into."

And there it was: the second reason for Blossom's visit.

"I don't have time to be trifling in your stupidness tonight," said Miss Hortense as she ushered Blossom out of her house.

"For all you know, I am next!" cried Blossom.

Hortense cussed her teeth. "*Crimewatch* is about to start and me have things fe do," she said as she pushed the door shut. Miss Hortense wouldn't tell Blossom that the things she had to do were connected to her own suspicions relating to Constance's death.

"Don't say me never warn you," Blossom shouted through the letter box. "I'm telling you, someone else is going to die! Someone else is going to be killed!"

13

Six Minutes and Fifty-Six Seconds

On Wednesday afternoon, Gregory pulled into the car park of the community center in the police car and took his time turning off the engine. The Bigglesweigh Afro-Caribbean Social Community Center sat on the edge of the Chatsworth Estate. It was a cinder-block one-story building built thirty-odd years ago and showing its age. Gregory knew that once upon a time his aunty had been involved in its establishment and he knew how important this place still was to the community.

As he stepped out of the car, he noticed two shifts in his surroundings. To his left, a young boy, about fourteen, on a BMX with red trims, riding off at pace. Gregory just about made out the word "Dyno" written on the chassis. He watched the boy disappear towards the Chatsworth Estate. The second shift was a hunched-up woman in a gray hoodie carrying a black bin liner. She climbed over a small wall and went off in the direction of the bus stop. It was these sort of subtle shifts that Gregory had become accustomed to; they told you about it when you first joined the police. It was the uniform, they said. While for some the uniform inspired confidence and signaled safety, for many it was the opposite, and that was the main reason he'd joined the force. Six years ago, he decided he wanted to make a change, and he knew he'd have to do it from the inside.

To survive, you had to interpret the shifts, and quickly. A young boy riding into the Chatsworth Estate could be just going back to get his tea; or he could be the CEI (Chatsworth Estate Intelligence). The woman was heading towards the ring road, to the End, probably in search of another fix. It was the boy he needed to take into immediate consideration. Gregory looked at his watch. Riding at that pace, three minutes to get to the back of the estate, four minutes to return. Gregory had about seven minutes, give or take.

He'd been called to the Chatsworth Estate many times. To reports of assault and battery, domestic violence, a few stabbings, sometimes fatal. He knew that there was a whole lot more that went on in that estate that police didn't get a look into, but he'd never been called to the community center while on duty.

He wiped his feet on the mat outside the entrance to the building and noticed the broken lock on the front of the door. He pushed it open.

"Hello? Anyone here?" he called out.

The woman who emerged from the large room to the right was about five-foot-ten, approximately 154 pounds, hair wrapped in a dashiki scarf, late thirties, could be older. He recognized her from the funeral. It was her mother, Miss Constance, who was buried two weeks ago. The hall she stepped out of reminded him of school dinners; dusty parquet flooring, a small stage, heavy curtains, folded-up chairs and colorful stickmen drawings and collage pictures on the walls. In the corner was a small table with the domino tiles still on it. It looked like it was only her in the room now. She wiped her hands down the front of her jeans, looked him up and down.

"Police Sergeant Jean-Baptiste." He put his hand out. She didn't take it. He glanced at his watch—one minute gone.

"It's through here." She walked towards a closed door in front of them, a brisk energy to her. He followed her down the hallway.

"I came in on Monday morning," she said, pushing the heavy door open, "to find this."

Gregory looked around the room, a kitchen. Red paint licked up walls, appliances including a cooker on its side. Cupboard doors pulled off hinges. A large fridge turned over.

"It's hundreds of pounds' worth of damage," she said. "Money we just haven't got. This kitchen needs to be up and running." She moved some broken plates into a bin and huffed loudly. "People rely on us."

"And they broke the lock at the front to get in?" Gregory looked at his watch. Two minutes.

"They got in at the front but the lock's been broken for months. We never bother to fix things like that."

"So you didn't have any security? Nothing to protect the building or its contents?"

"The building doesn't need protecting. It belongs to the community."

From the state of the kitchen, he disagreed. He walked over to the cooker.

"Anything missing?" he asked, studying the back of it.

"Not as far as I'm aware."

So, someone was sending a message, he thought, looking at the red paint; no words that he could make out.

He looked at her. Her scarf was expertly tied. He hadn't known her mother, Miss Constance, but he knew about the bad blood that had existed between her and his aunty. That her mother had replaced his aunty as the Pardner Lady after something, which no one would tell him about, had gone wrong.

"This is the first time you've had this kind of trouble?" he asked her, stepping forward towards the fridge, opening it.

She tucked a loose loc behind her wrapped scarf and shrugged.

"You've had this kind of trouble before?"

"Nowhere near this bad," she said.

"Any idea at all who it might have been?"

"Trust me," she said, "if I knew that I wouldn't have called you lot."

Gregory looked at his watch—five minutes.

"Insurance?" he asked.

"No. We can't afford insurance."

Gregory took a final look around the room.

"I'll do my best to find out who caused the damage." And he meant that.

There was a sound in the hallway. The door squeaked open. The hunched-up woman in the hoodie hobbled in.

"Here, Miss Camille," said the druggie, frowning at Gregory. "They didn't have black currant so I got you orange instead."

Camille smiled at the woman, took the can. "Hold on, let me get my . . ." She was gesturing towards the hall.

"No need," said the woman. She did a curtsy for Camille, cut her eyes at Gregory and left.

It was six minutes and fifty-six seconds when Gregory got back to the police car. Both front tires had been let down. The screwdriver that was used to do the damage was left on the pavement for good measure.

14

Spit in the Sky, It Going Fall in Your Eye

Later that evening, Camille paid a visit to her brother, Nigel, to find that only his wife, Yvonne, was at home.

"When might you expect him?" Camille asked, fiddling with a tassel on the velvet love seat in Yvonne and Nigel's sterile front room. For a man who professed to be an expert at developing property, Camille didn't think her brother had done a very good job with his own home.

"How should I know?" said Yvonne spikily, pouring herself a glass of something from the bar.

Camille was about to say something, but the sound of Nigel's obnoxiously loud car pulling into the drive stopped her. What a relief. Small talk with Yvonne was excruciating.

"Camille," Nigel said tightly, as he put down his briefcase and went to the bar to pour himself a drink. He shot his wife a stony glance as she moved from the bar back to her seat.

"Nigel, I've come to speak with you about—"

"Ah ah ah," interrupted Nigel, pointing his empty glass towards her like a gun. He looked to his wife.

Camille was slipping backwards on the love seat. She tried to recover herself, started again. "I wanted to ask—"

"How's that niece of mine? Not getting herself into any more trouble on the internet, I hope?" He looked across at his wife again.

Camille looked over to Yvonne too and cleared her throat. "We need to talk," she said. Nigel glared at her. "About arrangements . . . for Mum's house . . . because . . ."

Nigel blinked coldly at her.

"Because," she continued, struggling with the seat once again, "current arrangements might have to become . . . more permanent . . . with our . . . visitor."

Nigel shook his head. "Over my dead body. It's your problem, Camille. You find a way to get rid of it."

"Him," Camille said, and then looked over to Yvonne.

"It," corrected Nigel. He threw back the alcohol. "But if you don't do something, I will."

To her left, Yvonne shifted in her seat. Camille shifted in her seat too; no point in trying to have this conversation now. She had more pressing things to deal with.

"Also, I need to ask a favor. It's about the community center."

"What now?" Nigel huffed.

"I need to borrow some money. There's been a break-in."

Yvonne raised her glass to her mouth, bangles jangling.

"You should wean yourself off that place, little sister," Nigel said. "There's no profit in it."

"I'll pay you back," said Camille, slipping on the velvet once again.

Nigel turned, looked to the wall, shook his head.

"It's a no from me," he said, turning back to them.

Camille struggled to get out of the seat. She found her feet.

She raised her finger, pointed at Nigel. "What d'you mean, it's a no from you? I'm not bloody auditioning!"

He held his hands up like he was innocent. "I can't help it if I was Mum's favorite," he said. "It's not my fault that she left *everything* to me." Camille bit her tongue, literally. "But come on," he continued. "It makes sense, doesn't it? Given your track record."

"You're a fucking idiot," she shouted in his face. The "f" came out loaded with all the angst she felt at being repeatedly overlooked by her mother. Never being quite seen.

He looked her up and down and said, ever so lightly, "You couldn't even hold down a marriage."

Camille lunged towards him. Yvonne rose from her seat, stepping in between the two of them just in time.

"I think you'd better leave," Yvonne said to Camille.

"Don't worry, I'm going."

Camille gathered her coat and stormed out. If she stayed a minute longer, she was going to do something she'd regret.

15

An Unwelcome Discovery

It was the following afternoon when Sonia set off on the drive to Birmingham. As she reached the motorway, sheets of rain began to pelt down against the windscreen, the wipers working overtime, screeching their protest. When she passed a four-car pileup, she seriously thought about turning back, but she gritted her teeth and continued. She was already three-quarters of the way to her destination. And she wanted answers. She still had her mother's words swirling around in her head:

It's Bone Twelve. The Pardner Lady is watching. It's her fault.

She arrived just after 7 p.m. at 52 Percival Road, the address she'd found on the scrap of paper in her mother's bank book.

The house was a big Victorian one and stood on a pleasant-looking suburban street, in what seemed like a nice area, though there were some flats opposite that looked a little dodgy. The front garden needed some TLC, weeds sprouting out of a lawn that hadn't been mowed in a while. But she imagined the house was probably worth a bit of money. Sonia took a deep breath and got out of the car. The gate creaked as she entered the garden.

She rang the doorbell and stood thinking about what her first words would be, how she would explain herself. She knocked again, starting to feel panicked.

After some minutes of fruitless knocking, Sonia peered into the house through the front door, the frosted glass panels giving everything on the other side a funfair-mirror look. Then she noticed there was something on the floor. She couldn't make it out with all the frosting and distortion. Was that a . . . foot?

"Hello? Is anyone there? Are you okay? Hello?" There was no answer.

She twisted to try to see more but couldn't. It could be nothing; could be something. She peered in again and concentrated hard on the outline. Oh God. It had to be a person, and whoever it was wasn't moving.

She ran to the house next door and rang the bell: no response. She went back, got out her flip phone and called 999.

"Hello, 999, what is your emergency?"

"I'm outside someone's house. There's someone on the floor inside, I think. They aren't moving . . . No, I can't see them, not exactly." She gave the address.

They were sending someone out as soon as they could. But what if the person needed help right now? What if every second mattered? She began to use her body to shunt the door, but of course it was heavy timber and it stood unyielding to her weight. She could try to break the glass, she told herself. She saw a brick to the side and, unthinking, feeling like she was in a movie, reached down and hurled it at the glass as hard as she could. She reached her hand in, twisted the lock and the door clicked open.

"Excuse me, young lady?"

Sonia jumped. A little old man with pale skin blinked at her from the gate.

For a moment, Sonia thought he was white, but when he spoke again she realized his accent had a Caribbean lilt.

"What you doing there?" he asked.

"I think there's someone inside. On the floor." She pointed to the door, which was now slightly ajar. No sound from inside.

"Let me," said the old man, and he went past her into the house, the broken glass crunching under his feet. She followed him tentatively into a gloomy hallway. He reached down and she saw him pick up a piece of paper from the floor, then there was the foot, there was the leg, and then, there was the rest of the body.

Seconds didn't matter anymore. They were too late.

They waited in silence outside the house for the ambulance and then the police to arrive. It was drizzling. Sonia had a desire to be as far

70

away from all of it as possible, but she answered their questions as best she could and they took her details while she stood there shaking. The kindly police officer didn't think that she should drive all the way back to London in that state, and asked if there was anyone local she might stay with.

The old man confirmed that he didn't know Sonia but that he lived just over "deh so," and she could, he supposed, come over for a cup of tea to calm her nerves.

It was a relief to be walking away from the body and the house, as the old man, whose name was Mr. Wright, ushered her into a lift and up to his flat on the fourth floor.

"This is so kind of you," Sonia said, after a few sips of the weak tea he gave to her. "I don't know what came over me. It's just . . . It's a shock."

Mr. Wright was on the balcony, his neck cricked to the side, trying to see what was happening. She wasn't sure if he even heard her.

"I should be going," said Sonia, and when she didn't get an answer, she got up. But suddenly she felt weak again and sat back down.

"You all right, my dear?" said Mr. Wright, coming back into the room. He could see that she wasn't quite well, but he had no idea what to do with her.

"I tell you what I am going to do. I'm going to call a friend a mine."

The woman he called was at the flat in no time. She was in her sixties, Sonia guessed, with thin red lips and a bright scarf around her neck. Despite her complaints about her health, she whizzed around the flat, and Sonia found herself with another cup of tea, this time far stronger and not just from the tea bag.

"Tell me again?" Blossom said to Mr. Wright, joining him on the balcony. Police cars surrounded Constance's house.

"This young lady found the body," he said. "Hold on, them bringing it out now."

"You know who it is?" asked Blossom, crossing herself.

Mr. Wright shook his head. "No, I didn't recognize him."

"Who," shouted Blossom from the balcony, "were you looking for, young lady? At the house?"

71

"Oh," said Sonia. "I was wondering if someone called the Pardner Lady lived there."

Mr. Wright and Blossom looked at each other. How could this young lady know anything about the Pardner?

Blossom came back into the room, scrutinizing the girl more closely—there was something in the roundness of her head, and the way she held the tissue to it, that was familiar.

"The Pardner Lady?" she repeated.

"Yes," said Sonia, warily.

"Well," said Blossom, "she did live there but I'm sorry to say she died."

"Died? When?" asked Sonia.

"Well, about four weeks ago now," replied Blossom.

"Are you sure?" Sonia couldn't hide the disappointment in her voice.

"Oh yes," said Blossom. "Quite sure. As a matter of fact, I was at her funeral and nearly died there too."

That's when Blossom looked down and saw the red seeping through the sleeve of Sonia's blouse. She must have been so taken with the dead body that she hadn't realized she was bleeding herself.

"Lawd Jesus!" said Blossom, raising her hands to her mouth. "You're going to bleed to death! Come quick. I'm going tek you to a friend of mine, a nurse. She can fix anyting."

16

The Boy on the Red Bike

Despite the often fraught demands of being a police officer on the beat, Gregory was determined to find out who was responsible for the damage to the community center. His colleagues considered it small fry, but he knew more than most what the community center represented: patience, sacrifice and reward. His aunty was no longer involved in the Pardner that had acquired the land and built on it, but it was because of her and her generation that it existed. And yet, there was someone out there who was willing to trash it. He, for one, wasn't going to stand for it.

The bike he had seen riding away when he first visited the community center was very distinctive. It had bloodred trims, seat, handlebars, and pads wrapped around the main frame. The wheels were twenty inches with the same red around the tubing and *Dyno* in bubble writing on the chassis. It was, Gregory had found out when he'd got back to the station and did an Ask Jeeves search, a GT Dyno Detour, with Pacman Dropouts. Pretty rare in the UK, even rarer in Bigglesweigh. But when he asked around the station, he found out there was a boy on the Chatsworth Estate, well known to his colleagues, who rode exactly that model. When Gregory knocked on the door of this boy's flat, and looked through the letter box, there was the bike sat in the passageway. Gregory stood and waited for an hour and forty-five minutes for the boy who owned it to get home. Gregory knew the message had already gone around the estate that a pig was on the doorstep. He also knew that at some point someone in that flat had to come back and Gregory was prepared to wait. At ten to nine in the evening, the boy eventually turned up, dragging his heels.

"I haven't done nothing," said the boy, loudly enough so that the adjacent flats could hear and the echoes could travel to the opposite balconies.

"We can have this conversation here, or inside," Gregory said, low. He suspected inside would be the boy's preference. There was risk in talking out in the open, less opportunity to later protest one's innocence.

"No mum tonight?" asked Gregory, as the boy left the door open behind him and two-stepped inside.

Instead of Mum or Dad, Gregory spotted an ashtray filled with cigarette butts and a disused wrap. In the light, he found his initial assessment of the boy to be wrong. Close up, he was twelve at most. Gregory walked around the bare living room, looked in on the filthy kitchen. This was social services' territory. He'd call Lucy when he got back to the car. He hoped he would hear her voice and not the standard answering-machine message again.

"You need a warrant if you want to search," said the boy. His voice hadn't yet broken. He stood in front of a small sideboard and wasn't moving from that spot.

"You saw me at the community center, after the break-in. What d'you know about it?" asked Gregory.

"Nothing," said the boy, shrugging.

Gregory sat down on a broken chair.

"I can make it known to your friends that you were very helpful to me during this conversation," said Gregory.

That had an effect on the boy. "I didn't do it," he said.

"But you know who did?"

The boy considered. "Probably some druggies down at the End."

Too easy, thought Gregory. Either the boy was lying or there was more to it. "Why?" asked Gregory. "Who would they be working for?"

"Dunno," said the boy.

Gregory looked him up and down.

"D'you know what the maximum sentence for carrying a knife illegally is?"

The boy's hand instinctively moved to the area where the tool was tucked into his jeans, before he snatched it away.

"Detention, a young offender institution, at the very least. Ever been to one of them before?"

"Dice," said the boy quickly.

"Richard Dudney?" Gregory's heart sank. This was the second time his name had come up recently. The same man his aunty had inquired about. The last time his aunty had asked about a man who was at the center of one of his investigations, two men had ended up in the hospital, both with concussion and one with a broken leg.

"Take care, young gun," said Gregory as he left. He had a very bad taste in his mouth.

His car was parked twenty-two minutes outside the Chatsworth Estate. This time, when he got back to it, the tires were intact. After leaving a voicemail on Lucy's answerphone, he reconnected his radio and heard that a Black male had been found dead at 52 Percival Road, Musgrove Park. *Shit.* That was Miss Constance's house. The taste in Gregory's mouth got worse; now his aunty was definitely going to get herself involved.

17

The Body in the Bag

Hortense didn't have many visitors after-hours anymore and hardly any reason to open her door when it was knocked. However, the rat-a-tat hammering of Blossom was distinctive.

Miss Hortense had no idea why Blossom would be knocking down her door at 9:40 p.m. on a Thursday. But if it was anything to do with how she was dying, Miss Hortense would damn well help the Grim Reaper finish the job.

Hortense looked out of her curtain to see not only Blossom but the very pale paleness of Mr. Wright and a little coffee-colored woman stood to the side of them looking nauseated.

"Lawd Jesus," Hortense said, "I'm coming, I'm coming," as the door kept going with Blossom's hammering. Hortense, in nightgown and rollers, made her uneven way to the front door and unlocked the double lock.

"It's started," said Blossom, pushing her way into Hortense's house. "Come in," Blossom said to Mr. Wright and the woman behind her.

Settling into the settee, she said, "Hortense, this young woman has mashed up her arm. She needs a nurse to fix it."

The girl gave a brief smile. She revealed the cut arm still bleeding in a towel. Miss Hortense touched it gently.

"Is how you do this?"

"On the glass of a door," said the woman, with a London accent.

"Well, you might as well sit down," said Miss Hortense, "and you too, Mr. Wright. I don't bite."

Miss Hortense went into the kitchen and came back with a small medical box, a bowl of water, medical gauze, antiseptic and various

76

other bits and pieces that she kept in the house for emergencies. She carefully unwrapped the girl's arm from the towel.

Blossom began, "So this young woman, Sandra—"

"Sonia," corrected Sonia. Her voice was creamy like milk.

"Was knocking on Constance's front door when she heard a noise."

"I didn't hear a noise," interjected Sonia.

"When she saw blood through the letter box."

"I didn't see any blood," intervened Sonia.

"You didn't?" said Blossom, disappointed.

The girl flinched as Miss Hortense removed a tiny sliver of glass from the cut. Her big blinking eyes reminded Hortense of the potoo "poor-me-one" bird from back home.

"Have you always lived here?" Sonia asked suddenly.

"Long enough," answered Miss Hortense, picking up the arm again.

"Tell her what happened," said Blossom impatiently.

"Because no one answered, I called the police. But I decided to break in as well and that's how I cut myself."

"And the body?" said Blossom crisply.

"Well, thankfully this gentleman"—Sonia referenced Mr. Wright— "was passing, so he went in and felt for a pulse but there wasn't any." At this point the girl's voice broke.

Mr. Wright nodded to confirm her story.

Blossom continued the narrative. "And then he called me and we watched them take out the body in the body bag." "Body bag" was whispered and Blossom crossed herself.

Miss Hortense took out antiseptic wipes.

"The thing is, none of us know who the body in the bag is," said Blossom. Sonia shook her head, as did Mr. Wright. "But it was a man," said Blossom firmly.

"And what him look like?" asked Miss Hortense, starting to wrap the girl's arm in the gauze.

"Well, it was difficult to see," said Sonia. "It was quite dark inside the house and the body was sort of twisted. I only really saw a part of his face, but he looked old."

Mr. Wright nodded his head as if to say he agreed with all that the young woman had said.

"You mussy have long arms then, Mr. Wright," said Hortense, "if you can a tek a man's pulse and not see him face."

"Oh," said the girl. "And there was something else."

"There was?" Blossom leaned further in.

"Well, in the passage where the body was, it was messy—beer bottles and cans all over the place."

"He was both a drinker and a homeless man!" gasped Blossom.

"And there was a piece of paper with something typed on it. This nice gentleman, Mr. Wright, picked it up."

"You did?" asked Blossom, staring daggers at Mr. Wright.

"Don't worry. I put it right back," said Mr. Wright. He was thinking the girl talked far too much for his liking.

"Well, did it say anything?" asked Blossom.

"It said Exodus twenty: thirteen," said Mr. Wright quietly.

"Fourteen," corrected Sonia. "Exodus twenty: fourteen."

Miss Hortense didn't flinch, but Blossom gasped, stood up and put her hand over her mouth. Miss Hortense calmly finished with the arm.

"Thanks," said Sonia, cautiously rubbing the bandage.

"And what were you doing, knocking at Constance's house?" asked Miss Hortense.

But before the woman answered, Miss Hortense looked up and narrowed her eyes. She leaned forward and peered so intently into Sonia's face that Sonia felt suddenly raw and exposed, as if Miss Hortense were peeling her back like apple skin.

"Likkle? A you that?" asked Miss Hortense hoarsely.

Sonia looked up, double-blinked and then, peering back, in a hushed voice said, "You're the Pardner Lady?"

Mr. Wright said, coughing into the room, "Was."

It was at that point that Miss Hortense closed her eyes as if pained and said she needed to sit down.

"Lawd have mercy," said Blossom. "Likkle Bit? Errol's daughter?" She couldn't believe it. They hadn't seen the child in, well, thirty-odd years; not since the mess-up with Bone 12 when Errol had got into the car accident.

18

Old Friends in Low Places

The morning after Miss Hortense had wrapped up Sonia's arm, Fitz jumped when he turned to see Blossom standing just behind him in the bookie shop, her bright red lips almost pressed against his jacket.

"Morning, Fitz," Blossom said coyly, hopping in front of him. There was an invitation with it, as there always was.

Fitz dodged to the side of her, wanting to continue watching the 11:30 at Aintree on the screen overhead.

"Is what you want, Blossom?" he asked, without looking down at her.

The other men around him moved as far away as the small shop would permit. This was hallowed territory, the Caribbean equivalent to an English pub; a little sweatbox filled with smoke from the tobacco and funk from the adrenaline. A haven away from females except for certain kinds of females, like Donna the cashier and Tracey, who sat on her mobility scooter all day feeding the fruit machines. No refined women came into the bookie shop and none were welcome, and that suited Fitz just fine.

Fitz's dark eyes became intense as he watched the race, the low hum of the commentator getting more animated.

"And Hoof Hearted is on the run but being chased down by Laughing Lady and Laughing Lady isn't going to let Hoof Hearted get away and they are neck and neck but Laughing Lady is ahead and pulling away and Laughing Lady is going to take it, she's going to take it, and she's crossed the line."

"Rahted!" Fitz slapped his thigh, cussed his teeth and scrunched up another slip of paper in his arthritic right hand. It was the hand that he had relied on most for his uppercuts as a professional boxer; the hand was one of the few physical signs of his age. He threw the slip on the floor.

"Well," said Blossom. "You is needed."

"It's been a long time since I was needed, my dear," said Fitz. He had several other bits of paper with scrawls on them in front of him. He wasn't planning on leaving the betting shop until after the 2:15 at Doncaster, and he might, depending on his fortunes, also stay for the 2:45 at Chepstow.

"It's urgent," said Blossom. "It's about Hortense."

Fitz's shoulders squeezed in tight.

"What about Hortense?"

He looked directly at Blossom now, as much as it pained him to do so.

"I'll be waiting outside," said Blossom, a luring curl in her voice, and she swished out, her chest pushed up and her big feet prancing in front of her. He imagined she thought that there were heads turning in her wake; that he himself would be longingly looking after her. He was looking after her, but it wasn't longingly.

Ten minutes later, Fitz was outside. He had deliberately taken his time.

"Well," he said, meeting Blossom a few steps away from the door. "You tek me from me things. Now is what you want, woman?"

Blossom looked Fitz up and down, batting those thin eyelashes.

"Something wrong with Hortense?" he asked.

"Well, now you ask, there is something wrong with her. She's not seeing straight," said Blossom. "You hear them find a man dead in Constance house last night?"

"Me hear," said Fitz. "Anyone know who he was?"

"No," said Blossom. "But I think Hortense can find out."

"Oh, Lawd Jesus, woman," said Fitz. "You bring me out a me things fe dis?" He took his tobacco pouch from his breast pocket.

Blossom was feeling surprisingly lighter ever since the body had been found. Her hand wasn't hurting her and for the first time in weeks she could breathe without feeling tightness in her chest.

80

"There is a strangeness going on," said Blossom, "and we need Hortense to Look Inna it." The "Look Inna it" was whispered.

"What exactly are you expecting Hortense to find when she 'looks into' this 'strangeness'?" asked Fitz. He took out a Rizla paper and started to sprinkle tobacco into it.

Blossom hadn't got so far in her thinking as that, but said what she had been too afraid to say out loud before.

"Maybe it's obeah." And she said "obeah" in a whisper and crossed herself.

"If you call old age and life obeah," said Fitz, "then it look like it affecting us all. And you most definitely."

Never in all his days had Fitz come across a woman who was so hard in her head. He arranged the tobacco evenly across the delicate piece of paper.

"Now I think on it," said Blossom, "maybe it is a curse fe true. A curse 'pon the Pardner." She raised her hand to her mouth. "Maybe," said Blossom, "one of the Bones come back to haunt we because dey not happy with how things did turn out."

"Now you talking pure nonsense," said Fitz. He rolled the tobacco-filled paper with an expertise that came from decades of doing it and licked the edge.

"What about Bone Twelve?" Blossom whispered "Twelve." "Twelve is the only Bone that the Pardner never solve," Blossom said. "It could be Bone Twelve come back to haunt we for never getting to the bottom of it."

"Or maybe," said Fitz, "now all you husbands dead and gone . . ." He put the roll-up between his lips and lit it, curling his other hand around to allow the flame to take. He took a deep breath. "You don't have nothing better to do with you time then mek yourself a nuisance. Well, I do have something to do with my time, whilst I still got it," said Fitz, looking at his watch and then feeling the slips in his pocket.

"Or it could of course be one of us," said Blossom. "Maybe it's even you, trying to get your hands on the Pardner. If I recall, you didn't leave on any good terms."

"What could be me?" said Fitz, giving a brief laugh. "Nutting no happen, woman. A few old people drop down dead is all."

"And then of course there is the note," said Blossom, touching her hair.

"What note?" asked Fitz, inhaling again.

"Oh, just a note them did find with the body at the bottom of the stairs and it mention a verse in the Bible." Blossom paused, raised an eyebrow, and whispered, "*Exodus twenty: fourteen.*"

The color drained from Fitz's face.

"And there is also Precious," said Blossom.

"What about Precious?"

"Oh, I forget to mention?" said Blossom, batting the eyelashes. "We done find her too. She dead. We find de daughter as well. Well, she is the one found the dead man's body and us, and then she tell us 'bout Precious."

"Precious dead?" said Fitz, taking off his hat and scratching his short salt-and-pepper Afro. "And Hortense know about this?"

"Oh yes," said Blossom. "She knows, all right."

"And wha she say?"

"Well, that's the thing," said Blossom. "This morning, she disappear. We need to start finding out about all this strangeness, but she not taking me calls and she not opening the front door. But she might open the front door to you, Fitz."

19

Old Spice

As soon as Fitz had managed to get away from Blossom, he had rushed over to Hortense's house. He found it in darkness, with the curtains drawn. The hanging basket outside looked like it could do with watering. There were only three other times Fitz had come to Hortense's during the day to find her curtains drawn. All three had been some of the worst moments of his life.

He knocked on the door and waited; then, receiving no answer, he went around to the back, through the narrow side passage, and knocked on the back gate. He could hear her pottering around; he could even visualize exactly what part of the garden she was pottering around in: the part with the roses and where the daffodils bloomed in spring.

"Hortense," he called out. "Hortense? Me know you deh so." He waited; the pottering continued.

"Blossom come fe see me dis morning," he shouted into the fence. "She tell me you find Precious and the gal." The pottering and clanking got louder, then the sound of soil being dug deep.

"Me hear sey Precious dead," he said. "Nutting you or anybody can do 'bout it now." He gave her a minute.

The pottering stopped. After a few minutes more, the gate latch clicked and he pushed it open. The air was filled with the sweetness of the roses. He followed Miss Hortense into the kitchen, where he got pimento, garlic and scallion too. It was the smell of home.

"You winning?" Miss Hortense asked as Fitz followed her down the short passageway and into the living room. He hadn't been in the house for decades.

"I don't win nothing since morning, ma'am," he said, taking off his hat.

His Old Spice aftershave lingered like wisdom, a reminder of old times and what could have been. Fitz sat himself down at the oval table, the same spot he had always sat at when they were both still in the Pardner, and rubbed his hands together.

"You hungry?" Miss Hortense didn't wait for an answer. She rustled up something from leftovers and returned with a plate, which he quickly devoured. Even in a rush, she knew there wasn't another person's hands who could bring up food the way she could for him. He pushed the plate away and eased open a button on his waistcoat.

"You know what Blossom is saying?" He eased open another button and slouched back more. "From morning me never know a woman stupid like a she." Fitz had never made his dislike of Blossom a secret.

Miss Hortense cussed her teeth. "Blossom cares. There is no crime in that."

Hortense went into the tall sideboard and brought out the bottle of Wray & Nephew. She brought out a glass from behind the bar, poured a good measure into it and put the glass in front of Fitz.

He looked at the straight shot, picked up the glass, rolled it and downed the measure of clear liquid in one go.

He eyed Miss Hortense once more.

"Blossom tell you 'bout the note?" Miss Hortense watched him closely.

Fitz nodded. "Cha, man," he said, cussing his teeth. "That no mean nothing."

"Well, I going back inna it all the same," said Miss Hortense.

Fitz choked on the residue of the rum and got up abruptly.

"Now what nonsense you talking? You not serious, Hortense? You not following the stupidness of that woman?" He took the bottle of rum, threw himself a generous further measure and swallowed it quickly.

"Bone Twelve dead and finish!" He looked at Hortense more intensely as he intoned the word "dead."

"Yet somebody is sending me a message about it," said Hortense.

"You don't know that it is a message, and even if it is, that it is for you," said Fitz, his voice rising.

"Then what else you think it is?" she asked him.

"Coincidence," he said, finally.

Miss Hortense shook her head.

"You want me to list all the reasons why we can't go back inna that case?" Fitz cussed his teeth. He, like Blossom, believed that walls had ears, so he wasn't going to talk too openly, but he said again, more quietly, "It dead and finish. You is what age?"

Miss Hortense gave him a look.

"Well," said Fitz, "I'm seventy-one next spring. *Seventy-one*, Hortense."

Miss Hortense gave a sigh. "We old but we na cold yet, Fitz."

She moved to sit back down, and for a moment Fitz looked at her the same way he did when they first met, thirty-odd years ago, at that dominoes table. He was still handsome. A gold crown on his left incisor, lean, and always in a suit that hung off his body well. His skin was a rich dark leather that had weathered wisely with age. He was a strong-looking man. He commanded a space. The years had worn on him a little like everybody, but the fighter's stature was still there and Miss Hortense knew he knew it. Prostate cancer had taken its toll a few years ago, but he had beaten it, like so many adversaries. Nearly a cruiserweight champion, he would tell the Pardner when he felt in a talking mood. If you were on the wrong side of him, he could still be dangerous, as Miss Hortense well knew.

"Hortense," he said, his words slower. "Remember, it was Bone Twelve that nearly kill you." He looked pointedly towards Miss Hortense's leg and she brushed the side of her gown as if brushing his stare away.

"I'm not scared of dying, Fitzroy," Miss Hortense said.

"You making a mistake, Hortense." But he knew she'd stopped listening.

"And another thing," she said. "Is me one alone going back inna it, so no need to be concerned for you age."

Fitz cussed his teeth. "Oh Lawd now, Hortense."

"I mean it," said Hortense. "Nobody else, not you, not Blossom, only me one. I'm not going to let what happen before happen again. And you na bother tell Blossom what me a do, nider."

Fitz poured himself another shot of the rum, and though he tried to appear collected, his hand gave an involuntary tremor, so that the liquid almost overflowed in the glass. There wasn't much that frightened Fitz nowadays, but Bone 12 was one of the things that did. He still had nightmares about the case. He hadn't been entirely truthful with Hortense about his part in it, and if she ever found out, he didn't know if either of them would survive.

20

Washbelly

After Fitz left, Hortense went to the canal. When Hortense needed some-where to think, there were three places you might find her. Her kitchen, her garden and Quarter Point, on the eastern part of the Grand Union canal. To get to Quarter Point, she would take the 122 bus. That bus would take you right to the end of Jeffers Street and, from Jeffers Street, the canal was only a five-minute walk. Years ago, the buses didn't go farther than Christchurch. That was because no one had reason to go to the eastern part of the canal. Before the estate and shops were built, there were no neat, designated paths, no benches or pretty flowers. It didn't smell so good neither. There were deep recesses in that part of the canal. The water was so deep and thick with sludge and rubbish that to even stand too close to the edge, one felt oneself contaminated. If a body had ever been buried at that place, there was no way it was going to be found. Now, of course, it had all been cleaned up. Benches placed along it with walking paths. Pretty flowers sprouting all over the place. It was to one of these benches that Miss Hortense returned, time and time again over the years, to watch over the water and think about the past.

Miss Hortense was a washbelly. That was what the youngest child of a family in Jamaica was called. Washbellies were known for being spoiled and protected. She had three brothers and two sisters, most of whom were significantly older than her, and all of whom coveted her. She had been the surprise. A blessing sent to two of the best parents whom anybody could rightly wish for. Two of her brothers, Earl and Alan, went off to seek their fortunes in the Americas. Earl became an engineer in Canada, Alan a lieutenant in the US army, based in Texas. A third brother, Douglas, went to Panama. All three left long before Hortense could talk. The oldest sister, Patsy, was a big woman with two children of her own when Hortense was born. In time, Patsy took her children and went to join Earl. But it was and had always been Evie with whom Miss Hortense was the closest. She was ten and a half when Hortense was born, and Hortense slotted right into the small collection of her dolls. Evie whispered secrets into her ear and carried her everywhere she went.

"That there is Mass Johnson's house. Never go near him gate. That's where the Duppies live and Duppies snatch up children and eat them for breakfast."

Evie had loved to dance and Hortense loved to watch her sister twirling around in their room to the muffled radio sounds. She was Hortense's whole world until she picked up and left to seek her own fortunes in England. Fourteen-year-old Hortense was devastated. With no one to whisper secrets into her ear anymore, she started seeking them out for herself.

Being the baby, it was a long time before Hortense qualified to go anywhere by herself, even within the parish, let alone to a foreign land; but three days after her twenty-sixth birthday she packed her grip and went in search of Evie and—the lie she told her parents—to acquire a vocation. She squeezed her mother's small body tightly, Mamma's long plait dangling at her back, and embraced her father.

"Now remember, Hortense, everything we teach you," said Mamma, as Hortense rushed off the veranda.

In her rush to find her new world she forgot to look back at the one she was leaving. Even now, decades later, she would sit and think, oh, how she wished she'd looked back just one more time.

When she was met off the train by her sister, it wasn't the same Evie she had known twelve years before. She had the same high cheeks and gappy front teeth, her hair immaculately hot-combed and styled under her scarf, but when she squeezed Hortense and said, "Me glad fe see you come," it felt like more of a distancing than an embrace. There was more than just the barrier created by the extra layers of clothes and heavy wool coat.

For the first four months after Hortense's arrival, she stayed with Evie in her small room near Newington station with her husband, Reginald Jean-Baptiste. He was a man eleven years older than Evie, with a set jaw and deeply set eyes. Oh, he was all right, but he wasn't a Jamaican. He didn't speak much, boring if you asked Hortense, and was always watching Evie. No, Hortense and Reginald Jean-Baptiste never hit it off. Hortense looked forward to the times he was out so that she could speak freely with her sister, but there was no more whispering of secrets.

Evie and Reginald Jean-Baptiste were kind enough to show her how things ran in England. It was a very cold place, nothing sparkled and everything had a layer of dust or dew. And the thin-lipped people were in the main unkind and colder than the weather itself. She was instructed never to let the white people know her business and always to smile back sweetly, no matter the insult.

Before long, there were a whole heap of arguments between Reginald Jean-Baptiste and Hortense because Hortense would not keep her opinions to herself, particularly when it came to her sister. Evie was often caught between the two of them, but always seemed to come down on the side of her husband. She squeezed herself into something Hortense no longer recognized and there was no more dancing. Well, Hortense wasn't making herself small for the sake of anybody and got so sick and tired of seeing her sister do it that she decided to move out. Given Hortense hadn't really found her Evie, she decided she had better pursue a vocation instead. In the summer of 1961, she went off to Macclesfield teaching hospital to embark on a two-year nursing course.

During that time her older brother Alan, the lieutenant, passed away. He was followed by her father and then shortly thereafter by her mamma. The world felt like it was cracking in two.

"Guess what, Hortense," said Evie on the phone, shortly after their mother's passing. "Me belly full."

A light in a whole swamp of darkness. "But oh no, don't come, Hortense. It is very important that you finish you studies, you hear?" There she was again, it seemed to Hortense, pushing her away. At that time Hortense didn't know that it was the husband doing most of the pushing and pulling.

After the baby was born, a little boy whom Evie named Gregory, Evie called less and less.

This March had made it thirty years since her sister had died. Only three other people knew the real reason why. It was imperative to Hortense that it remain that way; the well-being of her nephew depended on it. She heaved herself up, patted the bench she was sat on twice, and left.

21

Miss Hortense Remembers

When Hortense got home from the canal, she climbed the stairs slowly, went into her bedroom and reached up to the top of the wardrobe. She pulled the grip that rested there towards her. The grip—or as the English called it, suitcase—that had traveled continents, weathered storms and carried whole lives within it. She eased the grip to the edge and brought it to the ground fast; it was heavy. Its red-brown leather was peeling in patches, but the black leather handle with the metal buckles was still attached and strong. Being with the grip was like being with an old friend. It had been her companion on her journey to England; it had contained everything she had in the new world. Now it contained her precious secrets, which were just as important to her. She pulled the grip up onto her bed with a heave and brushed the dust off the top. Taking a small key from her side table, she undid the lock. She clicked the catches and opened the top.

The envelopes peeked out at Miss Hortense like another set of old friends coming to say hello. Each envelope had the word "Bone" written on the outside in her neat handwriting, accompanied by a number. The numbers finished at twelve.

"Bones": the name of the tiles they used to play dominoes. Dominoes was a game of great skill, of reading your opponents and having confidence in your hand no matter what was dealt. It was also a game of bluff and puff. You had to plan three or four moves ahead and you had to be committed—it could be a long game. Hortense had played dominoes well, but Errol had also been a class-A player. No one ever expected him to lose. Throwing down his hand hard, licking the table

91

and rising to his feet when his bones had closed the game. "See it deh!" And there was that smile unleashed to disarm the most aggrieved of opponents.

Miss Hortense took the envelope that was marked *Bone 12*. Then she reached back into the grip and took out a small black notebook tucked into the side. She took the envelope and the notebook and made her slow way down the stairs, into the living room, and took a weary seat at the head of the oval dining table. Being sat in that position enabled her to have an overview of the whole room and to see who was passing by directly outside on the pavement. She slowly began to ease off the embroidered tablecloth, exposing the rich cherry and high sheen of the grain of the table.

This was the place in the room to which most people gravitated but where most were not permitted to sit. There was a solemnity to this table. It was stately and grounded and most importantly safe. This had been the place where serious business was decided, where the eight Pardners had come together to discuss the Looking Into business, the third and most serious function of the Pardner: the business of life and death.

Fitz would sit to her left. Then Mr. McKenzie and Pastor Williams. Then to Hortense's right were Blossom, Constance, Dimples and finally Errol. Miss Hortense looked at Errol's empty space opposite her now and saw the quick of his smile as he swiveled the chair around, leaned his body into the high back, and rested his head on the top like a pillow.

"Why the hell you just can't sit like the rest of us?" Hortense would say. "Don't you know how to sit 'pon chair?"

She missed him every single day.

22

P Is for Pearl White

Miss Hortense picked up the black leather notebook from the table. The leather was rubbed brown in places. She sighed and opened the book to the page marked with a *P*, where she had written the name Pearl White. So many people thought they knew Pearl, based on her profession, a "lady of the night." But nobody really knew Pearl. She wasn't a woman who gave anything away easily. Miss Hortense had gone to speak to her four weeks after the attack, which Pearl said took place on the night of June 14, 1969. Based on that conversation, Miss Hortense had six entries in her notebook:

- *Attacked walking home from a party on Silver Street.*
- *Attacker wore a balaclava.*
- *Attacker was taller than Pearl in her heels.*
- *Pearl slashed him on his chest with his own knife— drew blood.*
- *"6F"—two letters of the number plate on his blue car.*
- *Attacker whispered something into her ear: "Exodus twenty: fourteen."*

They were some of the most important pieces of information in the Bone 12 case.

Don't get involved, Constance and Pastor Williams had warned after Pearl's attack. *She is not the type of person the Pardner wants to be associating itself with.*

When the Looking Into Bones part of the business had started, Hortense had been in England for seven years and was thirty-three years young. On several occasions during those years, she was of a mind to pack her bags and go back home. She didn't need any badly spelled brick-wrapped diktat to tell her to. On several occasions she had actually packed her grip to do just that. But the question was always the same: Where is home now?

She had been raised, like many in her community, with high morals and a strong sense of self. Her mother had been a teacher, little like a pin, with bright eyes and brown buttery skin; she was firm but kind, and she taught Hortense:

"Never hang your head, girl child, raise it up high like a so."

Her pappa had been a well-respected businessman. He spoke three languages and had a particular interest in astronomy.

"If you look up deh so, Hortense, that is where true life begins."

At the heart of everything that surrounded Hortense was a sense of fairness and justice. Oh, her country had its problems, particularly when it came to the business of independence, and she would never pretend otherwise, but when she stepped off her veranda, she was never afraid. And she had confidence that if something wrong was done against her or any member of her family or community, justice would at least be seen to be done. But in England, for her people, it was another kettle of fish entirely. Because of that, it wasn't often that you heard of her people going to the police for anything. And if on the rare occasion a Black man or woman did go to the police, more often than not it didn't end well. If it wasn't assumed that they were the criminal, then they became the victim of the very people who were meant to be protecting them. Hortense had too many examples.

So the question was, where could her community go to seek justice?

Is we seek justice for those who can't seek it for themselves, she had said through gritted teeth to Constance and Pastor Williams, and Pearl White was no exception.

23

D Is for Daphne Stewart

In her notebook, Miss Hortense flicked to the page marked with a *D*. There she had written "Daphne Stewart."

For many years, Miss Hortense tried to imagine what that young lady would have been like before the attack. She tried to imagine the way in which her delicate feet, wrapped in shiny court shoes, would skip across a puddle, barely paying attention to the fact that it was something to be avoided, her thoughts on the thing in front of her, her future in this town and in this country.

In any case, whoever the girl had been before that night was not the person who Miss Hortense found on her doorstep in the early hours of October 11, 1969, barely conscious, moaning, creating the soft din people produce to cope with unbearable pain. She was wrapped in a large brown woolen overcoat, which hid the blood that was seeping below.

If she had been pretty, if she had been someone who would catch the eye of a man who had a perfectly good and loving woman and family at home, Miss Hortense wouldn't have known from the look of the person who came to her doorstep. There was an injury deep in her scalp where blood had started to clog up her hair, which no longer held any curls and had started to mat; her face was bruised and swollen to such a degree that her head shape favored a jackfruit.

"Jesus Christ," Miss Hortense muttered under her breath. At that unsociable hour, sometimes men did come to see Miss Hortense: those who had just been in a fight and needed something stitched, or those just running; but women rarely came. Daphne gripped tightly on to the overcoat as Miss Hortense led her gently into the house and rested her on the settee.

"I can see underneath?" asked Miss Hortense, immediately concerned about the dull pallor of Daphne's skin.

At that time Miss Hortense had been a staff nurse at the Queen Elizabeth Hospital for six years, though she had been nursing in total for eight. She was used to dealing with the injuries and patients that the other nurses didn't want to touch. But she was unprepared for what had been done to Daphne.

Daphne gripped the overcoat even tighter, but with Miss Hortense's gentle coaxing allowed Miss Hortense to open both it and the coat, which was Daphne's, that rested underneath it. Under the two coats were the remains of an emerald-green dress, torn and stained with blood and mud.

It wasn't the injuries that made Hortense stumble backwards at that moment. Hortense could deal with blood and guts and anything else that came from a person's insides till morning. It was the intention behind the injuries. The very particular intention. The attack could only have been motivated by hate. Only another woman could understand that.

The girl's hands hovered shakily about her lower waist and Miss Hortense knew whatever lay there was something unspeakable. Miss Hortense took the woman's hand in hers.

"I going have to take you to the hospital," said Miss Hortense. The girl shook her head no, but Miss Hortense suspected that there was bleeding inside that she couldn't get to.

As they waited for the ambulance, the light starting to seep through the curtains, Miss Hortense asked questions and Daphne did her best to answer with nods, one word here or there. Miss Hortense gleaned that she and her husband had arrived in the country only three months before. That her attacker was wearing a balaclava. The next time the girl spoke, it was blood that came up, not words. In the ambulance, Miss Hortense held Daphne's hand and continued to encourage her to talk. Any questions about the future fell into silence. A moan came from the girl as she tried to clear her throat.

"What is it?" Miss Hortense leaned in to try to understand.

Daphne swallowed and tried again. Miss Hortense leaned in closer. "He whispered something in my ear."

"There is a pattern," Miss Hortense told the other Pardner members at an urgently convened meeting. She was almost out of breath. "He's dangerous. We need to stop him right now before he strikes again."

24

E

Miss Hortense turned to the page in her notebook that was marked with an *E*.

There was no name written there because that was the secret that she had promised to keep.

The secret she wished to God didn't exist.

25

Exodus 20:14

Evie, her sister, was attacked on January 25, 1970, as she walked home from a blues dance. Only a handful of people knew what had really happened to Evie and that didn't include Blossom. For all her attributes, Blossom couldn't keep a secret to save her life. Fitz and Errol knew about Evie. It was unfair to keep a thing like that from them, given they were putting their lives on the line searching with Miss Hortense for the man who had inflicted her injuries. The man who was attacking women from their community and leaving them for dead, in assaults so horrendous that she had labeled him the Brute.

Mr. McKenzie knew about Evie, but that was because Miss Hortense couldn't keep it from him the afternoon she discharged herself from the hospital. She had, however, sworn all three of them to secrecy. Told them they couldn't even share the secret with their wives.

Under *E*, she had drawn an outline of a woman's body. The head was too big and the arms too long, but each mark inside the outline depicted a specific place where the Brute had left his legacy on her sister.

After Evie's attack, Miss Hortense had been sure that she knew who the Brute was. Not his exact identity, but the type of man that he must be: heavyset, in order to pull Pearl White from her normal walking path; large-spanning hands and thick fingers to make those slap marks across Daphne Stewart's mouth, hands strong enough to pin Evie down by her neck, to punch Daphne in her face and crack her jaw; tall, a minimum of five-foot-eleven to have the top of Pearl's head, who could reach that height in her three-inch heels, pulled up against his pointed chin; deep, black, dead eyes that gave nothing away as he spun Evie around to face him, eyes that didn't flinch to see Daphne's fear; the skin charcoal brown, flashes of which were revealed as he pulled and tore at clothes and flesh, the kind of brown that didn't reflect light and that might easily disguise scratch and bite marks. And wearing workman's boots, steel-capped boots, boots that could rupture the spleen of a woman, that could dislodge a fetus from its womb; boots stained with oil and cracked with mud, and then blood, the last thing his victims had seen as he walked away.

Miss Hortense looked again at the markings. She knew there were psychological scars that she couldn't record, but they all amounted to the same thing: death for every one of his victims. Somehow, some way.

Miss Hortense flicked to the last page of the notebook. On it were written the words the Brute had whispered to Pearl, Daphne and her sister Evie:

Exodus 20:14. The Bible passage that read, *Thou shalt not commit adultery.*

26

The Car Accident

Miss Hortense would never forget the day.

It was Friday, July 10, 1970. The preceding days had been so humid that Miss Hortense had gone without petticoats. The thick air clung to everything, frizzing up her hair, which dripped with grease and sweat. There was no breeze. That is what Miss Hortense hated about English weather: there was no respite to the never-ending heat when it did finally come.

The smell of people and their sicknesses in the heat produced such a stench that Miss Hortense had taken to walking the wards with her handkerchief, peppered with smelling salts, permanently held to her nose. She had been working the late shift, the sweat dripping underneath her freshly starched uniform. She pushed open the window as wide as she could next to one of her patients, but it made no difference; if anything, the room was hotter.

That night, when she got off her long shift, it was Errol who was waiting for her in his two-tone red Singer Gazelle on the corner of Paradise Street. They were working on their toughest case to date: Bone 12, which had been running for months with no real leads. The case consumed Miss Hortense around the clock.

As soon as she got in the car, the sky ripped open and the rains started like the rushing of a pregnant woman's waters. The windscreen wipers screeched as the heavy droplets pelted down, back and forth, back and forth in the darkness of the night.

When they pulled up outside 78 Church Street, she hadn't slept for almost sixteen hours. The windows of that small, terraced house were all misted up from the heaving, dancing bodies inside. The boom of the deep bass filled the car like a third heartbeat as they watched and waited, almost in silence. When they did speak, it was just some mumbled words. She was thinking, as she always did, about what she would say, what she would do when she finally came face-to-face with the man she was searching for.

At some point Hortense must have dozed off. When she next opened her eyes, they were moving. No longer anywhere near Church Street, but on the outskirts of town, chasing after a car.

"He in there? You sure?" she shouted over the noise of the engine and the storm.

She had imagined she would know if the Brute was in there; that she would feel the evil of his presence. Surely the Brute was too big for the blue car they were chasing down.

The car suddenly darted to the left. Errol darted to the left after it; she slid in her seat almost into him.

"It's the same car," he said. "Look. Look at the number plate."

But the car was barely visible through the rain and pulling farther away now. She could see the blur of the tail, the bright red of the lights. Concentrating hard between the windscreen wipers and the bright lights, she tried to see the number plate.

"EU . . . L . . . 20 . . . 6F. 6F," she said. It was him.

In each attack there had been a different car: a blue one, a green one, another car that might have been an Austin Morris, in blood red; but Pearl—Pearl had remembered a part of the blue car's number plate and that was the reason Errol had been able to make chase.

"Did you see who it was?" Hortense asked.

"No. Him fe park up but when him see our car, him shoot off!" Errol's voice was thick with adrenaline. There was no smile on his boyish face that night.

She held on to the seat as the car accelerated further and wove along a dark tree-lined street, Errol gripping the steering wheel, his focus all ahead. They were losing him.

"Go faster!" she shouted at Errol. "Put your blasted foot down. Him is getting away. Don't let him get away."

And then everything went black.

In her living room, Miss Hortense stared out the window. She could see the blurred images of the few people still left on the street, rushing to get out of a sudden downpour. She took the envelope off the table, and slowly pulled out the only thing it contained, a broken gold chain with a small gold crucifix at the end. She rested the chain with its crucifix in the palm of her hand. It was like having poison on her skin. After a few moments she had to drop it onto the table. The crucifix, a reminder of everything the Brute did to his victims. The broken chain, a reminder of what Fitz had done to him.

Now she was going to have to go back into Bone 12 and reach into all of its pain. She was going to have to confront the Brute and all his evil again.

27

An Apology

After visiting the canal, Miss Hortense stepped off the number 279 bus and walked at pace along St. Saviour's Road. For the first time in her life, she was carrying the heavy news of a promise about to be broken. But she had to do it. Now that Bone 12 was open again, she needed to end it before somebody else was hurt. She took a left at the bypass and kept walking until she came upon the row of shops on Chappel Road. Among them were the premises that she had helped source nearly thirty-six years ago. Just over eighteen thousand square feet of land and buildings. Premises that had access to a yard at the back and enough space to put in an extension, on a road that, back then, had enough Blacks to tolerate a man who would bring many more dead ones with him. As it happened, Mr. McKenzie's business was now located in the most desirable part of the "good" side of Musgrove Park.

The sign above the shop still read *McKenzie & Son*, despite the fact that there was no longer a son and hadn't been in many years. The shutters were down but a few hearses were parked up at the side. Despite McKenzie's strokes, they were still in business. Miss Hortense was led to believe there was a small cohort of mostly dedicated staff whom Mr. McKenzie had trained well. And of course there was his wife, Myrtle, who was determined to continue his legacy.

Miss Hortense knocked on the door next to the shop and waited. Mr. McKenzie had been so devoted to his adopted profession that he lived right next to it. The dead deserved his attention night and day. For a man who had no training in death, he had upskilled himself in no time at all. For the past three decades it was to Mr. McKenzie's that you went, even before the pastor was called, when there was a death in the family. He was a man who felt with you, who understood the pain that death brought; a man who had a deep love for his community and who made it his mission to treat the dead and the family of the dead with as much dignity as he would want for himself and his. If there was pride felt for any of the businesses that the Pardner had invested in over the years, then it was for Mr. McKenzie's undertaking business.

After several knocks, Miss Hortense turned to go and was about to begin back down the path when the front door opened and she heard a faint "Hortense?"

Hortense turned to see Myrtle McKenzie. Myrtle didn't have the Jheri curl or the half-and-half smile, but there was still something about the set of her face and the way the lines formed around the mouth that told you she was a relative of Constance. She was wearing a dull-looking buttoned-up cardigan, her hair in two plaits that looked like they hadn't been touched in weeks, and her olive skin had lost its sheen.

"How you do, Myrtle?"

Myrtle gave a tired smile. "Me deh ya. Me deh ya." Her voice was a high-pitched singsong, the accent a cross between their adopted Brummy and the Small Island she originally hailed from.

"Me na mean fe disturb you," said Hortense. "I heard you bring him home."

"Yes, me dear," said Myrtle.

"Well, me sorry me never come sooner," said Hortense.

Myrtle smiled. "He will be glad to know you come," she said. She led Miss Hortense into the front room to the left, which had become a makeshift bedroom. The hospital bed took up a third of the space. A bowl of unfinished soup giving off an unpalatable smell sat before the patient, and there was a sharp scent of bleach that was unable to mask it. A young woman with her back to Miss Hortense was busy leaning over and adjusting the bedsheets with jerky movements. Miss Hortense immediately recognized the elaborate hairstyle piled on top of her head. It was the young girl, Tamisha, from the flashy web page, the takeaway restaurant, and the flat that she had visited. It appeared that it wasn't just her boyfriend, Germaine Banton, who was a jack of all trades, and Miss Hortense wondered if Myrtle was aware of Tamisha's other talents, if you could call them that. Miss Hortense noted that Tamisha wasn't naturally talented at nursing Mr. McKenzie either. Whatever she was trying to do with the bedsheets didn't seem to be working out too well. One of the first things Hortense had been trained to do was crisp hospital corners, but this girl's corners looked like balloons. She touched her hair when she saw Hortense.

"This young lady is Tamisha," said Myrtle.

"We've already met," said Miss Hortense, eyeing the girl.

"She comes in twice a week now," said Myrtle. "I was very lucky when she came knocking on my door one day offering her services."

"Oh, I bet you were," said Miss Hortense. The girl smiled and lowered her head. Was it a coincidence that she was there too? Miss Hortense thought not.

A Bible was open on the tray in front of Mr. McKenzie, who lay on the bed with a white sheet pulled up to his chest, his face gray, eyes closed, breathing heavily.

"We going move the bed upstairs soon as him better," Myrtle said.

Hortense took Mr. McKenzie's hand in hers; it was unnaturally cold. She looked at him with a will, and his eyes slowly started to open.

"You hear me, Mr. McKenzie?" asked Hortense carefully. He grunted.

"Him hear everything, don't it, McKenzie?" said Myrtle. "His ears sharper than mine."

"How you do, sir?" Hortense asked.

He tried to nod.

"Is when you getting outta this bed?" Hortense asked him. "A whole heap of bodies is waiting for you." He tried to smile then, but it turned into a cough. Myrtle eased him forwards to release the phlegm.

"We using pencil and paper fe now," Myrtle said, motioning to the small notepad on the side.

When he had settled back down, Hortense spoke again. "I won't stay long, you hear, but I wanted to let you know." She felt him looking into her core. Then she leaned forward and whispered into his ear. She didn't want Myrtle to hear. "You remember I did promise you

106

something? A long time ago? Well, I have to break it. I'm going back into Bone Twelve." His grip tightened and there was a nod towards the notepad. Myrtle picked it up and placed a pencil in his hand. After struggling for a while, he flung the pencil as though it had failed him.

M-i-c is what Hortense thought she could read. Could be the first three letters of his son's name. But why was he raising Michael now?

"He's been talking about Michael a lot lately," Myrtle whispered to Hortense, as if she could hear Hortense's thoughts. That was understandable, she supposed. Her long nursing career had shown her that it was often on the deathbed that clarity about life was achieved.

Michael was killed in 1967. He was taken far too soon, and the reason for his death had never been properly recognized. The police had insisted it was a heart attack, rather than the beating he had received, that had turned his face black and blue and left him bleeding inside, his body broken. There was, according to his best friend, Danny Grant, a pretty girl whom Michael had been chatting to, and two white boys who had taken offense. A fight ensued, the white boys disappeared, and Michael never got up. It was the Pardner's first Looking Into case: Bone 1.

"It's difficult," said Myrtle, retrieving the pencil and paper and putting them on a table next to her. "But we trying." She tapped Mr. McKenzie's hand. "We trying."

Death clung to the air all around them and was edging further into the room. Mr. McKenzie's eyes started to close.

Myrtle motioned towards the door, and then led Hortense to the back room, which was filled with overflow furniture. A dining table was squashed up against the wall, the three-seater settee shoved to the window.

"It's been a long time," said Myrtle as she settled into a chair.

"It has," said Hortense. Much had happened since they had last spoken. Years of whispers, rumors and judgment. "How you coping?" asked Miss Hortense, sitting further forward in the settee. She knew that losing someone to a stroke wasn't easy and could be painfully slow.

"Me deh ya," Myrtle repeated softly. She rubbed her hands together. "Is what you think?" she asked Miss Hortense. "You the nurse. Him going get better, don't it?"

"Him doing just fine," said Miss Hortense. Her leg started to tingle. It was the same tingle she had that Thursday morning thirty years earlier, when she had told Myrtle and Mr. McKenzie that she had no leads in the disappearance of Danny Grant.

After Michael died, Danny, a tall, well-built boy, became like a surrogate son to the McKenzies. It was he who accompanied Myrtle to church every Sunday. He was the last person to be with Michael, the last to see him alive. It was understandable that Mr. and Mrs. McKenzie wanted to have him close, particularly as Michael's death had hit him hard too. He dropped out of his studies, and got into trouble with the police. When the McKenzies took him under their wing, that stopped. Then, July 1970, Danny disappeared. Myrtle had made it clear to Miss Hortense that she had never forgiven her for failing to find him.

"If I could swap myself for McKenzie, you see, I would do it in a heartbeat," said Myrtle now. Miss Hortense didn't doubt it.

Miss Hortense sat further forward in her seat and lowered her voice. "Watch that gal in there, you hear?" said Hortense, motioning to the front room.

"Tamisha?" asked Myrtle. Miss Hortense nodded.

"Her boyfriend is a very nasty piece of work." They both knew young women who had mashed themselves up by becoming involved with nasty pieces of work. "Watch him don't try tek advantage of you."

"Oh, my Lawd takes care of me," said Myrtle, defensive as ever. "You went to Constance's funeral, I heard," she said, changing the subject. She didn't wait for a response. "I couldn't make it, not with McKenzie. I was surprised you went, though. You never did like me cousin. In truth, what she showed the world," continued Myrtle, as though she could hear Hortense's thoughts again, "was not all that she was. You know she called me just two days before she died? We hadn't spoken for many, many years. It was as if she knew that the good Lawd was calling her. She told me, *If anything is to happen to me, Myrtle, you must get a grip of my affairs.* She was meant to call me back to explain what the affairs was but she never did, and what now with McKenzie, well, I can't deal in her business. I have my own problems. And anyway she have her pickney them." Myrtle shook her head and cussed her teeth. "Me na know. Life . . ."

108

Myrtle leaned forwards.

"You going back inna it, then?" she asked, looking directly at Hortense. "Into Number Twelve?"

Miss Hortense knew she didn't need to respond; that before she could, Myrtle would talk again. She always did talk more than she should.

"You is not a bad person, you know that, Hortense?" said Myrtle. "You just get a bad deal is all."

She rose and went to the fireplace, where she picked up a framed photograph that sat next to a glass ashtray. The ashtray was green and weighty, with sharp jagged edges. Strange, thought Miss Hortense; she'd never known Mr. McKenzie or Myrtle to be smokers. In the photograph were the two boys: Michael, his infectious smile spreading into the room, his arm around Danny, the two of them together, alive and full of life and youth, staring back at Myrtle and Hortense.

"Be careful, you hear? Mr. McKenzie always said that Twelve was going be the one to kill you."

She put the photo back, then looked at Hortense deeply, lowered her head and entered into prayer.

"Loving Jesus, please show Sister Hortense that pursuit of earthly vengeance is not the way of you, Lawd Jesus. For you say vengeance is yours and yours alone. Lawd Jesus, watch over Sister Hortense in her misguided endeavors. So she may rest easy and let go of things that are not for her to pursue. Bring peace to her, dear Lawd Jesus. Amen."

Hortense hadn't relied on God back in 1970 to provide her with the answer to Bone 12, and she wouldn't rely on him now. Fitz was the only other person who understood how Bone 12, Pearl White, Daphne Stewart, Evie, Danny Grant and Errol were connected; and he was a man who carried plenty of his own demons. Bone 12 reached deep and wide and swept up whole lives with it. She knew that in opening it up, in seeking to understand how it was now connected to the death of the man at the bottom of the stairs, it had the potential to sweep her away with it too.

28

Bulla Cake

When Miss Hortense got home, she went into the kitchen and started to take down baking trays and a mixing bowl. Beating, kneading and cutting calmed her nerves and gave her space to think. And she needed to think clearly now.

Bulla Cake

2 tbsp melted butter
3 cups all-purpose flour
1 tsp baking powder
½ tsp baking soda
225 g brown sugar (the darker the better) or molasses
some water
½ tsp ground ginger
1 tsp vanilla extract
1 tsp ground cinnamon
¼ tsp ground nutmeg
½ tsp allspice
¼ tsp salt

Miss Hortense put the sugar and salt into a pan on the gas fire and dissolved the mixture in some water on a very low heat. *Remember, Hortense, big fire don't cook food. Take your time.* She added the ginger, butter and vanilla, and stirred. She sieved the rest of the dry ingredients into a bowl. The pepper spice of the ginger tickled her nostrils. She used a wooden spoon to make a hole in the dry ingredients. She added the cool dissolved-sugar solution to the dry mixture to make the dough. She added a little water so that it was of the right consistency and kneaded; the dough for bulla cake should be heavy and on the wet side, not light. Miss Hortense floured the surface and put the dough onto it, adding some more flour. She used a rolling pin to roll the dough and then used a saucer as a template to cut circles. She greased a baking tray, put the bulla cake circles on it and put them in the oven.

While the bulla cakes were baking, Hortense dialed Gregory's number from the heavy rotary-dial phone on the hallway table, and waited for him to pick up.

"Gregry?"

"Yes, Aunty?"

"You know 'bout the body dem find at Constance's house?"

Gregory was quiet. "I'm not on that case, Aunty."

"I didn't ask you that," said Miss Hortense.

Gregory exhaled deeply. "I know that he was found at the bottom of the stairs."

"Yes, yes," said Hortense, rolling her eyes impatiently, "we all know that."

"I know that he was drinking, and from the state of him he must have been a heavy drinker."

"And what you think?"

"There'll be a coroner's investigation," said Gregory, "and we'll know more then."

"But what you *think*?"

"I think," said Gregory, "that he was a drunk that fell down some stairs."

"Do you?" said Hortense flatly. "And what him name?"

"I can't tell you that," said Gregory. He paused. "That is because at the moment the assigned officers are trying to ascertain his identity with relatives abroad."

"Abroad?" repeated Miss Hortense.

111

"Yes," said Gregory, again pausing. "They think he's from Texas."

"Texas. Um-hum. All that way," said Miss Hortense. "And what, him come all the way from Texas just to bruck into Constance house and drop dead?"

"No, Aunty, he didn't break in. Miss Constance's family invited him to stay in her house."

"Oh really," said Hortense. "And you have a name for the man dem invited in?"

"Oh, Aunty . . ." said Gregory, sighing heavily on the phone. "Donovan Miller, okay? But you didn't hear that from me."

"Donovan Miller, is that right . . ." said Hortense. "I did once know a man by that name, long, long time ago now."

"Please, Aunty," said Gregory. There was something like fear taking over his voice. "Don't get involved, okay?" History showed that her interest in police investigations didn't tend to end well for him. "I don't want—"

But Miss Hortense put the phone down before he had a chance to finish his sentence. The sweet, warm ginger of the baked bulla cakes was catching the back of her throat, a sign that they were ready to come out of the oven.

Gregory put the phone down.

If his aunty was back poking her nose into places she wasn't meant to, then that could only mean trouble. What did the community center, Richard Dudney aka Dice and this man Donovan Miller have in common? So far, it was his aunty.

He had pulled up Dice's file from the police database; it was, as he already knew, substantial. Petty theft, possession with intent, breaking and entering, grievous bodily harm, football hooliganism. He was a dangerous man. Dice took risks, but for his own advantage; the result was always that either something was taken or someone was hurt. The vandalism at the community center appeared different, as nothing was taken. Gregory also knew that Dice wasn't at the top of the food chain—he always worked for someone else. Who was he working for now? The fact that Miss Constance's daughter was the manager of the center also bothered him. Gregory's instincts told him that something bigger was afoot, and unless he solved this puzzle before his aunty did, someone else was likely to end up in the hospital or he would be looking for a new job.

29

Better the Devil You Know

The weekend passed without another visit from Blossom, but on Monday, she was back at Miss Hortense's house with appendicitis.

"It's the right side, don't it? It's a big aching," she said. "It's been giving me gripe since morning. It's right ya so; under here." Blossom pointed to her ribs. "What you think, it could be the liver instead?" But when Miss Hortense told her, as she sipped her sugar tea, "You had best find yourself in A&E because appendicitis is some quick and serious business," Blossom made a show of stretching and said: "It's all right, you hear, I think it's easing."

"I just come from church," said Blossom, settling herself onto the settee. "You know I still don't get my Pardner money yet? And them two Mavises wouldn't even let me past the front door to see the pastor. Something very fishy is going on. I want my money and I want to know what we going to do with the Pardner now that Constance is dead."

And then she said, "You seen what dem a do to the Bullring? Boy oh boy dem is mashing it up."

And then, finally, she said, "But, Hortense, why you don't go and Look Into the death of Constance and the man at the bottom of the stairs? The least you could do is to ask Gregory 'bout it the next time him come round?"

Miss Hortense shook her head and said, "No," which was a small word but one that grew and filled the whole of the room when Miss Hortense was the one using it.

Bone 12 was dangerous and Miss Hortense wasn't going to let

114

Blossom know anything about her secret reopening of the case because she knew Blossom wouldn't be able to resist getting involved.

"But . . ." said Blossom, who was always hard of hearing when it came to things she didn't want to hear, and she held up her fingers, about to list again all of the reasons why it was so important that Hortense start investigating.

"No," said Miss Hortense again, with a grave stare that would make an ordinary person quail.

"Well, if you not going to Look Into it," said Blossom defiantly, "I just going have to do it all by meself."

"And is what kinda Looking Into you can do, Blossom Henry?" Miss Hortense asked.

There was a reason why it was Hortense, Fitz and Errol who had got their hands dirtiest in the Looking Into. A reason why Black Cake was Black Cake. Blossom stood up and her bag fell off her lap.

"You don't think I can do Looking Into?" asked Blossom, wiping away at her lap.

"Blossom," said Hortense, softer now. "You going get yourself inna trouble." She was looking at Blossom over her glasses. "I don't have to remind you. Do I?" Miss Hortense didn't need to say the name Lester, or Bullfrog. They both knew who she was talking about.

One Friday in August 1968, Blossom had decided that her then-husband Lester (the one with the funny eye) had fathered three mixed-race children who lived around the corner. This finding was based on some dubious investigative work—she'd seen Lester talking to their mother at the corner shop. Blossom took it upon herself to declare her findings to the three children, the mother, and then the whole of Lester's dominoes group.

The real fathers—there were three—were none too happy to hear that they'd been paying upkeep for children who, according to Blossom, didn't belong to them, and Lester found himself in some very hot water on his way home from work. When he eventually made it home, he removed his coat and his hat, took out his fat fists and licked Blossom in the face and body and then started choking her. Blossom had taken to wearing scarves ever since. But still, Blossom boxed him back so hard that he hit his head on the sideboard and lost consciousness. When he recovered, his other eye was never quite the same, and *he* threatened to bring charges. It was Miss Hortense who had to clean the whole mess up. Firstly by proclaiming that Lester was infertile and therefore incapable of fathering any children—*Please, God*, Miss Hortense had thought—and secondly by giving Lester enough money to leave town; she had to hand over to him six months of her Pardner money.

Blossom sat down and took up her tea noisily from its saucer, only punctuating a sulky silence with the occasional slurp.

After five minutes of this, when the door knocker went, Miss Hortense was grateful for the interruption.

"Expecting company?" asked Blossom with a spikiness to her voice, as Miss Hortense rose.

Miss Hortense opened the door to find Sonia blinking on her doorstep.

"Hi," said Sonia. "I was just passing, and I just wanted to say thanks again, for looking after my arm." She pointed to it, moved it up and down like it was a wing, and then lowered it.

Hopping through the passage on twig feet after Hortense, she said, "I was just passing, really. Well, not passing, exactly. I'm up here now. For a bit. Sorting out the house. You know, the one my parents used to have on Ebley Street. The tenants."

Sonia nodded hello to Blossom.

"I'm not far from here, staying in a hotel called the Mirage? Just until I can get the tenants out, and the house sorted." There was a peck-peck-peck quality to Sonia's speech.

"The Mirage?" said Blossom, and she passed a glancing look at Hortense. "Don't you think it smell a bit funny in there?"

Sonia looked at Blossom.

"Well, I just thought it was the area."

"Oh, it's the area, all right," said Blossom, giving Hortense another look. "And what else is it you planning on doing while you staying in Bigglesweigh?" she asked, rubbing her chest at the girl's tentative smile.

"No particular plans," said Sonia. That milky, gummy voice again. "I'm just going to find out more about the accident that killed my

116

dad, really." Miss Hortense knew what the girl reminded her of now; it was the vulture bird, picking at flesh.

"Tea, Sonia?" asked Miss Hortense abruptly, and before anybody answered, Hortense was in the kitchen making up the teapot.

Blossom leaned over then and whispered conspiratorially to the girl, "Best not to mention anything to do with you father to Miss Hortense again, you hear?"

But Sonia didn't have the chance to ask her why, because then Hortense entered with the tea, and said, as easily as if she might have been asking if she wanted milk, "You can stay here."

The chair Blossom was sitting on rocked as she nearly fell off it.

"Really? Oh no, I couldn't," Sonia protested; Blossom was thinking the very same thing.

"I have a room—nothing fancy, just a bed and a wardrobe in it," said Miss Hortense calmly, as she handed a cup to the girl.

"Well, I don't want to impose?" said Sonia, hugging the cup close. Blossom looked at Hortense, her eyebrows nearly at her hairline.

"I didn't ask you that," said Miss Hortense sharply. "I said I have a spare room." Her tone indicated the conversation was over, take it or leave it.

Sonia hesitated for only a moment. "Well, that is very kind of you. Thank you. I'll take it."

Blossom's mouth fell open. In all the years she had known Miss Hortense, she had never, with one particular exception, heard her offer to share the space she was standing in, let alone her own house. Stanley Thomas had been the one particular exception, and clearly that was a very different situation. Hortense had felt responsible.

After Sonia had left, saying she was going to be back in a week with her things, Blossom turned to Hortense, all previous offense gone, her voice now urgent with confusion.

"Hortense, is what you doing?" she hissed fiercely. "Don't you know 'bout de dangers of letting strange people come live inna you house?"

30

People Will Talk

Gregory tended to visit Miss Hortense on a Tuesday evening after his shift ended. Miss Hortense would have preferred for him to come around more often because she knew that he didn't eat right, existing on all those takeaways since his wife had picked up and left him.

As they sat sipping tea after their meal, Miss Hortense asked, "You hear from Lucy?" That was the ex-wife's name, though it wasn't the name Miss Hortense called her in her own mind.

Gregory gulped down his tea. "It's complicated, Aunty."

What was complicated about your wife having an affair? It was pretty simple, if you asked Hortense. Hortense knew many men and women who had been mashed up good and proper by affairs. She was keeping a close eye on Gregory for exactly that reason. Gregory had always been resilient, but he could also be sensitive, and if Miss Hortense was honest, there was a small part of her that feared he might take after his mother.

"You find anything else more about the Miller case?" Hortense asked him casually.

"It's not my case, Aunty," he said.

"So you say," she said, "but you find out anything more?"

"No," said Gregory, but she could tell by the way he shifted in his seat that he was holding something back.

Six years prior, Gregory had decided to embark on a new career as a police officer, despite Hortense's very vocal opposition.

"Dem is all corruption," she had warned. Bitter experience had taught her this; after all, it was the reason she had got into the Looking

118

Into business in the first place. But he had mumbled something about "justice." Damn fool. She had advised him he was better off becoming a criminal. In any case, a policeman was what he now was.

"I can see the body?" she asked, as if she were asking him to take her to the theater.

"No!" Gregory cried out.

"Well then, I need you do to me a likkle favor," said Hortense. "There was a note with it."

"I don't know anything about a note, Aunty," said Gregory.

"Well, I need to find out about it," she said. Which meant that he needed to find out about it for her. That note had taken her back to a time that had brought her to her knees. She needed to see the note for herself. Make sure it said what Mr. Wright and the girl said it did, and then try to find out why.

"And how do you know about this note?" Gregory asked his aunty.

"Never you mind," Hortense returned.

"Well then, nope," he said. "I'm not jeopardizing my career again." The last time he did, and those two men ended up in the hospital, he was put on a warning that still had him under the watchful eye of Superintendent McGraf, the white man with the big nostrils who had been so interested in following his career.

But Miss Hortense was used to Gregory digging his heels in, so she opted straight for emotional blackmail.

"Listen, young man, I am the only aunty you got. And you need to respect me and respect that. When I speak, you listen. You hear?"

Gregory opened his mouth, an argument forming on his lips, but one hard stare was enough to shove it back in his throat. He coughed, looked down at his plate and picked up his fork. That was enough of a yes for Miss Hortense.

Ten thirty in the evening in Bigglesweigh made it 4:30 p.m. in Jamaica. In Bigglesweigh, darkness had already descended and it was cold and miserable. In Jamaica, tree frogs and crickets would be singing and there would be a cool breeze permeating the warm sweet air. Miss Hortense took out her international phone card and entered the long number before the operator told her how much credit was still available.

119

She dialed 00 and then 1 and then 876, and entered the long number that she knew by heart.

"Hello," said the echoey voice on the line.

"Tiny?" said Miss Hortense, imagining the bright sun beating down on the small house he had built for himself in Savanna-la-Mar.

"Yes, this is Tiny. Miss Hortense? A you that? How you do?"

Miss Hortense said she was doing not too bad, and Tiny said that, all being well, and if God spared his life, he was doing well too. Miss Hortense could hear it. One of a handful of them brave enough to actually go back home and lucky enough not to have dropped dead as soon as he stepped off the plane. Tiny, at six-foot-seven-and-three-quarters, had been one of the tallest sergeants in the Jamaican Constabulary Force before he came to England in 1962. In Bigglesweigh, he had stood up tall for more than a decade as security outside Safeway supermarket, freezing his pants off and being insulted by shoplifters, before he finally decided fifteen years ago to pack his bags; said he didn't want to be buried in no foreign man's soil. Ever since he had returned, he was Miss Hortense's eyes and ears back home.

"I'm calling to make inquiries," said Miss Hortense.

"Oh, yes?" said Tiny. They both heard the clicking on the line. There were things it wasn't safe to say into a phone. Probably it was just the connection, but neither of them took chances.

"You 'member a man named Donovan Miller?" asked Miss Hortense. "Him used to live in a boardinghouse with Constance Brown and her husband till the house did catch 'pon fire in 1965." There was silence.

Tiny came back. "Mek me tink. Donovan Miller? Yes. Wasn't he from St. Ann?"

"You ever come across him back a yard?"

There was a silence again. The clicking on the line.

"No, me na think so," said Tiny. "But leave it with me. If there is anything to find out, I will call you back."

"Thank you," said Miss Hortense.

"Oh dear," he said.

"Tiny, what is it?" asked Hortense. She could hear a slight alarm in his voice but there was a delay on the phone.

"Nutting. Me just see Jancro a circle is all," he said.

120

"Oh," replied Miss Hortense. There wasn't much to say to that. If Jancro, also known as John Crow, the scavenging vulture, was circling, it meant death was near.

"All right, then," she said. "Look after youself, you hear?" And she put the phone down and tapped it twice. Death had circled Tiny many times before, but still, she couldn't help but be a little concerned.

Miss Hortense went to the glass cabinet and stood in front of it for a moment. There was her reflection and a decision to make. She opened a drawer and took out a number of greeting cards addressed to *Dear Aunty Hortense*. Christmas cards, Thanksgiving cards, birthday cards, the announcement of a birth. She took the latest one from the top of the pile, opened it, redialed the long card number and this time entered 001, then dialed 512, and then the number at the bottom of the card. The number was written in big, sloping loops.

The ringtone was labored, the gap between the rings long. The phone clicked onto an answering machine. A woman's voice loud and broad with a honeyed American accent.

"Hi, this is Althea. I'm sorry we can't take your call right now. Leave a message and someone will get right back to you." Althea was her brother Alan's eldest daughter, the one who sent all the cards despite the silence back. It wasn't just her local community that Miss Hortense had shut herself off from.

". . . Althea?" said Miss Hortense. Miss Hortense didn't like leaving answering-machine messages. She shifted, careful. "It's me. Your aunt. When you get this, can you please call me back?"

The last time she had seen Althea was in April 1962, when she was just a young woman. Now Althea was a grown woman with grand-children of her own.

Hortense said, "I have something I need you fe do for me? You can make inquiries about a man named Donovan Miller? Donovan Miller." After a pause she said, "And me sorry to hear 'bout you grandson."

Miss Hortense quickly put the phone down. Things were hard for their young people all over, but for their young people inna that ya country, well.

31

The Twelve Rules

The following Monday morning, when fog was still creeping along the ground from the cold night before, Sonia moved her things into Miss Hortense's house. The curtains from across the road twitched as the girl teetered into the house with three large suitcases. Miss Hortense told her she hoped she didn't have too many more things to bring into the house and that she didn't understand why three suitcases were needed for what she was expecting to be a short stay. She said that she was going out to do some shopping and some visiting, and that she wouldn't be back for a few hours. She also left some very specific instructions.

First, that the girl needed to be responsible for her own cleanliness, which meant in the bath and the plughole and the sink; the girl could use the one half of the shelf Miss Hortense had cleared in the cabinet in the bathroom, but no more than that. Miss Hortense expected the girl to do her own laundry and linen—and one thing Miss Hortense couldn't stand was to see drawers hung up on the washing line; second, and it was obvious, but Miss Hortense's bedroom was strictly off limits—nobody other than Miss Hortense had any cause to be in it; third, that Sonia shouldn't move anything around in Miss Hortense's home, and particularly not in the kitchen; fourth, the girl was welcome to sit in the front room, except on a Wednesday evening, when Miss Hortense liked to concentrate on her program, *Crimewatch*; fifth, that the girl should take anything Miss Hortense's friend, Blossom, said with a pinch of salt; sixth, that any post for Miss Hortense was to be left on the sideboard in the front room; seventh, that if the girl saw any cats in the garden, she was to chase them off with the stick Miss Hortense left by the back door; eighth, that Mondays were market day and so Miss Hortense would leave early and be back around midday; ninth, that she wouldn't take kindly to Sonia coming in at all hours of the night and making up a whole heap of noise, disturbing Miss Hortense's good sleep; tenth, that Gregory, her nephew, was a very busy policeman, so Sonia wasn't to interfere with him at all at all; eleventh, if her nephew, Gregory, called that afternoon, Sonia was to tell him to call back at ten minutes past two exactly; and twelfth, that Miss Hortense wasn't somebody who liked to have strangers in her home (and she left it at that).

"Shall I write this down?" Sonia said, nodding but bemused.

Miss Hortense peered at her, disappointed.

"You can't remember twelve things?"

"Well, that's a lot to pay attention to. I didn't know I needed to listen so closely," said Sonia.

Miss Hortense sighed. "That's the problem with your generation. You don't pay enough attention." Miss Hortense opened the front door. "I pay attention to everything. And I don't forget a thing."

Every Monday morning, without fail, come rain or shine, no matter what guests she might have, Miss Hortense wrapped herself up in her heavy woolen overcoat (even in what the English called their summer), pulled her silk scarf over her head and ears, and made her way to Bridge Street Market, rolling her basket along the broken pavements and cobblestones, her handbag tucked into the crook of her arm.

Bridge Street Market had stood for at least two hundred years and had been the market that Miss Hortense had frequented for thirty-seven. There were a handful of familiar faces that would turn up every Monday morning just like her. The noise, the bustle, the colors and the smells—they reminded her that even on a gray day such as the one that she was now stepping into, there was a Caribbean Sea and a bright sun high up in the sky back in Jamaica.

Outside of Billy's fruit and veg, Miss Hortense spotted Mavis Buchanan feeling up an avocado. Mavis Buchanan lowered her head and said not a word. Ordinarily, Miss Hortense would have been more than happy not to engage with the woman, but on that Monday she had come with some very particular questions that she needed answers to. So she pulled up her basket alongside Mavis, reached for her own avocado, and said, "Morning, Miss Buchanan."

Mavis B was slow to respond. She turned slowly to face Miss Hortense.

"Oh, it's you, Miss Hortense. I did hear 'bout the body dem did find at the bottom of the stairs, at Constance house?" she said, as if waiting for a piece of gossip from Hortense that she could scurry back and take to her namesake. Miss Hortense, however, would not, at that present moment at least, oblige.

"Yes, I'm sure you did," said Hortense. "I wanted to ask you about Pearl White. You 'member Pearl White, Miss Buchanan, don't it?" Miss Hortense blinked away a sudden, vivid memory of Pearl whispering to her those two letters from the Brute's number plate. She carefully put down the avocado and picked up a piece of renta yam, focusing on the brown fur of the outside and the orange-yellow starchy flesh on the inside.

Mavis B looked at Miss Hortense with her beady eyes as if she had just had her tail snatched up. She cleared her throat and clucked, looking about her.

"Um, not really. Anyway," she said. She held on to the handle of her basket tightly, ready to push off.

"But you used to live in one of the little rooms on the second floor where she was in St. Clement's Road, back in the old days," said Miss Hortense, more loudly, after her. "So you must 'member her, you being in her employment and all?"

Mavis B pushed her trolley back and stepped in closer to Miss Hortense, her jowls bouncing with rage.

"That was a long time ago, Miss Hortense," she hissed, leaning into Miss Hortense some more. "A very, *very* long time ago." Mavis picked up another avocado, twisting it around in her hand.

"But all the same. You had one of the little rooms," continued Miss Hortense. "Did Pearl ever talk to you about the attack?"

"No," said Mavis B. "I hardly had any reason to have a conversation with that woman. Miss Hortense, you're talking thirty-plus years ago. Why would I remember anything about what you are talking?" Her eyes were popping in her head, the skin around her mouth tight. "If I remember rightly, you looked into all of this years ago and it never got you nowhere then neither."

"Well," said Hortense. "There may have been something or somebody that I overlooked." She was looking Mavis B up and down.

"Do you remember Donovan Miller?"

Mavis had a sudden intake of breath.

"Mr. Miller," continued Hortense, "was a very large man, tall and difficult to miss. I understand he used to frequent Pearl's very regular?" Hortense watched Mavis B carefully. She looked like she was about to explode. It was now that Miss Hortense would oblige. "They're saying it was Donovan Miller that was found dead."

"Donovan dead?" spluttered Mavis, and she reached a hand up to her chest. Miss Hortense almost wanted to reach out to her.

"But," Mavis said as if to herself, "he left in 'sixty-five . . ." She trailed off.

"Nineteen sixty-five, you say?" asked Hortense. "And you and him were close, don't it?"

". . . No, you have that wrong," Mavis said. "I don't remember the man you talking 'bout." Mavis dropped the avocado like it was a grenade. "I'd thank you not to raise Pearl White or the house she lived in, or anybody that visited it, ever again." And with that she rolled off her shopping basket and was gone.

After the visit to the market, Miss Hortense returned home for a cup of tea. The girl, Sonia, was out. She now had it confirmed that Mavis Buchanan, who she knew had been Donovan Miller's regular girl, hadn't seen Donovan Miller in thirty-five years, and that when he returned, it wasn't to find her. She now wanted to find out more about the note, so her second visit of the day was to the other Mavis.

"I can come in?" asked Miss Hortense at Mavis Campbell's door. The arthritis made Mavis lean against the door frame.

"I have me grandpickney with me," Mavis Campbell lied, filling the door with more of her ample body. "Grandpickney" was said in such a way to mean that she of course had them, whereas the woman in front of her didn't. That woman in front of her would never understand what it was to have grandpickneys or pickneys, because she'd never had a man to give her any and that was, as everyone said, the whole trouble. As far as Mavis was concerned, Miss Hortense didn't have a man of her own because no man would take her. Not only that, but she then went and managed to kill another woman's husband. Miss Hortense was bad luck. That is why Mavis didn't want Miss Hortense on her doorstep or in her house.

"What is this about?" asked Mavis gruffly, crossing her arms. She wanted to get back to her daytime TV.

"I want to talk to you about Donovan Miller."

"Who?"

"You don't know a man by that name?" asked Hortense.

"Why would I know a man by that name?"

"What about Daphne Stewart, then?" said Hortense.

Mavis stared at Miss Hortense hard. If the woman wasn't so dangerous, Mavis might even feel sorry for her, but the woman *was* dangerous and she'd clearly come to cause trouble.

"You been to church recently 'cept for funeral?" asked Mavis. It wasn't a man Miss Hortense needed; it was the Lawd Almighty himself.

"Daphne Stewart was a childminder—she used to look after you pickney them," Hortense persisted.

That was too many words, too much suggestion. Mavis leaned out the door looking left and right. "You living in the past, Miss Hortense," said Mavis. "I cannot help you with that." She held on to the door, firmly in her right hand, ready to shut it.

"Do you remember that brown coat you husband used to wear?" It was the most Miss Hortense had ever said to Mavis regarding Bone 12. Miss Hortense was watching her closely.

Mavis's skin started to prickle and get hot under her blouse. She pushed the door wide open and stepped her big body towards Miss Hortense with a rush of air.

"I hope you are not suggesting that my husband, Ralph, rest his soul, had anything to do with those attacks." Mavis was almost shouting, because it was important to set the record straight in case anyone was listening, including her late husband and the Lawd

126

himself. "Ralph was a good man. Not a better man than my husband would you find."

"I don't doubt that," said Miss Hortense, "but you've never liked me. And when they found that body at Constance's house, it came with a note beside it. Is you write it?"

"What is this now, my Lawd Jesus? You gone mad? What note you talking? You don't come a this house with your damned blasted"— Mavis signaled with her finger—"*lies*," she said. "Don't come back round hereso." Mavis was spitting now. "You. Is. Not. Welcome! Is you kill Errol." And with that Mavis slammed the door as hard as she could in Miss Hortense's face.

But Mavis's actions spoke louder than her words, and just before she pushed the door shut, she scratched at her neck. A nervous reaction. And Miss Hortense knew then, without a shadow of a doubt, Mavis Campbell was hiding something.

Gregory did call back at exactly ten minutes past two and Miss Hortense was ready by the house phone waiting. After her conversation with Sonia earlier, she couldn't trust the girl to so much as take a message.

"Gregry?"

"Yes, Aunty."

"Well?" Hortense asked.

"Yes, you're right, there was a piece of paper with some words typed on it found beside the body."

"I need to see it," said Hortense.

"But . . ."

Miss Hortense said, "Thank you," and without further ado, put the phone down.

After that, Miss Hortense left the phone off the hook. What she needed now was the space to study and decipher. There were many players in the new chapter of Bone 12. And just like a game of dominoes, Miss Hortense needed to watch each player carefully to understand their next move. At the present time, the players included all the members of Constance Brown's family: the disheveled daughter, Camille; the blubbering granddaughter, Jasmine; and, of particular

127

interest, the big-bellied son, Nigel Brown, with his crime-world entanglements with the dry-skin boy Germaine Banton and the tall mawga white man with the Aston Villa cap. She was undecided about the role of Mavis Campbell. But the pastor was definitely a player; there was something not right about his behavior at the funeral, and what was he mumbling about mortgage payments for at Constance's *plinkety-plinkety* table the day before she died?

32

Blossom Won't Be Told

Blossom's phone clearly wasn't working because nobody was answering her calls. Pastor Williams's phone kept cutting out after the first or second ring and Hortense's was completely dead.

Nevertheless, Blossom shouted into the receiver, "Hello? Hortense? This is the fifth time I'm calling you since morning. I will be expecting a return call from you at your earliest convenience. You hear? Can you hear me? Hortense? I have news. Big news. You there? You sure you are not there? Signing off now, then, unless you are there? Bye for now. Goodbye, then. It's Mrs. Henry—Blossom."

The big news was that Blossom, fed up waiting for Hortense to agree to the Looking Into, had launched her own investigation and was now three steps closer to finding out who the dead body at the bottom of Constance's stairs was and on the cusp of solving the mystery (as she saw it) of who killed Constance.

The three steps were provided by her hairdresser, Bola at Mane Attraction, just over two weeks after the body was found, during a rinse and set. Bola had said she could fit her in because Bola had just been having cancellations all over the place. On further discussion, it turned out that even their mutual acquaintance, Constance's daughter, Camille, had recently canceled. She had called Bola to say she couldn't make her 11:15 Saturday appointment because of the recent death of a family friend.

"A family *friend*?" repeated Blossom. So that was who the strange man was at the bottom of Constance's stairs. Step one. "What a crosses! And did the young lady say exactly who it was?"

"She did mention something," said Bola, "about him visiting from overseas." Step two!

"Oh," said Blossom. "What a shame."

They both agreed that it was just bad luck to have so much death happening to one family. And as Bola was fluffing up the back of Blossom's hair and showing it to her in the mirror, Blossom said:

"You wouldn't have a number for her, would you? Poor thing, she doesn't have a mother now to help her through." Step three.

It turned out Blossom's phone *was* working, because after several rings, a breathless woman on the other end of the line said:

"Hello?"

"Oh, yes, my dear, hello," said Blossom. "This is Blossom Henry."

"Yes?" said Camille, sounding irritated. The background was busy.

"Well, you probably don't remember me, my dear," said Blossom. "I come to the community center every year without fail for Independence Day and I was at your mother's funeral."

"Er, yes?" said Camille. "Listen, I've got a load of kids here and more coming any minute. Can this wait?"

Blossom was just about to say she was the one who had the funny turn at the funeral and nearly died when Camille said: "Look, is this about Pastor Williams?"

"The pastor?" repeated Blossom.

"Like I've told him before and I'm telling you now—it's not me he wants to be chasing down. Speak to my brother. It's Nigel that's dealing with Mum's bloody estate." And with that, the woman put the phone down before Blossom could ask anything about the body at the bottom of her mother's stairs.

Blossom still couldn't get hold of Miss Hortense, so she went to Mr. Wright's flat and told him about the strange phone call with Constance's daughter instead.

"Well, that don't surprise me one bit," Mr. Wright said, cutting into a watermelon. "I don't think that family is what it says on the tin." The melon juices dripped onto the plate. He sucked on the piece he had just cut out and spat out pips into his hand.

"Just thinking on it now, all the comings and goings that happened before Constance died," he said, digging between his teeth and wiping his mouth on the sleeve of his white shirt. "Well, that was a bloody disgrace if you ask me."

"How you mean?" asked Blossom. "What comings and goings you talking 'bout?"

"Well, you know me," he said. "I is not a man to spread gossip."

"Well, of course not," said Blossom self-importantly.

"But when I was taking my morning air on the balcony weeks before she died"—he spat out some more pips—"I saw the same daughter."

"Yes?" said Blossom, leaning in.

"And she slammed the front door shut."

"The front door was slammed?" asked Blossom.

"Yes," said Mr. Wright. "And don't forget it must have taken a whole heap of force for me to hear it clear up on the balcony. And then there is the granddaughter," continued Mr. Wright. Apparently there was no stopping him now.

"Jasmine? What about her?" persisted Blossom, remembering how much crying the girl did at the funeral.

"Well, she was always visiting her grandmother. She drives that little yellow car, which she puts in the wrong gear."

"Does she?" asked Blossom.

"Well, one time, when it was parked outside, I heard an argument coming from the inside of the house."

"An argument?" echoed Blossom.

"Raised voices," said Mr. Wright, "and maybe even screaming. Now, I know what families can be, but that don't seem right to me, to be slamming doors and screaming and carrying on such that I could hear it clear up on my balcony."

"What was the carrying-on about?" asked Blossom, almost bent at a right angle, she was leaning so far forward.

"Well, I don't know that part," said Mr. Wright, wiping some more of the juice from his mouth and then wiping the knife on a handkerchief, before flicking it closed and putting it in his pocket. "All I know is I didn't see that little yellow Fiesta parked outside the gate again."

"She stopped visiting?" gasped Blossom.

"She stopped visiting," repeated Mr. Wright. "What with all them family goings-on, it's a good thing Pastor was there to comfort her the night before she died."

"Pastor was with Constance *the night* before she died?" exclaimed Blossom, suddenly remembering what the pastor had said at the funeral. *I saw her the day before she sadly passed away.* He didn't say nothing about no night. "You sure?" she asked Mr. Wright.

"Oh, I'm very sure," said Mr. Wright. "I am not a man to make mistakes. And what about Miss Hortense, she start to investigate yet?" Mr. Wright licked the last of the melon juice from his lips.

"Hortense?" said Blossom, and she threw herself back and gave a humpf. "She not going to do a damned thing. She not interested in the death of Constance. She think it all natural. She not interested in the death of the man at the bottom of the stairs. And seem like she don't even care 'bout the note. And she only gone and invite that gal, Errol's daughter, come live at her yard. Honestly, I don't think she is in her right mind at all."

The following morning, Blossom sat at the back of the church with a pounding headache. It was from all the thinking, plus the singing and the tambourines. She watched the pastor sweat as he hopped about on the stage in front of her. A shake of the foot, a swivel of his hips and that pointy thing he did with his finger. Some women might find all that attractive, but not Blossom; she liked her men with hair.

She watched all the women on the stage behind him nodding and swooning as they followed his every move. It had taken quite a bit of resolve for Blossom to get herself to church that Sunday morning, and now watching the pastor's carrying-on, she was getting quite nauseated. He was shouting about the church roof again. How it had holes in it and how it was in desperate need of fixing. How it wasn't cheap. How any donation would be gratefully received but that the church accepted fifty-pound notes, checks and American Express.

Blossom had sat across a table from the man for many years but now she was looking at him different. Perhaps that little man wasn't quite all he made himself out to be. Perhaps he had something to hide, and that's the reason he was not answering her calls and ensuring Mavis C and Mavis B didn't let Blossom get anywhere near him when she came demanding to speak with him about the Pardner. Something very fishy was going on; her brief conversation with Constance's daughter, Camille, had also shown her that. It was something to do with money. Suddenly, for a man who so prided himself on the Pardner, the pastor had nothing much to say about it at all. But maybe it went further than that. What if it extended to actual murder?

He was shouting now about sacrifice.

"Are you prepared to give up your life for the Lawd Almighty?" he whispered fiercely at them.

What if, thought Blossom, he had sacrificed Constance for the church roof?

Blossom watched as the two Mavises behind him leaned into the sermon, ready to jump on his every word with their tambourines. One of them was bound to be on blood pressure water tablets, Blossom thought, so it was only a matter of time. After the first verse of the second hymn, Mavis C with her bad hip moved slowly off the platform and shuffled down the aisle with a handbag at her side. Blossom eased out of the row slowly behind Mavis and followed her into the ladies'.

"How de do, Mavis, it's Blossom," Blossom shouted towards the closed cubicle that Mavis had just entered.

"Mrs. Henry, a you that?" asked Mavis Campbell.

"Yes, my dear," shouted back Blossom. "How the arthritis?"

"Oh, you know," said Mavis. "Leaving it to the Lawd."

By the time Mavis C had finished dragging up her tights and pulling down her slip, Blossom had got what she wanted from the handbag that was left next to the sink and was sitting back down to the final verse. Her headache had now eased quite considerably. As she shuffled in her seat and looked about the congregation, she did a double take and narrowed her eyes.

Well, perhaps you really did get to see miracles in church, because in the very back row, in his pinstripe suit and freshly combed-out hair, was Fitz. He buried his head in a hymn book when he saw Blossom trying to make eye contact. *Blouse and skirt!* thought Blossom, stretching her neck to see more of him. Actually, he did look off-color. Oh dear, thought Blossom, raising her hand to her mouth. The prostate business was back, and this time it must be terminal. Poor Fitz, Blossom thought, and she crossed herself.

33

A Camel Goes Through the Eye of a Needle

At ten minutes past ten on that Sunday evening, there was a knock on Mr. Wright's door. He answered it in his powder-blue pajamas.

"Come," Blossom said, and marched away.

"Is where you going at this time?" he called after her, and before Mr. Wright got an answer, he found himself in his car, in his pajamas, heading towards the west side of town.

"Where we going?" asked Mr. Wright, watching his petrol gauge over the top of his glasses.

"Never you mind," said Blossom, and she switched on the radio.

Twenty minutes later she said, "Turn a left up hereso."

Mr. Wright recognized the road immediately. "Oh no you don't. I am not going to no blasted church." Mr. Wright couldn't adhere to places that teefed money off people and told them they could get their rewards when they were dead.

"Park up hereso," said Blossom, and she directed him to park on a side road a few yards from the back entrance of the church.

"I'm going in," said Blossom, and she wrapped her scarf around her head like a balaclava, so only one eye was visible, opened the car door and was gone.

"Into the church?" asked Mr. Wright, his voice an octave higher, looking at the building all dark and closed up. Before he knew it, Blossom was marching up to the glass front door and fiddling with a set of keys with a fluffy ball at the end, the security light beaming into her face.

"Is where you get those?" whispered Mr. Wright as he joined her and she tried another key.

"Me loan them," said Blossom.

Six keys later, Blossom had managed to undo the double lock on the big glass doors and the smaller lock on the inside and was pushing her way into the cold, dark church.

"Where you going now?" Mr. Wright asked, shivering and limping behind Blossom as she headed for the pastor's office, which was right at the back of the church, past the toilets and the music room, past the small kitchen and nursery, to the door with the gold plaque that read *Pastor Williams*.

She turned the handle of the door, but it was locked. She twisted it again, but it was still locked. She took out the set of keys with the fluffy ball on the end and tried all six keys, losing track of which ones she had tried. She tried again.

"What we doing here?" whispered Mr. Wright to Blossom, his voice echoey in the empty church.

Blossom pointed to the door she was trying to get into. When she'd finished trying all six keys for the fifth time, she said, "Bruck it down with your shoulder."

"No, sir," sneered Mr. Wright. "I'm not brucking meself up for nobody."

Blossom tutted and said, "Some help you are. I'll break the window instead." She was about to turn on her heels when Mr. Wright cussed his teeth, searched in his pajama pocket, and brought out his flip knife with the bone handle. He adjusted his glasses and bent to look closely at the lock, inserted his knife, held on to the doorknob firmly but gently like it was a lady's hand and twisted it to get a feel for the mechanism. He slipped the knife towards the catch with one swift move and the lock gave with a click. Blossom looked at him.

"You is full of tricks, don't it?" she said, before rushing into the room and switching on all the lights. She was amazed by what she saw. "Well, I never," said Blossom. An office that had more the appearance of a teenager's bedroom than a place of God's business: in the far corner, an unmade pop-up bed, clothes flung on it, suitcases on the floor and an unfolded ironing board.

The pastor's desk sat royally in the center of the chaos, covered in bits of paper. Blossom rushed to it and opened drawer after drawer, all of which seemed to be filled to bursting with opened, unopened and half-opened letters, plus items of men's clothing. When Blossom took more time to focus, adjusting her glasses to the bifocal bit for reading, she saw demands for payment, underpants, water rates, odd socks, red letters, string vests, rates from the council and letters from the bank. She stopped when she came across a crumpled-up handwritten letter in the last right-hand drawer.

"Hear that?" whispered Mr. Wright. "Someone is coming."

Blossom stopped.

The noise of a car engine came closer and lights flashed in through the window. Blossom stuffed the handwritten letter down the front of her top. Both moved quickly. Blossom flicked the lights off and Mr. Wright shut the door behind them before Blossom ushered them into the nursery, where Mr. Wright stepped on a squeaky plastic duck.

"Shh, na man," said Blossom. She could hear her own heart beating. Lawd have mercy, they were trapped. She was going to pass out. The pastor was going to kill the two of them, cut up their bodies and bury them under the car park.

Mr. Wright pointed to a back door. He was able to use the same trick to unlock it and both he and Blossom tiptoed out, crunching away over the gravel. They were out of breath by the time they reached Mr. Wright's car in the side road, which then took ten minutes to start. Mr. Wright cursed every second of the ten minutes and at one point held his chest. Blossom told him to stop being so dramatic. He told her that he hadn't come to this country to be arrested for being no damned blasted burglar. How dare Blossom involve him in an illegality, he puffed. Blossom said he should feel privileged to be accompanying her on a mission to uncover a murderer. She started to feel around her neck for the scarf that wasn't there.

"Bloody hell," said Mr. Wright, as they drove away, "I never said I wanted to go on no damned blasted mission to find no blasted murderer." And so it continued until Mr. Wright's car started spluttering and coughing, before it finally died in the middle of the dual carriageway.

As soon as the kind AA man dropped her to her house, Blossom read the letter. The contents were enough to bring on a heart attack. The letter read:

13 Cedar Avenue
Bigglesweigh,
Birmingham

May 13, 2000

Dear Pastor Williams,
I write in reference to the letters you sent to my husband,
Nigel Brown, on April 20th, 24th, 26th, 27th, 28th, 29th and
30th, and the letters that you sent to me on May 1st, 5th and
7th.

    I wish to correct you on a number of matters. As was
previously said to you on numerous occasions by my husband,
all of the Pardner property was legitimately transferred into the
sole name of my late mother-in-law, Constance Brown, her
holding the full legal title to the same. As he has previously
informed you, neither you nor any other members of the
Pardner have any further call on said Pardner assets, which
have now fallen into my late mother-in-law's estate and
therefore to her eldest son. It is of course up to you whether
you wish to instruct solicitors, but it's likely you would be
wasting your money.

    In respect of the matter you referenced in your letter to me
of May 7th, I cannot believe that a man who purports to be of
God would stoop so low. Please do not write to me again.
    Yours sincerely,
    Yvonne Brown

Every time Blossom read the letter, and in particular the line that read
*neither you nor any other members of the Pardner have any further call on
said Pardner assets*, she gasped and raised a hand to her mouth. She
couldn't believe it. How had all the proceeds of the Pardner investments
been transferred into the sole name of Constance before her death
and, now that she was gone, into the hands of her son, Nigel?

138

34

Caribbean Takeaway, Two Old Women and a Six-Foot-Four Football Hooligan

Pastor Williams was forever telling the Mavises that they needed to be more careful about locking up the chapel before they left. As he went around locking the doors they had forgotten, he considered his plan and all that had happened in the hours before. All that he had witnessed. He had headed to the garage on the Rushden Industrial Estate ready to confront the man who, since Constance's death, had made his life a living misery. But when he got there and entered—unnoticed—through the open door, the Lawd told him to hide behind a large crate and watch. Lawd have mercy, give him strength, he had asked, as he hid in the shadows and watched Constance's son, Nigel, sat at a makeshift desk, two feet up, swiveling from side to side. Then a number of other young men bounced in with loaded bin liners. One of them was in a shiny jacket, and the pastor blinked. It looked like the young man who came to see him before Constance died, all shook up because Miss Hortense had threatened him. Pastor leaned in further; it was that young man—what was his name again? Tremaine . . . No, Germaine! Pastor could hardly contain himself.

"Close the door, lads," instructed one of the men. "Let's get down to business."

Germaine Banton emptied the bin liners onto the desk. *Oh my God!* Pastor's knees suddenly went weak and nearly gave way. The bags were full of banknotes. More money than Pastor had surely seen in his whole lifetime. The pastor had a sudden urge to mop his brow, but was terrified of being heard. The men started dividing the notes into bundles.

It was obvious to Pastor that Nigel Brown, Germaine Banton and the group of men they were with were up to no good, that what was being done in that little garage was no good, and that where that money had come from, or was going to, was definitely no good. So much for Nigel Brown being Bigglesweigh's entrepreneur of the year!

And that is when it came to him like a flash of lightning, and he had started to formulate a plan.

The pastor shook his head because it was the plan he should have had in mind all along. A plan that would get him back in his house and get rid of all the debt-collection letters and bills that he couldn't bear to look at anymore.

"John five: twenty-four," he said out loud in the quiet chapel. The pastor was going to bring Brother Nigel and Germaine Banton into the fold. He suddenly had purpose again; for the first time in a very long time, he could see the light. He slapped his thigh. And just as he was about to switch off the light in the nursery, he noticed a spotty scarf lying beside the sand table, along with a squashed plastic duck.

The two Mavises were skeptical. The pastor had decided to station members of his congregation with flyers, to preach the word of God, in Rushden Industrial Estate. And at most unusual times of day and night.

"But nobody goes that way, Pastor," said Mavis B, "and what kind of time is that?"

"Oh, you would be surprised," was the pastor's response. "Even if it's just two lost souls, they will be souls worth saving," he said, confident in his plan.

When he stated that he would be stationing members of the congregation outside the patty shop on the corner of the High Street, there was less resistance, but still it was noted that the food in that shop was very bad indeed, and there was a rumor that it was overrun with rats. Still, the pastor had the answer: "*Blessed are they which do hunger and thirst after righteousness: for they shall be filled.*"

Although the pastor had full faith in God's plan, he decided it might not do any harm to have a little contingency one too, just in case, and for that he would need to start digging up dirt on Nigel Brown. After all, God helps those who help themselves.

* * *

140

It was Monday and Gregory's day off. So where else would he be but trailing a suspect, trying to get to the bottom of the damage at the community center before his aunty started looking into it? Over the past few weeks, he'd been staking out the Oasis nightclub on the High Street, following various suspects down to the canal, and keeping an eye on his aunty (easier said than done). He was definitely acting way outside his remit, in more ways than one. These were the things he so far knew and had jotted down in his notebook: the man at the bottom of Constance's stairs was Donovan Miller—his identity had been confirmed. He had a number of offspring in Texas but had lived a somewhat nomadic life before he departed for England, on a one-way ticket. He hit his head when he fell down the stairs and it was that injury that eventually led to his death. He was, as Gregory suspected, a drunkard; the state of his liver very clearly established that. As an aside, there were some financial issues with Miss Constance's house, a mortgage taken out in her name not long before her death.

Richard Dudney aka Dice had stopped working at the Oasis nightclub and it was Dice whom Gregory was now following. He had picked up his trail again at the Caribbean takeaway shop off the High Street. Dice seemed to frequent that shop every day, although Gregory never saw him actually eat any of the food. The owner of the takeaway was a Germaine Banton—also known to the police, but not clever enough to be a criminal mastermind. On the days Gregory was able to watch him, Dice entered with a plastic bag at twelve noon and left by 12:05 p.m. empty-handed.

The other recent activity of note came from two old church ladies stood in front of the takeaway belting out the Lord's Prayer and pushing out flyers. Gregory wondered whether they were all in on it: an elaborate scam that involved the Caribbean takeaway, two old women, and a six-foot-four football hooligan. At least his aunty didn't appear to be actively involved in looking into Dice's shenanigans, as far as he could detect.

Gregory hoped to God it would remain that way.

35

Miss Hortense Investigates Constance

Miss Hortense was very much in her stride with her secret investigation and was now focusing her efforts on one player in particular, a dead one. She was rooting around in Constance's life, as much as it pained her.

Miss Hortense had been to Constance's bank, to the offices of the local council where she used to work, to her solicitors, to her dry cleaners and to the local supermarket and corner shop where Constance had bought her groceries. She had also spoken to several mourners whom she had recognized from the funeral.

When Miss Hortense asked whoever she came across in various establishments if they knew a Constance Brown, she would show them the picture on page fifteen of the funeral order of service, the one that Miss Hortense thought showed the best likeness of Constance, where she looked old, and it was obvious her Jheri curl was dyed black by the staining on her hairline. Her teeth were showing, and if you looked closely enough, you could see a piece of food lodged between the front ones.

The owner of the corner shop said he remembered Constance as "a very pleasant old lady who liked to smile." He had no recollection of the last time he had seen her in his shop but was sorry to note that she'd passed away, and did Miss Hortense know who owned "the black M3 that parks on her drive, because it's banging"? An ex-colleague of Constance's, still working at the council, said, "I remember Constance as being very constant. An honest colleague who just got on with the job."

It seemed, apart from two exceptions, that no one had a bad word to say about Constance Margorie Brown, which was a surprise to Miss Hortense. The two exceptions were an old boss against whom a grievance had been lodged with HR. He was a white man, now in his eighties, with very white hair, who said, after some coaxing, "I just never got on with the woman. She thought too much of herself." The other exception was Camille's ex-husband, whom Miss Hortense managed to find in the telephone directory. When she mentioned she was calling in relation to his late ex-mother-in-law, he told her to "piss off" and put the phone down.

36

When God Closes a Door . . .

The only reason Blossom was not on the phone first thing to the pastor was because she was searching for her blue and yellow scarf, the spotty one, but she still left several messages for Hortense, whose phone was now ringing out. The first message simply said:

"Can you believe it? All of the Pardner gone to Constance? How we never know, Hortense? No wonder that blasted Pastor Williams has been running from me. This goes against every single principality of the Pardner. I don't know yet if he is the murderer."

Blossom's attention moved to "the matter referenced" in the letter of May seventh. The next message to Hortense said:

"What you think it could be? You think Constance's son and him wife murder Constance together so they can inherit all her tings dem? I going find out!"

Blossom omitted to leave any messages for Hortense detailing how she actually managed to acquire her information.

Blossom knew that it would only be a matter of time before Mr. Wright would be back at her door with his tail between his legs. It hadn't been pleasant for either of them waiting three hours in the middle of the night to be rescued by the AA, but some of the words that came out of that man's mouth, well, they made Blossom's eyes water. Only when she felt that he was truly sorry was she prepared to let him in and show him the letter she had borrowed from the pastor's office. But, if he continued with his bad-mindedness, she might just have to ask him to return all of the items she had loaned him—which included her Brother Deluxe 220, the George Benson LP and some compression socks.

Blossom tried to hide her disappointment with a plastered-on smile when, on Tuesday morning, she opened her front door to find not Mr. Wright with his cap in his hands but the orphan girl, Sonia. Her arm seemed to have recovered fully and her finger was stuck to the doorbell.

"Can I come in?" asked Sonia, sweet as honey pie. Well, Blossom wasn't somebody to leave an orphan on the doorstep, even if she did ring her bell like a hooligan, so she said, "Of course, my dear," and let the girl in.

"And is how you liking it at Hortense's?" Blossom asked, as she sat the girl at the kitchen table and started to eye her up and down. Blossom noticed the girl's eyes; they were a kind of marble black, and deeply set, just like her mother's.

"It's very nice," said Sonia, looking about her. "Miss Hortense is lovely."

"Lovely?" repeated Blossom as if she hadn't heard right. The word in her mouth had three clear syllables, and yet it still caught between her dentures. Blossom's eyes narrowed as she studied the girl further.

"Yes, she's been really kind to me," said Sonia.

"Oh. And what have you and Hortense been up to?" Blossom picked at the tablecloth and tried to sound less interested than she really was.

"Oh, nothing really," said Sonia. "She's pretty much left me to my own devices. She tends to be busy with the garden and cooking and whatnot."

"Whatnot?" said Blossom, wondering what the "whatnot" could be, now they were no longer involved in Black Cake.

"Actually," said Sonia, "I was wondering if you might help me."

"Well, I can always try," said Blossom.

"You see, the thing is," said Sonia hesitantly, "I'm in a bit of a bind." She brushed away some sweat at her hairline. "You said I shouldn't mention my father to Miss Hortense but—"

"Oh Lawd Jesus!" said Blossom, slapping her hand to her mouth. "And she tell you fe leave?"

"Oh no, that's just it, I didn't mention my father. Not at all," said Sonia, raising her hands defensively. "But one of the reasons I came back was to find out about my father and what really happened to

145

him. I understand he was involved in some sort of car accident? And was there something about Bone Twelve?" Sonia was remembering her mother's last words.

"Oh dear," Blossom said, as if the accident had happened all over again. "Oh my dear, oh dear me. This is terrible."

"I just thought," said Sonia, "it's been so many years now, that I might find out from Miss Hortense what she knows about it."

"Oh no, dear, I wouldn't do that."

Blossom didn't say anything else and there was an unexpected moment of silence.

"You're close to her," said Sonia, jumping into it.

Clearly not, thought Blossom sourly.

"Couldn't you just tell me what you know, then?" Sonia asked, her tone slightly sharper.

"It's one long story, my dear," said Blossom, shaking her head.

"Please," Sonia pleaded. "It's unfair that I don't know. He was my dad. Maybe I should just discuss it directly with her."

Blossom considered. "What you mother tell you 'bout de accident?"

"Not much," said Sonia. Even that was an exaggeration. Her mother had told her nothing. She wasn't a very vocal person but had still managed to make Sonia feel guilty all the time. In fact, the last moments of her life had probably been her most effusive.

"You can drive, don't it?" asked Blossom.

Sonia nodded.

"And your car working fine?" asked Blossom, remembering all the problems she'd had with Mr. Wright two nights before.

"Yes, it works fine," responded Sonia, confused.

"Then come back tomorrow same time," said Blossom. "I will have something more fe tell you then." Ordinarily, Blossom wasn't the sort of person to tittle-tattle gossip, but she needed a vehicle in order to continue her investigations. Plus, Blossom rationalized, she was providing charity. If she was going to talk to anyone about Bone 12, then it should be to the daughter of the man who died because of it.

37

Driving Miss Henry

The next morning was bright and sunny when Blossom stepped out to Sonia's silver Nissan Micra. Blossom had agreed she would tell Sonia what she knew (only the bits she wanted to tell, mind) on two conditions. One, the girl wasn't to raise the case ever with Hortense. Despite her resentment at being ignored, Blossom was still protective of her friend. And two, the girl was to drive her to just one or two places in her car.

Blossom made a point of inspecting the outside of the car, even though she knew nothing about cars. She noted the scratches and dents along the side. She kicked a wheel to test for its durability, before heaving a large insulated food bag into the passenger footwell, and then herself into the passenger seat. The car rocked with the weight of her and the bag. She inspected the inside of the car too, the pockets in the passenger door and around the gearstick, as she shuffled herself into a comfortable position. Only when Sonia started the ignition and Blossom had shuffled some more did she begin to talk.

"What I'm about to tell you is not an easy thing to tell." Blossom sighed. "And it must never leave this car. The night your father had the accident, he and Miss Hortense had gone to a dance together on Church Street. Turn a left here," said Blossom. "Church Street was a street well known for parties. That's because many of the people that lived on Church Street were Black and so there wasn't the same sort of trouble you might get with a party near Cuckoo Lane. Keep going, now tek that right. Months earlier, Hortense had started going to parties looking for men, and if she let them," said Blossom, vigorously pointing her finger for Sonia to go left, "Fitz or Errol went with her."

"Miss Hortense was looking for a man to date?" asked Sonia, surprised.

"Date? Oh no, oh no." What a stupid question, Blossom thought. "Hortense wasn't looking for a *man* man. No, Hortense was going to parties looking for one man in particular—turn right here—but Miss Hortense couldn't find him despite all the searching, even though," Blossom added in a whisper, *"Miss Hortense is normally very good at finding people she wants to find.* No, you gone wrong. Go back around again. I think it's this one. No, it's not this one. Go back around again. Well," Blossom corrected herself when they exited the roundabout on the second exit for the second time, "the truth was, this was one man Hortense just could never find." At this point Blossom stopped talking. She was finding it hard to give instructions and tell the story.

After a period of silence, Blossom said: "Stop right hereso. Back a bit. No, forward a bit. All right, then. Now stop."

They had apparently arrived.

"Look over dehso," said Blossom.

"What am I looking for?" asked Sonia, scanning outside the passenger window.

They were parked in a road, opposite a modern town house in a road of equally modern and characterless modern town houses. The one they were parked opposite, that Blossom was pointing to, had a big shiny black car poking out of the concrete driveway.

"This is Cedar Avenue," said Blossom in a posh voice, "and that is apparently where the daughter-in-law lives with the son, Nigel."

"Who's the daughter-in-law and who's Nigel?" asked Sonia, and Blossom had to explain the whole thing about Constance, before going on to talk again about how Blossom had nearly died at her funeral.

"It's a nice car," said Sonia, looking at the big shiny black car sitting on the drive.

"Me dear," said Blossom, "Constance was always boasting about how well-to-do her son was, *Nigel this* and *Nigel that*. It's a shame with all that money dem never spend none 'pon her funeral."

"So shall we get out?" asked Sonia.

"No, we are here to search for *the matter referred to in the letter of May seventh*," Blossom said, putting on the posh voice again.

148

"What's that?"

"Well, if I knew," said Blossom, "we wouldn't be here a look fe it."

"Shall we knock on their door, then?" asked Sonia, thoroughly confused.

"No, no, no," said Blossom, staring out the window at the house that wasn't doing anything beyond just sitting there as you would expect bricks and mortar to do.

"Well, what now, then?"

"We wait," said Blossom, folding her arms.

"Wait for what?" asked Sonia impatiently.

"We just *wait*." This girl asked far too many questions.

Blossom reached down into the insulated food bag she had put in the footwell. She had containers with fish, rice and peas and two sets of fritters in there. She took out the container of escovitched fish and offered some to the girl—who shook her head—before beginning to eat, her false teeth catching on the contents. The tingly whiff of onions and vinegar wafted into the air.

Resigned to the fact that they might be sitting there for some time and the fact that her car was now going to stink of fish, and being quite confused about what Blossom had just told her, Sonia asked:

"Could you just start from the beginning, then, please?"

Blossom explained, in between mouthfuls of fish, that she supposed the whole trouble began in the summer of 1969, when Pearl White found God.

Blossom said Pearl White ran a "good-time" house on St. Clement's Road, which, if Sonia wanted to know, was three roads away from Ebley Street. Blossom had never of course been anywhere near that house; no respectable woman would be caught dead there. But she had it on good authority that every night, for men who cared to indulge, traveling men, married men (*many* married men), Pearl's house was open to have a "good time."

A "good time," Blossom was led to believe, meant dominoes, of course, plenty of rum and music, and—Blossom cleared her throat because the pepper had caught in it—"other things too." That's why, Blossom explained, Pearl rented out all her upstairs bedrooms to girls who had no family and had just come off the boat or train.

Everyone knew what Pearl's was, said Blossom, finishing with the plate of fish and moving to the rice. Pearl's was always open, come rain or shine, every day, all days of the week, even on Sundays. But three weeks before Pearl White found God, her house shut down. That hadn't happened before as far as anybody could recall. Yet for three whole weeks no one saw a dicky bird from Pearl. The bottom of the house was all in darkness. Even the girls who rented the upstairs rooms said they hadn't seen or heard from her. Some folks started to say that Pearl was dead and some said she had caught something and some said she was in trouble and had packed up and left.

"Then, on the third Sunday," said Blossom, who bent down to put away the rice she had left and took out a fritter, "Pearl limped into church brazen as you like, just before the sacrament, and sat down in the front row. Well, as you can imagine," Blossom said, tearing off a piece of the fritter, "the whole church fell silent. Pearl's virgin hair was all up in the air for everyone to see, it hadn't been hot-combed or put in curlers, and even though she tried to hide it with makeup (and Lawd knows that woman knew how to put on makeup), her face was all mashed up and there was a big scar." Blossom illustrated with the piece of fritter in her hand. "On her cheek," she said softly.

Before Pastor Williams said, "God be with you," Pearl had left and was never seen in the church again.

"That was it?" said Sonia, opening her window, unable to take the smell anymore.

"No, that wasn't it," said Blossom. "After the service, well, everybody was talking. People were saying if you lie with dogs you going to catch fleas. And it seemed Pearl was never quite the same again. The house stayed shut. The girls gradually moved out—apparently Pearl was doing all kinds of strange things in the middle of the night, and she died a few years later of blood poisoning, which really means she drank herself to death. Lawd, the woman could drink."

"So what's this got to do with my dad?" asked Sonia, when Blossom finally fell silent.

"Everything," said Blossom solemnly. "When Pearl turned up at the church with her face all mashed up, Hortense wanted the Pardner to Look Into it. That means investigate," she said to Sonia's puzzled face.

"But some members, that is Pastor Williams and Constance Brown, were having none of it. They said Pearl had had enough 'Looking Into,' if you get my meaning. They said that it was probably one of her unhappy customers that had just had a bit of a misunderstanding with her."

"And?" asked Sonia. "What did Miss Hortense do?"

"Well, she spoke to Pearl, of course. And Pearl wasn't an easy somebody to speak to." Blossom wiped crumbs from the front of her blouse. "Pearl was able to tell Miss Hortense about her attack, details of a Bible verse and half a number plate. What use is half a number plate, though?" asked Blossom. "And apparently, she managed to slash her attacker with the same knife he was trying to slash her with, on the chest," and this time Blossom illustrated with a cut sign on her chest. "But to be honest with you, no one, 'cept for Hortense, much cared. But then, of course, Miss Hortense found Daphne Stewart on her doorstep and everything changed."

"Who was Daphne Stewart?" interrupted Sonia.

"Well, I'm coming to that," said Blossom, looking towards the house, which was quiet in its stillness. Blossom sighed and began to explain who Daphne was. When she had finished, she said, "Everyone thought it was Garfield Stewart, the husband, that had attacked Daphne."

"Garfield Stewart?" Sonia asked, leaning in more heavily over the steering wheel.

"That's right. Him used to beat Daphne up."

"So the police arrested him, then?"

Blossom stopped chewing and turned to Sonia.

"Po-lease?" said Blossom, like it was a dirty word. "Po-lease? Oh no, my dear. You don't get po-lease involved in a thing like that, back then. They wouldn't have helped." She looked at Sonia as if she were mad.

"But even though," continued Blossom, "everybody thought it was Garfield Stewart that attacked Daphne, Miss Hortense was very sure that it wasn't him because he wasn't in the country when Pearl was attacked. Miss Hortense kept saying, *There is a pattern*, and it was one man. The man that she was searching for. But some people were saying an attack on two women doesn't make any kind of pattern, and people couldn't understand why Hortense kept looking so hard,

151

given poor Daphne was dead and everybody thought it was her husband that killed her."

"Daphne died?" gasped Sonia.

"Oh yes, my dear. The morning after Miss Hortense found her on the doorstep. Something to do with the spleen."

"So, who did Miss Hortense think attacked Daphne Stewart if she didn't think it was her husband?" asked Sonia.

Blossom was about to answer when she saw a man trying, and failing, to hide behind a lamppost. He wore a wide coat, the collar of which was pulled up high over his neck, and a flat cap, but Blossom would recognize that man mopping his brow anywhere.

"*Pastor?*" she said to herself. "But wait, what him is doing looking at Nigel's house?" Sonia looked up to see the little old man.

"Who is he?" asked Sonia, but before Blossom had a chance to say anything further, Yvonne exited the house, dressed in an expensive-looking white jacket, with shades and large bouncy curls, looking like something out of a Destiny's Child music video.

"Well look at her na," Blossom said to Sonia. "Mutton dressed like lamb." The pastor beat a hasty retreat and started walking in the opposite direction; Yvonne seemed not to notice. She slid into the driver's seat of the shiny black car and started the engine.

And, as if on cue, as if she'd been practicing her whole life for the drama of this moment, Blossom sat up, stretched out a long manicured finger and roared, "Follow her!"

38

Too Many Questions

There were many things that had bothered Miss Hortense about Bone 12. In particular, she had many questions about the circumstances surrounding Daphne's attack. The first was how she ended up on Miss Hortense's doorstep.

The droplets of blood she'd left on the doorstep continued on the pavement for about fifty yards beyond her gate and stopped suddenly outside number 21. Clearly the attack hadn't taken place there, making it likely Daphne had traveled in a vehicle up to that point.

The large brown overcoat was left at Hortense's house when Daphne was taken away in the ambulance. It was the coat that had been worn over Daphne's own, her blood seeping beneath it, and was four sizes too big for the girl. It was well worn under the armpits and the lining was starting to tear. In the left pocket of the coat were two shillings, a half-empty packet of Benson & Hedges and an empty roll of bus tickets. It didn't take much for Miss Hortense to work out who the garment belonged to.

Miss Hortense replaced those items in the pocket, with the intention of returning it to its owner the next day: the Sunday that the pastor stood on the podium and announced, with deep regret, that Daphne Stewart, who had recently joined the congregation, had passed away.

He said, "Our thoughts and prayers are with her husband, Mr. Garfield Stewart." Most of the congregation, with the exception of Hortense, shifted awkwardly and muttered under their breath upon hearing Garfield's name.

Miss Hortense keenly observed Ralph Campbell, who was seated in a row adjacent to Hortense.

He was a muscular man in his forties, with skin the color of the mahoe furniture tree. His hands were always slightly raised by his sides, as if he were permanently carrying the Gibson ticket machine that he rang up on the buses. He was a quiet man, married to a homely woman who liked to sing, named Mavis; not to be confused with the other Mavis, who was Mavis Buchanan, who had lived in one of the rooms on the second floor of Pearl White's before she found God. Mavis Campbell and Ralph Campbell had three children. Hortense knew the family from Pastor Williams's church that she attended in the days when she too thought that God made the difference.

As Miss Hortense held out the heavy coat for Ralph to take at the end of the service, Ralph's eyes darted all over the place before resting on the brown fabric. He eventually rubbed his large hands down his freshly starched trousers and accepted her offering. How could he not? The coat belonged to him, after all. Mavis, only a few meters away, briefly looked in their direction and pursed her lips.

He had turned to go when Hortense said, "Brother Ralph? You can venture to my house a likkle later? I have a heater that is playing up."

His eyes darted around some more, but they had nowhere to go beyond their sockets, and they couldn't look in the direction of his wife.

"I don't think I need to give you the address, do I?" Miss Hortense asked. "You know where I live, don't it? Just like I know where you call home," she added for good measure. She knew where he lived, where he worked and where he worshipped. She gave him a knowing nod and was on her way.

Later that afternoon, he came into her home, gingerly, as if he half expected the poor girl he had left to still be there.

"Well?" said Miss Hortense, directing him to the paraffin heater she had brought into the room. His shoulders dropped as he sank to his knees before it. He weighed about 238 pounds, and she guessed his shoe size was a 12; if he wanted to, he could crush her in a heartbeat.

"The heater not been working properly for months," she said as she slipped the syringe from her handbag into her sleeve. "This one gives off the best heat when it's working." As he began poking and prodding, she looked around the top of his collar for any telltale scratch marks on his skin.

"Tell me about last night when you brought Daphne to my house," she said quietly. He was about to rise to his feet but she motioned for him to remain on his knees. He stuttered something about how he had come upon Daphne on the street and, seeing she was in such a bad way, brought her to Miss Hortense's. That was, of course, a lie. Miss Hortense asked him whether he was the one who had inflicted her injuries, syringe at the ready. She said they could always speak to his wife about it. He rose from his knees and slumped on the settee, hard tears falling down his cheeks.

He said he had started seeing Daphne Stewart three months before. That it had begun when she started looking after his daughter.

"I couldn't help myself," he said. "If only . . ." He gripped his hands into fists.

"And what happened last night when Daphne was attacked?" asked Miss Hortense.

He said he had car trouble, the carburetor was playing up. It had made him late to pick her up at their usual spot off Redman Road; when he got there, Daphne wasn't waiting for him as normal.

"I just had this feeling," he said, balling his fists some more, "that something wasn't right." He left his car and went looking for her and that's when he found her court shoe at the entrance to an alleyway. He found her lying facedown on the ground a few yards from the shoe.

He was the right build to overpower both Pearl and Daphne, and to drag them to their fates, but when Miss Hortense looked closely at his neck and face, there were no marks depicting a recent struggle. The heavy lines on his face were from something else, the weight of emotion—but was it guilt or something else? He wasn't a man who had recently been in battle with a woman fighting for her life, that was for sure. Why would he try to save Daphne by bringing her to Hortense if only minutes before he had tried to obliterate her? And then there were his hands. The distinctive cream patches at the fingertips and some speckles on his knuckles. If he had been the Brute, Daphne, as his lover, might have covered for him, but Pearl would surely have mentioned the vitiligo.

155

He looked directly at Miss Hortense and said, "I swear on the life of my children, on my daughter, that I could never do that to a woman," and then his voice broke. His shoulders rocked with a shuddering that couldn't be stopped.

Miss Hortense told him to take her to where he had found Daphne. It was an alleyway off Lynten Place, a five-minute walk from Redman Road. There it was, in broad daylight: the spot where Daphne had been violated and left for dead by the Brute. The place was discreet, not overlooked, serving no buildings; there were no windows that opened directly onto it. The ground was muddy with clumps of grass and weeds, glass and rubbish. Miss Hortense looked at what could have been heel marks in the gravel, and imagined Daphne being dragged along, begging for her life. She watched Ralph closely and saw him wincing too.

"Please," he begged. "Don't tell Mavis about this. It will kill her. I can't have another woman die on me." And there it was, his secret, another one for Miss Hortense to carry.

39

Garfield's Secret

Now, thirty years later, Miss Hortense continued to root around in Constance Brown's life. She had spoken to a sister from Constance's congregation, the one who had sounded like a foghorn at the funeral. The church sister said, "Constance used to drive me to service every Sunday. She was always smiling." And to Hortense's question about whether she noticed anything unusual about Constance the Sunday before she died, this church sister said, "Well, that's just it. She didn't go to church that Sunday. She said she had some business to attend to. That she was going to be visiting Garfield Stewart."

The sun was still shining on Wednesday afternoon when Miss Hortense decided to pay Garfield Stewart, Daphne's husband, a visit.

Miss Hortense took a deep breath before walking up the path to Mr. Stewart's house. The fact that there had been no resolution to Bone 12 had caused a kind of madness in him too. No matter what time of the day it was, the Stewarts' house was always in gloom. It clung to the house like sweat. Mr. Stewart's house was one of those houses Evie had warned her never to enter, "because of the duppies," bad spirits that caused nothing but trouble. It looked like it was about to fall down. It was one of those houses that children stood far back from and dared each other to touch the gate or put their foot on the path. And when people forgot why that was, the grandparents reminded them: "That man is the devil." That was because the grandparents still thought that he had something to do with Daphne's death, and the community dished out their book-and-key justice years ago—the sentence, a lifetime of exclusion.

157

"Mr. Stewart?" Miss Hortense leaned down to the letter box and shouted through it. The sound of her voice reverberated back on her. "You can let me in, sir?" she asked. Through the letter box she could see piles of mail in the passage.

She heard a shuffling.

"I know you in there," she said, knocking.

The shuffling came towards the door, which then opened just a crack. The stale whiff of dead skin and urine-soaked carpets assaulted her. Through the thin opening she saw Garfield Stewart. Deep lines were drawn down his face. He had on several layers of unwashed clothes, giving a false sense of size; underneath the knits he was skin and bone, where once he had been a substantial man. He was holding a worn, thin knife in his hand. He was probably in his late eighties or early nineties now.

"Go away," he shouted. "We don't want none of you people here."

"It's Miss Hortense," she said. "I bring bulla for you." She raised her bag to the crack in the door.

He mumbled something, then shouted out, "You lucky. She going let you in," then he turned and shuffled away from the door. Miss Hortense followed him back into the house, the full strength of the staleness coming at her.

His stained trousers bagged around the crotch and his feet were dry and bare as he shuffled through mounds of papers, plastic bags and other unidentifiable things on the floor.

"When last you eat, sir?" Hortense asked. The old man turned his head to look at her. She repeated herself, enunciating further. "When you eat, Mr. Stewart?"

He looked at her through watery eyes, blue with age but otherwise expressionless, and turned back.

"I tell you what I going to do," said Miss Hortense. "I going leave these things in the kitchen for you," and she veered left into the kitchen, a different smell of rancid meat and soured milk coming to her.

"Leave it," he said, a strength to his voice. "She going do it later." And he stopped still and stared into space at something or someone Miss Hortense couldn't see. Hortense left the things on the counter and followed him through the passage and into a back room where

158

he had picked up what looked like an old carburetor and was digging into it with the knife.

"What you doing there, sir?" Miss Hortense shouted at him.

He ignored her and continued with the digging, his hands bent with arthritis but still strong.

"Mr. Stewart?" Hortense said.

"Daphne said you fe sit down," he said to her. "Well sit down na man."

Miss Hortense looked around the room; there were no vacant spaces to sit. She moved aside some old newspapers and sat on a chair. He nodded and continued with his digging.

"I come fe speak to you, sir, about Constance Brown. Did she come visit you before she died?"

The knife slipped and he cut his finger. Blood dripped onto the floor.

"Let me." Miss Hortense rushed towards him.

"Stay back," he said, raising the knife. "I should never have brought her to this blasted country." There was a sudden clarity in his eyes. "If I hadn't brought her, she would still be alive."

Miss Hortense had long established both Mr. Stewart's guilt and innocence. A man who was significantly older than his wife, and bullied her, but couldn't have been the Brute, because he and Daphne didn't arrive in Bigglesweigh until July 1969 and the first attack on Pearl was in June. As most of the community never accepted that the attacks were connected, this fact didn't bother them.

"I'm asking 'bout Constance Brown, sir?" she said again, but he didn't answer her. "You ever hear of a man called Donovan Miller, then?"

"She say she seen him," said Garfield, resuming the digging despite the blood.

"Daphne seen Donovan Miller?" asked Hortense, ever the nurse, professional.

"That's right. She seen him. He is the one burning in hell."

"And Daphne tell you when she seen him, burning in hell?" Crossing over; entering into his world.

He paused. Nodded his head as if someone were talking to him in the silence.

"She said it's been years now he has been burning. Since the boardinghouse did catch 'pon fire."

"You sure you don't get it confused?" asked Hortense gently. He stopped the whittling.

"That's what she said, don't it? She seen him at the fire in Musgrove Park."

"But you and Daphne wasn't in England then," said Miss Hortense, sitting forwards.

"We was," said Mr. Stewart, turning to her.

Miss Hortense's face drained.

"How's that?" she said, a sudden urgency in her voice.

"That was our secret, don't it, Daph, but no need to keep it now. Mrs. Brown is dead and gone."

"What?" asked Hortense, who could barely breathe. "Me na understand?"

"Me and Daphne was living in that likkle room, the two of we," he said. "That white man let we stay in the basement because Daphne was young."

"Jesus Christ," said Hortense. "When?"

"Well, let me see. We was there from the June of 'sixty-four—*ain't that right, Daph?*—till the house burn down in 'sixty-five."

"Then what?" said Hortense.

"Then we moved to Walsall, but Daphne was still young."

"Young? How young?" shouted Miss Hortense, but he ignored her and continued.

"And then we moved back here in 'sixty-nine."

Miss Hortense felt her stomach churn.

If they lived in Walsall when Pearl was attacked, then it *could* have been him. But also, if Daphne was so young that they were living under the radar from at least 1964 until 1969, then just exactly how young was she? The thought of Daphne as a child bride made her sick to her stomach.

Garfield Stewart continued his digging.

Miss Hortense didn't know how she got out of that house. Hands on the wall feeling her way towards the front door, unable to catch her breath in the stench that suddenly seemed to sting her lungs.

160

She could hear him shouting, "We keep Mrs. Brown's secret, she keep ours!"

Once outside the gate, she tried to take in air. A man she had eliminated as a suspect, and even defended, could have been the Brute. How could Hortense have got it so wrong? Her breathing worsened, a pain bloomed in the center of her chest, footing all uncertain now and nothing to damn well hold on to.

40

You Can't Plant Yam and Reap Eddo

Pastor Williams was in his long johns reading 2 Corinthians, chapter 1, verse 4, and practicing for the Sunday sermon, when he heard the knock and the alarm call.

Two weeks after Constance's funeral, Pastor Williams had moved into his office in the church on Plevna Road, and since then had been permanently residing there. He might try to fool himself into believing that he had moved into his office to be closer to God; however, the repossession notice and the three bailiffs who came to his house to evict him would tell you something different.

When somebody knocked on Pastor Williams's office door, it was tricky. Very tricky indeed. The trickiness was in responding to the knock without actually opening the door. With deliveries, Pastor Williams would shout: "Leave it outside, I will get it shortly." For letters, it was: "Push it under the door, I will read it in due course." And there were many letters to be pushed under the door, so many, in fact, that on several occasions they all bunched up and got stuck and the pastor had another type of trouble trying to open it. For something that required his direct attention, he would say, "I'll be there in five minutes, I am just in the middle of prayer" (even if that wasn't strictly true at the time). But when someone knocked on the door on that Wednesday afternoon and said, in a voice that reminded him of a fire alarm, that it was "an urgent matter, a matter of life and death," well, he knew the five-minutes excuse wouldn't wash.

"Hello, Pastor? Are you in there? It's Mavis," the sister called out again. The difference between the two Mavises was normally clear in

162

the tone and timbre of the voice. Sister Buchanan was a high mezzo-soprano, whereas Sister Campbell was a contralto, deeper, with more control. Except the voice he was hearing was too high-pitched to be either a mezzo-soprano or a contralto, and there wasn't much control at all.

"Pastor Williams? I wonder if I could have a word with you, please?" said the voice beyond the door.

"I'll be there in a few minutes, my dear," Pastor Williams shouted, pulling on a sock and locating a clean pair of trousers.

"It really is of some importance," said the sister, her voice on the verge of breaking.

Pastor Williams was untangling the braces on a clean(ish) pair of trousers and finding a shirt without a stain.

"I'm not sure if I can go on like this," she continued beyond the door, knocking again.

"I will be with you shortly," he said as lightly as he could, given the gravity he could hear in the voice. He pinged on the left brace, then the right, stinging himself on the chest each time.

"I really do need to speak with you now," continued the sister whom he couldn't yet identify. "Could you open the door, please?"

He couldn't. That would reveal more than the sister on the other side would be bargaining for.

He had managed to locate the other sock. Now there was the task of getting out of the room without the sister seeing into it.

"Why don't you go down to the kitchen, my dear," shouted the pastor to the door. "Why don't you make us both a lovely cup of tea, settle you nerves?"

"A cup of tea?" came back the response, as if the pastor had suggested she take a minibreak in Sodom and Gomorrah. "I don't really want a cup of tea," she said.

"Well, then," said the pastor on the other side, trying hard to think on his toes, "let us pray."

"Pray now?" asked the sister in the same puzzled tone. "With the door in between?"

"Oh yes, my dear," shouted out the pastor. "Prayer can take place at any time with any number of obstacles in the way. You of all people

163

should know that. Now, let us move into prayer . . . Close your eyes . . . Are your eyes closed?" he asked into the door.

"Yes, them is closed," she said. And he began.

"Praise be to the Lawd . . ." And he inched the door open to see, on the other side with her head bowed, that it was Sister Campbell. He thrust himself out the door, almost into the woman, quickly shut the door behind him and locked it with the key he held in his hand.

"Um?" Sister Campbell now looked down to his feet and didn't raise her eyes from there. As he began to step off, he noticed what she was staring at. That he was without a shoe.

"My foot has been giving me trouble since morning," he said, again as lightly as he could, raising the shoeless foot a little. "I'm giving it air."

"Oh dear," said Mavis C, rushing to get down to his aid. He had to firmly let her know that there was no need for her to massage it, that the foot being without the shoe was relief enough. Then he ushered her down the hallway and into the main meeting hall. They sat at the front among the row of empty seats.

"Pastor Williams," said Mavis, "I want to speak with you about something I haven't ever spoken to anybody about before. It is something of the greatest importance." She looked at him, blinking hard. Her face was round and shining from the short walk from his office to the hall. He didn't want to think about what his own face might look like; he hadn't yet had time to sneak into the men's toilets to brush his teeth.

"Well, as you know, Sister," he said, "it is to the Lawd that you should be telling all things and one of the ways you can talk to the Lawd is through me, but before you go any further, is this about Nigel Brown?"

"Constance's son?" asked Mavis. "No," she said, looking at the pastor oddly.

The pastor pulled at his jacket and cleared his throat. "Then it's something else?"

"Yes," she said, and she looked hard into his face again. This time he felt himself begin to sweat. Had she discovered his big secret?

"I must confess something to you," she said. "I haven't acted in a righteous way at all."

164

"How you mean?" he asked, relieved.

"Ten days ago, Miss . . . a person came to see me and, well, I wasn't charitable to this person."

"In what way?" asked the pastor, getting into his familiar stride. He was used to teasing out information that didn't want to be teased out.

"Well, this person," said Mavis C, "made me want to say bad words. I had only bad thoughts towards this person and the words that I did say were . . . somewhat unkind."

"Oh, I see," said the pastor.

"But," continued Mavis C, "the words I did say weren't half as bad as the bad words I was thinking of. I won't tell you what those bad words were, but they were very bad."

The pastor reached out to touch Mavis on the hand. He had always been tactile with his congregation, got down on his knees to pray with them, put his hand on their shoulders. Held them sometimes in his arms. He didn't mean it in any way other than to share in the love and glory of the Lawd, but sometimes—well, sometimes—certain members of the congregation, particularly widowed women of a certain age, took the touching and the kneeling and the holding the wrong way, and Lawd, as a consequence, he had got himself into all sorts of situations over the years. Mavis shuffled closer to him and he made a concerted effort to shuffle away and removed his hand from hers.

Well, if this was the life-and-death situation that Sister Campbell was so eager to engage him with, he would prefer to get back to Corinthians. He would try to cut this short.

"Sometimes," he said with reassurance, "we all have thoughts that we regret. The fact that you regret is the important part." And he made to rise.

"Are you all right?" Mavis C asked him. He stumbled then, because it was rare for someone to ask him about his own disposition.

"It's just you haven't seemed yourself since Constance died, Pastor. You seem to have taken it very hard." She was right. He had. "You never seem to leave the church nowadays. And your office is always locked. Wasn't locked before. Whenever I come, no matter how early, you are always here and whenever I leave, unless you are on your rounds, you are here too."

He nodded and smiled. "The Lawd's work is never done and it requires commitment, no matter the time of day or night. This is my calling," he said.

"I know what you mean," she said. "This little church"—and she looked around the hall—"means the world to me. With me pickney them all grown-up. And me husband, Ralph, dead. It's coming here, carrying out this work that gives me purpose every day. Without it, I don't know who I would be."

"Indeed," said the pastor, tapping Mavis on the hand again, then removing his hand quickly. It was exactly at these types of moments, moments of connection, that the misunderstandings started to creep in.

"But the thing I wanted to discuss with you was to do with my late husband, Ralph, rest his soul," continued Mavis.

"Your husband?" asked the pastor, sitting down again. Ralph had died almost twenty years ago. He was a God-fearing man.

"This person I was talking to you about was asking questions about Ralph and I didn't like what they were insinuating."

"And what were they insinuating?"

"Well . . ." said Mavis carefully. "This person was insinuating that I might know something more about what happened to Daphne Stewart. You remember Daphne, don't you?"

The pastor nodded; he did. Everyone who was around in the community in the 1960s knew about Daphne Stewart, but the Pardner and its members *definitely* knew about Daphne Stewart, whose death was part of the never-solved Bone 12.

"It was an unfortunate business," he said.

"This person was asking whether my husband might have 'known' Daphne Stewart—intimately."

"Ah," said the pastor. "Well, I could see how that would be upsetting." He was reminded of all the upset that "the person" Mavis was referencing had created throughout the years with similar "insinuations," which she called investigations. He shook his head.

"But the thing is, Ralph . . . *did* know Daphne Stewart that way," said Mavis, nodding.

"Ralph?" asked the pastor, alarmed. Ralph was a man who, as he recalled, was quite steady.

Mavis nodded her head. "Yes," she said. "He *knew* knew Daphne Stewart. He never knew that I knew, but I did. I found out almost as soon as it started. A wife knows these things, you see."

"I see," said the pastor, shifting in his seat.

"It was me who invited Daphne into our home." Mavis shook her head. "You know sometimes you can't see a thing coming. I had some very bad words for her too, but you wouldn't wish what happened to her on anybody."

"No," said the pastor, remembering exactly how "the person" had described what had happened to Daphne Stewart.

"And then there was the baby," said Mavis. "Daphne never told me directly, of course, I'm not sure she was that far along. But I knew; plus, the week before she died, I dreamt about fish. And you know what dreaming about fish means."

He did. He also knew that Daphne Stewart was pregnant when she died as she had confessed the same to him two weeks before she was attacked. But he had no idea that it was Ralph's.

"The thing is, my confession is that, well, for thirty-odd years, I have held a secret."

"Right," said the pastor. There was nothing really nowadays that could shock him. He had been listening to confessions for most of his life, but now here was Mavis telling him all sorts of information, which perhaps even Miss Hortense hadn't been aware of.

Mavis took a deep breath.

"I'm going to tell you something I've never told another soul," she said, swallowing hard, as if she had a brick in her throat. "It was my husband, Ralph, that did the attacking."

"Ralph that did the attacking?" said the pastor in a hoarse voice. "Oh dear, are you sure? Did you raise your suspicions with him?"

"Well, that's just it," said Mavis. "I never did." She folded her arms in her lap. "You see, I like my life, Pastor. All I worked for was my family, a little house, to know my God. I never asked for much. Now, if I'd have mentioned it, he would either have had to lie or tell the truth, but then what would have happened to my family? Well, I suppose," she said, looking up at the crucifix looming above their heads, "I didn't want to rock the boat."

"So, you looked the other way," said the pastor, trying to remove judgment from his voice.

"Yes, I suppose I did," said Mavis gravely. She looked at him again. "Am I a bad person, Pastor? All these years I've lived with the guilt that my husband was the attacker. And now Miss Hortense is asking questions and, well, Ralph is dead. What difference does it make now?" she pleaded.

"Let us pray," said the pastor, and he took Mavis's hand firmly in his again and knelt down in prayer.

"Before we pray," said Mavis, "I have one more confession. One time, a very long time ago, just after Miss Hortense bought that house of hers on Vernon Road, I sort of accidentally on purpose threw a brick at her window."

41

A Truly Bizarre Stalking Expedition

Sonia and Blossom were still in hot pursuit of the daughter-in-law, Yvonne. They weaved in and out of traffic as Sonia tried her best to catch up. Blossom was out of breath just holding on to the dashboard. Sonia yanked the gearstick into fourth. With her one-liter engine she did her best to keep up, but the woman they were following clearly didn't respect the speed limit.

Yvonne Brown pulled away hard at the traffic light as Sonia struggled to put the car in gear again. Sonia almost didn't see the little boy as he stepped out in front of them; she swerved to avoid him and was within millimeters of missing another car on the other side.

"Come on, come on," chided Blossom. "I thought you could drive."

Thankfully it was clear, by the road signs, that they were heading towards the shopping center. When they entered the car park, Sonia released her breath. They parked in a bay two rows behind Yvonne.

They followed her, at a distance, through the big department store. Blossom hid behind a mannequin as Yvonne stopped to look at a pair of men's trousers before purchasing some socks. Finally, Yvonne entered a restaurant that offered all-day breakfast and took a seat at the back.

Sonia and Blossom perched at a table several rows to the side of Yvonne's, out of her eyeline.

"No, nothing for us," Blossom said, as a young waitress waved a menu at them. "Don't you know I've just had me breakfast?" She shooed the confused-looking girl away.

"The thing with Hortense," whispered Blossom to Sonia, as if they were still sitting in her car talking and were not on a truly bizarre stalking expedition, "is she can't let a thing go. Pastor and Constance said it couldn't be the same person that attacked Pearl and Daphne. But Miss Hortense said it was the same man she called a brute, and when she couldn't find him, she started to follow the women dem."

"The women?" asked Sonia, confused.

"Miss Hortense was protecting dem," whispered Blossom. "But you see, those kinds of women didn't want her protection."

"What kind of women?" Sonia whispered back.

"*Married* women," Blossom said with a shudder. "Married women in the area who Miss Hortense said was in danger."

"But why would being married mean the women were in danger?"

"Because of what the Brute whispered in Pearl and Daphne's ear and what it said in the Bible."

"What did it say in the Bible?" whispered Sonia.

"Exodus twenty: fourteen. *Thou shalt not commit adultery*," said Blossom, as she scratched her neck. "Because nobody didn't want anybody knowing their business, and Hortense is very good at finding out about your business. The women dem all started complaining about Hortense to the Pardner: how she was following dem home and ting. And Miss Hortense said she didn't want to make her following a secret, because she wanted the Brute to know."

"So," asked Sonia, thinking that her instincts had been right all along and Blossom had a few screws loose, "what happened next?"

"Good question," whispered Blossom, getting into her stride.

At that moment, a smartly dressed young man entered the restaurant, his hair neatly drawn into cornrows and his face cocoa-butter shining. He was like a breath of fresh air. He looked around the restaurant and caught Sonia's eye for a moment before he spotted Yvonne waving at him. As he moved towards her, she rose up to touch his face and embraced him so wholeheartedly that the world stopped for a minute, even for Sonia.

"Is that her husband, then?" whispered Sonia. "He's young."

"No, my dear, that very definitely is *not* her husband," whispered Blossom, who had placed her insulated bag on the table and was hiding behind it. "Well," she continued, "I think we find the matter referenced in the letter of the seventh of May." And somehow, to Sonia's bemusement, after all the food Blossom had consumed in the car, she heard Blossom's stomach growl loudly.

On the drive back to Blossom's house, Sonia was full of questions. But Blossom was too busy connecting dots.

"If she is seeing that young man . . . then Lawd have mercy, if the mother-in-law did find out she is seeing him, and Nigel is a big shot . . . And if Constance didn't like it . . ." continued Blossom, thinking out loud, perhaps creating more dots than connections.

"So Miss Hortense was following married women home back then as part of her investigation into Bone Twelve?" Sonia said, remembering her mother's reference.

"Oh, yes," said Blossom. "Well, and then her sister did die."

"Whose sister?"

"Miss Hortense's sister Evie, of course."

"Miss Hortense's sister died because Miss Hortense was following married women home?" Sonia rubbed at her temple. She was getting a headache.

"No, no, no," said Blossom. "That don't have nothing to do with that part. The sister, Evie, died in an accident. She fell down the stairs and bruck her neck." Blossom shook her head. "Hortense took it hard. Very hard. Evie was the only family she did really have, apart from Evie's son, Gregory."

"And what did that have to do with my father?" asked Sonia, ravenous for answers.

"Well, we couldn't find the Brute; he had already attacked two women, Pearl and Daphne. Who was next? Miss Hortense had all that 'pon her mind. And then her sister Evie bruck her neck, and that was 'pon Hortense's mind too, and that's what made her do the next thing, which wasn't really like Hortense at all."

Sonia pulled up outside Blossom's house.

"What next thing?" asked Sonia.

Blossom sighed. "Come into the house," she said, exhausted from the afternoon's shenanigans and all the explaining. "I going show you."

* * *

171

Blossom spent a long time upstairs. Sonia heard the sound of strange bangs through the ceiling and things being dragged along the carpet.

After ten minutes Sonia shouted up, "Can I help with anything, Miss Blossom?"

There was no answer for a while, and then, "No, my dear," shouted Blossom. "Me nearly there."

Blossom came down twenty minutes after that with a single piece of paper in her hand, which she passed to Sonia. On closer inspection, it was a page from a newspaper, the paper yellowed with age, the print blotchy. Sonia read.

Bigglesweigh Daily Herald

April 22, 1970

Brute on the Loose

A large, well-built colored man has been on the rampage attacking and terrorizing vulnerable women. This man has been attacking women at knifepoint and leaving them for dead. Many of these women have been too afraid to come forward and report these horrific crimes. The police are treating the reports very seriously but have said that a conspiracy of silence is hampering them in their search for the dangerous colored man who carried out the attacks. They have warned lone women to be vigilant at all times and have urged anyone with information to come forward.

"Oh . . ." said Sonia. "Was Miss Hortense the source of the article?"

"Yes," said Blossom. "Hortense spoke to a journalist at the local newspaper. She was only trying to do right."

"So . . . what happened?" asked Sonia, hoping that things would start to make sense soon. She handed the paper back to Blossom.

"A whole heap of blue fire is what happen," said Blossom. "And poor Stanley Thomas was arrested."

"So this Stanley Thomas was the man Hortense was looking for that night with my father?"

"No, no, no!" cried Blossom. "It wasn't Stanley—couldn't have been Stanley, and Miss Hortense proved that beyond doubt. Him was in po-lease custody when Daphne was attacked. But them na care, them get him on someting else instead."

"Oh," said Sonia. "And then?"

"So, after Hortense's sister died and after the ting with the newspaper, Miss Hortense became kind of . . ." Blossom paused, searching for the right word.

"What?" asked Sonia, impatient.

"Well, she did feel the case even more hard. She became . . ."

"Obsessed?" prompted Sonia.

"Um," said Blossom, looking for a better word. "More . . . passionated. She couldn't let it go. And the Pardner, well them did kind of lose trust in her. What with the newspaper ting . . ."

"But not my father? He didn't lose trust in her?"

"Your father and Miss Hortense was like brother and sister. Them was close."

"He was loyal to her."

"Yes, him was," said Blossom cautiously.

"So, when no one else would help her, he went with her to search for this attacker, the Brute man, and like this Stanley Thomas, he got caught up in her obsession with finding him?"

"Well . . . I suppose so," Blossom said. That was how most saw it, how the community saw it, and why they never forgave Hortense. "After you father died, people blamed Hortense. But it wasn't fair. She didn't make him do anything he didn't want to do. He wanted to find the Brute just like the rest of us. It was an accident."

"Thank you," said Sonia, rushing out of Blossom's house before the woman could see her tears begin to flow.

42

Thirteen Months

When Hortense had managed to catch her breath outside Garfield Stewart's house, she caught the 122 bus and found herself back at the canal. The sun was beating down. She was sitting on her bench and trying to process what she had just learned. How could she not have known that Garfield and Daphne Stewart lived in Walsall when Pearl was attacked?

There were thirteen months between the Brute's first attack on Pearl White and the death of Errol. Thirteen months that enabled the Brute to go on inflicting his pain and terrorizing the women of Bigglesweigh. Every time Miss Hortense thought about it, even now, her breath caught. She had tried so hard to find him during those long months. Finding out as much as she could about the attacks; reconstructing what she knew of them, and where they had taken place; and following leads, so many leads. Stopping the Brute was more important than anything, even if her efforts brought shame to those she was watching. But then there was the terrible series of events that led to Stanley Thomas's life being ruined. When Stanley Thomas was arrested in April 1970, Miss Hortense spent hours outside the police station on Fairfoot Road demanding to speak to the detective on the case, DS McGraf, after they had escorted her out of the building.

"Tell him it's Miss Hortense. Tell him he has the wrong man holed up inna him cell. Someone better tell me what is going on," she shouted at the hard-faced man at the reception, and then at the brick wall that so resembled him.

"Tell him if he doesn't speak to me, I will tell everybody 'bout all the cases I helped him to solve."

But her interpretation of events didn't suit DS McGraf, and he refused to speak with her. She'd gone home dog-tired after Fitz had persuaded her to leave.

An extraordinary Pardner meeting was called for the next day. A meeting that was going to be held at the pastor's church on Plevna Road, not at her house as usual.

That evening, Hortense, Fitz, Errol and Blossom were sitting around Miss Hortense's table, pensively nursing glasses of rum.

"I'm not going," said Hortense.

"You better go," said Blossom.

"The pastor and Constance is up to something. You better go," repeated Errol.

"If them going try and get rid of you, Hortense," said Fitz, his strong fists clenched, "I'm gone too."

In the first row of seats in the church hall were Constance, with her shark teeth very visible, Mr. McKenzie, accompanied unusually by Myrtle, prim and proper with her hands in her lap, and Blossom. The pastor was stood at the front with Errol. Fitz, who arrived later than everyone else, had taken a seat some rows behind the others. Pastor shook his head when Miss Hortense entered the hall. Errol nodded at Hortense and mouthed to her, "*No worry 'bout it.*"

"I'm not part of this circus," Fitz said to Hortense as she walked past them all slowly.

Someone told her to sit down, but Hortense remained standing, and then there was silence.

Pastor knocked on some wood. "Them still not release Stanley yet," he said, looking at Constance.

"But Miss Hortense proved the Brute is not him?" That was Blossom.

"Them charging Stanley with breach of the peace and assaulting an officer." Constance. "Him going before the magistrate on Tuesday."

"Now, Hortense." The pastor. "You can't go on like this. This thing tekking you over. Mekking we look real bad."

"Bone Twelve going kill you." That was Mr. McKenzie, quiet. "The passing of Evie has hit you hard."

"You see, this Pardner"—the pastor—"it is an institution. An institution like no other."

"It is not, never has been, a one-person thing." Constance. She looked like she was enjoying this.

"It looks bad on all of us." The pastor again.

"You should never have gone to any newspaper."

A shaking of heads. "That wasn't good at all at all."

"The Pardner rests on its discretion." This was the pastor.

"Twelve going kill you." A female echo in the room.

"We don't think you is a fit and proper person to be leading this Pardner anymore." Constance couldn't help herself.

"But Hortense started the Pardner." That was Blossom.

"Her judgment of late has gone questionable." That was the pastor. "And we can't have that."

Nods.

"Innocent people are getting caught up in it now." More shaking of heads.

"And how many people has Hortense helped over the years?" That was Errol.

"None of the women wanted her to follow them." Constance.

"You mekking this thing out to be more than it is." Pastor.

"You searching for a man that doesn't exist." Constance.

"We know why Pearl White was attacked."

"Garfield Stewart attacked his wife." The nodding of heads.

"It's a shame, but them is isolated events."

"And thank God, no one else has been attacked." That wasn't Errol or Fitz.

"You're not protecting anybody." The pastor.

"Protection is for the Lawd." That was Myrtle.

"Hortense, it is time for you to step down." This was Constance.

"Constance has agreed to take your place as the Pardner Lady." Pastor Williams.

Miss Hortense glared at the ignorant, false-smiling, goat-mouthed woman, and right at that moment wished her dead.

* * *

After the ambush, Miss Hortense had resolved to deal with the case: just her, Errol and Fitz. Blossom was married then, and a potential victim, so Miss Hortense wouldn't let her get involved, no matter how many times she asked. Miss Hortense resolved to continue to watch over the women the Brute was targeting, finishing her long shifts at the hospital so tired she could barely keep her eyes open and going to the places that she knew he might be—dances, darkened alleyways, outside the door of secret liaisons, her in full view. The Brute would see her and know that she hadn't given up. But she hadn't been able to stop him for over a year. Pearl was attacked in June 1969, Daphne in October of that year and Evie in January 1970. She hadn't been able to stop him during that time or the five months after and that failure sat in her stomach and churned. She had no idea if there were more victims.

It was only when the Brute made his one and only mistake that Miss Hortense and Fitz found him. After the car accident, when Errol's life hung in the balance.

Sitting now, quietly watching the slow movement of the canal, Miss Hortense felt a great darkness settle over her. She thought back on the words that Constance had said to her across her glass table at what was to be their final meeting:

Miss Hortense is not a suitable candidate for this Pardner . . . And we don't need to remind ourselves what happened the last time she interfered, do we? People get hurt. People get killed.

She was right.

43

Catching the Brute

After the accident, it took Hortense twelve days to find out who the person driving the car in front of them was. That was the number of days she was in the hospital as a patient. The number of days she couldn't fully raise her own body weight. Twelve days for Hortense to replay the last conversation she had had with Errol before they crashed, over and over again.

They'd had the Brute in their sights. They'd had him in front of them, less than four meters away. There had been the sleeting rain, the darkness of the night, the side of Errol's face illuminated by the streetlamps, concentrating on the car in front, her gripping on to the dashboard and trying to read the number plate. In the first days of being in the hospital, through the haze of the painkillers, she twisted it around in her head and still drew blanks. Who was driving the car in front? Nothing. The way he was driving, erratic. But nothing.

"Did you see who it was?" she had asked Errol in the car, and he had said no. But there had to be something there that she had missed—but she couldn't see beyond the small stretch of road in front. When she closed her eyes, she saw a monster, but it was a monster of her own making, ten feet tall, heavy, leaning down on her leg, snapping it in two.

Hortense turned to the page in the notebook with the folded corner. On the page, scrawled by a hand that could barely write, was the number plate, EUL 206F, the *F* sitting several lines beyond the rest. Written by a hand for whom a pencil was a lead weight. After the car accident, it had been two days before she'd been strong enough to write down those seven figures and letters. She'd held on to them for dear life through the blackness, determined that they would help reveal the answer of Bone 12 to her.

She had two new things. The full number plate, EUL 206F, and the fact that he had used the same car twice. While she was staring up at the ceiling with the small patch of damp in the corner, she reflected on what she thought might have been the Brute's mistake. That small thing, that he had used the same car twice.

As soon as she was able to talk, she begged Fitz to find out from the policeman McGraf who the owner of that number plate EUL 206F was. McGraf still owed her for Stanley's wrongful arrest, and she reminded him she wasn't scared to carry out her threat to expose his incompetence.

A week after that, Fitz came back. "A two-door Ford Cortina. Belongs to a white woman, lives on Mountbatten Street. Goes by the name of Mrs. Brady."

"You sure?" Miss Hortense asked, barely audible. He nodded.

"And?" she pressed.

"Nothing. She lives with a husband. Him is white too."

He couldn't be the man they were searching for. That man was Black; Pearl, Daphne and Evie were sure of that, despite the balaclava he wore to hide his identity.

"Nobody else living at the house," continued Fitz. "Just a young family."

But Hortense needed more than a dead end.

"Go inside," she said.

"Into the house? No. Lawd Jesus, Hortense. Cha man. They don't have nutting to do with dis. Get yourself well first."

Miss Hortense shook her head then, and tried to rise from the bed, the pain shooting down her left side. That car was their answer now. But what did it mean if the car that the Brute had used twice belonged to a white family? Fitz had gone back to the Bradys at her insistence.

"Dem wouldn't let no Black man drive them car," Fitz had said afterwards. "That is for damn sure."

It was while Miss Hortense was looking at the damp patch on the ceiling that it came to her.

She remembered the carburetor and how Ralph had said it was because it wasn't working that he had been late to meet Daphne.

"What if he works on them?" she said to Fitz. "The cars. What if he fixes them, or knows how to break them? A man that works on cars that wears steel-capped boots, stained with oil."

Fitz took his hat off and rolled his hand through his hair. He was seeing what she was. It was the breakthrough they had been waiting for for over a year.

"Go back to the Brady house," Miss Hortense demanded. "Find out which mechanic them tek them car to. Then we going find the Brute."

Three days later, Fitz came back to visit Hortense in the hospital, and when he came, he moved slow and heavy. It was death he brought with him and it was death that weighed him down. It clung to the back of his head, the lines in his face, it was in the way that he shuffled the only chair in the room closer to the bed so that it scratched and scraped along the floor. There were fresh bruises on his knuckles. Miss Hortense didn't know it immediately, but it was the lives of two people that he carried on his back that afternoon.

"Well, me find him," he said, low, as he took a seat next to Miss Hortense's bed and shook out his trouser leg. There was once a time when they could have been so much more. The scent of his Old Spice drifted over to her. He cussed his teeth. "The Bradys get scared, seeing a Black man on dem doorstep again—and closed de door in me face." He took off his hat and scratched his hair, then started fiddling with the crease of the hat in his hands. "But I find the nearest car garage to them house. A garage just off Slade Lane. You know the one? Only one Black somebody work there anyhow."

Miss Hortense held her breath. Fitz swallowed hard and said, "Danny Grant." The boy who was so torn up about his friend Michael's murder. The boy the McKenzies had taken in as their own.

In the hours and days since Fitz had left, Miss Hortense had been running through all the men she knew to be good with cars, who worked with cars, who she had known were interested in cars or worked as mechanics. There was Eamonn and Patrick, Silverton and Adolph, there was Daphne's husband, Garfield, there was even Fitz himself. But she had been running men in her head, not boys. Her mistake. Her mistake for nearly a year was that she was looking for a man, not a boy.

"Him don't fix cars," Fitz continued as the world fell apart around Hortense. "But him do the valeting. Is him them give the keys to clean the cars and the key to the yard." He looked at Miss Hortense. "Now you see it?"

How could someone so young have done the damage she had seen? Why? Why would he have attacked women? It didn't make any sense.

Miss Hortense stared at Fitz. "What more you not telling me?"

Fitz reached into the pocket of his jacket and handed her a gold chain. It fell lightly into the palm of her hand, as if it were barely even there. The links to it were narrow, with a small gold crucifix at the end. The chain had been snapped from its clasp as if it had been snatched from the neck to which it belonged. In her mind's eye, she saw Fitz do it. There was no engraving on it, nothing to set it apart from another chain and crucifix. And yet it began to feel oddly heavy and hot, so that Miss Hortense had to drop it down onto the side table.

"Him baptized now," said Fitz. "Is me who baptize him." He couldn't look at her then. He sat back and rubbed at his hands with the bruised knuckles.

He wouldn't say any more, not in a white person's hospital with only a thin cubicle curtain drawn around them.

"Where?" she asked, needing to know the answer, despite the risk of the words being admitted out loud.

"Down by Quarter Point. The canal," he said.

They had solved the case. They had discovered the Brute. He wouldn't attack another woman again. Danny Grant didn't fit her description; the Brute was meant to be a big old man, bigger than life itself, not a young boy with hardly any years to his name. He was meant to have wild eyes, not to be human, because she couldn't see how anything human could do the kind of things that he did. She was meant to have recognized him. Felt him. Miss Hortense felt sick to her stomach remembering the injuries. Had she been too caught up looking for the wrong clues in the wrong places? She'd spent so long thinking about what she wanted to see done to him. And now he was dead.

"Hortense . . ." Fitz said, leaning forwards. And then he told her about the second death he had brought with him. "Errol's gone. He passed this morning."

The sound that came from Miss Hortense was like no sound that had come from her before. It came from somewhere deep down inside, a place she didn't even know existed. A scream so chilling that it made Fitz, a man who didn't show emotion when his own mother died, sob his heart out.

On July 22, 1970, they had caught the Brute. Danny Grant was dead. But now, given what Garfield Stewart had told her, there was the possibility that there might be more than one attacker or even potentially that they had caught the wrong person. She looked at the time on her watch and realized she'd been sitting on the bench at Quarter Point for hours. This was the place she came to be close to Danny Grant's swollen and decomposing body, that had been held down under the weight of the water, in the deep recesses of the canal, for thirty years.

44

A Pastor Comes to Call

Sonia had been up in her room for most of the afternoon, thinking about what Miss Blossom had told her. Sonia refused to believe that Miss Hortense wasn't in some way responsible for her dad's death. Her mother had said, *It's her fault.* Something just didn't add up. Why did her father go with Miss Hortense that night? What did her mother's last words about "the Pardner Lady" mean? As she continued to ruminate, there was a knock at the front door.

A little old man with a sweaty bald head was stood on the doorstep. She recognized him from outside Yvonne and Nigel's house. Sonia insisted that he must come in, notwithstanding that Miss Hortense wasn't at home and probably wouldn't have approved because of her rules.

"Well, I don't know," said the old man, mopping his head with a hanky. "I could always come back another time?"

"Oh no," insisted Sonia. "I'm sure Miss Hortense will be back soon." Even though Miss Hortense had shouted up on her way out that she wouldn't be back until the evening.

The man came into the house reluctantly, and sat down. Sonia made herself comfortable in Miss Hortense's armchair. It whined in protest at the unfamiliar body.

"Uh, sorry, but who are you?" Sonia asked, deciding not to mention the lamppost that she had seen him trying to hide behind. "I didn't catch your name."

"Oh," said the old man, wiping his head, "I'm the pastor. I have a church in Plevna Road. You know the one?"

183

Sonia shook her head. A pastor who hides behind lampposts? This place got stranger and stranger.

"And you are?" he asked back, blinking at Sonia.

"I'm Sonia," she said. "I'm staying with Miss Hortense for a while."

"Oh, you are?" said the pastor, a surprise in his voice. "Family?" She looked familiar.

"Oh no." Sonia cleared her throat. "I'm Errol and Precious's daughter."

"Oh!" said the man. "Oh . . ." he said again, mopping his head and rising. "Well, I'd better be going now."

"No, please," she said to him. "Please stay." And she rose too, and then sat down as if to tell him that is what he must do.

"Well . . ." He sat back down too. Finally he said, "I hear that Precious did die."

Sonia looked at him then, expecting something more from this man of God, but he went quiet and stared at the coffee table.

"Yes," she said. "She did die. Did you know my dad—Errol?"

"Well . . . not really . . . a little," said the pastor, mopping his head again.

Sonia leaned in, waiting for him to say something more, but he didn't and so she said, "What was he like, my father?"

The pastor adjusted in his seat.

"Well . . . He had a good strong voice. It was a baritone, if I recall." Sonia sat further forward. The pastor gulped. "He could play a game of dominoes."

"And my mother?" she asked, given that he seemed to be short of words about her father.

"Um, well . . ." he said, looking at a hand. "I didn't really know you mother . . . No," he said with a tremor.

"Oh," said Sonia. That surprised her, because if anyone should know her Bible-thumping mother, it would be this man of God.

"And Miss Hortense?" she asked.

"Yes?" he said, clearing his throat.

"You came to see her?" encouraged Sonia.

"Oh yes," said the pastor, as if just remembering.

"I haven't heard Miss Hortense ever say she was going to church." It wasn't one of the things on Miss Hortense's list.

184

"Well, no," said the pastor. "Miss Hortense stopped coming to my church many years ago . . . after the thing . . ."

"The thing?"

The pastor balked. "Um, well . . . yes, um, a thing that happened as things do happen . . . many years ago." Sonia just knew he was talking about her father. The accident.

"And you know Miss Hortense well, then? You're close?"

"Um," said the pastor. "Well, we was, I suppose, to an extent, close, yes, once. Not now."

"But you've come to see her now?" Sonia said. "Maybe I can help?"

"Oh no. Me na think so," he said, and this time he rose very firmly and started to make his way to the door. "Myrtle . . ."

"Myrtle?" Sonia repeated. What did this Myrtle have to do with anything?

The pastor felt an urgent need to explain himself: "Myrtle used to clean the church before her husband took sick. I must go and visit her now. Do let Miss Hortense know me did call." And he quickly shuffled to the front door and opened it.

"So . . . who should I say visited?"

"Yes," said the pastor, hurrying out. "Pastor Williams." And he rushed away.

"Williams!" exclaimed Sonia after him, but he had already disappeared down the road.

Sonia "forgot" to mention the pastor's visit to Hortense when she arrived home later that day. Instead, she spent most of the evening locked in her room, staring at the recurring payment from *A. Williams* in her mother's banking book and wondering what the first name of Pastor Williams could be, and how bad a "thing" had to be to make you lose your faith.

45

The Brick

Her hours of contemplation at the canal had convinced Miss Hortense that she needed to further investigate Garfield Stewart. She decided to speak to the pastor the following morning.

On a non-church day, without the pomp of a ceremony and the throng of its people, the building on Plevna Road looked deserted. When the pastor had decided to locate his church at that spot, thirty-odd years ago, it had made much more sense. Back then, the council wasn't trying its best to deter people from coming down the road where it sat and it had generally been a pleasant place to find solace. But now the church was stuck between the Tasty Grill kebab shop to its right, which took its best takings when the Oasis night-club shut on a Saturday night, and the William Hill bookies to its left. It was now very much a bad location for a church and there were probably a number of its newer neighbors who hoped it, with its hallelujahs and clapping of hands, would simply be flattened and disappear.

Save for the day before Constance died, Miss Hortense hadn't had a meeting with the pastor since 1977. But he seemed strangely unsurprised to see her.

"It's all right. It's all right," he said when one of the Mavises blocked her way into the meeting hall. "Let Sister Hortense come through." And as she walked with him into the building and down the corridor, he said quietly, so that the Mavises didn't hear, "We can talk inna my office."

186

The office was in chaos. Miss Hortense was taken aback that he was letting her in. He quickly closed the door behind them.

"So you congregation know this is where you live?" she asked, eyeing up the camp bed and the scattered clothes, as the pastor went to check if anyone was listening at the door. "What happened to your house?"

"Please," he said, his voice lower, the assurance he had in front of the Mavises gone. "Take a seat." He swiped some papers off a chair in front of his desk, let them fall to the floor and motioned for Hortense to sit. "I going answer all you questions."

He got out his handkerchief and mopped his balding head.

A bright piece of women's wear caught her eye. A familiar-looking scarf, blue with yellow spots, lying on a pile of clothes in the corner.

"Whose scarf is that?" she asked.

He looked over. "Oh, me find it in the nursery. Why, you know who it belong to?" he asked shrewdly.

"I have no idea," said Hortense, the tingling in her leg starting again.

"I was wondering when you were going return my visit," he said.

"You came to see me?" Hortense asked.

"Yes, yesterday. The girl staying with you didn't tell you?"

"No." *Damn girl*, she said to herself as she thought of Sonia scavenging around, picking away at her flesh.

"I can't give you what you asking for," the pastor said.

"What am I asking for?" she said, her face puzzled.

"The money you demanded in your letter?"

"What letter?"

He opened a drawer and handed Miss Hortense a typewritten letter. She read:

Dearest Pastor Williams,
Since Constance is no longer with us, I demand
that you provide to me, and Blossom, a detailed
account of all of the Pardner monies and property
or I will be forced to reveal to your concregation
where I got much of my information for my Looking

187

Into cases from many years ago. PS I also want to be reinsulated as the Pardner Lady as soon as possible. Yours waiting for a response, goodbye for now, Miss Hortense.

After Miss Hortense had read it, she said, "What the . . . ," and was on the verge of saying the bad word beginning with *b*, but stopped just short of it.

"I have no problem with you rejoining the Pardner, Hortense," said the pastor, mopping his head. "In fact, as I said, I think that would be a very good idea, but you might as well know . . ." He went to the closed door and put his ear to it once more. "I and the Pardner don't have a penny."

"This letter?" said Hortense, holding it in the air. "Is when you receive it?"

He looked at her, puzzled. "You left it under my door the day of Constance's funeral."

Did I now, thought Hortense, remembering how Blossom had left the service early to go to the toilet and how they had found her in the lobby when it was all done. She was going to kill Blossom.

Miss Hortense laid the letter back on the desk. The pastor looked to the window and shook his head.

"You know me, Hortense. I am a man of God. I don't deal inna this," he said, motioning to the papers on the desk. "Never have done. Constance got me to sign a whole heap a papers for the Pardner about a year ago. I just signed them. I didn't study them properly. I wasn't expecting this. And, well, it look like me gone and signed away everything but these clothes me is standing in to Constance, and now her boy Nigel have it all. It all gone, Hortense." His narrow shoulders drooped some more. "The whole damned lot, and now Sister Blossom is calling every day, dem threatening to send in de bailiffs and I tekking from Peter to pay Paul." He looked at the many empty tithe plates scattered about the office. "I don't know how much longer I can go on. Me na know wha fe do." He shook his head. "I don't care about the money, Hortense; I don't care about the house." His tone was flat, none of his usual theatrics. "But this place"—he looked around the room and tapped on the desk—"is where people come when they don't have anyplace else to go."

"How could you sign away *all* the Pardner to Constance?" Miss Hortense asked in disbelief.

The pastor was coy. "I don't deal inna paperwork, Hortense. Never have." He cleared his throat and mopped his brow. Miss Hortense felt there was something Pastor Williams was not telling her. She noted the irony; that they had kicked her out of the Pardner thirty years ago, supposedly to protect it, and here he was pretty much telling her that the Pardner was dead.

"But wait, if it wasn't about the letter, and the girl never tell you about my visit, what was it you wanted to see me about?" he asked, suddenly curious.

"Garfield Stewart," said Hortense.

"Oh, Mr. Stewart," he said, shaking his head.

"Him ever confess anything to you 'bout . . . Bone Twelve?"

"Mr. Stewart? You mean confess to killing him wife? No, sah. Him never confess nothing like that to me. Even though at the time, as you know, I did think him did have everything to do with it," said the pastor. He moved to the door and put his ear to it again. "But that is why I was coming to see you. I now know who killed Daphne Stewart and it wasn't her husband."

And then, just like old times, he went on to explain to Hortense all that Mavis Campbell had confessed to him, first about her husband Ralph Campbell and then her second confession, about a brick she had thrown at Miss Hortense's window in the summer of 1966.

"You," said the pastor, "was the first of us to really make your mark, to buy that little house on Vernon Road. Is not everyone likes to see others get on, and well, at the time, that did lead to some jealousy on the part of Mavis. But she is very sorry for her actions now."

Hortense remembered the feelings she had at the time, the loneliness of living on that street, the creeping fear.

She took the letter from his desk and put it in her handbag. She gathered her things and walked out of his office-cum-bedroom-and-laundry-room, or whatever it was now, hoping, for their sakes, that she didn't see either of the Mavises on her way out.

46

A Resurrection

Coco Fritters

1 tsp baking powder
1 egg
3 cocos
1½ tbsp flour
pinch of salt
2 scallion stalks
oil

On Friday morning, Miss Hortense decided to make fritters. After she peeled the cocos, she set them under the tap, washed them and grated them. It was the washing and the grating that focused Hortense's mind. Cocos look like yam but they taste more like a potato and are nutty and earthy. There was a time when it was hard to get coco in Bigglesweigh, but not anymore. Miss Hortense beat the egg and mixed it together with the grated coco, the flour, a pinch of salt and the cut-up scallion. She put a deep pan on the stove and poured in oil. When the oil was sizzling, she put drops of the coco mixture in, one spoonful at a time, and fried the fritters until they were golden brown.

Garfield Stewart admitted that he was living in the West Midlands when the Brute had attacked Pearl. Meaning the Brute could have been him. Mavis Campbell, on the other hand, believed it was her husband, Ralph Campbell, who had killed Daphne. Meaning there were two suspects that she had discounted back in play. Was it possible that there could have been more than one attacker, as the community, as Pastor Williams and Constance, had said all along?

If she understood him right, Garfield Stewart was also saying that it was Donovan Miller who died in the fire at the boardinghouse in 1965, which then begged the question of who the man at the bottom of Constance's stairs was, because he couldn't have died twice.

Something was beginning to dawn on her, and it had to do with the ghost she thought she saw at Constance's funeral. She needed to speak to a member of Constance's family to find out more. She covered the fritters and tidied the kitchen, then put on her coat, picked up her handbag and headed to Bigglesweigh Community College.

Soon she was waiting beside a little yellow car that was badly parked a few hundred yards from the entrance to the college.

The day was a balmy one, so Miss Hortense didn't mind the waiting. Looking in through the dirty windows of the car, Miss Hortense was able to determine that Jasmine liked too many fizzy drinks and chewy sweets, and didn't like or didn't care about cleanliness.

The details of the college had been on a flyer advertising a fashion show stuck up on the noticeboard in Constance's kitchen on the day of the ambush—one of the designers, Hortense suspected, being Constance's granddaughter. Given everything that had happened, she also suspected that the show had come and gone without much fanfare.

Just as Miss Hortense had anticipated, Jasmine approached the car. She was carrying a large, black, flat art case and some books. Her step slowed when she saw Miss Hortense.

"I can have a word, my dear?" Miss Hortense asked as the girl neared, broad forehead on show. "If you don't mind, let's talk in you car?"

After a moment, Jasmine got out her keys and unlocked the passenger side.

"I don't know if you remember me," Miss Hortense began, looking out the windscreen, "but I was at you grandmother's funeral."

Jasmine nodded.

"I won't beat about the bush, young lady," said Miss Hortense. "At the funeral you said something about a regret you had. What was the thing you wished you hadn't done?"

Jasmine swallowed. "Oh, it's nothing. I was just . . . upset." She cleared her throat unconvincingly.

"Did it have anything to do with the man they found dead in your grandmother's house?" Miss Hortense asked now, looking at the young lady, who swallowed and licked her lips.

Jasmine lowered her head and her breath caught.

"I have my sources, you see," continued Miss Hortense, "and one of them was able to tell me that the man staying at the house, who was found at the bottom of the stairs, was a Mr. Donovan Miller. Came all the way from Texas, USA. Landed on the day of the funeral," said Hortense. "I met a Mr. Miller once, a very long time ago, nearly forty years now. That was before the fire. He was boarding at the same house your grandparents was staying in." Miss Hortense looked again at the girl. "You know 'bout the fire at that house, don't it?" The girl nodded. "What I can remember of Mr. Miller was that he was a tall man," said Miss Hortense. "I also met your grandfather, Mr. Brown, on a few occasions. You couldn't really forget meeting Mr. Brown. Of course, he passed away in that fire, years before you was born. You know one thing: he was a rather short man."

The girl was looking down at her lap.

"Me and you grandmother Constance didn't get along, but I wanted to say my farewells. But on the day of her funeral, well, I thought I saw a ghost. A very short ghost."

"It's not him!" Jasmine blurted out, and then, frightened, slapped a palm over her mouth.

"Who, child?" asked Hortense steadily. "Because the ghost I thought I saw looked very much like your grandfather that died in the fire, a man with the same broad forehead you and your mother and uncle all share."

Jasmine shook her head.

"I'm sorry," she said, her voice as emotional as it was the day of the funeral. She was looking around as if watching for someone. "I don't know what you're talking about. Please, *please* leave."

Hortense straightened at the girl's voice.

"Please," said the girl again.

Miss Hortense nodded and left the car. She had her confirmation. But when Jasmine eventually got the car in gear and drove off, Miss Hortense wondered what could be making the girl so afraid.

47

Clean

"This is nice," said the man sitting next to Nigel in the passenger seat. His long legs had to wrap around themselves to give them enough space. "This is very nice." He pushed the button on the glossy black inlay under his elbow and the electric window lowered with a buzz. He stuck his long arm out and it hung there loosely and precariously as Nigel put the car into third gear and pressed down hard on the accelerator. The g-force sent both of their heads flying back.

"Yes!" said Dice, adjusting his Aston Villa baseball cap. Nigel pressed down harder and shouted over the roar:

"Six-speed, 343 horsepower, S54 straight-six." He pushed a button and there was a further jerk, and the roar got louder.

Nigel slowed. Except for the purr of the car and the wheels on the shingles, it was quiet; 2 a.m. quiet, when the police were tucked up in their beds and Nigel felt like he could be in his car with this man and go over eighty-five miles an hour.

"Now tell me," said Nigel as they came to a stop, the shingles crunching under his nineteen-inch alloy wheels. They could just see the canal. It was black and shining. "How's my business?"

"Good," said Dice, taking out a cigarette.

"Not in the car," said Nigel.

"Yeah, course," said Dice, putting the cigarette behind his ear.

"Business is good," repeated Dice, twisting his foot in the footwell to get some more space for the long legs and the big trainers.

"And the man that was at my mum's funeral?"

"Cuttah's pony?" said Dice, scoffing. "Nothing to worry about."

"But you will take care of them?" queried Nigel, watching Dice closely. It was, after all, what he was paying him for.

Dice shifted. Cuttah and his crew weren't men you took care of. The old man was known as "Nine Lives." He couldn't be killed. Made of Teflon. No point trying. Last time someone did, it was them ended up six foot deep. But no point in saying that to his boss.

"Old-timers. Trust me. No one bothers with 'em anymore. They're harmless," said Dice. It was partially true. Nigel pondered.

"And you're not hearing anything else?" he asked, looking out at the canal, cautious, careful.

"No, Nige," said Dice. He sniffed. "Well, you know, just talk on the street, murmurings, but nothing worth listening to."

"Murmurings?" Nigel traced his hand around the steering wheel.

"Crackheads, that's all. Running their mouths down at the End. One of 'em said an old lady was asking about me, but it's nothing to worry about; it's an old lady, for fuck's sake. I can deal with her."

Miss Hortense again, Nigel thought. An interfering old battleaxe, according to his mum. She'd already tried to warn Germaine off. But he had nothing to fear from her, now that all of his mum's assets were safely in his hands.

"I hope there's nothing else, because I'm starting to get a little anxious, Richard." The use of his real name made Dice sit up.

"No need," he said, trying to loosen his shoulders.

"Nothing or no one can get in the way of my plans. D'you understand?"

"Yeah . . ." said Dice.

"My job is to be clean, legit. And that means you need to do your job and keep me out of it. D'you understand me?"

"Course. Yeah, Nige," said Dice, shifting again. "No problem."

Patience and sacrifice got rewards. After weeks of covert surveillance, following Dice to any number of locations throughout Bigglesweigh at all times of the night and day, Gregory had watched as Dice got into a black BMW that was driven away at speed. And who was in the driver's seat? Gregory pulled out his notebook and looked at the name he had written: Nigel Brown. The man at the funeral who wasn't

195

very good at giving speeches. Not only the son of Miss Constance but—Gregory had looked him up—a big-time property developer and Bigglesweigh's entrepreneur of the year since 1998!

Now Gregory wondered how the puzzle fitted together. There was the break-in at the community center, which was orchestrated by Dice, who he now knew was working for Nigel Brown. But why the community center? Nigel's mother had been a significant figure in the community up until she died and his sister, Camille, ran the center. The man found dead at the bottom of Constance's stairs, Donovan Miller, had been invited to stay at her property "by her family." Did that mean Nigel? How was it all connected?

One thing he did know was that, whatever Nigel Brown, Dice and Germaine Banton were up to, it had to be illegal. Now he just needed enough evidence to prove it.

48

You Are What You Hide

It was a chilly day considering the time of year, and Miss Hortense was back at Constance's big old house. Miss Hortense hadn't wanted to set foot anywhere near that house again after Constance took out her whetted knife and tried to stab her with it the day before she died, but after what Garfield Stewart had said—that it was Donovan Miller who died in the boardinghouse fire in 1965, and the confirmation of sorts that she got from Jasmine, Constance's granddaughter, that Donovan Miller was not Donovan Miller—she was coming to Constance's to investigate her security arrangements. If someone had killed the man who wasn't Donovan Miller, she wanted to find out how they might have got into the house to do it.

She looked at the house from the pavement, still pushed up and pretentious. She entered the gate again. Rubbish had accumulated since Constance's death, and the weeds looked like they were having a party. Two dead bodies had been found at the house—that meant two restless duppies prowling around, and at least one of them was cantankerous and provoking. She went up to the big old timber door. The glass where Sonia must have thrown the brick and reached her hand through was now boarded up with wood. She pushed on the door firmly, but it was solidly locked. She couldn't see a great deal through the remaining frosted panels. She took some steps backwards to examine the window to the right of the front door. The gray net curtains could do with a wash. She remembered how they had moved the last time she was there when Constance opened the door to them. The windows that might open were all at the top and didn't look like they could enable anybody other than perhaps a small child to squeeze through them. It was the same with the window on the other side. She walked to the side gate next to the house. She pushed on it and it clicked open. She felt like she was being watched from the street, but when she looked back she couldn't see anyone.

The gate squeaked shut behind her as she walked down the narrow pathway, broken tiles and more weeds underfoot. When she got to the end of the path and entered the back garden, there was the smell of something foul and she was careful where she walked. She stepped towards the big glass patio doors and peered inside to see dust sheets covering the furniture. She tried the patio door. It was firmly shut with a modern lock, steady and solid. She went to another back door and came to the same conclusion. The window to the kitchen was also firmly shut. They didn't look like locks that had been recently installed. Miss Hortense didn't believe that Constance Brown would have taken her security for granted and, save for the back garden gate, she was right. If someone did push the man who was not Donovan Miller down the stairs to his death, unless one of the doors to the property was left open, the person had to have picked the lock or been invited in.

As she walked back up the path to leave, she heard a voice calling after her from the adjoining property.

"Hiya?" said a woman with blue-rinsed hair, wrapped in a dressing gown, leaning over her gate. "You were here the day before Constance died?" She looked Hortense up and down.

Miss Hortense lied and said she was a friend of Constance, and the blue-rinse neighbor, who introduced herself as Barbara, invited her around for a cup of tea. It transpired she had been Constance's neighbor since 1973.

As Hortense sipped her tea, Blue Rinse Barbara said, "The man that lived there for a time was just awful. He left lots of beer cans and empty bottles all over the front garden. We had to call the council. I was so upset by it all I had to go and stay with my daughter for a few days. Then we heard that he had died. Terrible, just terrible, but what a relief!" Then Blue Rinse Barbara said, "You were Constance's friend, so you know she was a lovely woman." Miss Hortense nearly choked on her tea.

"When the awful man was living there"—Miss Hortense took this to be the man who wasn't Donovan Miller—"did you notice that he had any visitors?"

"Only Constance's children," said Blue Rinse Barbara.

"And the day before Constance died, did you see any other people visiting her?" Hortense asked.

"Well, I don't really pay much attention," lied Barbara. "But there was you, and then another lady who wore a bright scarf." *Blossom*, thought Miss Hortense. "And just before I went out shopping in the morning, there was another visitor, a man." *Ah, the pastor*, thought Miss Hortense, remembering that he was already at the house when she and Blossom arrived, sat in the kitchen mopping his head.

"I remember because there was a bit of argy-bargy on the doorstep," said Barbara. "But eventually Constance let him in."

Perhaps an argument about the Pardner finances, thought Hortense.

"Was the man bald-headed?" Miss Hortense asked, to confirm it was Pastor Williams.

"Oh, no," said the woman. "It wasn't the church man. No, the church man came much later in the evening. The man that visited in the morning had quite a lot of hair, and he was, well . . . you know . . . like me."

"White?" said Miss Hortense. Barbara nodded.

Well, well, thought Miss Hortense, and she wondered if the two exceptions from her rooting-around investigations into Constance Brown—Constance's old boss with an HR grievance and Constance's ex-son-in-law who told Miss Hortense to "piss off" over the phone—might be more significant than she had originally thought.

49

Featherweight Round

Even though most of Gregory's spare time was occupied with putting together the final pieces of the puzzle in his secret investigation into Nigel Brown and Richard Dudney aka Dice, his Tuesday evening visits with his aunty continued. The woman who had found the deceased man at Miss Constance's was now staying at his aunty's house.

"Who is she?" Gregory asked, impolitely, about Sonia.

"Never you mind," was the response.

"Well, apparently," he said, after he had polished off his plate of curry mutton and rice, "your body at the bottom of the stairs is proving quite popular."

Miss Hortense gave him the look, which, despite him now being thirty-seven years old, could mean *Don't play with me, child*, or *You is not too old for me to put you over my knee*.

"Apparently, someone at the betting shop has been trying to find out about the body and in particular whether there was a scar on the chest."

Just then the doorbell went.

Gregory's Tuesday visits were a fact that Blossom knew well. So, when Blossom's voice was heard saying "Kuya!" through the letter box, Miss Hortense wasn't much surprised.

"Oh, fancy seeing you here, Gregory boy," she said, pushing her way into Miss Hortense's front room.

"Hortense." She sniffed, and then proceeded to the phone in the hallway, picked it up, listened, and made a dramatic "Oh" of mock surprise before she dropped it with disdain. It was working. Miss

Hortense folded her arms. When they reentered the front room, Gregory looked between the two women waging a silent war of recrimination and, knowing better than to speak, bowed his head over his plate.

Without taking her eyes off Miss Hortense, Blossom settled herself at the dining table, right next to Gregory.

"I have a hypocritical question," said Blossom as she was easing off her coat. "I want to know how you would go about proving somebody kill somebody else when them may not have actually killed the person."

"Gregry don't have no time for you stupidness now," said Miss Hortense, sitting back down and clinking her cup against her saucer.

"I can ask him a question if I want to, don't it?" said Blossom, nodding at Gregory with a spike in her voice. "It's only a hypocritical question. You don't have the monopoly on hypocritical questions," she said, the spike getting sharper. "I watch *Crimewatch* too. You na mind, do you?" Blossom asked Gregory, nodding some more, her voice sweeter.

"No, I suppose not," said Gregory, making himself as small as possible in between the two women.

"So how would you do it? Kill somebody without actually *killing* them killing them."

"When you say not *killing* them killing them . . ." asked Gregory.

"Not touching them," said Blossom quickly. "The killer in one place, the dead body in another."

"Well, I suppose," said Gregory, "there might be any number of ways that a person could kill another in that scenario."

"Like wha?" said Blossom, looking at Gregory intensely.

Hortense tutted.

"Well, we've come across cases where people have been poisoned, for example," said Gregory.

"Oh, yes," said Blossom. "Could be poison, but me na think so. What else?"

"Well," said Gregory, shifting in his seat. "You have cases where somebody pays another person to kill."

"A hit-person," said Blossom, knowingly. "No, that is not this. What else?"

"Blossom Henry," said Hortense. "If you don't stop you foolishness now, me going have fe tell you fe come outta me house."

201

"Out of your house?" said Blossom, pushing up her mouth. "Of course you would put me *out of your house*. And yet you'd rather have strangers holed up inna it." She motioned to the ceiling. "You and Fitzroy is acting very strange. Very strange indeed. I mean, I can understand, what with all him is going through, with the diagnosis and all, that him would want go to church."

"Diagnosis?" asked Gregory quietly into the room. He was ignored.

"But with you," continued Blossom, "there is no excuse. Not recipe-creating my phone calls and now you threatening *to kick me out*. Ha. Some friend." And she gave a big huff, but it quieted Miss Hortense.

"And what about motifs, Gregory boy?" continued Blossom. "If you could prove a person had a motif to kill somebody."

"Well," said Gregory, still small, dodging the bullets, "I suppose if you have evidence that a person had a *motive* to kill someone, that might go some way to showing that the person could have been killed by the person with the motive."

"Oh," said Blossom. "So, if one"—she looked at Hortense—"hypocritically could get evidence of a motif, then that might be enough to prove a murder?"

"Maybe," said Gregory. "It would be a long shot. You'd need a body, and the evidence of a *motive* would have to be very strong, but maybe, hypothetically speaking."

"Evidence? Like photographs?" asked Blossom.

"Depending on what the photographs were of, yes, maybe?"

"Blossom," said Miss Hortense, looking at her again from over her glasses. "You must stop. Now."

Blossom ignored Miss Hortense and said to Gregory, "Okay then, thank you. Thank you very much, you hear."

And she put on her coat and headed out the door.

After Blossom had left noisily, Gregory turned to Miss Hortense and asked, "What was that about?"

Miss Hortense shook her head and cussed her teeth.

"Me na know, but that woman going get herself into a whole heap of trouble."

50

Melvin "Red" Bright

Miss Hortense's own investigation continued slowly but surely. On the first Saturday of the month, Tiny called, at 8 a.m. Jamaica time, with an update.

"No trace of Donovan Miller in St. Ann and as you know, that's where his people come from. Which is the surprise, really," said Tiny, the crackly line making his voice sound tinnier still, "because him still have family all 'bout ya so. But the funny thing is, if he was living in Texas, none of his family don't know 'bout that. Seem like him go a England and just disappear."

She wasn't surprised to hear Tiny confirm what she already knew.

There was something else that might interest Miss Hortense, though, said Tiny: "One of his aunties said that he was childhood friends with Melvin Bright."

"Melvin 'Red' Bright?" asked Miss Hortense, checking she was hearing correctly, given the long-distance phone call.

"You hear me right," said Tiny. "And we all know 'bout the badness of Melvin 'Red' Bright."

"Melvin Bright carried out dem robberies and murders in Jamaica when? Forty years ago now?"

"Yes, though you know people still talk 'bout the wickedness of that man? And dem never catch him."

Tiny was sorry not to be of more help, but he did tell her that she wasn't the only one searching for a man who had disappeared off the face of the earth. Someone else had been making inquiries about Danny Grant.

"Who is searching for Danny Grant?" Miss Hortense asked with urgency.

The best place for Hortense to be after a phone call like the one with Tiny was in her garden. Miss Hortense took a deep breath. The small north-facing garden was Miss Hortense's pride and joy. It wasn't an easy garden. She had inherited a mess when she bought the house off the old racist fool-fool man in 1966 and the garden had retained much of his bitterness. But Miss Hortense had worked hard on her knees with her hands in the soil, which was far too dry with far too much clay, and it had slowly surrendered. Now the air was filled with the sweet spicy aroma of lavender, thyme and rosemary and the musky scent of the Deep Secrets. She knew the garden's crevices, where best to put a plant if she wanted it to get sun or shade. Then there was the back of the garden, which she let grow wild; that was where she buried her other secrets, which would remain secrets as long as those damn blasted cats stopped digging. It was to the back of the garden that she looked now.

"Can I get you something?" A milky voice came from behind her, jolting her out of her reverie.

"No," said Miss Hortense, and she cussed her teeth. She rolled up her sleeves and moved to the rosebush.

"I could make us some pasta? With cheese?" said Sonia. "Or even with tuna. Do you have tuna?"

"No," said Miss Hortense, just as curtly. Pasta! "I understand I had a visitor." Hortense had been waiting over a week for Sonia to tell her.

"A visitor?" said Sonia. "Oh. Yes, the priest. Sorry," she added, "I completely forgot."

"And Rule Twelve?" inquired Miss Hortense.

"Sorry?" said Sonia.

"No strangers," said Hortense.

"But I thought he was your friend?"

Miss Hortense exhaled and rose from her knees. On rising she saw something in the potted hebes that made her blood boil.

"Damn blasted cats," she mumbled. She brushed past the girl, went into the shed and pulled out a spade and some small black bags. She scooped the poop that was sitting in the hebes into a bag, twisted the top of the bag into a knot and flung the bag high over the fence to the left.

"Dem fe do them dutty business in them own blasted garden. Not mine!" Miss Hortense said, and marched straight back into the house.

Later that night, when Sonia was sound asleep, Miss Hortense went out to the back garden with her flashlight in one hand and the spade in the other and started to dig. Ten minutes later she pulled out a small plastic bag. She took it into the house and blew off the residue dirt. Inside the bag was an old rusted tin. She opened the tin and several old notes, old shilling coins and halfpence burst out.

51

The Body in the Canal

In the morning, Miss Hortense called Blossom but the phone went to voicemail and Hortense didn't leave a message. She was starting to worry about what that woman was up to. But right now she needed to deal with somebody else. Hortense headed to the canal. She sat on the bench and looked over at the water. She had never known Fitz to be late and yet here he was, fifteen minutes late for a meeting Miss Hortense had summoned him to. Yes, that was right: "summoned." As she waited, a seagull pecked away at an old chip on the ground.

When he arrived, he approached slowly and took a heavy seat but left a gap between them.

"I've been coming here for years," said Hortense. "You know that?"

A cyclist whizzed past, the pebbles scattering on the path. The gull, who hadn't been disturbed, was still with them.

"How you get him here?" Miss Hortense didn't wait for him to answer. "You put him in a van?" Fitz shifted in his seat. "Who you borrow de van from? When he went in the water, how him stay? How quickly him sink? Him go deep, you tink?"

Fitz hung his head.

"Gregry told me a man in the bookie shop was trying to find out if the dead man at the bottom of the stairs had a scar on him chest. So, I am thinking perhaps it's Fitz and perhaps Fitz isn't so sure anymore that we got the right man. I can deal with that. I've had my doubts over the years too. How could a boy do all of that damage? And Blossom told me she see you in church. Well, Fitz doesn't go church. He didn't even mek it to him own child's christening. Even

206

if he was dying, Fitz wouldn't go church. But here is me thinking, maybe you just regretting what you did. Looking for some kind of forgiveness. And then I speak to Tiny, and him tell me somebody is asking around for a man named Danny Grant. Him tell me dat somebody was you, Fitz! Dat don't mek no blasted sense because Fitz said Danny Grant is dead. Is Fitz put Danny Grant in the canal thereso. So why you looking for a dead man, Fitz, in every nook and cranny 'cept for the one place you said you bury him in?"

Miss Hortense's voice was stiff with anger as the water gently lapped at the side of the canal.

Fitz was chewing his cheek. He cussed his teeth, took off his hat and twisted it in his hand.

"Hortense," he said, a tremble in his voice. "Let me explain."

Hortense folded her arms stiffly and stared straight ahead.

"When me find out it was Danny that worked at the garage on Slade Lane," Fitz began, "I went home and took the cutlass off the kitchen wall where it hung. I went to the boy's yard and waited outside out of sight. I watched as he entered. I only had one thing 'pon my mind, Hortense: to kill him. At around midnight, when I saw him turn off the lights, I went to the boy's door. The door busted open easily as I barged my shoulder inna it. The boy was on the floor on a mattress. He had no time to avoid my fist landing the first punch on him jaw. The boy, still half asleep, tried to get up but I hit him again and he stumbled back. I pulled him up, slammed me fist inna him body, and inna him ribs—bam, bam, bam—he stumbled back 'pon de floor. He had no time to raise his own fists in defense; no time to protest his innocence. I ripped off his undershirt and pulled him to his feet and back towards the light. I switched it on.

"There was the scar, rising like a tick on the boy's chest. The scar Pearl had told you she had put 'pon him body. That was his guilt. It wasn't big but it was there," Fitz said. "I hit him in his face again, harder this time, all of me weight behind it, rising to lean in more—bam, bam, bam—until I heard the boy's nose crack. I didn't give him no time to ready himself. I hit him again and he stumbled back, this time heavier. He knocked his head 'pon the wall as he went down. I couldn't see him. I couldn't hear him. Just the sound of my fists punching, breaking, busting open, for Pearl, for Daphne, for . . . Evie. I beat the boy so bad that my own body started to ache. And that's when I pulled out the cutlass. But when I looked down at the boy's bloodied body sprawled on the floor in front of me"—he swallowed hard—"I knew I didn't have to use it. I snapped the chain off the boy's neck, put the door back in place quietly and left.

"Now, like you said," said Fitz, combing his hand through his hair, "I needed a vehicle to move the body. But I couldn't get hold of a van until the evening the next day. But when I got back to the bedsit now, ready to move the body, well . . . I went in and, well . . ." Fitz combed his hand through his hair some more. "The body wasn't there."

"The body wasn't there?" asked Miss Hortense, in disgust.

"The place was clean, Hortense. Everything gone. And the body gone too. It was a professional job."

"All these years. Lawd, Fitz," said Hortense. Her face was twisted with anger.

"That boy had enemies, Hortense," said Fitz, "and is one of them clean up him body, so I didn't have to."

"How you know that, Fitz?" said Hortense. "How you even know he was dead?"

"He was dead!" protested Fitz loudly.

"You're not so sure anymore, Fitz, and that's why you searching for Danny Grant now. Why you couldn't just tell me the truth?"

Fitz shook his head. "Look how you were, Hortense." He still remembered the way her scream had chilled his blood. "You needed it to be over and it *was* over. It was just the body that disappear."

"But it wasn't bloody over!" she said to him with such force that the persistent gull flew off.

"So, what you think, Danny Grant is still alive?" he asked her.

Finally, she turned to look at Fitz.

"None of our inquiries have established that him is still alive and I have this." From her handbag, Miss Hortense pulled out the tin, recently dug up from her garden, and handed it to him.

"I found it when I went to his place after I left the hospital."

Miss Hortense had gone straight there after discharging herself, after Fitz had told her that Errol and Danny were dead. It was a

208

bedsit on Clarence Street. One room and a bathroom in a basement. The place where the Brute slept after he had destroyed so many lives. Entering it, she expected to feel closer to him, closer to his victims, but the place was clean. So clean in fact that it was the cleanness that she remembered most; the caustic smell of hydrogen peroxide and bleach.

"There wasn't a hair that I could look at, not a toothbrush, not a button on the floor," said Miss Hortense. "All traces that he had lived there, gone. But I did notice something as I stepped to leave. One of the floorboards creaked. I bent down and pulled at it and underneath I found two things—a Bible and that tin."

Fitz understood. "A dead man can't take his money with him, but a live man always will."

She raised herself heavily from the bench.

"Hortense? What you going do now?" Fitz called after her, but she left him and didn't look back.

52

Evie

The next morning, Miss Hortense went straight to Fitz's house. Despite her anger at his lie, she needed him. He seemed surprised to see her as she walked right in. She hadn't been to his house in many years. But it was just as she remembered. Sparse. He wasn't a man who was interested in comfort or modern conveniences. The front room had a settee and a table. The back room had a cooker and a fridge. The microwave must have been a recent addition, though he was clearly still suspicious of it, as it wasn't plugged in. There were no pictures of his children or his two wives. It was functional. Everything had a specific purpose. A half-empty bottle of whisky and a glass had their place on the table in the front room.

"You going have to go to Mr. Stewart's house," she told him as she sat down at the table.

He shook his head. "No way. I'm not going into no duppy house."

Miss Hortense continued as if she couldn't hear him.

"You are going to have to see if he has the scar."

"You think Garfield Stewart could be the Brute now?" he asked, shocked. "But you said—"

"Well, I could have been wrong," she interrupted, and gave him a look that made him quail. "Maybe the attacks were carried out by more than one man."

He couldn't believe what he was hearing come out of Hortense's mouth. She had been so sure the Brute had been responsible for all three attacks. He shook his head trying to take it in. "There is another man? And you tink is that man kill the person found at the bottom of Constance's stairs?"

Miss Hortense looked at him. She didn't yet know the answer.

While Fitz went to Mr. Stewart's house, Miss Hortense took another trip to visit Mavis Campbell. As she knocked on Mavis's door, she held in her hand a gift. And when Mavis C opened the door, she raised the small brick into Mavis's eyeline. The woman flushed a deep red and moved, with her head down, to let Miss Hortense in.

When Fitz came into Miss Hortense's house later that day, he was breathing out as if a bad smell rested underneath his nose. He looked like he'd been through a war, his normally slick suit was askew, and he was twitching.

"That man and that duppy you see," is all he said before he reached for the bottle of Wray & Nephew in Miss Hortense's cabinet without asking and poured himself a very large glass.

"The man don't have no scar on him chest," he said finally, still twitching. "But him have a whole heap a likkle fleas a crawl 'pon it." Fitz scratched himself some more.

"Mavis Campbell also confirmed that her husband didn't have a scar on his chest."

"Ralph?" asked Fitz, looking confused.

"Never mind," said Hortense. "At least we can eliminate the both of them from the attack on Pearl White."

When Sonia came in at a quarter to nine just after Fitz had left, she called in from the front room: "A letter came for you this afternoon when you was out, Miss Hortense. Did you see it? It was hand-delivered?" Sonia reached down to a drawer where Hortense would never have looked for a letter and pulled it out.

Miss Hortense grabbed the envelope from the girl. She noted it was already opened. She read the letter inside. As she read, she had to sit.

"When this come?" she asked Sonia urgently.

"This afternoon—I think one, maybe two. Just before I went out."

"You think?" said Miss Hortense sharply. "You see who post it?"

"The back of him," said Sonia. "A man, maybe."

"Old, young, tall, short?" asked Hortense, her voice quivering.

"Young, I think," said Sonia. "I think. He was wearing a hoodie or something. It was just a delivery boy. Is everything all right?"

The next morning, before daylight, Miss Hortense was back at Fitz's house. He blinked away the sleep in his eyes as he opened the door to her. She put her handbag down, but she didn't sit. She told him what Sonia had told her about the typewritten letter and how it had come to be delivered.

"Useless," said Fitz, wiping his eyes. She put the letter on the table in front of him. He got out his glasses and read:

Dear Mrs. Hortense,
Acts 2:38. Then Peter said unto them, Repent, and be baptized. I'm truly sorry for attacking your sister. Stop your investigating now or somebody else will get hurt.

"Lawd have mercy," said Fitz. He turned the letter over in his hand. "You think it's from Danny?"

"No." Miss Hortense was shaking her head and pacing the floor. "I think it was made to look as though it was from Danny."

"Who would do that?" Fitz asked. "Why you just don't get Gregory to do him police thing 'pon the letter and get de fingerprint dem?"

She looked at him then like he was crazy. "You don't see it?" She gestured at the note in his hand.

Fitz scanned the words again.

"Oh . . ." he said.

"Apart from me, unless there is another attacker, or Danny Grant is alive, which is unlikely, there is only three other somebody that is living know 'bout my sister. Her husband, Mr. Jean-Baptiste, Mr. McKenzie, and . . . you." She looked at Fitz. "Any of you could have sent me that letter."

"Me?" He looked at Hortense, incredulous. He sat down heavily and, despite the hour, poured himself a drink from the rum bottle on the table.

"You ever tell anyone 'bout what happen to Evie?" asked Miss Hortense to his back.

"No," said Fitz heavily. "I never tell a soul."

"You sure?"

"No," he said more loudly. Their relationship was changed. He had to repeat himself now, where a word would have sufficed before.

"You think is me send the letter, Hortense? You think me involved in Bone Twelve?"

"I going find out," Miss Hortense said, and she snatched the letter from Fitz and left.

Going back into Bone 12 meant Miss Hortense was knocking on a whole heap of doors she had closed a long time ago. And one of those doors belonged to Mr. Reginald Jean-Baptiste, Gregory's father.

Mr. Baptiste slowed as he reached his door and saw Hortense. He had aged but not enough to shed that same judging look.

"Well, you coming in?" he asked, not moving from the door.

"No," said Hortense. "I'm not staying. I just wanted a word with you."

Miss Hortense had never graced this house before and she hadn't gone to his second wedding twenty-nine years ago, either.

"Hortense," he said. "Everything all right?"

The night of Evie's attack, Reginald Jean-Baptiste called for Miss Hortense. There was a frantic knocking at Miss Hortense's door as Evie's husband stood in front of it. It felt like the coldest night Miss Hortense had ever experienced since coming to the country.

"Hortense? Come. Please, will you? Bring you bag."

Hortense's mind immediately jumped to Gregory. Just a little boy at that time and sickly as a baby. Reginald Jean-Baptiste assured her—"It's not the boy"—but said no more.

They drove in near silence, him driving too fast for the icy roads.

He drew up in front of their little rented house and pulled on the brake abruptly. They both rushed out, feet slipping and sliding on the path.

Gregory was sat on the stairs. "Go to bed, little man," Miss Hortense told him firmly. "I going come in in a minute to say you prayers with you. Go on now." He rose groggily and went in the direction of his room.

"She came in late," the husband said as he opened the door to their bedroom. A dim lamp on in the corner. He backed away and closed the door behind Hortense.

Evie's face was turned away from the door. The bedspread was covering most of her body. Miss Hortense saw the blood on the pillow in the dim light. On the side of Evie's cheek, the wound still weeping and oozing. Even before Hortense removed the bedspread, she knew what she was going to find underneath: everything she had seen on Daphne Stewart's body and heard about from Pearl, the places where the Brute had hit, slapped, kicked and bitten her. The places where he had yanked and pulled out her hair and held her down at her neck.

"Go to the hospital, please, Evie," Hortense begged, suddenly the little sister again.

"Nothing they can do to fix this," Evie said from wherever it was he had taken her. She never left that house alive again. Shame, shame written on her body and between her legs and on her face.

Evie's eyes were open but she wasn't focused on anything. She was gone. Her Evie who had loved to dance, who had been the life and soul, who could feel the rhythm more deeply than anyone Hortense had ever known. Her Evie, who had whispered secrets in her ear, who grabbed on to her hand so tightly as they ran past Mass Johnson's house, their hearts thumping in their chests. Hortense wanted to take the pain away, to tell her sister, *Come, we go home. Let's go back.* Back to the warm, life-giving sun, back to the veranda, back to Mamma and Pappa's. Back. But she couldn't say those words to her sister because that home didn't exist anymore; there was nothing to go back to. Hortense didn't know how to comfort her. Pearl had been angry; Daphne had tried to hold on to life; but Evie, Evie had already left them.

"Did you ever tell anyone 'bout what happened to Evie?" asked Hortense urgently. Mr. Jean-Baptiste pulled Hortense to one side. His voice was low.

214

"I would never," he said fiercely. "I would never speak to anybody about that. No one. Neither of that nor what happened afterwards. Why you come fe ask me now? You find out who it was?" he asked harshly.

Hortense was silent.

"I loved your sister. I wouldn't do anything to hurt her. And I wouldn't do that to her memory," he said.

Miss Hortense didn't doubt the love. If anything, that man had loved her sister too much; suffocated her with his damned, blasted love.

He lowered his voice. "I don't know is what you got going on, Hortense. I don't want to know neither. But I don't want Gregory caught up inna it and I don't want him knowing nothing about this, you hear?" His tone was still low but threatening now. "Gregory must never know. He must *never* know."

53

The Promise of Mr. McKenzie

Later that evening, after Gregory had eaten and left, Miss Hortense called Blossom and, getting her answering machine again, left a message. "Blossom, you there? It's Hortense. When you get this you must call me back. You hear? Immediately." Miss Hortense put the phone down and shook her head. Blossom was one stubborn woman. She was starting to feel uneasy about what Blossom might be up to. She went into the kitchen.

Gungo Peas Soup

½ pt dried green gungo peas
½ pt corn
½ pt salted pig's tail
½ quart water
1 onion
1 scallion stalk
1 pt coconut milk
1 tbsp flour

Miss Hortense had already soaked the peas overnight and the salted meat for a good four hours. The letter didn't come from Mr. Reginald Jean-Baptiste. She boiled water. She was almost certain that Danny Grant was dead, even if she didn't know yet who had killed him. If Danny Grant was dead, then he couldn't have sent the letter to Miss Hortense. Either it had come from another man who was the attacker, or it had to be from one of the two people she had confided in, or someone they had told.

When the pot was boiling vigorously, she put in the peas, meat and corn and cooked until the meat and the peas were tender. There was Fitz, the man she had once trusted with her life. And there was Mr. McKenzie, who was incapacitated on his deathbed. He had been the last one to see Evie, Daphne and Pearl. To prepare their bodies for the grave. But why would either of them send such a letter? What would either of them gain by stopping her investigation now?

Miss Hortense made and added the dumplings, then poured in the coconut milk and allowed the pot to simmer gently.

The next morning, Miss Hortense went to Blossom's house and banged on her door. But if Blossom was in, she didn't answer and Miss Hortense headed to the McKenzies. She asked Myrtle if she could talk to her husband.

"Well, he is not too good," said Myrtle, shaking her head and barring the entrance to their home.

"It's important," pleaded Hortense.

Myrtle looked Miss Hortense up and down but then her gaze rested above Miss Hortense's right shoulder.

"Myrtle? What is it?" asked Hortense.

"Him stop use the pencil," she said.

Miss Hortense moved into the house and held on to Myrtle's hand. No words were said. Myrtle wiped her face, sighed and opened the door to the front room.

Hortense slid her bag down on the chair. She wetted her lips and leaned in close to Mr. McKenzie.

"Did you ever tell anybody about what happened to Evie? Please, it's important you try to tell me the truth."

Myrtle leaned in close too.

McKenzie opened his mouth, but nothing came out. He tried to shake his head and it looked like he was using every ounce of his energy to do so.

"Thank you, sir," Hortense said. She gently held his hand for a moment and left the room.

217

Outside in the passageway, Myrtle took Miss Hortense to one side. "What the problem?" Myrtle asked.

"Did Mr. McKenzie ever talk to you 'bout Bone Twelve? 'Bout the details of the attacks?"

"Oh no," said Myrtle, shaking her head. "He kept all that part of Pardner business to himself."

"Thank you," said Hortense, touching Myrtle's hand before she left.

On July 22, 1970, after she went to Danny Grant's bedsit, after the news of Errol's death, it was to Mr. McKenzie's that Miss Hortense dragged her aching body. She stood breathless, bent over on his doorstep, a hand on the wall to support herself. He told Myrtle, who had rushed to the door and was shaking her head at him, that he would handle this, and ushered Miss Hortense into his home.

She went to his house because he was the man you went to when someone died. She knew he would be handling the funeral arrangements for Errol and she wanted to see what she could do to support Precious and her daughter, Likkle Sonia. "Is there anything?" she asked. The words still hurt, but she had to get them out. "If there is anything at all?"

He had stopped her then, sat her down and told her carefully what she already knew.

"Hortense, people is blaming you. Okay?" He looked at her deeply. "You need to give people time, okay? And you need to give Precious time. It was her husband that died." He gave her another moment. "You can't go to the funeral. Okay? You must stay away."

They sat in silence for a long time before he moved over to her and took up her hand in the softness of his, the warmth radiating up almost to her heart, but not quite.

"You know what you have to do, don't it?" he said after a while, looking at her directly. "If you don't let this thing go, it going kill you."

He said he had seen death in all its forms, from bodies mangled by traffic accidents to the unsated appetite of cancer, freak accidents that caught the body by surprise, asphyxiation at the hands of men in authority.

"One of the worst deaths," he said, "is the living one. People walking

218

and talking and breathing but for all intents and purposes them is dead too." He looked at her then.

"It will eat you up, Hortense, and bury you alive, okay? Here you are chasing down a man when what you is really looking for is you sister. Well, you not going find her, you hear? No matter how hard you look. She gone, Hortense. She gone."

Hortense let out another guttural sound, from where she couldn't tell, but it was everything she hadn't let out since Evie died.

And then she told Mr. McKenzie what she had told only two people before. "She ended her life because of what that Brute did to her," Hortense said. "And he got to her because I wasn't watching."

Miss Hortense's body heaved as the words came out.

"I am not a Bible man," Mr. McKenzie said, leaning over to steady her. "I leave all that kinda thing to me wife. None of us know what lies on the other side of the breath, what judgment or reckoning we face. But is not for we to seek that which is bigger than us."

"Do you think she was in pain?" Hortense asked.

He considered and then said, "When a person come to me, they are as much the person in death as in life. I touch them like how I'm touching you. And I am as close as I am to you now; closer. I wash them down and I talk to them. Okay? Yes, I talk to them. And I did talk to her."

He let that land.

"I thanked her for her life. No matter who they are or what they have done, I thank them. I thank them for the gifts that they gave to the people around them. She did give you gifts. She gave you a nephew. I thank them for the time that they served because we are all serving time. I wash down their body and you know that when I'm looking at the person, there is only peace. She was at peace, Hortense. Whatever despair there was inna her life, whatever torment, there is only peace now and it's one of the most beautiful things inna this world to have. You trying to control this thing but it's not within your control, Hortense. You trying to understand what you cannot see. She made a decision to end her life. Now you must live with it and stop blaming yourself for something you couldn't have done nothing about."

"She's not coming back?" said Hortense, the question surprising her.

"No," said Mr. McKenzie. "She's not. And you going have to let her go. You hear? Promise me, Hortense. Promise me that you going let Bone Twelve and her go."

At the time she had lost so much that she had promised him. Planted the roses to never let herself forget. Hidden away from everybody.

But as she thought about it now, she wondered why, even as she knew what she did about Danny Grant, it had been so important for Mr. McKenzie that she stopped her investigation then.

Miss Hortense was still trying to contact Blossom, but the phone was now ringing out. Fitz came to visit her later that day. He brought with him a guilty conscience.

"That girl gone out?" he asked, shaking the rain off his hat. He meant Sonia.

Miss Hortense nodded but she knew he already knew Sonia had left the house five minutes prior, as she'd seen him watching. Miss Hortense went into the kitchen and continued peeling her onions.

"You find out more about the letter?" Fitz asked.

"Is that why you come visit?" asked Hortense.

Fitz scratched his hair and played with his hat.

"Why would I send the letter? What benefit is that to me?" His jaw was tightening.

Miss Hortense crushed some garlic with the back of a knife.

"Why would you tell me 'bout a man dead in the canal?" She watched him closely. "The note with the dead man in Constance's house, the letter, the girl coming to Bigglesweigh, it's all pointing to something."

"And that's why you have the gal in your house? Because you think she have something to do with all a dis?" He shook his head. "You should never have let her come inna your yard bringing bad luck, Hortense."

"You telling me?" asked Hortense, a light amusement in her tone.

"All I'm saying is that girl is trouble."

"Trouble which part?" Hortense sounded only mildly interested as she squashed another clove of garlic with the flat of her palm on the knife.

"That girl looking fe some kind of revenge," said Fitz, watching.

"You don't think I know that?"

"Well, I been doing some investigation of my own," said Fitz.

"Oh, you have?" said Hortense, now peeling an Irish potato. Fitz could find out things when he wanted to, she knew that.

"That gal isn't who you think she is," he said. "She couldn't wait for the mother to die. Flung out every piece of her belongings before Precious was cold in the ground."

Miss Hortense smiled to herself, wondering where Fitz got his information from.

"She's dangerous. She is not some poor pickney. Just like Stanley, you trying to fix something that is not in your gift to fix. Cha man, Hortense, you can't see what happening?" he said, shaking his head. "She taking you for a damned fool and you letting her do it."

Miss Hortense took a seat at the kitchen table opposite him.

"You hear yourself, Fitz?" asked Hortense. "This isn't about Sonia. This is about you."

He looked at Miss Hortense, shook his head, then grabbed his hat and stormed out of her house, slamming her door behind him for the first time in his life.

54

Watch Stinky Na

That morning, Gregory walked into the station at 9:16 with all the evidence he'd gathered over the past weeks neatly tucked into his backpack. He had details of all the trips to the takeaway shop, the nightclubs and the canal. He headed to Superintendent McGraf's office. This sort of case, well, it needed to be dealt with at the top. McGraf was one of those for whom policing ran in the blood; a famous grandfather and father looked down on him from the wall. All had similar red noses and plenty of hair.

"Well, take a seat," McGraf said to Gregory. "What can I help you with, son?"

"I've got evidence, sir, of what I think could be illegal money-laundering activity." Gregory went into his backpack. Took out the pictures. "Nigel Brown. And those are his associates, Richard Dudney and Germaine Banton. Both are known to us, sir."

McGraf breathed in heavily.

"You see," continued Gregory, "I was investigating a break-in at the community center on the Chatsworth Estate, which led me to investigate Richard Dudney, and he led me to Germaine Banton. I think they're using his takeaway shop as one of the businesses to wash the money, sir. And the mastermind behind it all is this man, Nigel Brown." Gregory pointed at his picture. His finger landed on his forehead.

Gregory showed McGraf the logs he'd been keeping. "You see, that's where Dudney and Nigel Brown have made contact with each other, and here's where Banton and Dudney do the drop-offs."

Gregory pointed at various entries in the log.

"And that's it?" asked McGraf when the backpack was empty.

"That's everything, sir," said Gregory, leaning forwards. "In the pictures you can see large bags filled with cash, sir."

McGraf picked up one of the pictures. A hazy image of the side of a man carrying a bin liner.

"Hold on, son," he said. "How d'you know it's cash in the bag? Nothing in this picture shows that."

"Well, it's obvious, sir. If we could just get a warrant to—"

"Who authorized this covert surveillance?" interrupted McGraf.

"Well, sir, because of the sensitivity, I took it upon myself to carry out the investigation."

"So no one else has been involved?" asked McGraf, scratching his gray hair. He raised his head. You could see up his nostrils.

"No, sir, not to date," said Gregory. "Just me." Well, there was his aunty as well, but he didn't know the extent of her investigations and it wouldn't do to mention her.

McGraf ran his hand through his hair. After a moment he said, "Well, I'm disappointed in you, Jean-Baptiste." He turned towards his family on the wall. "We've been here before, haven't we, son?"

"But that was different, sir," interrupted Gregory.

"Off on a frolic of your own," McGraf shot back. "Sounds familiar to me."

Gregory sometimes really wished his aunty wasn't his aunty.

McGraf rolled his chair further into his desk. "This could get you into an awful lot of trouble, young man. Illegal surveillance, the targeting of innocent members of the public."

"But—"

"This isn't evidence, son," said McGraf, scattering the papers on his desk. "This looks malicious to me. Against an upstanding member of the community? A successful businessman at that."

So Superintendent McGraf knew who Nigel Brown was? "But, sir—"

McGraf interrupted him again. "Do you know the flak we'd get? It would be a bloody nightmare. Why are you going to all this trouble, son?" McGraf narrowed his eyes at Gregory. "Do you know him? Have you two got a connection?"

"Me?" asked Gregory, incredulous. "Why would I know him?"

"Well," said McGraf, leaning in as if he were about to divulge a secret. Instead, he raised his caterpillar eyebrows, making his nostrils flare even wider.

"No," said Gregory, leaning back. "I don't know him. I mean, his mother was an acquaintance of—"

"Well, there you go." McGraf folded his arms as if he had solved a far greater crime. "First rule of policing," he said. "Don't let personal relationships cloud your judgment."

"But, sir—"

McGraf raised his hand again, and with his other hand slid the photographs, the logs, all Gregory's hard work into the bin next to his desk.

"I'm doing you a favor here, son. This could be a disciplinary. You'll take some leave. Immediately. Then come back fresh and ready to do *your* job." McGraf raised his head, the nostrils flaring again, and pointed to the door.

That evening, Camille was running a bath and thinking about her mum. She missed her voice, even if it had been mainly used to sing her brother's praises. *Did you know, Nigel has just bought a new house, and now a fancy car?* Camille was really trying to find peace with him. It was her mum's decision to leave him everything in her will. That wasn't his fault. And maybe that was the right decision. Nigel was, after all, a successful businessman. And look at what was happening to the community center under her management. She hated to admit it, but it was on the brink. What if it had to close? How was she going to explain that to the community? To all those people who relied on it? Another epic failure to add to her list.

When the door knocker went, she threw on her blue dressing gown carelessly so it just about covered the bare skin underneath and her recently loosened locks tumbled about her shoulders and down her back. It wasn't her daughter, Jasmine, on the doorstep as she had expected, but the policeman from the community center, staring back at her. The one who had been obsessed with his watch. He looked almost normal without his uniform on. She saw him glance down at her shins, ankles and feet, free of the polish she had just taken off. She tucked the left behind the right.

He cleared his throat. "Sorry to bother you at home," he said. "I said I'd get back to you about the break-in at the community center." His voice was low. He had dark circles around his eyes—she did too, she knew.

"Yes," she said. Her voice was tight.

"It was a man called Richard Dudney, otherwise known as Dice."

"Who?" she said, clutching at her dressing gown, alert to the gushing tap upstairs.

"I'd, um, ask your brother if I was you." There was a brief moment when their eyes met, just as the rage she had been hoping to soak away ignited again.

"Don't let anyone know you heard this from me, okay?"

And he turned on his heel and left.

55

The Roasting Tin

At 4:45 a.m. the following morning, Miss Hortense woke abruptly, drenched in her own sweat. Unanswered questions were swirling about in her head and she hadn't heard from Blossom in over a week. She had a sudden urgent desire to look in her black notebook, but she searched high and low and couldn't find it. She got up and went to the kitchen and made a pot of strong tea. She needed something more to line her unsettled stomach, so she reached into the back bottom cupboard to pull out the roasting tin for the breadfruit, but it wasn't there with the Dutch pot and the grater.

There was one hell of a clanging and banging as Miss Hortense flung open drawers and turned them upside down looking for the roasting tin, which was not where she always left it, where it had stayed for the past twenty years.

Miss Hortense hadn't lived with another somebody since her student nursing days. Not since she was stuck in that one box room with one bathroom between the ten of them squawking white girls, and was asked more than once why she didn't wash with soap.

Is that why it doesn't come off?

She had been so lonely then, living with those girls, that she had packed her bags and gone to the train station, ready to go all the way back home to Jamaica. And then as the train pulled in, she had the same thought as always: *But where is home now?*

Miss Hortense could just about put up with Sonia's strange ways. Coming upon Miss Hortense suddenly in the garden when she was having her alone time; watching Miss Hortense in the front room as she sat in her chair and watched her program; leaping up the stairs and into her room when Miss Hortense put the key in the front door. Miss Hortense could just about put up with the space the girl had taken in the bathroom—two shelves, not the half of one she had left for her—and the cigarette ash she found on the windowsill, and the clutter she had started to gather around the coffee table. But Miss Hortense had no tolerance for any changes in her kitchen. That was unforgivable. The sugar pot moved to the left instead of the right, the eggs put in the fridge rather than in the cupboard, the spoons put where the forks should be, and now Miss Hortense was flinging plates and cutlery, serving spoons and plastic serving jugs, the Dutch pot and the mortar and pestle all over the place, because if she couldn't find where the damned blasted roasting tin was, then everything might as well go to pot.

Sonia was woken from her sleep by an almighty commotion downstairs. In her half sleep she thought someone was robbing the house and smashing it up. As she crept down the stairs carrying hair tongs in her hand for protection, she only just remembered to avoid touching the walls and banister; the soil was still hitched up in her nails and staining her fingertips. She was expecting a confrontation with an intruder, only to find Miss Hortense in the kitchen flinging several plates into the sink. One by one they cracked on each other.

"Um, is everything all right, Miss Hortense?" she asked, tiptoeing with her words and hiding her hands behind her back.

"Can't find me blasted roasting tin," said Miss Hortense, not turning around. She was now opening the washing machine.

"Your roasting tin? Um, I don't think it's in the washing machine?" Sonia said, in a small, cloggy voice among the cacophony.

"Well, if it's not where I put it, where it should be, where it's meant to be, where make most sense, that means it could be any damn blasted place where it don't mek sense including here." She was in the fridge now; out came the butter but, thank God, not the bottle of milk.

"Um," said Sonia. "Was it the big roasting tin that you keep in the bottom there?" She pointed to the back bottom cupboard. "The one that had black all over it?"

Miss Hortense moved on to the cupboards underneath the worktop. Bags of grain and cornmeal were dashed onto the floor. They burst open.

"Because if it was that one," said Sonia quickly, "I thought it was a bit old? So . . . I kind of threw it away?"

Miss Hortense slammed the cupboard door closed and backed onto a chair by the small table. The kitchen was in disarray, plates broken, the contents of the cupboards lying everywhere.

"God, I'm sorry," said Sonia. "I didn't think it would mean so much."

Miss Hortense raised her hand to tell the girl to hush. For her own sake more than anything else. Miss Hortense rose in one swift movement and went towards the back door.

"I can buy you another one tomorrow," said the girl after her. An ice-cool breeze came into the kitchen from the open door. And then Sonia heard an intake of breath and "Oh my Lawd Jesus!"

Sonia rushed out the back to find Miss Hortense kneeling in front of one of her plants.

"Oh God!" said Sonia, raising her hand to her mouth.

It was the rosebush. The one that she had seen Miss Hortense so tenderly nurture. The red petals lay scattered on the small path like droplets of blood. The plant itself was completely pulled out of the ground. Large holes had been dug around it and several stems were snapped in half and coming out at angles. All her other plants near the rosebush looked fine.

"The cats? Why would they do that?" Sonia asked, bending down to touch what was left of the plant.

"It's dead," said Miss Hortense, from a place deep in her belly.

"Maybe if we just . . ." Sonia reached down to try to right the plant, but as soon as she let go, it fell back to the ground like a fatally wounded soldier.

"Leave it. You know how long this ya bush been here? You know why it's here?" Hortense asked, her voice shaky.

Sonia shook her head.

"Go back to bed," she told Sonia.

"But—"

"Go," said Hortense firmly. Sonia turned and went back into the house.

Hortense rose to her feet.

"I planted that rosebush in the soil years ago," she said softly to the morning light, her voice cracking. "To remember two of the most important people inna my life. Them both dead and gone. And is me one to blame."

56

The Attack

That evening, Blossom called Sonia on her mobile. "You can come and get me please?" she asked. Sonia could barely hear her. "I'm at the po-lease station. I want to leave here as soon as possible. Something very bad has happened. But don't tell Hortense."

Of course, Miss Hortense insisted that Sonia tell her everything, after she overheard Sonia shouting, "Miss Blossom? I can't hear you. Police, did you say?" She also insisted that she would accompany Sonia. Her heart was pounding in her chest the whole journey in Sonia's fishy-smelling car. What harm had Blossom come to now?

Hortense was surprised to hear when she got to the station that Gregory wasn't on his shift as usual. Once they had found Blossom in a small interview room, Miss Hortense was relieved to see that, at least on the outside, her friend looked okay, if a little shaken. Miss Hortense took out her bottle of rum from her handbag and insisted Blossom take two long swigs from it.

"Now tell me everything that happened," she said.

So Blossom told Miss Hortense and Sonia the story.

"I found out, through following Constance's daughter-in-law, that she went to the leisure center every Tuesday and Thursday at seven o'clock. So this evening at six o'clock, I caught the number 84 bus to the leisure center and waited with me likkle camera in the car park to get evidence for the motif. I was going snap photographs of her and her young lover that we did see her with at the shopping center. I was going show that she had a motif for killing Constance and therefore prove beyond all and any reasonable doubt that that is what she did."

230

Miss Hortense cleared her throat.

Blossom blinked at her, and then continued. "I was in the car park and I watched her get out of her car. A man approached her. He was tall, a mask covered his face and a hood was pulled over his head, and he grabbed her from behind. He said something to her and then he hit her and she dropped. Then he came towards me, pulled at the camera and ran away with it."

"And it was you who called the ambulance for the daughter-in-law?" Sonia asked.

Blossom nodded.

"Well, is she badly hurt?" asked Sonia.

Blossom nodded. "She wasn't moving when them took her away."

"And this person, did you get a good look at who he was?" Sonia asked.

"No, not really," said Blossom, ashamed.

When Blossom saw the man hit Yvonne, she just froze. She could have shouted, approached him to frighten him off, but she froze. She felt such shame as she explained this to the policeman with a large pimple on his nose who had interrupted her covert operation and taken her to the police station.

On further questioning from Miss Hortense, and three more swigs from the bottle of rum, Blossom remembered three details she had, in all of the confusion and anxiety, forgotten. One, that the attacker was wearing a shiny jacket; two, that he had on a sparkly gold watch; and three, that he smelled of takeaways.

Miss Hortense reached across and patted Blossom's hand. She realized she had been wrong. Excluding Blossom from her own investigation had done the opposite of what she had intended and driven Blossom right towards the danger.

"Hortense, I can't do it on me own," said Blossom in a very little voice, and Miss Hortense looked at her with such kindness, Blossom felt something in her break. "Me heart can't tek the violence," she said. "I don't think the Looking Into Bones business is for me again, after all."

57

The Queen Elizabeth

The next morning, Hortense asked Sonia to take her directly to the Queen Elizabeth Hospital.

"Only family allowed," said the nurse at the station, not looking up. "Are you family?"

"We aren't," Sonia said too readily. "But we know the woman that found her after the attack."

"Well, I'm sorry," said the nurse, her head still buried in her form.

"We won't be long," said Sonia, with a sweet smile that the nurse refused to see.

"Sister Hortense?" said a plump white woman bounding towards them. "It is you, isn't it, Hortense? Oh, my goodness, I knew it was you. You haven't changed a bit. I haven't seen you in—"

"Twenty years," said Hortense with a smile.

"Twenty years. Is it? No," said the woman coming upon them. "It can't be? Well, I suppose it must be. Bloody Nora."

The woman was soon ushering them away from the nurses' desk.

"It's all changed. Like bloody drill sergeants now," she said, looking in the direction of the nurse, who was still buried.

"I'm back in the café. It's been nearly three years since I've been back working there," continued the woman. "We went to Majorca. But then the same thing that happened to your sister happened to my Len." And the nurse leaned forward and mouthed a word silently to Miss Hortense.

Miss Hortense stopped and took the woman's hand in hers.

"Well, it was a long time ago," said the woman. After a moment she removed her hand from Hortense's. "But I had to return because of Len, and lucky for me I got me old job back. Been here ever since." She beeped a card on a set of double doors that said *No Entry—Staff Only.*

She looked at Sonia and said with a wink: "Be careful of this woman. She doesn't miss a trick. Through there to the right," she said, pushing the door open.

When they reached the room they needed, Yvonne Brown was sleeping. She had a large purple-red swelling down the left side of her face. Miss Hortense took the notes from the bottom of the bed and studied them. Yvonne started to rouse.

"Anthony?" she shouted.

"That must be the name of her lover," Sonia whispered to Miss Hortense.

Sonia moved closer to the bed. "We are friends of the woman who found you. Blossom? She called the ambulance for you?"

"Is Nigel here yet?" Yvonne asked groggily.

"I know this is a difficult time fe you," said Miss Hortense, looking at the bruising, "but we wanted to ask you some questions about the attack."

"I've already said what I need to say to the police," said Yvonne quickly. "I don't remember anything." She eased herself up in the bed. "Who did you say you were again?"

"My name is Miss Hortense."

Yvonne opened her eyes wider to look at Hortense, then leaned back. "You were at the funeral," she said.

"Is there anything more you remember about the attack?" asked Hortense gently.

"No," said Yvonne.

"Miss Hortense can help find the man that did this," said Sonia. "She's very good at finding people." Miss Hortense gave Sonia a side-eye.

Yvonne sat up some more.

"Look, I don't need your help. My husband will sort it," she said shakily.

"The man that attacked you," said Miss Hortense. "He said something to you. Do you remember what he said?"

"I don't know," said Yvonne. "Something from the Bible."

Miss Hortense's stomach started to turn. "Can you remember the words?" she asked with dread, already knowing the answer.

On the way out of the hospital, Sonia said, "But that's the same verse on the note found with the body at the bottom of the stairs. That means there's a connection?"

"Well now, that's obvious, isn't it," said Miss Hortense, irritated. The better question was why.

Then Sonia started to nudge her. She was looking towards the front desk, where a good-looking young man in a matching tracksuit with neat cornrows was engaging in conversation with the same nurse who had barred their entry.

"That's her lover, *Anthony*," whispered Sonia. "The one Miss Blossom and I followed."

The man was let through with no problems at all.

When they got to Sonia's little silver car, Miss Hortense eased herself into the passenger seat. She rubbed at her throbbing leg.

Sonia suddenly started patting herself down. "Oh, no," she said. "I must have left my phone on the ward. Don't worry." She looked at Miss Hortense's leg. "You stay here. I won't be a minute."

Miss Hortense raised an eyebrow as she watched Sonia make her way eagerly towards the hospital entrance that directed patients towards A&E and the café, and not towards the entrance that read *Outpatients and Minor Injuries* from which they had just exited.

58

Till Death Us Do Part

When Yvonne arrived back at home, it was gone midnight. Nigel had sent one of his minions to pick her up from the hospital. He didn't even have the decency to come and get her himself and—surprise, surprise—he wasn't at home when she arrived. She didn't even get to shout at him. The house was in darkness; all surface-shiny and put away, but on the inside it was rotting, just like her.

She climbed the stairs slowly. She pulled a suitcase from under the bed in their room. She opened drawers and flung his things in: pants, shirts, ties, shoes, his prized watches. She dumped them all in the open case. She was hurting. Not just the soreness of where she'd been hit and had fallen, but deep inside too.

She slid the suitcase, jam-packed with his things, down the stairs. She watched it tumble down, step after step, banging onto the walls, chipping the Almond Eggshell and the glossy skirting boards, scuffing up the brown leather of the case as it went. She left the case where it landed in the hall, half on its side, waiting like a dog for its master to come home and take it out.

She poured herself a glass of whisky. Then another. She took long, hard swigs and after a while it did what it always did, which was to numb her from the inside out. Her mouth felt dry. She lay on the couch and dozed until she heard the loud rev of the engine on the drive and then a minute later his key in the door.

As he came in, she threw the glass at him. Of course, it missed, bouncing off the armchair and landing intact on the carpet, its concentrated contents spilling.

"You couldn't even come and get me from the hospital." Her voice was hoarse, as if she'd been shouting for hours. Feeling the effects of the whisky and groggy from the pain medication, she slumped further in the chair.

"I've been at work," is all he said.

She laughed. "Work?"

He walked right past the suitcase and poured himself a glass of the whisky.

"Have you found out who it was? I could have been killed," she said to him. In her head, the words sounded brutal. But when she heard them, heard how he would hear them, they sounded whiny, nothing more than pinpricks; the sound rather than the words causing discomfort.

Out of habit she bit her lip. But he wasn't looking.

"And yet here you are," he said coolly.

"You're a pig. The world sees one thing, but behind closed doors, I know what you are." She was shouting now, losing her voice with it.

"What does that make you, married to me, then?" he asked.

It was a good question and Yvonne cried. She hadn't meant to. She still had so much to say to him. She knew his secrets, she wrote his letters, and yet now she could hardly get any words out. There was a time when he would have at least sought to comfort her with something shiny. He looked her up and down and then across to the empty glass on the carpet.

"Didn't they put you on medication or something?" The words were bitter as he said them; accusing. Getting to the place that all their arguments got to in the end: that it was her fault that the rooms upstairs were empty yet overspilling instead with her clothes and jewelry.

"The police came to see me," she said. "And they took a statement."

"You said nothing," he said, turning to her for the first time. "You know if anything happens to me it will be bad for you."

She hated him more than she had ever hated anybody. She wanted to get up and scratch his eyes out, slap him about his head. Take the skin off his face.

"And that friend of your mother's, Miss Hortense, came to visit me too," she said, the words like venom.

For the first time in the conversation, his shoulders tensed.

He came up behind her on the settee, could have reached out and touched the back of her head with his smooth hands. Instead he said:

"Don't ever drive my car again. You're messing up my clutch. And cover that up—you look a mess." And he picked up his briefcase and went back out the front door, leaving her curled in her own hate and desperate loneliness.

59

Split Bridges

So far, in the search for the culprit in Yvonne's attack, Miss Hortense had a tall man with his face covered by a mask and a hood pulled over his head and the three additional bits of information that Blossom had provided: the shiny jacket, the gold watch and the smell of take-aways. It wasn't hard to put two and two together and come up with the dry-skin boy, Germaine Banton. Either the boy was stupider than Miss Hortense had thought (and the bar was already quite low), or there was more to Germaine Banton's involvement in the attack than met the eye—because how would he have known about the Bible verse?

Germaine Banton, as she saw it, had two connections to her case. The next evening, just after 10 p.m., Miss Hortense went to the Rushden Industrial Estate to explore the first.

She found Nigel Brown's shiny car at the front of Unit 44, the door unlocked and him hunched over a makeshift desk studying a set of architectural drawings.

When she reached the desk, he looked up at her and said, "Well, look who it is, the busybody."

She saw from the corner of her eye the black bin liners. "On Thursday evening, your wife was attacked. Did you hire somebody to do it, Mr. Brown?"

He reached his arms behind his head, leaned back. His big belly popped out.

"Why would I hire somebody?" he said, and sat forwards in his chair.

"Thou shalt not kill," Miss Hortense said.

238

"Are you accusing me of something?" He tapped his big forehead with a pencil.

"Thou shalt not . . ." Miss Hortense repeated, and left space for him to finish the next verse. A man who knew the Bible, who had instructed Germaine Banton to whisper it into his wife's ear, who believed in its sentiment, was likely to finish the sentence without even thinking, or at least shift uncomfortably under its weight.

Instead he said: "Is it true what Mummy said? That you drove a man to his death?" A broad smile appeared on his face. He had the big forehead, yes, but he also resembled his mother around the goatish mouth.

"Do you know your wife is having an affair?" Miss Hortense asked.

"Is she? Well, good on her." The smile turned into laughter. The laughter seemed to take over his whole body. Miss Hortense turned to go. It was clear that the attack on Yvonne had nothing to do with him as a jealous husband.

"But now, your turn," he shouted after her. "Who else do you think carried out the attack on my wife, Miss Hortense?"

She had no allegiance to Germaine Banton and so she tossed his name into the room like a bomb. Nigel stopped laughing then.

"You know something?" said Miss Hortense, coming back to his desk. She looked squarely at him. "You see you likkle plan dem?" She referenced the architectural drawings on the table, where, clearly laid out in red, were plans for demolition of the community center, church and undertaker's, and for new blocks of flats in their place.

This made Nigel sit up. Miss Hortense leaned in. "Over my dead body will you touch so much as a brick in any one of dem Pardner buildings." And she left, not bothering to shut the door behind her.

Later that night, Nigel drove Dice to the car park again, the one that faced the canal. He hadn't said a word to him on the drive until now.

"Know who built the cut?" asked Nigel.

"Nah," said Dice. He wasn't touching up the interior this time. He was sitting quite straight, long legs tucked. He'd heard Nigel was on the rampage.

"Sir George Lovely. A canal built for commerce. Know what they are?" Nigel pointed to two steep winding paths adjoining the canal then rising to a bridge. "Split bridges for horses. To minimize interruption of profit."

"Oh yeah," said Dice. He couldn't really see what Nigel was going on about. Why would you need a horse to go over a canal?

"There's two irritants affecting my profit now. Germaine Banton is one of them," said Nigel. "So you know what to do."

Dice nodded.

"And that old busybody, Miss Hortense, is the other."

Dice nodded again.

Nigel started up the engine, it roared underneath his foot, and they sped off.

60

Donovan Miller

Althea called Hortense from Texas the following evening at a quarter to eight. Miss Hortense wasn't expecting to hear from her.

"Aunty Hortense?" she said. The round, honeyed voice at a distance, but pushing through the receiver.

"You left a message on my answerphone a few weeks ago?" It had been nearly five.

"I did some investigations about this man, Donovan Miller? Well, if it's the same Donovan Miller," she said broad and treacly, "there is quite a lot of information I found out about him. Do you have time now to talk?"

After she put the phone down, Hortense rolled up her sleeves and raised her skirts to her knees. She put the metal bowl between them and leaned down hard on the grater. Many of the threads of Bone 12 and its new incarnation were starting to reveal themselves, but there were still a number of outstanding questions, and it was going to take her at least two batches of the gizzadas to work through them.

Gizzadas

½ tsp rose water
1 tsp mixed spice
½ pt cold water
1 coconut
1¼ lb brown sugar
¼ tsp nutmeg

2 cups flour
¼ pound cold shortening
¼ pound cold margarine
salt to taste

Miss Hortense grated and grated the coconut, until small white flecks filled a third of the bowl. She reached up, took out the all-purpose flour from the overhead cupboard and sieved it and a pinch of salt into another bowl that she took down from the cupboard to her left. She cut the shortening and margarine into the white floury mixture and beat it until the mixture started to give and formed a light crumble. She got the mug of water and added drops to the flour, slimy on her hand. She used her right hand to roll and roll the dough, something she had been doing since before she could remember; she knew instinctively it had to come good, you just needed the patience.

She floured her hand once more, rolled the dough into a ball, covered it in some cling film and put it in the bottom of the fridge. She lit the gas cooker, boiled brown sugar and water until it formed a syrup in the bottom of the pan, running smoothly along her wooden spoon, shiny and golden. She added a drop of rose water, the fragrance that reminded her of her mother, floral and sweet; she grated nutmeg, the nutty, peppery scent tickling her nose like her father's cigars. She mixed it all together before adding the grated coconut and watched the sugary syrup soak it up. When the pastry had been in the fridge for about eighty minutes, she took it out, rolled it on the floured surface and used a saucer as a template to cut the dough into circles. She molded each circle into a small case and used her fingers to pinch around the edge. She filled the coconut mixture in the little cases and baked.

After the second batch, the milky voice said: "Miss Hortense, I just wanted to let you know, it's getting late. I just wondered if you needed help?"

"No thank you, child," said Miss Hortense to Sonia.

"Are you okay?" asked the girl.

"Yes, my dear, I nearly finish," she said in the sweetest voice she could muster. She had the measure of Sonia, but for now she had bigger fish to fry. And she continued with the grating. Repeating the process she had done twice already that night. She had been mistaken. It was going to take at least three batches.

61

A Crab Will Find His Hole

A quick visit to Mane Attraction on the High Street to get a wash and set (although there was no such thing as a "quick" visit when it came to Mane Attraction) was all that Miss Hortense needed to cement the conclusions she had reached the preceding night.

Miss Hortense made sure she was the first customer to arrive as Bola was pulling up the shutters. She didn't apologize for the fact that she didn't have an appointment but instead presented her with a freshly made tray of gizzadas, which Bola squealed at. "No! My favorites? I love these!"

Bola leaned over the sink and was applying shampoo to Miss Hortense's hair. "So, any gossip, Miss Hortense?"

"Well, my dear," said Miss Hortense, "it is carry go bring come gossip that I wanted to talk with you about, actually. I have a favor to ask."

Bola leaned down to hear the favor that Miss Hortense wanted.

After Hortense had described the girl she was looking for and what she did (which took a while to explain), Bola confirmed that yes, the girl was indeed one of her regulars and went to her client book to see the dates that the girl had been in and who else had been in the salon at the same time as her.

Miss Hortense went home to redo her hair after Bola had put it into a "style." Too many curls for Miss Hortense's liking; it made her look like a shaggy doll. She had just smoothed it down and was putting on her coat to go back out again when the doorbell rang.

It was Constance's granddaughter. "I'm sorry to disturb you, but can I come in?" Jasmine asked, looking over her shoulder onto the street before Miss Hortense led her into the front room.

"Grandma did talk about you sometimes," she said, settling into Miss Hortense's settee.

"Hmm," said Miss Hortense, knowing that whatever was said wouldn't have been favorable.

"I need your help, please," said Jasmine.

And then the girl explained what had happened in the preceding months and how the dead man at the bottom of the stairs had come to be in Constance's house.

"For college, I took a module in history and one of the assignments was to find out about your own family? There's this genealogy site you can go into and put in your details, and you get connected to people from all around the world?"

"Oh," said Miss Hortense, thinking that sounded like it could be dangerous. She also thought that young people these days seemed to speak with too many question marks.

"I was talking to loads of people, and then I came across a girl in Texas, in America, with similar interests to me and she was, like, my age, and we did this DNA thing and it turned out we was connected?"

"Oh," said Miss Hortense. "Dangerous indeed."

"She told me about her grandfather."

"Him have a whole heap a pickney them and a whole heap a women."

"Yes," said Jasmine, puzzled. "How did you know?" Althea had spent nearly an hour on the phone telling Miss Hortense all about the seeds that "Donovan Miller" had planted throughout Texas.

"This girl I was in touch with forwarded me a picture of him. There were no pictures of my granddad around, but I found one in my mum's stuff."

She took out two pictures and showed them to Miss Hortense. The first was the old photograph of Constance that was in the funeral brochure. The other side of the photograph unfolded to reveal Mr. Brown, his arm around Constance, and her with that look in her eyes. As Miss Hortense studied the photograph now, she could see that it wasn't fear but loathing. The second photograph, well, it looked very much like Mr. Brown too, but he was much older, with his top off and his arm around a woman looking much younger than him.

"Can you see, he looks the same, doesn't he, except older?" said the girl.

Miss Hortense nodded. "This must have been a shock for you," she said.

"It was," said Jasmine. "I was told my granddad died in a fire, and the reason that Grandma never spoke about him and didn't have any pictures of him was because it was too painful for her." She took back the photographs.

"The girl I was communicating with had an address for him?" said Jasmine.

"In San Antonio, Texas."

"Yes," said Jasmine, looking at Miss Hortense, confused. "I got in contact. At first he didn't answer my letters but then he wrote back asking financial stuff about Grandma's pension and the house and said that he'd had a really bad accident many years ago and he couldn't remember who he was before the accident."

Miss Hortense cussed her teeth.

"I was really excited because there was a possibility that he might be my granddad, even though his name was now Donovan Miller, and I'd found him for Grandma? But when I told Grandma, well, I wasn't expecting her to react the way she did?"

"She wasn't happy 'bout it," stated Miss Hortense.

"I was expecting her to be kind of shocked, but I thought she might be, like, happy or something, but she was just really angry. Angry in a way that I've never seen her before? And then she shouted at me that I shouldn't have interfered. That was the last time I saw her alive."

"I'm sorry to hear that," said Miss Hortense.

"After she died, I told Mummy about the man that I'd found, and Mummy was really shocked too and said as much as Grandma might not have liked him, that we had a moral obligation to tell him that Grandma was dead? And we did, and he asked if we could send money for him for a fare to come over. And so we did, and he came over."

"On the day of the funeral," said Miss Hortense.

"He missed his flight the day before? So he had to get another one? And then he lost all the money Mum sent him, which meant she had to send him some more? And then he couldn't find the right cemetery and then got lost because he said the cemetery isn't the same cemetery that he knew in 1965, but he found it eventually."

Miss Hortense remembered the ghost with the broad forehead that she saw relieving himself against a tree before Blossom had her sudden turn.

"He didn't have anywhere to stay? So Mum said he could stay for a bit in Grandma's house? Then he said, well, technically it was his house anyway, given that Grandma was dead."

"And why you want my help now?" asked Miss Hortense, studying the girl, who was playing with her fingers.

"Because I don't think he fell down the stairs by accident," she said. "I think he was pushed. Uncle Nigel was really mad with my mum for inviting the man . . . my granddad, over to stay in Grandma's house. He said he was a gold digger. He told us that if anyone asked we was to say he was just an old family friend. That if anyone found out who he was, he would claim all of Grandma's property. He said Mum better keep her mouth shut because otherwise she'd lose the community center."

"Did he," said Miss Hortense.

"Then last night, Uncle Nigel came over to our house. I was listening at the door. He was well angry about something my mum texted him. Then Mum asks Uncle Nigel if he had anything to do with the kitchen getting mashed up at the community center. And guess what? He laughs. Mum gets really mad and starts shouting about how could he when he knows how important that place is to the community and was to Grandma. He says he's just helping her run it into the ground. He can't wait till it gets bulldozed and he can turn it into flats! And that's when Mum called him a"—Jasmine looked at Miss Hortense sheepishly—"a good-for-nothing bleep bleep bleep, and then . . . she punched him and said that she'd be telling the whole world exactly who Donovan Miller was. And that's when he said if she didn't want to end up like Donovan Miller herself, she'd better keep her mouth shut."

"He threatened you mother?"

Jasmine nodded and started to cry.

"I think he had something to do with my granddad falling down the stairs," she said in between sobs, "and I think he's gonna do the same thing to Mum."

62

Mr. McKenzie

So now Miss Hortense knew beyond any doubt that it was Mr. Brown at the bottom of the stairs, but why had he run off to America and pretended to be Donovan Miller? And how could he be connected to Bone 12 if he wasn't even in the country back then?

After the girl left, Miss Hortense called Fitz, because if there was one thing she could still rely on him to do, it was to protect, and she needed him to protect Jasmine and her mother. Then Miss Hortense caught the number 279 bus. She got off at Widmore Street and walked until she got to Chappel Road, which was of course where Mr. McKenzie lived. There was someone she needed to see, and it wasn't Mr. McKenzie.

Hortense had been sitting with Mr. McKenzie for nearly half an hour when she heard Myrtle return. During those thirty minutes, Hortense had watched Mr. McKenzie's every breath, each one like a mountain climbed. She had studied his face, chiseled and drawn; a face that had once been so full of dignity, now reduced to skin and bone.

She had also been studying Tamisha, with the piled-up hair on her head, who had let her in when Miss Hortense said she was more than willing to sit with him for a few minutes until Myrtle returned. There had been a kind of relief upon the girl's face. "I'm so snowed under with next door," she said. "Paperwork. And Miss Myrtle doesn't like him left alone."

"Well, him is not alone with me by him side," Miss Hortense had reassured her, taking off her coat.

She and the girl had some small talk about the girl's many talents until the girl revealed, beaming, "Mrs. McKenzie has just offered me a share of the business, actually."

"Oh, really?" said Hortense. "That's generous of her. No doubt Myrtle must feel you have done something to deserve it?"

The girl flushed a soft pink.

"But you don't feel a way working in the dead people business?" Miss Hortense asked.

"Well," said the girl nonchalantly, "when you've seen one dead body, you've seen them all."

Quite a different philosophy to Mr. McKenzie's, thought Miss Hortense.

"And anyway," said the girl, visibly excited by this new business venture as her face brightened, "we've—I mean, I've—got plans. Probably, it won't always be an undertaker's. Would you like a cup of tea?"

"Oh no, thanking you kindly," said Miss Hortense, and she settled herself down next to Mr. McKenzie's bed. "Maybe a likkle later, my dear." It was now clear to her that Tamisha was very much the "T" of "G&T."

Myrtle heard Miss Hortense quietly murmuring before she saw her sat at the side of her husband's bed.

"How you do?" Miss Hortense called out. Myrtle brought an outside draft and two plastic shopping bags in with her.

"Don't worry. He has been well looked after," Miss Hortense reassured her.

"You didn't call to say you was coming," Myrtle said primly, still with her coat on. Had she known Miss Hortense was planning on making a surprise visit, she said as she went around the bed smoothing the sheets, she wouldn't have bothered to go out. She had just popped to the shop to get a few essentials and she didn't pop out very often. What bad luck it was that Hortense had happened to come by just as she must have been leaving. "You were just passing?" Myrtle continued.

"No," said Hortense. "I came specifically for a visit."

"Oh. That's good of you," Myrtle said, smoothing more of the sheet, which wasn't creased. "You get to speak to him?"

"Not much," said Hortense. "He sleeping now."

"Oh," said Myrtle, whispering lower. "He might be a while yet, you know."

"I can wait," said Hortense.

"You sure?" asked Myrtle. "These days he is asleep more than him is awake."

"Very sure," said Miss Hortense, and the two words dropped in the room like two immovable weights.

"Well, come on through to the back till him wake," said Myrtle. She led Miss Hortense through to the back room, where the air was less dense.

Tamisha came in, singing, "I thought I heard the door."

"Excuse me one minute, Hortense," said Myrtle as she moved the girl into the kitchen. The hushed voice of the girl drifted in.

"But I didn't leave him alone . . . But I thought you said . . . But I'm not raising my voice, I just . . ."

Myrtle came back into the room, smoothing down the front of her coat. She shook her head. "These young people of today, you see."

"You know what, my dear?" Hortense called out to Tamisha. "I will have that cup of tea now, thanking you very much.

"Still chilly out?" Miss Hortense asked Myrtle as she shook off her coat.

"Yes, my dear, the wind a cut. Well," said Myrtle, settling into her chair. "I heard about the attack on Nigel's wife." A long sigh followed that. "I suppose that has been occupying all of you time. It's a worrying thing."

"Yes, it is worrying," agreed Miss Hortense.

While Myrtle was adjusting herself into the armchair, Hortense made her own adjustments in the seat, knowing that what was coming next wouldn't be comfortable for either of them.

"Myrtle? I believe you know is why I'm here."

Myrtle shuffled in her seat some more. "You see," said Miss Hortense, "where I get to is this." She cleared her throat. "Everything comes back right ya so . . . to Mr. McKenzie."

"Is what you saying?" Myrtle asked.

"Bone Twelve. Danny Grant was the attacker." She noticed how

251

this information didn't seem to surprise Myrtle. She showed no emotion. "But," continued Hortense, "I now know Mr. McKenzie was the one telling Danny Grant what to do."

Now Myrtle gripped the sides of her armchair, then leaned forwards like a cobra, towards Miss Hortense.

She hissed wildly. "My McKenzie?"

"Yes," said Hortense. "Mr. McKenzie." His name landed heavily in the room and sank somewhere just around their feet.

Myrtle gave a bitter laugh. The air carried it sourly away.

"Well, Miss Hortense," she said. " 'Nuff people say is bad luck to let you inna them house. At one time, I even said it. It was McKenzie let you in after Errol died. 'Member? And after everything him do for you? You want to accuse a sick man?"

Hortense watched Myrtle closely. Accusing her beloved husband of the Bone 12 attacks was something the woman wasn't going to take lightly. Particularly now Miss Hortense knew the lengths she would go to protect his legacy.

"I know all you been through, Myrtle," said Hortense. "I know what you had to put up with and I'm sorry to bring this to your door. But at your door is where this thing has landed."

Myrtle shook her head.

"All the time I had been looking for bad apples but never did I stop to think that the cart itself was rotten. I always wondered how the Brute escaped me with everything I had for him, all of the looking and watching I did. But it was because there was somebody inside the Pardner directing him. Directing me even. Somebody who was letting Danny know about my investigation. And somebody who was making sure that my investigation stopped. No wonder he made me promise. It was Mr. McKenzie all along. But the question is, why? And I think you must know the answer to that."

Myrtle gave another bitter laugh. "It's not possible. What about the attack on Nigel's wife? Can a man who can't even talk be responsible for that too?"

"No," said Hortense, looking directly at Myrtle. "That was all you."

Tamisha entered with a tray containing two cups, a milk jug and bowl of sugar, much of it spilled. Miss Hortense watched as the girl

252

put the tray clumsily down on the coffee table and turned towards the door.

"How do you sleep at night?" asked Miss Hortense after her.

Tamisha turned around. "Sorry?"

"With that thing 'pon you head?" Miss Hortense looked up at the elaborate hairstyle. "How do you sleep at night?"

The girl touched her hair. "Oh, you get used to it," she said with a quizzical smile.

"Who do it fe you?" asked Hortense.

Tamisha looked from Myrtle to Miss Hortense.

"Just a hairdresser, on the High Street. Were you thinking . . . ?" She smiled at Miss Hortense and looked to Miss Hortense's hair.

"Oh, no, my dear, I couldn't put that concoction 'pon my head. Funny, though, don't it?"

"Sorry, what is?" asked Tamisha.

"Things you hear in a hairdresser," said Hortense. Myrtle stared in front of her.

"A woman was attacked five days ago," Miss Hortense continued.

"Terrible," said Tamisha, looking at Myrtle. "Really bad."

Miss Hortense watched the girl closely. She had noticed her tendency to rock on her left foot when under pressure, and she was doing that now.

"You know the woman who was attacked?" asked Miss Hortense. Myrtle adjusted in her seat.

"No," said Tamisha. "But I know Mrs. McKenzie said it was a relative."

"Oh, yes," said Hortense. "There is that. Constance is Myrtle's second cousin. Yvonne is Constance's daughter-in-law."

The girl rocked.

"You know it was a copycat, don't it?" said Hortense.

"Sorry?" said Tamisha, looking towards Myrtle.

"Copycat," repeated Hortense. "Following the footsteps of attacks that happened many years ago before you was even born. Attacks on married women. The same Bible verse said to them."

"About adultery?" said the girl. She didn't even know she'd given herself away, but Miss Hortense looked to Myrtle, who scratched the back of her hand.

"No, I didn't know that," continued Tamisha, also looking at Myrtle.

"Well, why would you?" said Miss Hortense, reaching for the cup on the tray. She continued to watch the girl closely. "But," she went on, "it couldn't really be considered a copycat because it wasn't, in many ways, as brutal as those attacks that took place years ago. Me mean in terms of the violence used." Hortense looked closely at Myrtle and sipped her tea.

"No?" said Tamisha, her voice shaky.

"Oh no," said Miss Hortense. "You see, the thing is, the attacker would have slashed the woman's face for a start." Hortense made a cutting-slash action at her own cheek.

"God, that's awful," said Tamisha, looking like she might be sick. "Who does that?"

"Who indeed?" said Hortense.

"Well," said Tamisha, "I suspect this attack was probably just to warn the woman off, to scare her just a little bit. Nothing like those other attacks."

"Oh," said Miss Hortense, nodding. "Well, yes, maybe you right, because in those attacks, Yvonne Brown would have been mashed up so badly"—Miss Hortense paused—"that she wouldn't be able to walk straight again."

"Stop it," said Myrtle, sharply.

"I didn't know about that," Tamisha said, chastened.

"You wouldn't. It wasn't intended for you to know that." Hortense turned towards Myrtle. She was staring ahead and wringing her hands.

"The thing is," said Miss Hortense, "you, my dear, was probably told the attack was because Yvonne, Nigel's wife, was having an affair. An affair that you thought you knew 'bout because of a certain conversation you overheard from an old woman with bright nails, who talks too much and talked too loudly under a hairdryer when you visited Mane Attraction on the High Street. You overheard that conversation on the afternoon of Saturday, July first, because that's when you got all that hair 'pon you head re-piled up. Na true? You came back here, and you carried that piece of gossip to Myrtle. I'm presuming that was part of your job, because you is not a very good nurse."

Tamisha rocked again.

254

"I wondered what your motivation could be, particularly as you know what it is like for a man to put his hand 'pon you."

Tamisha's shoulders shrank some more.

"I wondered," continued Miss Hortense. "But now I know you was getting paid. Very generous of Myrtle to give you a share of the business."

"Oh God," said Tamisha, raising her hands to her face.

Myrtle shook her head. "Leave us."

The "buts" returned as Tamisha protested.

"Now," said Myrtle, and the girl twisted around and fled from the room.

When the door closed, Hortense looked at Myrtle again.

"It was Mr. McKenzie told you about the attack on Evie, years ago I'm presuming. It was you who sent me that letter six days ago, typed by that girl pretending to be Danny Grant, warning me off. It was you who staged the attack on Nigel's wife—so that I would look away from McKenzie. A man on his deathbed could never have organized that. What an evil man he is to get Danny to do the things he did."

Myrtle gripped on to the side of the armchair. "No," she said, "not my McKenzie."

"What an evil man he is to get you to do the same," continued Hortense.

"I won't let you say those things about McKenzie. No, d'you hear?"

"What an evil man he is, and when he dies, how he will burn," said Hortense finally.

"It was me!" Myrtle screamed. "Nothing to do with McKenzie." She recoiled into her armchair.

And finally, finally, there was the truth. After all this time. A gate had been unlocked and her mouth was moving and she was speaking, speaking into the room, and Myrtle wouldn't, couldn't, for the life of her, stop.

63

The Belated Song of Miss Myrtle

"Sometimes I could barely get out of bed in the mornings after Michael died," said Myrtle. Her voice was fragile.

"McKenzie already find him peace. Bury himself inna the dead. But me? I was the one couldn't get on; couldn't move. Stuck at the doorstep with the policeman and him news: *There is something we need to tell you about your son.* My faith was the only thing keep me going. I went to church every day.

"I saw all kinds of people coming into the church, searching for their peace. Then one time when I was in the church cleaning behind the altar, a woman walked in that I'd never seen walk in before; she had on plenty color in her clothes, on her face. I knew who she was. Everyone knew about her place on St. Clement's Road. She sat down with the pastor and she said: *I don't think I'll send for them now.* She was talking about her pickney them. Can you imagine? Four pickney, and she left them all back home in Jamaica. *I don't think I'll send for them now, Pastor,* she said. Like it was a choice she was mekking. *Does that mek me a bad mother?* she asked him. And when the pastor told her to pray on it, she thanked him and pranced right past the altar where me deh, and out the church. She didn't see me, but I saw her."

"Pearl White," prompted Miss Hortense.

"Yes, Pearl White," confirmed Myrtle. "I knew who she was and what she did. And I was thinking, how is that fair? There she is in all her color, choosing whether or not to bring her pickney come; not a care in the world so far as I could see, and here am I, in all a this darkness,

256

not even one pickney. But when she came in the church the next time, well, she wasn't so colorful. I watched and I saw. And I thought, that is God's punishment for what she was." Myrtle raised her hands to her mouth. "I didn't know what Danny was doing, I swear, Hortense. I thought it was God's work. His vengeance upon those sinning women fe their sinning ways. All part of God's plan, I thought. All I said to Danny was *That woman don't deserve to be a mother*."

"And Daphne Stewart?"

"I was putting out some flowers at the back of the church and there was a young lady sat down in the front. She looked troubled. I remember seeing her at church before. A good-looking young woman. We had a talk. *I heard what happened to your son, Mrs. McKenzie. I'm very sorry for your loss.* She was going pray for me. What could her trouble be, I wondered. A nice-looking young lady with good hair. I listened at the pastor's door: *Me get myself in trouble. Me miss me monthly. I can't keep it. It's not fe me husband. What me a go do?*"

Hortense felt her stomach turn, thinking of Daphne's pain, what lay underneath the emerald dress, though her face remained blank and smooth.

"We had a Bible study meeting, just Danny and I, every Wednesday evening. And I would just talk to him, about sinners and worldly people."

"Married women," said Hortense.

"Women that didn't deserve to be mothers," said Myrtle defiantly.

"Mothers?" said Miss Hortense, aghast. "This was about that?"

"McKenzie knew nothing about any of it. You must believe me."

"And what about my sister Evie?" Miss Hortense asked.

"Mr. Jean-Baptiste went to see Pastor too," said Myrtle. "Poor man. He said he wanted his wife to love him. That he thought she was seeing another man . . ."

"He was wrong. You were wrong!" said Hortense loudly, unable to stop the words. A sliver of a crack in her composure. She stilled herself. She said, barely above a whisper, "What did you do?"

It was then Tamisha ran into the room shouting, "It's Mr. McKenzie!" Myrtle ran out. Her scream was unmistakable. Miss Hortense couldn't move. How many years and decades had she wanted an answer and here it was. The truth at last. She looked at the room as if it were a canvas: the vase, the doilies on the settee, the table and chairs pushed up to the window. And that picture next to the ashtray on the mantelpiece of Michael, with his arm around Danny, both smiling innocently into the room.

64

The End of Hope

Mr. McKenzie was right, death brought peace. Gone was the tension from his face. Miss Hortense had spoken to him at length in the makeshift bedroom for the thirty minutes or so before his wife had returned. Told him everything she knew about the case, everything she'd discovered about his surrogate son. It was possible that he had already put two and two together before his stroke. That he knew about his wife's role too. That she was the reason he made Hortense promise to stop her investigation after Errol died. He had looked tortured then, but now he looked free.

Myrtle was crumpled up beside the bed and hollowed out. Miss Hortense looked at Tamisha and the ridiculous mess on her head. She gathered up her coat and handbag, and left.

So much had happened that she almost forgot that it was July 10.

After Miss Hortense had treated Evie's wounds and given her something for the pain, she sat by Evie's bed. Evie said, "Hortense . . . this isn't." She touched her face, her hands shaking as she neared the mean-looking scar, still oozing. "I'm not . . . I only wanted to dance."

"It doesn't matter now," said Hortense, hushing her sister. But Evie turned fully to look at her then, as if a realization had washed over her. "How will I get anybody to believe me?" Evie had said, and she turned her back to Hortense and never left that house again alive.

When Evie died, a part of Miss Hortense died with her. The part that wished for good, that believed in possibilities and hope. Miss Hortense had been so busy trying to find the Brute that she had taken her eyes off her sister. If she had been there watching Evie, her sister would still be alive.

It was eleven in the evening by the time Miss Hortense banged down Reginald Jean-Baptiste's door. Lights in the house switched on one by one. He came downstairs, slowly, and opened the door, wrapping a belt around his dressing gown and his big old baggy pajama bottoms.

"Lawd, Hortense," he said. "It's late."

Miss Hortense pushed her way inside his house.

"You," she said even before he reached the room she was stood in, "went to Plevna Road to visit the pastor before Evie died."

"The pastor?" Mr. Jean-Baptiste rolled his hand through his hair and took a seat. "Well, I think I did one time," he said.

"You told him Evie was cheating on you?"

"Well, yes, Hortense." Beads of sweat formed on his upper lip. "I think I did. At the time, well, I suppose I thought she was."

"You thought?" said Hortense. "Do you know what you did?" She spat the words at him.

She wanted to smack the man in his mouth, to get the belt around his waist and wrap it around his neck. Instead, she told him everything, and left him sobbing on the settee, his head in his hands with his woman standing by the door, looking on.

65

Blood Follows Vein

On Monday morning, Sonia had answered the phone in the hallway to hear a deep voice.

"Hello, Sonia? This is Sergeant Gregory Jean-Baptiste. Miss Hortense's nephew. I need to speak to you. Can we meet later today?"

Sonia agreed to meet him in the evening at a bar in Musgrove Park, not far, it turned out, from the house she had found the dead body in. Before he put the phone down, he said, "Don't mention our meeting to my aunty. She doesn't need to know."

Sonia spent the rest of the afternoon deciding what not to wear. She arrived twenty minutes early, in a navy jacket with a cream blouse underneath, sat on a barstool and ordered herself a gin and tonic; something for Dutch courage. Gregory turned up twenty minutes late, with no apology for his tardiness. He sat down heavily on the barstool next to her. His eyes scanned the lines of bottles in front of them and he kept his head low. When his pocket vibrated, he took out a pager, studied the message displayed on it, looked at Sonia briefly, and then put it away. He exchanged pleasantries with the woman behind the bar and nodded at a short, shaven-headed man in a group that passed behind them. The same man came to the bar several moments later and glanced at Sonia before passing Gregory a brown envelope, which then sat on the counter in front of him. Gregory ordered "my usual."

He'd been to the house a few times on a Tuesday when she was there; she'd seen the way that he deferred to Miss Hortense. Now he looked taller, broader, his jaw squarer, his movements more considered. It was the side profile she was getting, though, and the occasional reflection from the mirror in front of them. Not a young face, not an old face either. Giving little away. He smiled at the bartender and took up his pineapple juice. Sonia adjusted her jacket over the frilly blouse.

"You don't drink?" Sonia asked him, her voice sugary.

"No."

Sonia wondered why. He rolled the ice in the glass.

"You're not trying very hard, are you?" he said.

"Pardon?" She pulled her jacket together.

"With your mother's house," he said. "I thought the plan was to get the tenants out?"

"Oh," she said, sipping from her glass. "It takes time. To evict. And—"

"Fitz," he interrupted, "thinks you're taking my aunt for a ride."

She adjusted. "The old man she has over at the house? Look, I'm not trying to pull a fast one, or whatever it is that you and Mr. Fitz think I'm doing. I love your aunty, really, I do." She smiled sweetly.

He scoffed. She knew the word was wrong as soon as it slipped out. "Love" wasn't a word that sat in the same sentence as Miss Hortense. She knew that now; she'd seen how Miss Hortense operated.

"So, I made some inquiries of my own," he said.

Fuck, she thought.

"You're running, Sonia," he said finally.

"Me? I'm not running." She shook her head. The smile again, but she swallowed hard, and he was staring at her in the mirror and saw. "Oh, are you talking about the bank?" she said lightly. "It was just a colleague I didn't get on with." She gulped some more of her drink. "A misunderstanding. No. A vendetta. Against me," she said more seriously.

He pushed the envelope towards her and nodded for her to open it. She did so, slowly. She knew what was in it even before she looked inside. A trap: the photocopied signatures—all hers. She looked around for the man who'd handed them to Gregory. He'd gone.

"Forgery is a very serious business, particularly for an accountant."

"No charges were ever brought," she said quickly. Her voice was changed. There was a sourness to it, the sugar gone. She let the envelope drop to the counter.

"Doesn't mean you're not guilty, though, does it?" She felt his stare

262

in the mirror. "Why are you here, Sonia? What is it you want with my aunt?"

"Okay then," she said. "Fine." She took a deep breath. "I just want to find out why my dad died. That's all." It wasn't "all," but she wasn't going to share with him that she was also here to make the woman responsible for his death pay. And that the payback had already started.

Gregory pulled away from the counter in front of them. Even he, it turned out, knew there was power in the mention of her father.

And now it was her turn.

"And I've already found out a great deal," she said, and went on to describe everything she'd learned from the old woman, Blossom, about the cases of the women that were attacked.

"They call it Bone Twelve. What I don't understand is why it was never solved. Surely something like that, the police would have been all over it. And then there's the attack that happened on that woman at the leisure center."

"What's that got to do with any of this?" asked Gregory.

"Don't you know?" she asked him. "Apparently, it's all connected."

The jacket came open; she didn't try to adjust it this time.

He put his head back and dashed the rest of the juice down his throat.

"There's something else," she said. "About your aunt, actually."

She motioned for another of the same for both of them. The bartender looked at Gregory and he nodded.

"The other night, Miss Hortense just went crazy," she said, and went on to describe the incident with the roasting tin. "She just . . . lost it. This is how it starts. My mum went through something similar. Maybe because Miss Hortense hasn't had anyone living with her . . . being on her own for so long. I suppose no one's been watching her that closely." She swigged a whole mouthful of her new drink. "And there's history, isn't there? Of her becoming 'obsessive,' people getting hurt as a consequence. It could all stem back to the thing that happened with your mother."

Gregory sat up straighter.

Sonia looked at the brown envelope still on the counter, the buff of it. She fiddled with a corner.

"Did you know your mother took her own life?" She watched in the mirror as he stiffened more.

Before he had a chance to respond, she told him about the encounter she'd had with the woman from the hospital when they went to visit Yvonne Brown and she had to go back to retrieve her mobile phone.

"I know Miss Hortense told everyone that she fell down the stairs." Sonia watched him in the mirror. "But this woman was at the hospital when they brought your mother in, so she knows . . . And," she said, moving in closer, "I think she might have done that to herself because she was one of the victims . . . you know, one of the women attacked in Bone Twelve, because"—Sonia passed her tongue against her teeth— "she was having an affair. There was a letter, you see, addressed to Miss Hortense, delivered to the house. In it was an apology for the attack on your mother." She saw his eyes, hurt, like a little boy's. "Look, I'm only telling you because I think you deserve to know. No one told me about the circumstances surrounding my dad's death, and . . . well, it's unfair being the last to know."

Gregory's stool scraped hard along the floor and it fell backwards in slow motion as he roughly got up. He grabbed his jacket and rushed out of the bar.

Number 37 Vernon Road was Miss Hortense's house. Every part of it was hers, she'd paid for it, every brick and all the mortar, so she didn't feel any way about being in one of its rooms, even if it so happened to be the room that the girl was temporarily staying in. And she didn't feel no way about going through things in the room, even if they happened to be Sonia's. Miss Hortense didn't do anything unless it was necessary, and she felt that going through Sonia's three suitcases was a necessity now.

Miss Hortense knew the girl was there with reasons of her own, but she'd had bigger fish to fry before McKenzie died. Now Miss Hortense was determined to find out what the girl was up to. She had only given the girl a few instructions when she'd first come to stay and she knew at least five of her rules had already been broken. Oh, Sonia was all smiles and sweet milky words to Miss Hortense's face, but Miss Hortense knew that was for show. She opened the first suitcase, put her hand in and riffled through it: hair tongs, lipsticks and other bits of makeup, perfume and a cigarette lighter. Miss Hortense cussed her teeth.

The second suitcase contained too many clothes, but nothing that Miss Hortense found particularly offensive. She went into the last one. This one looked like it was used to conduct her business. In it was some stationery, a small typewriter in a case, and correspondence regarding the house on Ebley Street. She undid one of the side compartments and pulled out a bank book, which looked like it had belonged to the girl's mother. Miss Hortense flicked through and saw the recurring payment from an "A. Williams." *Well, well,* thought Miss Hortense.

Finally, she dug a bit deeper and pulled out her own notebook, the one that she had been looking for for the past week.

66

Pastor Denied

The saving-of-lives business could be a very long one and there were no guarantees. It was now the end of July and it had already been nearly six weeks since Pastor Williams had formulated his plan. Even though there was still a small dedicated group that went to preach every Monday lunchtime and Friday evening at the two remote locations he had specified, and even though they had moved into Psalm 11:6 and other hellfire verses of the Old Testament, and even though they had committed to staying an extra fifteen minutes longer each time, there were still no signs yet that a life had been or was about to be saved. In the meantime, the red letters kept piling up on the pastor's desk and the gas people were threatening to switch off their supply. Pastor Williams couldn't let his congregation go without hot water, and so he decided belatedly that he needed to move to plan B: that was the plan that involved the dirt. He drove all the way to Rushden Industrial Estate and waited outside the garage for Nigel Brown to arrive.

"Mr. Brown," he called after the shiny black car as soon as it pulled up at 9:16 p.m. "Young man?" he said more loudly, knocking on the window. Nigel turned the engine off and got out of the car.

"I demand you return to the Pardner all what is rightfully ours."

Those were the words the pastor had been practicing in the car for the past hour. He was stabbing Nigel in his chest with his index finger as he said them. They were about the same height, but Nigel was heavier and of course younger. If anything was going to kick off, the younger man was guaranteed to come out the victor. Nigel looked down at the finger, brushed it aside, and then looked at the pastor, who noticed he had a purple eye that was turning black.

"I know what you are doing, young man, and I won't stand for it," said Pastor. "I am a reasonable man and I do believe that everybody deserves second chances, but this has gone too far." Some more of the words he had practiced.

"If you've got a problem, old man, why don't you take it up with my solicitor." Nigel clicked his car door shut and strutted towards the garage.

"A solicitor?" Pastor called after him. "Do you really think a solicitor would be a good idea, given all your illegalities?"

Nigel slouched menacingly back towards the pastor, looking nothing like the upright businessman he had long claimed to be.

"Whatever 'illegalities' you are referring to, old man, know this." He whispered in the pastor's ear: "They've been washing through your collection plates for years."

Pastor Williams mopped the sweat from his head with his handkerchief.

"Condemn me, and you condemn yourself, old man."

Nigel laughed then, and patted the pastor on the back, hard.

The pastor felt his heart beating in his chest and leaned into Nigel. Sweat was dripping from his head. "You think you is the only"—and he said a bad word beginning with *b*—"one who can do something? You think you is the only bad man in town? You want test me?" These were words coming out of the pastor's mouth, but they were not the ones he had practiced.

Nigel grinned. "What can you do to me, old man?" he asked, before he turned and sauntered away. It was the one question that needed no answer because there was simply none to give.

67

The Wages of Sin

For three Tuesdays in a row, Gregory didn't show up at Miss Hortense's for dinner. Miss Hortense had cooked bully beef on the first Tuesday and susumber soup on the second, and waited for the doorbell to ring. It didn't. The same three weeks passed before Mr. McKenzie was buried in the corner of Westmill Hill cemetery in the same plot as Michael. Mr. McKenzie's funeral was a subdued affair, with a humble coffin made of walnut, a minimum of religious texts and one song. Neither Tamisha nor her boyfriend was anywhere to be seen. According to Mavis C, according to Mavis B, the takeaway shop had been closed for nearly three weeks now and no one knew where the owners were.

At the funeral, there was a loyal flock of mourners who remembered Mr. McKenzie, the gentle man who never had a bad word to say and was always there to share in their grief.

"He was always in the undertaking business, you know."

"Yes, him come from a long line of undertakers."

"You won't find another undertaker like him."

It was clear that the passing of Mr. McKenzie had a profound effect on his wife, Myrtle, too; she had started having half-finished conversations with her late husband and asking him for his opinion in a way she hadn't ever asked him in life.

"Don't that right, McKenzie?"

Miss Hortense thought about Garfield Stewart and his ghost, Daphne.

"Such a shame," whispered Blossom to Miss Hortense. "How grief can take you."

"So that's it," said Fitz, leaning into Hortense and away from Blossom as they made their way out of the cemetery. "Danny Grant was the attacker. Myrtle was the instigator. Bone Twelve finally done and finish," he said to her quietly. Miss Hortense had told him and Blossom what she had found out the day Mr. McKenzie died.

"But . . ." said Blossom, raising her manicured fingernail into the air. She could hear very well when it suited her. "Myrtle's entanglement in Bone Twelve don't explain the body in Constance's house nor the note found beside it."

"A common tactic," said Hortense, looking off towards the graves.

"Eh?" asked Blossom.

"Of distraction," said Hortense, walking on.

Blossom looked at Fitz, who would not oblige her with an explanation, then down at the muddy ground, before following Hortense. Hortense could be a very funny creature, thought Blossom.

After a small gathering at the house, the mourners made a quick retreat. If the husband had been caring and effusive, making death seem a natural part of life, the wife made it seem like something to be avoided at all costs.

Fitz accompanied Miss Hortense home. As they stepped off the 279 bus, he said, "Me have someone a watch Constance's daughter and the granddaughter, round the clock."

"And you have any concerns?" asked Hortense.

Fitz removed his hat, scratched his head and nodded. When they got to 37 Vernon Road, he explained, and then also explained why he had accompanied her all the way home.

"Word on the street is that a man named Dice will pay heavily for somebody to do harm to you."

"Oh, really," said Hortense, unsurprised. Not the first time someone had threatened her life. "Mek them try."

"Hortense," Fitz said, "I did warn you. We too old fe this."

Since the discovery of Myrtle's part in Bone 12, Miss Hortense was finding it harder and harder to settle at night. Her thoughts were loud. She'd had it wrong; all along, Bone 12 had been in many respects about grief. About a woman losing a son, who couldn't bear other

269

women having what she didn't. But the note by the body at the bottom of the stairs—that, she believed, was something else. She knew it was a distraction, but she hadn't quite worked out why.

It was just drawing towards midnight, as her thoughts quieted and she started to drop off, when there came a faint knocking at the front door. It was the sort of knocking that wasn't quite sure whether it was a knock or not, apologetic but persistent enough to stop a person from getting their longed-for sleep.

"That damn blasted gal you see," Miss Hortense said out loud. Why was she out so late anyway? That's why Miss Hortense didn't live with people. Because people forget keys and woke up other people from their good, good sleep when good sleep is hard to come by. She cussed as she pulled herself from her bed and swung her heavy legs around to the floor. As Hortense pulled on her dressing gown and slipped her feet into her slippers, she cursed the girl from her foot to the tips of her relaxed hair. She was still cursing when she swung the front door open, but it wasn't to find Sonia without any keys, but Tamisha, her hair still piled high on her head, a sleeping child draped over her shoulder and mascara streaks staining glistening cheeks. In the small bit of light that reached her doorstep from the streetlamp, Miss Hortense saw two things—the girl's eyes, fear etched in them, and a look Miss Hortense couldn't mistake: the girl was running.

Miss Hortense curled her right hand into a fist. When she had broken into his flat and drunk tea from his mug, she had warned that stupid boy not to lay a finger on the girl. All right then. Miss Hortense was already plotting her next move when she heard a rustling to the side of the girl. As Miss Hortense leaned out further, she saw, standing in the shadows, the outline of another person. They had a hood pulled up over their head and were curled slightly forward, looking like they could barely hold up the weight of their own body: Germaine Banton. Miss Hortense thought he didn't look so full of himself now.

"Please," said Tamisha quietly. "We didn't know where else to go."

"Come," said Miss Hortense as she ushered all three of them into the front room. She instructed the girl to lay the sleeping toddler on the settee. Germaine slumped into the chair by the door. As Miss Hortense reached for the light switch, Tamisha pleaded: "Please don't."

Miss Hortense clicked the light on anyway. As she looked from the girl to the boy on the chair, she saw the reason Tamisha had wanted to remain in darkness. The whole front of Germaine's jacket was splattered in a dried redness that could only be blood.

"Lawd Jesus," said Miss Hortense to Germaine. "You hurt?"

Tamisha said soberly, "It's not his." And Hortense knew then why the two of them were running.

Germaine didn't say a word; only squeaking noises came from his shiny jacket as he shifted from time to time. His head bowed into his hand.

It was Tamisha who explained why they had knocked on Miss Hortense's door at ten minutes to midnight.

"G went to the garage on the Rushden Industrial Estate. It's where they run the business from," she explained, though she didn't need to. Miss Hortense nodded.

Tamisha looked at her boyfriend, took a deep breath. "A few months ago, G found out about plans for the development of property in Musgrove Park. We just wanted to take advantage of the opportunity." That's why the girl was working at McKenzie's, thought Hortense; the undertaker's was part of the plan. "They found out. We had to close the shop, stay at my mum's. G was just going to tell them that we'd made a big mistake and to leave us alone. I told him not to go." The girl looked across to her boyfriend again. He was rubbing his temple. "But when G got there, something was off. He saw someone on the floor. When G reached down, the body was covered in blood. He'd been stabbed. G found him like that," she said. "I swear. He found him."

When Miss Hortense asked if they were sure, Tamisha replied, "He was dead."

"You *sure* sure?" asked Miss Hortense, turning to Germaine. A man might look dead, but without checking his vitals, that might not be the case.

"G said he was dead," repeated Tamisha. "He left him there and drove home to me."

"You didn't call an ambulance?" asked Miss Hortense, already knowing the answer.

"He's got a record, Mrs. Hortense."

"Miss," Hortense corrected.

"If they think it's him"—she shook her head and started to cry—"they'll lock him away."

Germaine's first words in the room sounded like gravel, dry and coarse:

"*For whatsoever a man soweth, that shall he also reap.*"

Tamisha shook her head, her pleading eyes directed at Miss Hortense.

"He's in shock, that's all," she said.

The child was starting to stir. Tamisha went to him and patted him back to sleep.

"Who is the man you found dead in the garage?" asked Miss Hortense.

"Mr. Brown," said Tamisha, cradling her son. "Nigel Brown."

With the girl and her young child in the front room, a dead body bleeding on the floor of an industrial estate somewhere, and a blood-stained boy on her chair, there were limited options at her disposal. She told the girl to follow her into the kitchen with the little one where she said she would get him some milk.

"How you so sure that it wasn't him?" Miss Hortense whispered to the girl.

"I know him, Miss Hortense," she said. "He might not be the best person in the world, but he's not a killer." But they both knew he was capable of violence. Miss Hortense had seen it under the sunglasses, in the plastic bag in their flat, and the bruise on Yvonne's face.

"And what if he was in a temper?" asked Miss Hortense.

Doubt crept into Tamisha's face and her bottom lip trembled. Miss Hortense nodded.

"Tek the baby upstairs," said Miss Hortense. "Put him to bed in the first room you come to."

Miss Hortense used the phone in the kitchen to dial Gregory's number. It took a number of rings for him to pick up.

"I know, for whatever reason, you are not happy with me, Gregry," she said quietly into the phone. "But this is not the time. There is a man lying dead in the industrial estate up at Rushden and I have a boy covered in his blood sitting on my settee."

Gregory was at Miss Hortense's house in less than twelve minutes. It was him who rushed in and tackled Germaine Banton facedown onto the carpet.

"It's not you doing this," Miss Hortense said to Tamisha as she collapsed to the floor, the sound of sirens surrounding the house.

As he was led out in handcuffs, Germaine spoke. "Exodus twenty: thirteen. *Thou shalt not kill.*"

When Sonia returned home, keys at the ready, she found herself unable to get within one hundred yards of Miss Hortense's front door. Five police cars surrounded the property, and in the crowd that had gathered around the periphery, a rumor was circulating that a murderer was inside.

68

A Third Death in the Family

The dead body at the industrial estate was Nigel, all right. The police found him on the floor at Unit 44. He was, according to Gregory, stabbed in the neck once and the back four times, with a knife that had at least a five-inch blade.

It turned out that quite a number of people wished Nigel dead, including several gangland rivals, several business owners to whom he owed substantial debts, and someone he had cut up at a set of traffic lights—not to mention his wife, his sister and Pastor Williams.

The tall white man with the Aston Villa baseball cap was also missing and a warrant was put out for his arrest, but it was Germaine Banton who was charged with Nigel's murder. There was motive: Nigel Brown had somehow found out that Germaine Banton had been responsible for attacking his wife. Germaine had a propensity for violence—his record was longer than an arm, including three charges for grievous bodily harm and an arrest for possession of a knife. In fact, the knife in the plastic bag Miss Hortense had found in his flat had a five-inch blade. His DNA was over everything, including Miss Hortense's settee, which Hortense had to spend an afternoon cleaning.

"Any money found with the body?" Miss Hortense asked Gregory over a second cup of tea on Tuesday.

"No, not a penny," he replied. And then he started to shift in his seat.

"And? There is something else. Well, out with it."

". . . Why didn't you come in and say my prayers with me?" he asked.

"What nonsense is you talking 'bout now?" said Hortense, raising her cup to her lips, but clashing it against her teeth.

Gregory cleared his throat. "Before Mum died, there was this night when you rushed into the house with Daddy, and you told me to go to bed. You said you would come in and say my prayers with me. You never did."

Miss Hortense rose quickly, her cup of tea in hand, and rushed to the kitchen as though there were a pot about to boil over. She stood in the little kitchen trying to quell the shaking by gripping on to the table. There was no pot boiling on the stove but thirty years of silence and pain. The bedspread, the pillowcase covered in blood, the little boy sat at the bottom of the stairs. She wanted to go back into the front room and tell him . . . but she couldn't move, and then she heard the front door quietly open and close and Gregory was gone.

69

Jamaican Independence

Despite all the dramas and deaths of the last few weeks, it was still August 5, which meant the next day was Independence Day. For twenty years now, the Bigglesweigh Afro-Caribbean Social Organization (BACSO), of which Constance Brown had been a trustee and the chair, organized various fundraisers including Independence Day celebrations, and early August meant it was that of the Jamaicans.

As the community hall only sat ninety, and for health and safety reasons that had to be reduced to eighty-four, to get an invitation to the BACSO Jamaican Independence Day dinner and dance was quite the accolade.

Despite the death of Constance (who wasn't a Jamaican, in any case) just over three months earlier, and the man at the bottom of the stairs (who was Mr. Brown, though most people didn't know that yet) four weeks later, and the passing of Mr. McKenzie five weeks after that, and the murder of Nigel almost three weeks after Mr. McKenzie died, the fundraiser was still going ahead. Indeed, for the past ten years the Independence Day celebration had acted as a kind of obituary for the recently deceased.

For certain members of the community, it was one of the most important events of the year; a chance to remember a time when they could jump up and down and had sung or cussed at the signing of the Declaration of Independence by Bustamante. It was an opportunity to watch one another and commiserate with one another and eat too much food and complain about the food and the cost of the ticket and sometimes to dance. At £25 a pop, those who bought their ticket were going to make damned well and sure they attended, no matter who was dead.

For obvious reasons, Miss Hortense wasn't normally one of the eighty-four, but this year Blossom had made a determined effort to get a plus-one and had organized for her and Hortense to catch a ride with Mr. Wright, who had recently upgraded his vehicle for something that actually worked: a red Rover with four previous owners and 90,000 miles on the odometer.

Mr. Wright had picked up Blossom first despite the fact that Hortense's house was closer to his than hers. When Mr. Wright pulled up to collect Hortense, she could tell something wasn't right with Blossom, who was sat in the front passenger seat. Hortense had seen her most days for black cake (no more Black Cake, though) and thought she had recovered from the shock of Yvonne Brown's attack, but after Hortense had maneuvered herself into the back seat behind Mr. Wright, Blossom said not one word about her ailing health. There was no mention of her arm hurting her or her stomach and its gas; nothing about her swelling foot or rheumatoid arthritis. In fact, Blossom was uncharacteristically quiet. Mr. Wright had on a chirpy powder-blue overcoat that looked new, but Blossom was in a black dress that looked remarkably like the one she'd worn to Constance's funeral. From the back seat, Miss Hortense could see that Blossom's skin looked washed out and her lipstick wasn't the normal bright offering. Miss Hortense leaned forwards to look for the nails. Oh dear, she thought as she leaned back—not the magenta pink.

"So, this is the new car Blossom been talking 'bout. It mussy set you back a few bob?" Miss Hortense said to Mr. Wright. He was touching the steering wheel like it was on fire, his hands on and off every few seconds.

"How many years since the Independence?" asked Blossom. Her voice cut across Hortense's.

"Nineteen sixty-two—well, that would make it . . ." said Mr. Wright.

"Thirty-eight years," said Hortense.

Blossom cussed her teeth. "Thirty-eight years, is it? Already? And look what we come to," she said morbidly. "Well, is just like you said, Mr. Wright. We getting on." And that admission, coming from

Blossom, made Hortense's stomach churn. She saw the gray streaks like blasphemy at the top of Blossom's nodding head. If Blossom was letting the gray show, something was wrong, wrong, wrong.

"Hortense, you was right," she said. "Apart from that business with Myrtle, there wasn't anything to Look Into after all." Her voice was an echo. "Except for Constance's boy, Nigel, everybody else die of old age. Um-hum." Blossom folded her hands in her lap. "Constance died from the heart attack."

"Even young people can die of heart attack, you know," said Mr. Wright. Blossom nodded sagely.

"And Mr. Miller was a drunkard and he did fall down the stairs," Blossom continued. Miss Hortense coughed because she knew what she knew about Mr. Brown but hadn't yet divulged the same to Blossom.

"Plenty people fall down the stairs nowadays," said Mr. Wright. "Particularly when they is old. And drunk."

"And poor Mr. McKenzie. When the stroke catch you, you see." And this time Blossom rubbed her left hand. Miss Hortense would almost have rejoiced to hear Blossom say how she couldn't feel her own left side or wasn't able to raise her arm above her head or had woken up with her mouth leaning, but instead Blossom said, "Old age going kill we all one way or another. We all heading for the grave."

"Everybody getting old," said Mr. Wright, to reiterate the point. "And the generation of today going put we in the grave before we time. Dem is a damn shame. We fought for our independence," he said, like there had been a war and he had personally been in it. "And what them do with it? Teef and murderer, the lot of them. Like that blasted boy, what's him name?"

"Germaine Banton," said Blossom.

"Ger-maine Ban-ton," repeated Mr. Wright. "Killing our own, like damn fools. You see, when I came to this country, in the summer of 'sixty-five, things was hard. But this generation nowadays have it easy and dem still a mess it up. Well, wasn't no easy street for me."

"No, sah," agreed Blossom. "We didn't get no easy streets."

"Hopefully, that young man gets what him deserve anyway," said Mr. Wright.

Miss Hortense folded her hands in her own lap and stared out the window as the rain droplets touched it and rolled down like tears. The conversation moved on to reminiscing.

"I wish we could go back," said Blossom.

"Yes," said Mr. Wright. "There are certainly some tings I wouldn't have waited so long fe do."

"I need to go pee-pee," called out Miss Hortense from the back seat, interrupting them.

"We going be there soon," said Mr. Wright, tightly. But in this traffic, that wasn't true.

"Well, I need to pee-pee now," called out Miss Hortense.

"It's the old age," said Blossom, looking across to Mr. Wright. "When the urge tek you."

They were now about fifteen minutes from the community center, about six minutes away from Mr. Wright's.

As the lift wasn't working properly, they had to climb four flights of slippery stairs, as the rain continued to fall and enter the leaky stairwell, to get to Mr. Wright's flat.

"The council won't fix a damn thing," said Mr. Wright as they passed the second floor. Miss Hortense was sorry to see the state of his block; clearly people in it didn't wait to go to the toilet like she did. When they reached Mr. Wright's front door it was a relief for all of them. Each needed to catch their breath, but Mr. Wright was particularly wheezy. Blossom told him to stop being so dramatic, but when Hortense returned from the bathroom, she could see he needed something more than just a seat.

"Angina?" she asked.

"Really?" asked Blossom. "Angina?" He nodded at her.

"You have tablets?" Hortense asked. He clamped his mouth shut.

"If you have tablets, let her find the tablets na man," said Blossom, helping him to undo a top button. "They in your pocket?" He shook his head and pointed to his bedroom.

Mr. Wright's bedroom was neat and tidy, minimalist, with white sheets and a shaver on a side table. Miss Hortense found two sets of tablets. She picked up the angina ones. After a few minutes, Mr. Wright's breathing settled.

He grunted, "Thank you," while looking at Blossom. Miss Hortense noticed quite a few of Blossom's items seemed to be lying around his flat, including a pair of compression socks that Miss Hortense had loaned her. Miss Hortense went to the window and stepped out onto the balcony. It was pelting down but the view was beautiful from up there; one could almost forget where they were. And when she looked down she could see that, even in this weather, Constance's house looked like it was shining, almost like it was bathed in gold; from this height, you couldn't see the weeds and you couldn't see the rubbish. Miss Hortense cussed her teeth. Property. Why did it make people jealous so? She was thinking about what a wicked thing jealousy could be. Particularly for those who had very little to lose.

After the last course of a stodgy bread and butter pudding at the Independence Day dinner, Mr. Wright sat digging out his fingernails with his pocketknife, its gold embossed lettering glinting under the lights, and Blossom continued complaining about the temperature of the food. "Don't them have a cooker? Look like everything mek in a microwave." She complained about the size of the tables, the cutlery, the tablecloths, the music, its volume, the smell, the soap in the ladies' loos and the roughness of the toilet paper.

When Miss Hortense managed to get a word in, she informed Blossom that she would be making her own way home later. She was aware of Mr. Wright's uncharitable feelings towards her; feelings that, in all fairness, she knew he wasn't alone in having. In fact, the whole evening had been a reminder of why she never attended such events, with the sly looks from the other partygoers. A big old dutty man sat opposite her tried to play footsie under the table. He leaned over and said, "Hello, darling. What you name then?" Hortense lifted her head even higher and ignored him. "Me name is 'M' fe Maurice," he said. "But you can call me Daddy." Miss Hortense cussed her teeth. The only thing she would be calling him was "dead" if he continued to gyrate his crotch in her direction.

Such was Blossom's continued bad mood that she didn't notice the brazen old man and didn't put up too much resistance at Miss

Hortense's insistence on leaving alone. She and Mr. Wright, along with a rather nice-looking little glass he slid from the table into his side pocket, left at a quarter to ten. Miss Hortense sat and waited until the hall was almost empty before she rose from her seat and made her way to the front reception area, where Constance's daughter, Camille, was busy pulling down bunting and balloons.

"Excuse me, my dear?" called out Miss Hortense.

Camille looked over, a glint of recognition in her broad face.

"You can order a taxicab for me, please?"

Camille rose to her feet, obliged, and told Miss Hortense the cab would take about fifteen minutes to arrive.

"Thank you, my dear. I can wait here?" Miss Hortense asked, pointing to a chair beside the table Camille was using to sort out the decorations, and sitting herself down before Camille could answer.

After a while, the only sound the rustle of bunting being sorted, Miss Hortense said, "I am sorry about the loss of your brother, Nigel, my dear."

Camille said, "Thank you." But she didn't want anybody's sympathy. She had hated her brother.

"Your daughter, Jasmine? She's a good girl. You doing a good job," said Hortense.

"Thank you," said Camille again, blushing this time, continuing to pile the bunting into a box. "To be honest, I feel like I'm failing. In everything."

Miss Hortense reached across and squeezed Camille's hand. An olive branch that had skipped a generation.

"You doing a good job with this place, too," said Miss Hortense, looking around at the building she had helped to create.

"Well, it doesn't matter. This place is gonna be closed down soon anyway," Camille said, removing her hand. "The one place we have and my brother's debts mean it's going to be taken away." Some bits of bunting slipped onto the floor. "And it's probably stupid . . . No, it doesn't matter."

"Go on, child," encouraged Hortense.

"I'm probably being paranoid, but I've just had this strange feeling that I'm being followed," Camille said.

"Well, you are," said Miss Hortense, looking intently at the woman. Fitz had already established that. "You and your daughter are in danger," Miss Hortense said.

Camille's jaw dropped. The bunting she was holding slid to the floor.

"Inheritance and property," said Miss Hortense, "is one dangerous thing. When money is involved, people lose them minds."

"But my brother's dead?"

"Well, exactly," said Miss Hortense.

"Who? Who's following us?" asked Camille, panic entering her voice.

Miss Hortense moved her chair in closer to Camille, reassured her that she already had protection in place in the form of both Fitz and Cuttah, and then she started to explain how she was going to catch the person who she believed was responsible for quite a number of deaths. It was a plan that involved her mother's house.

70

An Old Woman Goes Hunting

By the time Miss Hortense got home, it was almost a quarter to midnight, which made it almost 6 p.m. in Jamaica. In Bigglesweigh the rain was pelting down. In Jamaica, it was doing the same. Hortense picked up the phone and called Tiny.

"Tiny, it's me, Hortense."

"Nice fe hear from you again."

"Please, I'm begging you another favor," said Miss Hortense.

"Yes?"

"Find out anything you can about Melvin Bright."

"Melvin Bright? The teef and murderer? Is this 'bout him being friends with Donovan Miller who you asked me to Look Into?"

"Me na sure quite yet," said Miss Hortense. "Me come across a very forward man tonight, who get me thinking 'bout names dat start with 'M.' I think I may have found out what happened to Melvin."

With help from Joel at the library, she found thirty-seven nursing homes listed in Bigglesweigh and surrounding areas. Millicent Granwaithe was quite an unusual name and, given her age, Miss Hortense bargained on her either being dead or in a nursing home. It turned out the latter and it wasn't long before Miss Hortense tracked her down as a resident of St. Thomas's nursing home in Harborne. It had taken Hortense a few days to locate her, another two hours to reach the nursing home, and only one minute for Hortense to use the forged staff identity pass in her handbag to gain entry at the nursing-home gate.

In 1965, Millicent Granwaithe had been fifty-nine, which made her ninety-four now. She looked like a little white feather surrounded by a mountain of duvets and large pillows. The room she was in smelled of Dettol.

When Hortense entered, she didn't seem to notice. After a time, she said, "Is that you, nurse?"

"Yes, Miss Granwaithe?" Hortense went up closer to the bed. "My name is Hortense."

"You're another one of those darkies," she said in a small but determined voice. "Have you taken any of my lilies? They're only for us, you people are not allowed."

"I haven't come about any lilies. I come to ask you about the post office. You remember, the one you worked at on Lancet Road?"

"The post office? Oh yes," she said. "Is it time for work? Am I late?"

"No, my dear, you're not late," said Miss Hortense.

"What day is it? Is it a Monday?" Millicent asked.

"It's Thursday, August nineteenth, 1965," Miss Hortense lied.

"Oh dear," said the woman. "Is it that day again?"

"You remember what happen on that day?" Hortense asked.

"Oh, it's awful," she said.

Hortense put her handbag down. "Why you don't tell me all about it, then?"

When Millicent had finished recounting the events of the famous Lancet Road post office robbery, she said, "Do you think the robber is going to come back?"

Miss Hortense reached down to touch the woman's hand. "Oh no," said Miss Hortense. "I think he has his sights firmly set on other treasures now."

Despite a significant rise in their number, supplemented by eighteen grandchildren ranging from twenty-three years to eight weeks old, the Richardsons' headquarters remained the little house on Vernon Road, opposite Hortense. This was despite the fact that five of the daughters had acquired eight council properties between them and a sixth had emigrated to Australia. For the past eleven years, half of Mr. Richardson had been buried in the back garden. His ashes were evenly distributed

284

between his two favorite places, the other being on the top of the Guinness tap at the Tiger's Head.

The house was still the heart of the family. A thoroughfare of cars parked out front and across the road and around the corner (though no one parked in front of Miss Hortense's gate). Family of various shapes and sizes and ages came and went twenty-four hours a day.

Even before Miss Hortense could knock, the door swung open and a little girl with jam smeared across her left cheek looked up at Hortense.

"Nan?" shouted out the girl. "It's Aunty Horty." Each of the Richardsons had the same familiar look, variations of the flaming red hair, squinty black eyes and a ruddy skin tone that could weather any storm, hands ready to slap any man down.

"Well, don't leave her on the bloody doorstep, send her through," belted out her grandmother, now confined to a wheelchair, except when she needed to go on holiday or into the kitchen to get her Fruit & Nut.

"Help yourself to a Lou-ee Vee-ton?" said Maggie Richardson as Miss Hortense entered the front room. She motioned towards the colorful array of fancy handbags spread over the carpet. The place was bursting with toys, knockoff designer bags and an overlarge state-of-the-art TV that took up most of the room.

Miss Hortense shook her head. "No, thank you, Mrs. Richardson. I have enough handbags."

"Maggie, Horty, Maggie. I see you've got yourself a lodger now," said Mrs. Richardson. "That must be nice for you? Is it your niece?"

"No," replied Hortense.

"Well, she takes after you anyways, doesn't she—with her love of gardening. We saw her out front. She was busy studying your roses." Miss Hortense didn't look surprised.

"And she must like your clothes too, cos we've seen her in your bedroom, a couple of times now. Switching all the lights on as soon as you've gone out and searching in your wardrobe. Wonder what's in it that she's so eager to borrow?"

Hortense nodded a thank-you to Maggie Richardson for the information. Such surveillance had more or less saved her life during Bone 8.

"So, sit down then," said Mrs. Richardson. Hortense moved a brightly colored Lego construction and took a seat.

"Laquisha?" Mrs. Richardson bellowed, and the little redheaded girl who answered the door came running in with a half-eaten piece of toast and a rat-like dog that sniffed at Miss Hortense's feet; she kicked it away. The girl leaned against her grandmother. "Get Aunty a cup of tea, will you, love?" And turning to Hortense, Maggie Richardson said, "So what can we do you for?"

Thirty-three years earlier, Miss Hortense had knocked on their door and Mr. Richardson had asked her the very same question. She had explained that there was a young man called Michael, only nineteen, who had been attacked and left for dead just down the road, and then Mr. Richardson had supplied her with the names of the two feral cousins, Mark and Christopher Chapman, who lived near the Chatsworth Estate. After he had given her the names he said, "Wait till I tell you a funny story, Horty."

"You've told her this story already," Maggie Richardson had said. The story was about the famous post office robbery that took place on Lancet Road in 1965.

Now Miss Hortense was here to ask another question.

When Miss Hortense described a tall, skinny white man who wore a baseball cap and who had recently disappeared off the face of the earth, Maggie Richardson said:

"Nasty piece of work, that Dice. Give us a few days, Horty, and we'll find out where he's got to."

Miss Hortense asked her, "Did Mr. Richardson ever find out who stole from the post office?"

Maggie gave a chuckle and said, "Oh Jesus. Now you're going back. No, we never found out who committed the famous Lancet Road post office robbery, even though it was only down the bloody road. Dad used to say he'd buy the Yam Yam that did it a drink. And you know, he never bought a bloody drink for anybody." Maggie Richardson laughed.

71

The Tall Mawga White Man

True to her word, two days later, Mrs. Richardson sent her grand-daughter to knock on Miss Hortense's door. The little girl handed her a piece of paper before smiling at the piece of cake Miss Hortense gave her in return, and skipped back across the road with the cake already smudged on her face. The piece of paper had an address and the words: *Be careful. He's dangerous.*

Miss Hortense didn't have to travel far to find Richard Dudney. He was a short bus ride away, holed up in the Mirage Hotel, which always had that sickening sweet odor of hydrogen sulfide. He wasn't in any of the rooms that looked out to the main road and were used for unsuspecting tourists, nor was he in any of the back rooms on the second floor that were supposedly used for the oldest profession in the world. He was in a room on the third floor, a floor that the lift didn't service and that had easy access to external stairs for a quick getaway.

"Housekeeping," said Miss Hortense in a thick West Indian accent. She had her handbag firmly tucked into her side, her cleaner's blue tabard on and a trolley full of linen.

"Don't want none," said a coarse voice a few seconds later.

"Bed need changing," said Miss Hortense. "It probably stink." The accent still thick.

After a few more seconds, the door clicked and swung open. There was no one behind it. Unperturbed, Hortense rolled the cart with the clean linen into the room and the door slammed shut behind her. The mawga man jumped out from the bathroom pointing a gun in her direction, but she kept her head low.

"I said I didn't want any"—he swore—"room service." He pointed the gun at her chest.

Miss Hortense mumbled under her breath about dutty people and began to take the sheets off the bed. The man mumbled back, "Bloody foreigners," under his breath. He sat down on a chair by the side of the bed and put his gun down on the table next to him. Miss Hortense watched him from the corner of her eye and moved further in.

"I am looking for information about the killing of Nigel Brown," said Hortense.

They both looked at the gun. She was closer than him now and even though she was perhaps slower, she had a decent chance of getting to it before he did. He did a double take.

"You're that fucking busybody. Should have taken care of you my bloody self."

She explained why she was there. They both watched the gun carefully. But he should have been watching the hand that was in her bag.

"Funny how when them find Nigel Brown's body them never find no money with it," said Hortense. "What do you know about the murder of Nigel Brown, Richard?"

"Don't know nothing about it," he said, straightening and eyeing the gun.

"But you know that it wasn't Germaine killed him, don't it?"

"Germaine?" he sneered. "He couldn't hurt a"—he swore—"fly. Germaine's gone soft. Ever since those religious nutters started hanging around and quoting Bible verses. Serves him"—he swore—"right to get"— he swore—"caught. Him and that"—he swore *again*—"wifey of his."

"The thing is, wherever money is, you is there same place too. And being as no money was found with Nigel's body, I think either is you kill Nigel or you saw who did it. Either way, you took the money."

"Piss off, Grandma," he said, eyeing her up, and then lunged for the gun.

She reached him with the needle just in time, even as the gun went off.

"Now," Miss Hortense said again, as he writhed around on the bed screaming. "Tell me what you know about the murder of Nigel Brown."

"All I know," said Dice, rolling around and starting to slur his words, "is when I got there, a car drove off. Someone wearing a dark jacket was at the wheel."

"What car?" asked Hortense, leaning over the bed.

"One of them pissy little Nissan Micras. Silver or something. Now fucking help me!"

It took three nurses, two doctors and a security guard at the Queen Elizabeth Hospital A&E to remove a tall lanky man in an Aston Villa baseball cap from a room where keyhole surgery was being performed. He was demanding that it should be vacated to treat a bullet that had grazed his left big toe. Security alerted the police, who, upon answering the call, were surprised to find that the man was actually Richard Dudney, aka Dice, wanted for burglary, using forged money, possession with intent to supply, and breach of bail conditions. When they asked him how he had come about his injury, he clamped his mouth shut and didn't say another word.

72

She Have Things to Say
(Quite a Lot Actually)

Those who knew Miss Hortense knew that she wasn't a woman who was quick to make known any conclusions that she might have come to, and certainly not without sufficient time to verify her findings. She would say, *Big fire don't cook food*; who wants undercooked or burnt food? And her nursing training had taught her to be cautious before rushing to and then communicating a diagnosis. Miss Hortense had certainly taken her time to watch the game, the players at the table and those in the room, and now she had come to some very definite (and verified) conclusions, which she would be sharing, all in good time.

It was mid-August, and yet the rain pelted down and gray shadows drew across the stormy sky. The local newspapers had been full of the details of the murder of Nigel Brown and speculation about his many crimes ever since. It seemed he was not the legitimate businessman that he made himself out to be, and the council was seeking solicitors' advice on how they could retract his many accolades. Twenty nights had already passed since Nigel Brown was killed and there hadn't been any traditional nine-night celebration for him, as was usually done for the dead. His body was still lying in the police mortuary, not looking like it would be released for burial anytime soon, and his wife, Yvonne, was rather more occupied in the celebration of his passing. Blossom had it on good authority that Yvonne's lover, Anthony, had already moved his things into Yvonne and Nigel's house. And she and the young man were seen looking very happy together gallivanting all over town in his car.

Although no one was much minded to remember the life of Nigel, there was going to be a remembrance of sorts. Camille had decided to organize a small gathering to remember her late mother and those (except for Nigel, really) who had recently departed. Since Constance's death, pretty much everything had gone to pot; proof of what a powerhouse she had been in life, the most upright member of their community, the linchpin when it came to charitable and civic life—a big hole had been left in her wake. Those in attendance were only too willing to be invited, and only too willing to put on their mourning suits again and get a peek inside the woman's big house before it was sold.

It seemed fitting to Camille to have the memorial at her late mother's house: Constance's pride and joy, and the place where she drew her last breath before she tragically passed away.

The guest list was reasonably small. It consisted of family—Constance's daughter, Camille; her granddaughter, Jasmine; her daughter-in-law, Yvonne; and her second cousin Myrtle; a handful of church brothers and sisters, including Pastor Williams and the two Mavises; current and former Pardner members Blossom and Fitz; and Mr. Wright, a neighbor from the block of flats across the road. It also included the hairdresser, Bola, who hadn't known Constance personally in life but was very well informed about the woman from the daughter, the granddaughter and Blossom. But rather unusually for such an intimate affair, the guest list also included someone who might best be described as Constance's number one enemy, Miss Hortense, who was accompanied by two of her own guests: her designated driver, Sonia (whom Miss Hortense was keeping a particularly close eye on); and Miss Hortense's nephew, Gregory (the policeman), who didn't look too happy about being summoned to attend the memorial—he came into the house grumpy and helped himself to a bottle of beer, which Miss Hortense noticed with a purse of her lips, as he was meant to be teetotal.

Outside the house, the *For Sale* sign had been blown sideways, a bit of it hanging off the pole. When each attendee entered, they were sodden, and left a bit of a puddle in the hallway.

Miss Hortense had arrived early with her guests, so she took the opportunity, when she thought no one was watching, to go up the grand staircase and into what she believed was Constance's bedroom, a large room at the front of the house. All signs of Mr. Miller (or, as a select few now knew, Mr. Brown) had been removed from the room, and it was, in many ways, a bedroom similar to Miss Hortense's own—an overlarge queen-size bed for one, well made; a wardrobe, empty now except for a grip pushed up into a corner on the top shelf; and a dressing table at the front with a large ornate oval mirror.

Miss Hortense moved the curtains and looked out the window at all the people she had chosen so carefully for the guest list, who were arriving. She looked across at the council flats opposite. She wondered if Constance ever looked out and thought how lucky she was. These past weeks spent rooting around in Constance's life had revealed more to her about the woman than she would have wished to know. She had to admit, though, up until recently, Constance hadn't done such a bad job as the Pardner Lady. It was sad to see things come to this. Regardless, she had entered the Looking Into business to seek justice for those who couldn't seek it for themselves, and now Constance fell into that category. She took a deep breath. "Goodbye, Constance," she said as she left the room. "Unfortunately, I'm going to have to get right up inna you business now."

The shadows followed the attendees up the path to the front door and gathered with them in what Constance used to describe as the drawing room, the place where all the best furniture and crockery were on display. When Constance was alive, it was a room only open to "good" guests. But "good" guests clearly hadn't included Miss Hortense and Blossom on that Tuesday morning before she died; then, Constance had made a concerted effort to make sure the door to that room was well shut.

When the last of the guests entered, Camille discreetly double-locked the heavy timber front door and Jasmine, not so discreetly, clicked the lock on the back door shut and popped the key into her pocket. Miss Hortense seemed to be the only person to notice.

The drawing room was decorated in chintz and patterns and was full of crystal glasses and china ornaments and things that shouldn't

292

be touched or sat on. In fact, it was one of these ornaments, a large hand-blown fish with its forever gaping mouth and its vivid rainbow colors, that Miss Hortense was intensely studying now as it sat on the fireplace. There was a nice little English spread put on, with crisps, sausage rolls and the like, plus a selection of alcohol including several tins of Guinness. Fitz was standing in the corner with a good view of the room, but particularly of Camille, who was stood nearest the door, and her daughter, Jasmine, who was now sitting cross-legged on the settee. For anyone discerning enough, they would have seen him nod once at Miss Hortense.

At such gatherings, there was normally a religious invocation at the beginning, a prayer for the dead to mark out the sacredness of the event, but Pastor Williams remained stony-faced on a chair in the corner and everyone else waited in a sort of limbo for the whispered prayer that didn't materialize.

Although Camille was the host, it was Yvonne who rattled her long acrylic nails against a half-empty wineglass and slurred, "I'd like to say a few words. Please, I want to speak."

The room hushed. "This is a gathering for the late mother of my late husband, Mrs. Constance Brown."

It seemed she was enjoying the word "late." There was a chorus of "um-hums."

"My late husband, Nigel, introduced me to his late mother in 1981 after our second date, in this very house." More "um-hums." "She didn't even bother to look at me the first time we met. I was *too dark-skinned for her Nigel*, Nigel had said." She laughed then. The glass she was waving about was now four-fifths empty, with more of the contents spilling onto the carefully preserved patterned carpet. The room's "um-hums" had disappeared and were replaced by an intake of breath, eagerly sucking up the scandal to come.

"She used to call me 'the Baron,'" said Yvonne, "on account of the fact that I never gave her a grandchild."

"Oh, is that the reason?" said Blossom too loudly. "I thought it was because she was too uppity," she said more quietly.

"I was married to her and her son for nearly twenty miserable years and every one of them was hell. God, I hated them both." More intakes of breath.

"This isn't the time or place," said Camille quietly.

Yvonne looked at her sister-in-law with wavering, dilated eyes, then continued.

"Oh, sweet innocent Camille. Your brother was a cheat and a liar. He bled your mother dry and cheated you out of your inheritance and you know it." She pointed at Camille, but her eyes couldn't properly focus. "I never wanted his kids and I'm not sorry he's dead. There you go." She gulped some more of her topped-up drink. "Do you know, Nigel used to come here early in the mornings to stash his merchandise? D'you all know how Nigel made his money?"

It was Gregory who moved to hush her, as how Nigel made his money was still at the center of an open investigation, and he helped her to a seat.

In the gap, Miss Hortense rose to her feet.

Gregory looked across to her and mouthed, "*No, Aunty*," but Miss Hortense cleared her throat.

"Excuse me, please. Excuse me, everyone," she said. A hush descended on the room again. "Many of you know who I am. Constance and I never did get along. Many of you know that." There were some coughs of acknowledgment and derision.

"Although we are here to remember the life of the departed, I always think it is important to talk the plain truth." Gregory coughed loudly. "And therefore," continued Miss Hortense, unfazed, "it is time we start to talk the plain truth now."

Someone shouted out, "Who invited her here?"

"In particular," Miss Hortense insisted, "we need to talk the plain truth about the murders of Nigel Brown, Donovan Miller and Constance."

There was a shocked gasp from the other attendees after each name.

"Aunty," warned Gregory. "We have someone in custody for the murder of Nigel Brown. And," he said, with gritted teeth, as if placating a badly behaved child, "this isn't appropriate."

"I believe and can verify," said Hortense, scanning the room, all eyes on her, "that the young man in your custody is innocent." There was another collective gasp.

"And I believe that the guilty culprit of all of the murders is right hereso in this very room."

There was another gasp and each of the guests looked at one another, and then someone who sounded like Mavis C said, "Me tell you sey she not righted. She gone clear!"

Gregory made a director's "cut" gesture with his hand at his own neck. Miss Hortense blinked right past him and continued.

"So," said Miss Hortense when the noise had settled down again. "Let us begin with Nigel's murder. Stabbed in the neck once and in the back four times with a knife at least five inches long on the evening of Friday, July twenty-first, at his garage number forty-four, on the Rushden Industrial Estate. Estimated time of death—nine to ten p.m.?" she said, looking at Gregory.

He took a swig from his beer bottle in response.

"There were any number of people outside of this room who wanted him dead," she continued. "There are also a number of people inside this room who wanted the man dead." Miss Hortense scanned the room—various people, sitting or standing with plates or glasses in their hands, dotted around the place. "Including you, my dear." Miss Hortense turned to Yvonne, who was raising a full glass to her mouth.

"Didn't me tell you," said Blossom, clicking her fingers.

"We all now know you hated your husband, and you also had the opportunity: you knew better than anybody else his movements. Perhaps you'd simply had enough of an uncaring, wicked husband."

"If I wanted him dead," Yvonne shouted into the room with a laugh, "I would have killed him years ago." A soberness passed over her then as she took in the gaping stares.

"I didn't kill him," she said under Miss Hortense's clear gaze. "I was with . . . Anthony."

There were several more gasps in the room.

"Me tell you," said Blossom, smiling broadly. "Me tell you she have a lover."

"He's my son!" said Yvonne defiantly. "Yes, I've got a son," she said to the room, as if she were sticking two fingers up at it. "It's not a crime, is it, Pastor, to have a child outside of marriage at fifteen?" She stared at the pastor, who looked down at his feet. "To have a child when I was just a child myself . . . And no, Nigel did not know about him . . ." She trailed off. There were lots more whispers in the room. "No," she said, to the vicious whispers, "Pastor Williams is not the father, just someone I confided in years ago whom I shouldn't have trusted."

The matter referenced in the letter dated May 7, thought Hortense.

"Well," said Blossom, "the way she greeted him didn't look like a mother to me."

"I can verify it. She is telling the truth," Miss Hortense said to the room.

Yvonne looked at the pastor and screwed up her face.

Miss Hortense cleared her throat again. "If we have to look at all suspects, we must also look to you, Miss Camille, and your daughter, Miss Jasmine there." All eyes now rested on Camille, who looked back at Miss Hortense, mouth agog.

"We didn't kill Nigel," she said after a moment, a redness rushing into her face.

"He was wicked towards you, though," said Miss Hortense. "And I suspect, even when you told your mother, Miss Constance, about his wickedness, she still dismissed you."

Camille wrung her hands.

"You were desperate," continued Miss Hortense. "The damage he had been responsible for at the community center was the last straw."

Gregory looked down at his shoes. Camille rolled her hand in and out of a fist.

"This isn't what we agreed to," she said in a faltering voice to Miss Hortense.

"We must eliminate all suspects," said Miss Hortense.

Camille sighed. "I hated my brother for what he did to me and the community center, so yes, I gave him a black eye." Camille looked at her fist and nodded. "I'm not proud of that. But it couldn't have been me or Jasmine that killed Nigel. We were both at the hairdresser's when he was stabbed." She looked at Jasmine and nodded.

Then Bola put up her hand tentatively and Miss Hortense motioned for her to speak. "That's correct, Miss Hortense," said Bola. "On Fridays we open late. A condition wash and retwist for Camille and extensions for Jasmine. We left the shop together at about eleven p.m.?" She smiled at them both and the room, happy to have been of assistance. "And, if anyone is thinking of getting their hair done, first appointment ten percent discount." She was ready with business cards, dishing them out to reluctant takers.

"I didn't kill my uncle Nigel," said Jasmine, her voice soft in the room. "But I did kill Grandma."

There was another gasp from the attendees.

"Sit down, Jasmine," said Camille with a voice full of grit.

"No, Mummy," said Jasmine, raising her hands. "If we're gonna do the truth? Then the truth is that? If it wasn't for me, Grandma would still be alive, and you know it."

Camille shook her head but tears began to roll down her cheeks.

"The last time I saw Grandma," Jasmine continued to the room, "I upset her so badly that she screamed at me to get out of her house . . ." The girl tapered off; the blubbering started.

"That is the truth," said Blossom, as if she had been there too.

"If I hadn't found out about Granddad . . ."

Mavis C looked at Mavis B and whispered, "Which granddad? Mr. Brown? I thought him was dead?"

Mavis B said, "Must be the father's father."

Miss Hortense said kindly, "Sit down, child," and Jasmine slumped back down in her seat.

"Let us continue thinking about who had the motive and opportunity to kill Nigel." Miss Hortense looked over to the person sat in a chair in the corner, still mopping his brow and looking at his feet.

"Pastor?" invited Miss Hortense.

The gasp of shock in the room was the loudest yet. There were many whispers as Pastor Williams sat up in his chair.

"It's true," he admitted, "that I had some very negative feelings towards the man."

"Indeed, your very significant financial difficulties are as a consequence of his actions," said Miss Hortense. There were further murmurings in the room.

"It is true that there were some financial difficulties," the pastor said to the room, quelling that fire again.

"I told you," whispered Mavis C to Mavis B.

"But nothing that the good Lawd himself cannot help to conquer," the pastor was quick to add.

There were a number of "Amens."

"You were upset that all the church and Pardner property fell into Nigel's ownership, given he was the sole beneficiary of Constance's will. A result of her tricking you into signing ownership of the Pardner assets over to her." There were further gasps.

"Yes," said the pastor, his voice tight with shame, "I was very aggrieved by that. That is true."

"It's also true that you were at Constance's house the evening before her body was discovered," said Hortense. Eyes rested on him more intently.

"He was here in the evening," confirmed Blossom.

"I was here along with you and Sister Blossom, Miss Hortense, the day before she died," he said sharply.

"In the evening," said Blossom again to the room.

"After we left, you remained," Hortense said to the pastor.

"That is true," said the pastor, a man who normally had so many words now with so few.

"And you may have been the last person to see her alive," said Hortense.

Pastor Williams considered his next move, his jawbone rolling.

"What happened after Blossom and I left our meeting on Thursday?" asked Hortense, studying him intently, as was Blossom.

"Well, after you left," Pastor Williams said, his eyes desperately looking for succor, which was obstinately refusing to come, "I talked to Constance about some discrepancies with the accounting, and then I left too. I visited Sister Myrtle and Brother McKenzie, which you can check."

"And you left on good terms?" asked Hortense.

"Well," said the pastor, "I wouldn't say good terms exactly."

"But she was alive when you left her?"

"Yes, of course she was bloody alive," said the pastor with a click in the jaw. There was a further gasp from the room because of the "bloody."

298

Blossom stood up, pulled out from her bosom the handwritten letter that she had stolen from his office and waved it about. "This letter is proof he wasn't on any good terms."

"Is where you get that?" the pastor asked Blossom. Blossom sat down.

"Okay, yes, there was still some unresolved business," the pastor said quietly. "I came back to the house looking to sort it all out . . . a little later."

"A little later? What time was that exactly?" asked Hortense.

"After I visited Sister Myrtle and Brother McKenzie. Around nine p.m."

"And?" asked Hortense, studying the sweat beads forming a pearly chain about his brow.

"She didn't answer. Her car was on the driveway, but no one was in. The house was in darkness."

"If her car was on the driveway and it was nine p.m.," said Camille, "then she must have been at home. But"—she turned to the pastor—"are you saying no lights were on in the house at that time?"

"That is what I said," said the pastor. "The house was in darkness."

"So, what that mean?" asked Blossom.

"It means," said Jasmine, "that Grandma might have been dead before it got dark because she didn't turn on any lights and she never went to bed before ten p.m."

"Yes," said Miss Hortense, "in May, the time for turning on lights is around eight thirty p.m., don't it?"

"Me lost," said Mavis C. "Didn't Constance die in the morning time?"

"My brother, Nigel, found Mum dead the next morning," said Camille patiently. "Miss Hortense and Miss Blossom, you left the house at what time the day before?" Camille turned towards them.

"Between four and four thirty in the afternoon," said Blossom.

"And, Pastor Williams, you left the first time at what time again?" asked Camille.

"About fifteen minutes after they left," he said.

"Which means," said Jasmine, "that Grandma could have died anywhere between four forty-five and eight thirty p.m. the night before she was found."

"Providing," said Mr. Wright, who had so far been very quiet in the corner, "the pastor is telling the truth."

"But does it matter," asked Mavis C, "what time she died? Are you saying, Miss Hortense, that it wasn't a heart attack?"

Camille turned to Miss Hortense. Everyone in the room did too.

"I have no reason to dispute the medical evidence that it was a heart attack that eventually killed her," said Miss Hortense. There was a sigh of relief in the room.

"But," said Blossom, raising her finger in the air, "all kind of things can *eventually* cause heart attack. Me did tell you so, don't it?" she said, looking at Mr. Wright.

"Indeed," said Miss Hortense. "And what about the night that Nigel was killed? Where were you, Pastor?"

"Doing the Lawd's work like every night," he said to Hortense.

Mavis B, who was still with him, despite the word he had used earlier that wasn't in her Bible, said, "Amen."

"That was a Friday and on Fridays I'm at evening prayer. Any number of the congregation members could vouch for me," he said, tapping his hand on his knee. Mavis B's mouth was opening and closing like a fish's, but no noise was coming yet.

Miss Hortense turned to her because she looked like she couldn't wait any longer.

"That's true," Mavis B said. "And if you was still attending church you would know for yourself." The other Mavis gave a satisfied huff.

"And were you at the same evening prayer service, Mavis?" asked Hortense, turning on her now. Mavis B's beady eyes blinked rapidly under Hortense's scrutiny, because it wasn't a question that anyone had asked her before.

"Well," she said, "I was doing the Lawd's work too."

"And where was that?" asked Hortense.

"Well, that was at the Rushden Industrial Estate."

"Where Nigel was killed?" asked Camille.

"Well . . . yes," said Mavis reluctantly. There were further gasps around the room.

"I was there on Pastor's strict instructions," said Mavis B, pulling up her jacket, "to hand out leaflets and preach the word of the Lawd."

300

"Amen," said Mavis C.

"And what did you see at the Rushden Industrial Estate?" asked Gregory, suddenly interested.

"Well," said Mavis B, thinking carefully, "I saw Mr. Nigel drive up and get out of his car and enter his little garage unit."

"At what time?" asked Gregory.

"Well, I would say 'bout nine p.m."

"And was there anything else?" asked Gregory, leaning forwards, because this was a witness he didn't know about.

"Well," said Mavis B. "Nothing out of the ordinary. Just one or two cars coming and going."

"Any particular cars?" asked Gregory.

"Well, now you asking," she said, "there was a little silver car that parked up."

Gregory got out a notebook from his pocket and was writing something in it.

"Well," said Hortense. "That leads me on to my final suspect." Hortense scanned the people in the room, and her eyes finally rested on Sonia. Sonia itched her scalp and shuffled nervously.

The church brothers and sisters exchanged looks. Bola bit down hard on a piece of celery; she hadn't been this entertained since O.J. decided to drive away.

For this part, Miss Hortense smoothed down the back of her skirt and took a heavy seat on the chair behind her. Now all eyes rested on her again.

"If I can have a glass of water?" she asked Jasmine.

Jasmine unfolded her legs and said, "Yeah, of course."

Miss Hortense looked at her watch.

A long minute and a half later, Jasmine returned with the water and Miss Hortense took a sip. "It is no secret that I and Constance never did get along and it was no coincidence that I was summoned to this house the very day before she died. It was a meeting that was carefully engineered by you"—and Miss Hortense now shuffled fully to her left and said—"Blossom."

73

She Have Things to Say (Plenty More Things)

All eyes in the room now rested on Blossom, who had responded "Eh?" when Miss Hortense called her name. Half a sausage roll was caught in her mouth.

"You, more than anybody, did know," said Miss Hortense, "how much Constance and I disliked each other. So I was the perfect tool to use to raise Constance's blood pressure."

Blossom choked on half of the sausage roll. It ended up on the floor in front of her.

"I was Constance's weak spot. I was the thorn in Constance's side, and with me present she was weakened and backed into a corner."

"What dat?" asked Blossom, coughing now, as the other half of the sausage roll went down the wrong way.

"You haven't been honest with me at all, Blossom," said Miss Hortense. At this point, Blossom could barely swallow.

"Let us think on how all of this has come about." And Miss Hortense turned her chair further towards Blossom. "The meeting we had with Constance, conveniently placed the day before she died. Your disappearance at her funeral service, ten minutes before it ended, and the blackmail letter that Pastor received shortly afterwards that was supposedly from me. You were instrumental in the attack on the daughter-in-law—it was your false rumors about her having an affair that led to her getting knocked down in the car park."

"I never knew dey was false!" said Blossom.

"Hold on," said Yvonne, suddenly sober again. "What did you do?" she said to Blossom, leaning towards her.

Blossom rose from her seat. "Oh no, no you don't, Hortense." And now with the sausage roll gone in a number of directions, one load of bad words rushed out.

Such was the color of Blossom's words that both Mavises started to hum. Fitz began to laugh.

"And," Blossom said, when it seemed there could be no other bad word left to say, "all of the times I stood up fe you when nobody else did." She was shaking with fury. "When everybody said you was bad luck and an obeah woman!" She looked at both Mavises. "Is me one stood by you. Is me one! All a de times when I came to your corner even though it cost me dear, even though people was telling me that you was nothing but trouble. And you going to call me out?"

Gregory stood up and gently coaxed Blossom back to her seat. Miss Hortense took out the letter that the pastor had shown her in his office from her handbag. She cleared her throat and continued, but there was a slight tremor in her voice.

"You see, you slipped this under the pastor's door the day of Constance's funeral." Blossom turned red. "Making accusations about the Pardner business. Even when you type, your *c*'s and *g*'s. It was the same typewriter that was used to write the note found with the body at the bottom of Constance's stairs." Miss Hortense took out a plastic wallet containing the note.

"Aunty, that's evidence," said Gregory in an embarrassed whisper.

"You see the *s*? See how it smudge?" She waved both the letter and the plastic wallet at the room and then handed both to Bola, who was standing next to her. "That's because the ribbon of the typewriter sticks where the *s* is."

Bola was turning the letter sideways with scrunched-up eyes. She passed the letter and the plastic wallet with the note in it to her right, and so it continued until the letter and the note eventually ended up in the hands of Mr. Wright.

"I didn't write that note," said Blossom, crisp with hurt.

"But you did write the blackmail letter," said Hortense.

"I only wanted to get the Pardner money back," said Blossom, sounding small.

"When you came to see me that morning after Constance died," Miss Hortense continued, "I knew that it was pure lie a come out of you mouth. You said you had just come from the market. But the number 64 bus from the market would have arrived at 10:16 and there is no way with your bunion foot that you would have brought yourself to my house in four minutes—even at a rush." Blossom cussed her teeth.

"But," continued Miss Hortense, "the number 234, from your house, that is a different matter entirely. That bus arrives at 10:04, and it took you sixteen minutes to get to my yard from the bus stop. So why lie about where you were coming from, Blossom? Because," she said more softly, "your relationships have a tendency to get you inna trouble. You see," said Hortense, now addressing the rest of the room, "I think it started with the big shiny black car. The one that belonged to Nigel. I think that was the straw that broke *your* back."

And this time, Hortense turned even further to her left to face Mr. Wright.

74

She Have Things to Say
(Yes, She's Still Talking but Almost Done)

"Me?" said Mr. Wright, looking over both shoulders as if to find who she could be addressing.

"Yes, you," said Miss Hortense. Blossom was looking down at the carpet, her face all flushed. "The morning Constance died, Blossom didn't just bump into you at no market. You went to her house, and you let yourself in with the key she gave you."

There were several "Oohhs" from the room.

"Seeing a woman is not a crime. But maybe you is jealous," Mr. Wright said, smiling meanly at Miss Hortense, who merely scoffed.

"Jealous? Of what? I wouldn't deal with a dried-up, washed-out, frowsy-smelling, shriveled-out old man like you if you was the last man alive." And Miss Hortense recomposed herself and adjusted her jacket. "It must have been difficult for you, though," she continued, "to be the bystander, always watching what you thought was opulence and wealth not a hundred yards away from your own front door. What did you have? A mashed-up car, a moldy flat with renk stairwells, a dodgy heart and, quite importantly, a life-threatening diagnosis."

There was an exhalation from the room.

"It wasn't Fitz, Blossom, whose health you should have been concerned for. I found two sets of prescribed medication in Mr. Wright's yard. Angina tablets and capecitabine tablets, five hundred milligram. Chemo tablets recently prescribed fe cancer—causes sore hands. I noticed how you was handling your new steering wheel, Mr. Wright."

"Malcolm?" said Blossom to Mr. Wright.

"There was Constance and her spoilt pickney them a live the life of Riley whilst you suffered across the road. And then came the brand-new automobile on the drive, combined with your recent diagnosis—well, that is the straw that broke your back."

"I don't know what you're talking about, woman," spat Mr. Wright.

"On the day Blossom and I came to visit Constance and Pastor Williams, there was somebody else in this house with us besides the pastor."

"Was there?" said Blossom, momentarily piqued out of her anger.

"I didn't know that," said the pastor.

Miss Hortense motioned to Blossom. "You remember that the curtain twitched when Constance did open the front door?"

"I'm not talking to you," said Blossom, remembering her anger once again.

"The curtain moved in this room," said Hortense, as she moved towards the very same curtains and touched them. "Pastor was sitting all the way in the kitchen back thereso when we got here." She pointed in the direction of the kitchen.

"It took this young lady"—Miss Hortense motioned to Jasmine—"ninety seconds just now to go to the kitchen, get me a glass of water and come back. This is a big old house and that kitchen is far. So the curtain couldn't have been twitched by the pastor."

"No, sir, I couldn't get from thereso to hereso like that," said the pastor.

"Which means there was at least one other person in the house when we entered. That was further confirmed," said Miss Hortense, "by the fact that Constance pulled the door to this room shut as we walked through the passage and followed her into the kitchen."

"Meaning there was someone or something in this room that Grandma didn't want you to see?" said Jasmine.

"Exactly so," said Miss Hortense. "You, Mr. Wright, was in this room, and it was you that Constance didn't want us to see."

Miss Hortense went into her handbag and took out her black notebook. She opened it and took out another piece of paper. She looked at Sonia, who blanched.

"I have something here that might explain why Constance was in so much fear of us seeing you. Young lady, please can you read

306

this out?" Hortense held out the piece of paper for Jasmine, who nodded.

Bigglesweigh Daily Herald

August 20, 1965

Gunpoint Raid on Post Office

Police are seeking a man who raided the post office on Lancet Road yesterday about 20 minutes after opening. Approximately £5,000 in cash and negotiable documents including postal orders and stamps were taken. Sub-postmistress, Millicent Granwaithe, of Hazelwood Road, who has worked at the post office for 15 years, said the man forced his way into the safe, grabbed the money and ran off. It appears the gunman vanished. The police description of the raider is aged between 25 and 35, about 5ft 5, wearing a dark coat, trousers and a balaclava.

Jasmine handed the piece of paper carefully back to Miss Hortense, who said:

"I spoke to Millicent Granwaithe the other day. She still alive, did you know? To this day them never find the man who did that." Miss Hortense allowed her gaze to rest on the cans of Guinness on the side table.

"What relevance is this?" asked Mr. Wright, digging dirt out of his fingernails.

"Well, you should know," said Hortense. "You being . . . Melvin Bright."

"Melvin 'Red' Bright?" said Mavis C, agog.

"Badman Red?" said Mavis B.

Jasmine looked at them both with big eyes.

"A man that is still wanted in five parishes in Jamaica for theft, armed robbery and murder that took place between 1959 and 1965," said Miss Hortense.

"Not me," said Mr. Wright, kissing his teeth. "I don't know what you talking 'bout. This woman is damn crazy, you hear?"

"The article you just read," said Miss Hortense to Jasmine. "You find anything strange 'bout it?"

Jasmine shrugged.

"You notice how the robber was described?" asked Hortense.

"Between twenty-five and thirty-five. Five foot five. Wearing dark clothes?" said Jasmine.

"That's quite a broad description," said Gregory.

"Yes it is," said Hortense. "You notice the one thing it didn't mention, though?"

Miss Hortense looked around the room; the attendees shrugged.

"Him color," said Fitz in a monotone.

"Um-hum," said Miss Hortense. "And boy, oh boy, if Millicent had thought it was a 'darkie' that had terrorized her so, she would have shouted that out from the rooftops. That mean to say the police was only looking for a white man and that, Mr. Wright, was your party trick. The police wasn't looking for no Black man, even one as fair and pale as you."

"Maybe if they were, they would have looked plenty harder," said Fitz.

A scoff of agreement from the attendees.

"You'd had a long record back in Jamaica as Melvin Bright and so I am presuming that led to the one mistake that began this whole story. You had only recently absconded to England on a false passport, changing your first name to Malcolm and the *B* of your last name to a *W*, and you wanted to make sure no one suspected you of the robbery. Murder in Jamaica then was punishable by hanging. So you gave the stash, the five thousand pounds, to your longtime friend and accomplice Donovan Miller to look after until things died down. Your best friend from back home, the one who was living alongside the Browns in the shared boardinghouse in Musgrove Park. The house that did catch 'pon fire two days after the post office robbery."

Mr. Wright stayed silent.

"And then after the fire, the one that was reported to have killed Mr. Brown, your longtime good friend Mr. Miller disappeared with all you money. All of the money gone, or so you thought. But you had your suspicions when Mr. Brown's widow, Constance, bought this big old house. You wondered, like so many of us, 'bout how she could afford to buy this big old house when she didn't have two pennies to rub together before. And so you managed to get yourself a little council flat opposite and you watched what you suspected was Constance spending all the money that you had stolen from the post office. Your greatest triumph being enjoyed by somebody else? You watched her for thirty-five years from you little balcony and I suspect that when the big shiny black car arrived, along with the shocking news of your diagnosis, you decided it was now or never."

Hortense once again looked at Blossom. "It was Mr. Wright that encouraged you to set up a meeting between Constance and me, na true?"

The fury that had been consuming Blossom seemed to abate; her bottom lip started to quiver and there was the smallest nod. Hortense turned back to Mr. Wright.

"Constance wouldn't want to be exposed in front of me, the thorn in her side. If you could get me into the same building as her, you knew you would have greater power. You knew with me in this house Constance would do and say anything not to expose herself, so just before Pastor arrived, you knocked on her door. It was you who the neighbor saw having 'argy-bargy' with Constance. The morning we came here, there was a smell of burntness inna the kitchen; as the toast burned and the bottom of the pan caught under the porridge, you stood on the doorstep and told Constance that you suspected she was living off your ill-gotten gains and that you would expose her right then in front of her guests unless she did what? Transferred her house or a sum of money equivalent inna your name, as recompense for your thirty-odd-year silence?"

There were gasps around the room.

"The woman died of a heart attack," said Mr. Wright. "Anybody can die from a heart attack."

"Constance died of a heart attack, yes," said Hortense, but now she turned and addressed herself to Camille. "Your brother, Nigel, said he found Miss Constance in this passageway?" Miss Hortense opened the door to the passage.

"Yes," said Camille.

309

"But seems to me, before she ended up there, that there was one hell of a struggle that took place right hereso inna this room. I suspect, Mr. Wright, that after I, Blossom and the pastor left, Constance came back into this very room, where she had hidden you, and told you exactly where you could go with your ransom demand. And I bet you didn't take to that too kindly.

"Bola, please step forward here." Bola stepped forward. "What would you say that is behind Mavis C on the armchair over deh so?"

Bola bent down to study it. "Hard to say exactly, but I'd say that was hair activator?"

Mavis looked down to see the greasy imprint of a pattern of small curls.

"Do we see that anywhere else in the room?" asked Hortense. Everyone looked around on the furnishings and agreed they couldn't.

"Mum hardly ever came in this room," said Camille. "She would never have rested her head anywhere she knew it would leave a mark."

"But if she was pushed into the chair and her head hit the side there, then the activator from her curly perm would leave a residue, don't it?" said Miss Hortense. "And finally this." She pointed to the ugly fish statue on top of the fireplace with its big old mouth. The one she had been studying earlier in the evening.

"Grandma loved this," said Jasmine, picking it up.

"Look closely," Miss Hortense said.

Jasmine raised and studied the fish. She clasped her hand to her mouth. "The fin, at the bottom, it's broken off."

"Perhaps it was knocked and chipped when you had your struggle, Mr. Wright? You told Blossom that the ambulance men had been working on Constance for one hour and thirty minutes on the morning Nigel found her, but that was a lie."

"Just to confirm," interrupted Camille, "that is definitely a lie. When Nigel found Mum, she was dead."

"Her body was stone cold when the ambulance arrived in the morning," continued Miss Hortense. "That's because when you left this house in the early evening of that Tuesday, Constance was either dead or gasping for her last breath, and that is why, when you returned to the house, Pastor, it was in darkness. She died or was severely incapacitated before it got dark."

All accusing eyes now rested on Mr. Wright.

"And then there is Mr. Miller. You saw the same ghost I saw, didn't you, at the graveside at Constance's funeral? The ghost you saw wasn't your longtime friend Mr. Miller but Mr. Brown, Constance's husband, who was meant to have perished in the fire thirty-five years ago, except the ghost was well and truly alive and, after the funeral, started staying in *this* house, the house that you'd been watching for years. You knew then for certain what he and his wife had done, and you couldn't stand it. He'd come back to claim the house that you believed was rightfully yours. So you entered from the back garden, you picked the lock, and you went upstairs. You probably had some kind of argument and then you pushed him down the stairs. Is that how it go? You went home then, and you watched and waited, to see who was going to be the first to come to the house, and when you saw a young lady at the front, in distress, you rushed out of your flat and assisted her. Whoever it was who entered the house, you were going to enter with them so your fingerprints would be over everything, in case you'd missed any—the note you put there and now picked up, his neck and clothes as you took his pulse—not as a murderer but as a helpful Samaritan. It was you who typed the note on Blossom's typewriter and pretended to find it at the bottom of the stairs in front of Sonia. Blossom had told you about Bone Twelve, and what better way to stop me Looking Into you than to distract me with a case that had never been solved. And finally, let's talk about Nigel. You ever hear the saying 'Teef don't like to see teef with long bag'?"

Jasmine and others in the room below the age of forty shook their heads.

"It means," explained Camille, "that a thief doesn't like to see other thieves succeed."

"Where is that old black coat of yours, Mr. Wright?" Hortense asked. "After you killed his father, you decided to approach Nigel and demand what you believed to be rightfully yours. Any other man might have been scared to approach a big-time criminal like Nigel, but that would be forgetting that you are Melvin 'Red' Bright. You told him that you

311

wanted the house or you would expose the dodgy dealings you had witnessed at that garage of his on Rushden Industrial Estate, but I bet he laughed in your face. So you went to Rushden Industrial Estate, and you stabbed him to death. There is still power in those arms of yours, and Nigel wasn't expecting your company."

"You're ridiculous, woman. You can't prove any of this," said Mr. Wright. "What an imagination this woman has."

"You were seen," said Miss Hortense.

"Who saw me?" challenged Mr. Wright.

"On the night Nigel was murdered, you were still without a car." Miss Hortense turned to Sonia. "So you borrowed Sonia's little Nissan Micra. I presume that you two bonded when you discovered you both had in common a dislike of me. Though, I presume, Sonia didn't know that she was aiding and abetting a murderer. We now have two witnesses who saw Sonia's car parked up around the back of Unit Forty-Four."

"Two?" asked Gregory.

"Mavis and that tall mawga white man, Dice."

"Aunty!" said Gregory.

"Son," Mr. Wright said to Gregory. "Take your aunty home before she makes an even bigger fool of herself. This woman hasn't got one thing on me. She better sort her own house out before she starts fiddling with other people's."

Mr. Wright lunged suddenly at Miss Hortense. Both Fitz and Gregory moved quickly. Gregory got there first, though Miss Hortense made no attempt to move. He grabbed Mr. Wright's right arm in a hold and forcibly encouraged him to sit.

"All right, all right, young man," Mr. Wright said, deflating.

Sonia stood up. "I've got something I'd like to say." Sonia cleared her throat. "I agree, there is a murderer in this room," she said, turning to Miss Hortense. "And we both know it's you."

75

Sonia Has Things to Say Now

All the weary eyes in the room now rested on Sonia. She continued addressing Miss Hortense. "Not only did you murder my father, you attempted to murder Mr. Wright. Tell them, Mr. Wright."

"Well, that's right," he said, shaking out his sleeves. "She came to my flat and she tampered with my pills. They didn't taste the same after she'd been at them. I threw the bottle away. I don't know whether it was cyanide or what it was."

Miss Hortense rolled her eyes. It wasn't true. She had something in her handbag that was far more effective than tampering with any pills.

"A few days before Nigel Brown was murdered, that girl Jasmine over there"—Sonia pointed to her—"came to see Miss Hortense at her house. I overheard her tell Miss Hortense that she was scared of her uncle, and Miss Hortense said she was going to help her deal with him. That's right, isn't it?" asked Sonia, looking at Jasmine.

"Yes," said Jasmine.

"Well, what better way to deal with him than to have him killed and to get Mr. Fitz to do it?" said Sonia to the room.

"What damn foolishness is she talking 'bout now?" Fitz said, clenching his fists.

"Hold on," said Jasmine.

"What's to say Miss Hortense, or Mr. Fitz, wasn't at the Rushden Estate at the time Nigel Brown was murdered? She could easily have told her supposed witnesses to 'see' my car. And it's not the first time that she's got another man to do her dirty work for her. Isn't that right, Pastor Augustus Williams?"

Sonia looked at the pastor, who gulped.

"You paid my mother a sum of money every month for years," she said to him. "Was that because you was paying blood money for what Miss Hortense did to my dad?"

Miss Hortense rolled her eyes again. Now, that didn't make any blasted sense. The bank book she saw was dated 1963 and Errol died in 1970—unless the pastor had the same foresight as Blossom.

"Um, oh Lawd." The pastor fell back into his chair. There was an intake of breath in the room and the two Mavises rushed to his aid. "I'm all right, I'm all right," he said, fanning himself with his hand.

"Then let's talk about Mr. Miller, shall we? Because what proof do we have that this man wasn't who the police say he is?" Sonia continued. "You were seen creeping around the outsides of this very house weeks ago, Miss Hortense. Mr. Wright saw you."

"I did," said Mr. Wright. "From my window."

That's who was watching me, thought Miss Hortense.

"What reason did you have to do that unless there was something you'd come back to try to hide? And you were seen in the market by Mr. Wright, making inquiries about Mr. Miller to a Mavis Buchanan. Who is Mavis Buchanan?" Sonia asked, looking about the room.

Mavis B tentatively raised her hand. She wasn't going to say anything more. Most people had forgotten that she had rented a room from Pearl White, and she wanted to keep it that way.

"Why were you so interested in the man that was living here? What's to say it wasn't you that came in the house and pushed Mr. Miller, or whoever he was, down the stairs?" asked Sonia.

"And what reason would I have to do that?" asked Hortense softly, but Sonia wasn't listening.

"And then there is Constance Brown. That poor lady," said Sonia. "You were at this house the day before Constance died. Did *you* leave here on 'good terms'?"

"No," said Hortense lightly.

"No surprises there, then," said Sonia, no sweetness now. "What's to say you didn't cause her heart attack? In fact, that makes the most sense," she said to the room, nodding. "And then there's my dad," Sonia added, her voice like curdled milk.

314

Gregory went towards Sonia, but Hortense raised her hand to stop his approach.

"Years ago, you made him get in that car. You and your obsession with those attacks, just because they involved your sister."

Blossom said, "Eh? What?"

"You killed my father back in 1970. It was your fault. You've killed once, so you could do it again."

Sonia sat back down on her seat, her eyes rimmed red. Miss Hortense hung her head. It was so quiet it sounded like church.

She finally cleared her throat.

"I'm truly sorry for what happened to your father. He was like a brother to me. I know you want somebody to blame. But I did not kill him. I'm sorry about your mother, but I didn't cause her unhappiness either."

Miss Hortense felt like something heavy had been lifted from her chest. She had never said that before, not to herself or to anybody else. For years, others had blamed her for Errol's death and in truth she had blamed herself. But looking at Bone 12 again in the weeks and months since she had reopened the case, she could finally recognize it for what it was. Bone 12 had been one of the worst cases Hortense had dealt with. It had been the case that had ripped the Pardner Network of Bigglesweigh apart. But she knew now that Bone 12 wasn't her doing, that it wasn't her fault and that she had to get out from under its shadow.

"See, the thing is," said Hortense, addressing herself to Mr. Wright again, "you could have got away with Mr. Brown. You could have got away with Nigel. But you underestimated Constance—the one killing you thought you didn't even have to try to cover up. *It was a heart attack after all.* But you never factored in Constance. She was one hell of a woman."

76

Constance and Myrtle

Miss Hortense sat down. She wasn't the only one in the room who felt exhausted. She sighed and continued: "Constance was a woman who wasn't going to be pushed around by anybody without a fight. Isn't that right, Myrtle?"

Miss Hortense turned to Myrtle, who was sitting in a chair in the other corner looking into the distance. "The funny thing is," said Hortense, addressing Mr. Wright again, "you were in significant danger yourself and you didn't even know it."

Myrtle rose from her seat and shuffled into the center of the room.

"Is it my turn?" she said, looking around at all the faces. She began: "Constance was my second cousin. We shared the same great-granddaddy." Then, speaking to the distance: "*They might not know that, McKenzie. I'm telling them so they know.*" Back to the room. "Blood is thicker than water, and blood is thick."

Some nods in the room.

"But Danny . . . well, he became like a son to we." Myrtle stopped then and looked directly at Hortense.

"He said to me once, 'Why do you believe in God, Miss Myrtle, after that thing that happen to Mikey?' From then on, we did Bible study together. I talked to him." Off to the distance: "*I schooled him in the Bible, McKenzie. John five: twenty-nine, Revelation twenty: four-teen and ten, all the verses about damnation. I was trying to mek sense of it meself, but I didn't mean . . .*"

"Shall we get someone to take her home?" asked Camille, concerned.

"No," said the pastor quietly. "Let her continue."

"One morning, soon after Errol died in the car accident, Danny called me. He was crying. He told me to come to his bedsit right way. The boy was almost dead." She turned to Fitz, her eyes wet with tears. "You beat him up badly, he could barely move, but you didn't kill him." She paused. "*No, but you don't know this part, McKenzie. Let me tell the story.*"

Myrtle found a seat, sat down and folded her arms in front of her. She carried on talking to the air.

"Danny said he thought Mr. Fitz was going to come back for him. 'Why,' I asked, 'why did Mr. Fitzroy do this to you?' *Then he told me, McKenzie.*"

"Told her what?" asked Mavis B.

"Shh, she's talking to her dead husband," Mavis C said to her.

"He had been the one to carry out the attacks on those women," said Myrtle, her face twisted with anguish.

"Who?" asked Jasmine.

"Shh!" cried Mavis B.

"You see, during our study, I told him all about those sinful women. The ones who left or threw away their pickney them and carried on with married men. I told him how terrible it was that they didn't care about the children God had seen fit to provide for them. When the attacks started, I thought all that trouble they were having was part of God's good and gracious plan. That everything happens for a reason. Proverbs sixteen: thirty-three." Myrtle was wringing her hands. "What a wicked boy to tek that from the Lawd. It was my Savior, my great Redeemer, who told me what I must do next. There was a green ashtray on the mantelpiece. I grabbed it."

"Whose ashtray?" asked Mavis B.

"Doesn't matter, she grabbed it," said Mavis C, cussing her teeth. "Shh, na man!"

"I raised it like so"—Myrtle illustrated—"and reached up and I brought it down on Danny's head."

"Oh Lawd," said Mavis B.

"Him legs went from him. He fell to the floor. I watched him. The gurgling stopped after a while."

317

"Oh, dear Lawd," said both Mavises together now.

"I got up and came here to Constance's house."

"You came here?" asked Blossom.

"She owed me for something I had helped her with many years before."

77

The Truth About the Pardner Lady

Several of the faces in the room were now staring agape at Myrtle, waiting to hear from the old woman what on earth she did next. Blossom was almost bent at a right angle, she was leaning so far forwards in her chair towards Myrtle. Mavis C was crying, though nobody else except the pastor and Miss Hortense could really understand why. Mavis B was fanning herself frantically with a lacy fan she'd found in Constance's display cabinet, Sonia was shaking, and Bola was chewing so hard on a piece of gum that she was in danger of causing her cheeks a serious injury. But Mr. Wright sat, as cool as any cucumber you might see, as Miss Hortense looked at Myrtle again and said:

"You got the idea from Bigsy, didn't you?"

"What idea?" asked Blossom, looking confused. "Bigsy? Dimples's husband?"

"The mix-up with the bodies," said Hortense. "And this is where you come back in, Mr. Wright."

Mr. Wright sneered. There was nothing new this has-been detective busybody woman could tell him.

Myrtle looked drained as her Brummy-cum–Small Island accent entered the room again, as she continued her confessional to her husband. "It wasn't Constance's husband who died in that fire in the boardinghouse in 'sixty-five," said Myrtle, "but she was tired of him, a good-for-nothing philandering fool, forever embarrassing her and couldn't keep him thing in him trousers. Constance had always been a woman that liked to look over people's shoulders, and she had previously been watching over Mr. Miller's. He lived in the same boardinghouse as she did. She saw him bury something in the garden, and a day before the fire, she found the something: a large bundle of money. The money belonged to Donovan Miller. It was he who had perished in the fire, no doubt searching for it. She hid it and told Mr. Brown that if he didn't take the half she was going to give him and leave, she would tell the police he started the fire and killed Donovan for the money. *She came up with the idea, McKenzie, not me.* Mek the man in the fire look like it was her husband and send him go long 'pon him way as Mr. Miller. Him could get a new life in America. She could get a new life, free from him here. *Constance was my second cousin, McKenzie. I had to help her. I didn't tek a penny for it. I made sure you wasn't working when the body came in. You would have noticed the difference—even though there was hardly any body left to look 'pon after the fire took hold.* Mr. Miller was tall, Mr. Brown very short. So, when Danny died . . ."

"Is you kill him," shouted one of the Mavises. "Him never just die."

"I came to Constance and I begged her to help me with him body. If we could just get him to Chappel Road, to our undertaker's, I could tek care of the rest."

She stopped abruptly and her face twisted again. Her hands were shaking.

"On the Monday before Constance died, she did call me. She said she had received a letter from somebody called Melvin Bright."

"Oh, Lawd Jesus, not another letter," said Mavis C.

"She said," continued Myrtle, "that she needed another favor from me. That the man was going to be visiting her in a few days. That she was going tek care of it. I never heard from her again."

"What that mean, *tek care of it*?" asked Mavis B, aghast.

"Well, kill him, of course," said Mavis C, "and the favor mussy was to help bury him body."

The smile had disappeared from Mr. Wright's face and he looked whiter than anybody in the room had seen him look before.

"You still don't have any evidence that I am Melvin Bright," he managed to say.

Miss Hortense rose again. "Well, you wrong there," she said. "When Constance called you, Myrtle, she said something else, didn't she?" she asked.

Myrtle nodded.

"She said for you to take a grip of her personal affairs should anything happen to her."

"Yes," said Myrtle. "That is what she said. But I didn't know what—"

"Well," said Miss Hortense, interrupting. "There is a grip upstairs in Constance's room."

"What's a grip?" asked Jasmine.

"A suitcase," said her mother. "But that old thing? I was going to throw it out. It's empty."

"Well, a good thing you didn't. You see, there was something in it. In the lining." Miss Hortense produced another letter from her handbag. "The letter from Melvin Bright to Constance. You see, the same smudged *s* in the word 'house' as in the letter Blossom pretended was from me and the note that was found with Mr. Brown's body." Miss Hortense gave the letter to Bola, who looked at it, nodded and circulated the letter to the group.

"That still na prove nutting," said Mr. Wright.

"You don't think so?" said Miss Hortense. "Well, that knife you keep inside your pocket does—the one that come in handy for all kinds of things—to clean your fingernails, to gain entry into churches and people's houses."

"What knife?" Mr. Wright said, jigging his foot. But when Gregory started to pat Mr. Wright down, the familiar-looking flip knife fell out of his left trouser leg.

"Leave it," said Gregory, as Pastor Williams was about to pick it up. He kicked it away, and Miss Hortense picked it up with her handkerchief.

"If you were to look at it closely," said Hortense, "you will see engraved in the bone handle, the letters . . ."

"MB," said Blossom, slowly. "Melvin Bright."

"Gregry," said Hortense. "I think you better call you little friends now."

Mr. Wright made a decent effort at lunging for the front door, but the fact that both the back and front doors were locked, and that he was now without his knife to pick any locks, meant neither Miss Hortense, Gregory, Fitz, Camille nor Jasmine was too alarmed. Mavis B did scream, though Gregory apprehended Mr. Wright again with ease, twisting his left arm behind his back and bringing him with his feet shuffling into the front room while he dialed the station.

Mavis C had stopped crying but Sonia started; both Mavises were shaking their heads in disbelief and busily chatting away to themselves about the magnitude of what had just unfolded; Bola couldn't help it, she was smiling, she'd had a hoot; Myrtle was humming "Nearer My God to Thee"; the pastor was saying a quiet prayer for her; and Blossom was busy trying to get one of the gaudier-looking rings off her right middle finger.

As Mr. Wright was led away, Blossom threw the ring she had eventually got off at him and said, "You lucky you is in handcuffs or I would box you from here to next year," and she kissed her teeth at him.

Myrtle was also arrested and led away, although she went ever so quietly, still humming. As she passed Hortense she said, "I'm going to keep praying for you, Miss Hortense. Praying for your peace." And she smiled as she left amid the curses of Mr. Wright that echoed up and down the driveway.

78

Loose Ends

Thanks in large part to the way the two Mavises and Blossom were running their mouths, the whole of Bigglesweigh was still buzzing with what had happened at Constance's house a week later. It was all that anyone was talking about at Mane Attraction, and Bola had started giving five percent discounts for piled-up hair. Pastor Williams also put on a special clarificatory service to the effect that "free will did not mean freedom to murder people."

On Friday morning, Miss Hortense let Sonia come to the house to collect her belongings. She called her into the front room.

"Your father was number four for receiving the Pardner draw—the sum of the money that I collected when I was the Pardner Lady," Miss Hortense said. "It was Dimples first, second Blossom, third Constance, and fourth was Errol. For a long time, I couldn't say your father's name." Then she said, "I saw it, you know. When you was likkle and you said you tripped and lost you mother's money fe de Pardner. I saw the roll of money tucked in the top of your sock. It wasn't lost."

Sonia looked at Miss Hortense with her big eyes.

"I thought you were stealing all our money. I never thought you knew?" Sonia lowered her head.

"Well, of course I knew, child," said Miss Hortense. "Just like I knew that when you came back to Bigglesweigh it was because you wanted to cause me harm." Miss Hortense sipped some more of her tea. "You know why I did plant the daffodil bulbs by the side of the rosebush?" Miss Hortense asked. "Because not the damned blasted cats from next door, nor squirrels, nor any of the foxes will go near them. They don't like daffodils at all at all."

Sonia looked at Miss Hortense then, shame washing over her.

"I just wanted to hurt something you cared about."

"I know," said Hortense gently. She reached for the girl's hand. "Don't mek my mistake, you hear. Don't live in the past, because no good can come from it." She looked at Sonia. "Visit me anytime you like and I will tell all about you father—but you not staying in my spare room again."

Sonia smiled. It was the first time Miss Hortense had seen her do that.

79

Resolution

On Tuesday evening, when Gregory came to look for Hortense, all of the girl's things had gone, save for a glossy magazine with Naomi Campbell on the front. Gregory was thumbing through it as he sat perched on the edge of the settee.

"So you know," he shouted out towards the kitchen, where Miss Hortense was making the tea, "we've charged Mr. Wright for the manslaughter of Constance and the murder of Nigel Brown. We found a five-inch knife stuffed into a compression sock in his flat. We've also informed the Jamaican authorities that we have Melvin 'Red' Bright in our custody. I looked him up, Aunty. He carried out some horrendous crimes in his time."

Miss Hortense entered with the cups. He blew on the tea and took a sip.

"Myrtle McKenzie also told us everything. Apparently Danny's body was carted off to the crematorium, so not much evidence left there. We dug up the grave that was meant to belong to Mr. Brown, though, and are investigating the remains. I didn't know," he said, "that it was her son that had the heart attack on Cuckoo Lane."

Miss Hortense gave him a look because they both knew well and good that it wasn't no damned blasted heart attack that killed poor Michael McKenzie.

"She's gone, then?" he said, putting the magazine back under the table. "Sonia?"

"Well, what does it look like?" asked Miss Hortense.

"And you knew all along she was just here to cause you trouble?"

"Better the devil you know," Hortense said.

Gregory shook his head. "You had me worried there for a minute."

"As did you," said Miss Hortense. She looked at him. "I know I wasn't the only one Sonia tried to hurt."

Miss Hortense shifted in her chair. After a pause, she said, "You know Evie wasn't leaving you?"

The hurt came back into his jaw.

"She was in a lot of pain," said Hortense. "But she loved you."

Hortense gave him the space to ask the question. And if he had asked it, despite everything she had vowed, she would have responded with the truth. But he didn't.

He looked at her. "Did I tell you that a man came into the station wanting to speak to me? He had a briefcase filled with details of the illegal dealings of Nigel Brown—money laundering, fraud, deception. The man disappeared before we could get his name."

"But him did have big ears and wore a leather jacket?"

"Aunty?" he said. "That wasn't you too?" Miss Hortense scrunched up her mouth but didn't answer. She was thinking that at least Cuttah's Donkey was good for something.

"Well, whatever it was," he said, looking at her closely, "I'm grateful." He adjusted his collar. "You do know that you're too old to be involved in this type of business? It's dangerous. So, promise me, no more. This is it now."

There was a knock at the door. The familiar hammering. Gregory did not want to be caught up in the middle of another war between his aunty and Miss Blossom and he rose quickly to make his excuses.

"I better be getting back to the station," he said. "Criminals to catch, and all that."

Miss Hortense cussed her teeth and said, "Well, you won't have far to look, then."

When the man with the big ears and leather jacket brought all the evidence of Nigel's money laundering into the station, Superintendent McGraf took a sudden and extended holiday. There was nothing in the evidence brought in to suggest that *he* knew Nigel Brown, but Gregory was working on finding out the connection.

80

We Two

Blossom was sat on the settee nearest the door while Miss Hortense was in her favorite armchair. The Wray & Nephew sat on the coffee table in front of them and they were both nursing half-full glasses. The crumbs from a piece of demolished black cake sat on the coffee table in front of Blossom.

"Well," said Blossom, sighing heavily, "I haven't slept fe days." She rubbed her foot and the bunion that protruded from the tights. "You know, I had a feeling I was going be next." She shuddered.

"What I can't understand," Blossom continued, "is how nobody never know that the man Constance bury wasn't her husband and really the husband was gone overseas a breed up a whole heap of pickney. All this time when Constance Brown was blowing her own crumpet in her big old house, all along she knew she get the money to buy it from a dirty post office robbery. Well," said Blossom, "that could have been the perfect crime."

"Except," said Hortense, "that Mr. Brown came back to life."

"Why you think Mr. Brown came back to life?" asked Blossom.

"Run out of money, of course. With Constance dead, he could claim all of hers."

"You think all those years ago is Constance and Mr. Brown start the fire on purpose and it wasn't that bad landlord after all?" asked Blossom.

"No, me na think so," said Hortense. "The landlord admitted to me it was fe de insurance. Constance just saw an opportunity is all."

"But wait," said Blossom. "If Daphne and Garfield Stewart knew all along that it wasn't Mr. Brown in the fire, why dem never say nutting?"

"Constance knew Garfield's secret—that Daphne was underage when he married her. She must have gone to visit Mr. Stewart after she'd received Mr. Wright's letter, to make sure that he wouldn't be her weak link."

"Garfield Stewart is a dutty wretch!" said Blossom.

She put the glass to her lips and tipped her head, but was interrupted by a sudden revelation, and she spluttered.

"But, you said it, didn't you?" said Blossom. "The day we went to visit Constance. You said it, at the table. *Don't think I don't know who you are, Constance Brown.*" She looked at Hortense, her eyebrows raised in those black arches. There was no more gray showing at the top of her head. "You knew she was a liar?"

"Me know enough," said Hortense honestly. "Cobwebs and dust is visible if you know where to look." She took another sip. "I remember the very first time I met Constance at your house. When Mr. Brown won that dominoes game, and everyone was questioning how he did it."

"I remember," said Blossom. "That was the night we started the Pardner."

"Well, Constance was the answer."

"Won the game for Mr. Brown?" asked Blossom, puzzled.

"It was she who was peering over shoulders and telling her husband what fe play."

"How?"

"Signaling to him with her mouth and teeth. I don't think she liked her husband but there was a reason the two of them were together."

"Both of them was cheats and liars!" said Blossom. She reached for the bottle and poured herself another glass.

"Hortense," she said. "You don't tink is I deliberately helped Mr. Wright, do you?"

Hortense reached over to touch her hand. "Of course not," she said, and smiled. "You were just being Blossom."

"Is how you do it?" Blossom asked, once she'd had another sip of the rum. "How you keep all them secrets and don't tell nobody? It don't weigh you down? It don't make you tired?"

Miss Hortense took a sip of her rum. It did make her tired and it did weigh her down.

"We all have our own crosses to bear," said Miss Hortense, and hers was a lifetime of secrets buried in her wardrobe and in the back garden. "Anyway, Constance wasn't all bad," she added. "Mr. Wright was right 'bout one thing; this ya life was never easy. 'Member how it was when we first come a England?"

Blossom nodded.

"Constance did care for this community, and she tried fe mek it a better place."

"Speaking of which," said Blossom, readying herself to ask the question she had really come to ask.

But Hortense intercepted her. "Don't ask me no blasted questions again about the Pardner."

Miss Hortense had promised herself she was never going back into it. And Miss Hortense was not someone to break her promises.

81

The Price of Peace

From Sunday morning to early in the afternoon, Miss Hortense was busy in her kitchen cooking. She had mutton to finish seasoning, fish to fry, the peas to finish soaking and carrots to grate for the coleslaw. And as she did these things, she was thinking about the bank book that she had found in Sonia's things.

At 2:45 p.m., Miss Hortense's first guest, Pastor Williams, arrived. Miss Hortense had summoned him to come before the rest. She was rolling dumplings, and shouted out to him with her floured hands: "Push de door, it's on de latch. Come through."

He came into the kitchen, shaking off the rain. Miss Hortense directed him to sit at the little table in the kitchen while she continued her rolling.

Still with her back to him, Miss Hortense said, "Now, Pastor."

"Yes?" he said, tentatively.

"You have something to confess?"

"Um . . ." he said.

"You didn't just sign away all the Pardner, did you?" asked Hortense.

"Um . . ." was his response again.

"Your signature was the price you paid for Constance agreeing to keep your secret for all these years. The money you sent to Precious every month. For your daughter. Starting the year she was born."

His body started to shake with the sobbing.

"I don't know how it happen, Hortense . . . I mean, I do know how it happen . . . but it wasn't meant to happen. It started after a

330

prayer service. She said she wasn't happy in her marriage. I said she should pray 'pon it. I put my hand 'pon her shoulder and, well . . ."

"*Who here is without sin, raise your hand?*" said Hortense, playing back to him a part of his sermon from Constance's funeral. She knew all those years ago what she had witnessed. "Maybe you should get in touch with you daughter. She could do with some guidance now." He looked at her and gulped.

She was disappointed but not surprised, and said, "Your secret is safe with me as long as you choose to keep it." The same words she had said to a number of others over the years.

Fitz was next to arrive. He pushed open the front door and walked through to the kitchen with his cool broad walk, concealing something behind his back. He looked at the pastor.

"The onions," said the pastor, who wiped more water from his eyes.

"You winning?" Miss Hortense asked Fitz.

"Cha man, me na win nothing since morning but me get you this anyway." He presented her with the little rose plant he had hidden behind his back. "It's a Deep Secret," he said.

Miss Hortense found she was sniffling now. "Damn blasted onions," she said, and took the plant quickly from Fitz.

Blossom came in shortly after with her nails freshly manicured; the nails matching the earrings, both matching a new scarf. "I'm having problems with me left eye," she said, coming in blinking. "Glaucoma runs in my family, did you know?" She eyed up Fitz keenly. "You feeling better, my dear?" she asked him. He cussed his teeth at her.

Camille entered after with Jasmine and a bunch of petrol station flowers already wilting. "I'm sorry, we can only stay for a half an hour or so." She really didn't have a clue as to why they'd been invited.

Miss Hortense sat at the head of her dining table and directed her guests to take a seat around it. Fitz in his usual seat by the radiator rubbing his hands. The pastor sitting next to him. Blossom in her usual seat next to Miss Hortense. Camille was told to sit next to Blossom, in her late mother's chair; it had a broken foot, which made it wobble. Jasmine was told to sit in Mr. McKenzie's chair. Errol's seat remained empty.

"Well," said Fitz, as his tummy started to rumble, "we come to nyam food or what?" The smell of the curried mutton was making his mouth water.

"So, this what I think it is?" asked Blossom, beaming across the table. "The Pardner?"

"With no money or property, we is not much of a Pardner, don't it?" said the pastor.

"And whose bloody fault is that?" snapped Blossom.

"What's a Pardner?" asked Jasmine.

"Oh yes," said Miss Hortense, "me nearly forget."

Miss Hortense went to the glass cabinet, pulled out the drawer and took out a thick piece of paper. She handed it to Camille.

"That grip," said Miss Hortense, "that was in your mother's bedroom, this was in the lining of it too."

Camille read the front of the document Miss Hortense had given to her. "A last will and testament?" she said. "But Mum already had one?"

"Well, it looks like she got herself another one," said Hortense.

"It seems to be dated after the one she did with Nigel?" said Camille.

"What's it say, then?" asked Jasmine.

Camille was reading the document. She stopped reading and started to shake her head.

"What is it, Mum?" asked Jasmine.

"It says that the house is given to Nigel, but . . . her residual estate . . . well, it says . . . that goes to me?"

"*Residue estate*, what's that?" asked Blossom, leaning in.

"It looks like it's everything else?" said Camille. "All the investments. The property."

"Well, that will be the Pardner, then," said Fitz.

"The church hall!" said the pastor.

"The community center!" said Jasmine.

"Constance was a difficult woman," said Miss Hortense, "but she wasn't blasted stupid. She knew what your brother was."

Camille sat back with her mouth agape. Her daughter rushed around the table to give her a hug.

"Right, then," said Hortense. "Let we nyam." She was just about to step into the kitchen to start bringing in the food when there was a frantic knocking.

She opened the front door to find the Donkey on the doorstep. Sweat was dripping off his head and onto the leather jacket; his face was all beaten up and his jacket torn. He could barely catch his breath.

"Miss Hortense, you have to come quick," he said, trying hard to find his words. "It's Mr. Cuttah. He's dead . . ."

Acknowledgments

This book has been a dream come true.

Firstly I must thank my husband, my beautiful children, my sisters and Bleu, for their support and patience. To my dad, thank you for instilling in me the belief that I could achieve anything; I miss you. To my mum, thank you for your quiet inspiration.

To Aunty Grace, thank you for that burning bush and forever backing me. Thanks also to Penny and Ferdy for your encouragement. To Auntie Peggy, when I think of you I smile; forty-three years of service to the National Health Service—you inform how I want to be remembered and therefore live. To Mrs. Ivy, Gennie, Jocelyn, Jannie and Joan, thank you for your wisdom and humour.

To Meeta, Lisa and Eme: your friendship means the world to me. Thank you to Arlene and Judith for answering my random queries and for the energy and inspiration you bring, and to Lisa and Inyang for answering my random medical queries with patience.

To my phenomenal agent, Nelle Andrew, no words will do you justice. Thank you for enabling my dreams. I knew that when you agreed to represent me there was a possibility that my life would be changed for ever. To Rachel, Charlotte, Alexandra and everyone at RML, you are brilliant!

To the team at Baskerville and John Murray, thank you all for believing in this book and helping me to craft it and bring it to the world. To my UK editor, Jade Chandler, you've been amazing to work with. Thank you for the passion you've shown for Miss Hortense and the Pardner Network. Special thanks also go to Nick, Jocasta, Yassine,

Corinna, Zulekhá, Ellie, Sarah, Megan and the whole team. Thank you also to the wonderful Katy Loftus and Nick de Somogyi. To Sumuyya, thank you for capturing the essence of Miss Hortense for the UK book's cover.

To Lisa Lucas, you were one of the first to believe in this book. The memory of that call from Nelle at two in the morning still stuns me! Thank you for your enthusiasm, insight and investment. Having you in my corner was so important and I'm sad we didn't get to continue the journey.

To the team at Pantheon, my wonderful US editor Anna Kaufman, it's been great getting to know you. Thanks also to managing editorial, Lisa D'Agostino and Kirsten Eggart; production editor Kathleen Cook; publicist Ciara Tomlinson; marketer Julianne Clancy; cover designer Vivian Lopez Rowe (I love my cover so much); and editorial assistant Natalia Berry.

I must share my gratitude for Hachette UK and Tamasha Theatre Company, who were involved in a new creative writing scheme in 2018 and to the authors and other creatives that gave their time so generously. The stats speak for themselves. We need more of the same! To Katie Ellis-Brown, as my mentor on that scheme, the enthusiasm you showed towards my work still makes me feel warm inside.

To the Tamasha Theatre Company—Pooja, Valerie, Harris and the team—theaters like yours, which champion underrepresented voices, are so important. Thank you for the opportunities. To the Jack Studio Theatre, thank you for the investment you provide in new writing and for giving me one of my first breaks.

To tiata fahodzi, thank you for allowing me to be a part of your story, and the Alfred Fagon Award for the important work you do.

So many creatives have been involved with my work over the years. I must thank Fin Kennedy, Anastasia Osei-Kuffour and Debo Adebayo for creating opportunities for me and many others. I am also grateful to the talented actors who have breathed life into my words.

To Richie Campbell and your cousin, thank you for opening a door.

To Sir Lenny Henry, thank you for sitting in a room with me and asking me about my dreams. Thank you to Dana for your encouragement; to Amy for your card reminding me every day that the journey is the destination; and to Gary for my flowers—they meant a great deal.

Last but definitely not least, thank you to every reader, bookseller, librarian and blogger who has picked up this book. I'm so excited to share Miss Hortense and the Pardner Network of Bigglesweigh with you. I hope you enjoy being with them as much as I do.

ABOUT THE AUTHOR

Mel Pennant is a playwright, screenwriter, and novelist. She graduated in 2014 with a master's in screenwriting from the London College of Communication. In 2013 she won the Brockley Jack Theatre's Write Now Festival with her play *No Rhyme,* and was involved with the Tamasha Theatre Company, writing for the Barbican Box. Pennant has written audio plays with Tamasha and the National Archives, and in 2018 she was awarded a place on the Tamasha × Hachette scheme for aspiring playwright novelists.